Thalia gazed at Justin through the fringes of her eyelashes.

His profile was strong, emphasized by the radiant moonlight, and his eyes took on a silvery color. He was magnetic. Her hand was drawn to his face almost as if by marionette strings, and she found herself touching his cheek.

Justin dared not move. Thalia's hand brushed his cheek gently before she caught her breath and jerked it away. Why had she done that? Had she been as affected as he by the little kiss on her forehead that night at her gate?

Deciding to be brave, Justin slid his arm around her and gazed down into eyes glistening in the moonlight. He knew that if something didn't happen quickly, he'd kiss her.

He knew he was inching closer, but couldn't stop— didn't want to stop. He wanted to kiss her, maybe more than he'd ever wanted to kiss a woman.

Dear Reader,

April brings us a new title from Lynda Trent, *Rachel*. In this Victorian love story, a young, impetuous woman falls for a mysterious man with more than a few skeletons in his closet.

With her book *The Garden Path,* we welcome Kristie Knight to Harlequin Historicals. When Thalia Freemont marries a handsome sea captain to escape her scheming brother, her new husband turns the tables on her.

A courtship that begins with a poker game soon blossoms into full-blown passion in Pat Tracy's *The Flaming.* A contemporary romance author, Pat's first historical is guaranteed to please.

Be sure not to miss *Dance with the Devil* from Pamela Litton. This sequel to her first book, *Stardust and Whirlwinds,* is the story of eastern-bred Libby Hawkins and Comanchero Mando Fierro.

We hope you enjoy all our titles this month, and we look forward to bringing you more romance and adventure in May.

Sincerely,
The Editors

The Garden Path

Kristie Knight

Harlequin Books

TORONTO • NEW YORK • LONDON
AMSTERDAM • PARIS • SYDNEY • HAMBURG
STOCKHOLM • ATHENS • TOKYO • MILAN
MADRID • WARSAW • BUDAPEST • AUCKLAND

Harlequin Historicals first edition April 1992

ISBN 0-373-28720-8

THE GARDEN PATH

Printed in the U.S.A.

KRISTIE KNIGHT,

a native of South Carolina, believes that laughter makes the world go round. Though she resolved long ago never to take herself too seriously, the one exception to that philosophy is her writing—which she takes very seriously. Kristie, a former secretary and office manager, now makes her home in Decatur, Georgia, with her husband, Bob.

To my good friend and agent,
Adele Leone.
Through the years her constant encouragement and
unfailing support have been mainstays of my career.
Nothing I say or do can ever repay
her generosity of spirit, or her wise advice.

I also dedicate this book to one of my best friends,
Peggy Mitchell.
For more years than I can remember,
Peggy has been a good companion, either when
traveling or just poking around shopping malls.
She's a wonderful friend to writers everywhere—
because she's an avid reader.

Prologue

Justin Lee rode stiffly through the swirling mist, wondering how events could have come to such a horrific ending. His heart ached, burned with rage, over the unnecessary death of his fiancée. He continued on to the glade his best friend, Peter Kimball, had indicated. He had never felt so alone in his life.

Pain knifed through Justin as he considered what was about to happen, something he'd tried valiantly to prevent but could not. Alicia Kimball's death—her suicide—was a result of an affair she'd had with a man Justin didn't know. The man had fled the Richmond area, and Alicia's heart was broken. Had he known in time, Justin would gladly have offered to bow out of their impending marriage. Society women, he'd discovered too late, cared little about others. They were self-centered and vain, always trying to make a better match or find a richer husband. He wanted nothing to do with them—not that it would matter after today.

But there had been more than her disillusionment about the man who had made love to her and left her. Alicia Kimball had been carrying the other man's child. When Justin had discovered that Alicia was pregnant, he'd told her that the marriage would still take place. He owed her father that much for saving Justin's mother from drowning when her carriage had slipped off the bridge. But Alicia had refused to consider "burdening him with another man's child."

Now she was dead. Buried on the day before their wedding would have taken place.

And matters were even worse. Peter Kimball suspected that Justin was the father of Alicia's child, and he had sworn vengeance against him. Justin had pleaded with his friend to see reason, but the two men who had been friends since early childhood couldn't resolve the issue. Justin couldn't besmirch Alicia's reputation by telling Peter about the man she had been seeing. He refused to hurt his friend further.

Peter Kimball insisted that the only way to avenge his sister's death was to kill the man who'd caused it. Secretly Justin agreed, but Peter suspected the wrong man.

Yesterday, standing beside Alicia's fresh grave, Peter had required satisfaction.

He demanded a duel.

No matter what argument Justin had used, Peter had refused to hear it. Justin, a far better shot than Peter, was now on his way to kill his best friend.

The chosen spot was about halfway between the two men's plantations. Justin's family didn't know anything about the duel, except for his younger brother, Samuel. As was customary, the two participants in the event were to select men to act as their seconds. Samuel had offered, even begged, but Justin had refused. He would have no second.

Justin approached the spot where either he or his friend would likely die. The outcome of today's duel was already decided. Justin, already grieving over the death of his fiancée, couldn't take the life of his best friend.

After he found a safe place to tether his horse, Justin walked slowly around the little glade. The sun, which should have been well into its morning climb by now, was nowhere to be seen. It was almost as if the sun were refusing to witness the killing, hiding behind the mist.

Justin heard a twig snap and turned in the direction of the copse nearby. There he saw Samuel, moving furtively among the low-hanging limbs. He'd undoubtedly come to be Justin's second, whether Justin wanted him or not. Without warning, Justin ran over and caught his younger brother by his shirt. "No, Samuel. Go home. I won't have you here to witness this."

"Please, Justin, let me stay." Tears rolling down his cheeks, Samuel stared up into his brother's eyes. "I . . . I know what you're going to do. Please, I want to be with you."

"No," Justin said softly, hugging the boy close. Samuel would do anything for Justin, even to the point of watching him die, if necessary. The boy wanted to be like Justin and copied everything his older brother did. Justin refused to allow violence to infiltrate that hero worship, even though he intended to cause no bloodshed here today. The impact on Samuel of watching his brother shot—without defending himself—would be too great. "Go home. You're almost a man now. Mother and Father will need you in the next few days. You can tell them I did as I saw fit, that I refused to kill my best friend. Now go."

Justin watched as Samuel trudged into the mist, almost silent except for an occasional muffled sob that shook his shoulders. Only when he heard Samuel's horse galloping in the direction of home did he return to his place on the fringe of the glade.

Time passed slowly. Justin had come here early, to give himself time to think. He'd considered every possibility and had reached the only decision he could.

The sound of horses came from the direction from which Peter would be riding, and Justin turned, his heart hammering in his chest. Two men dismounted and tethered their horses nearby. For a moment, Justin stood as still as possible. He could leave the area, leave Virginia, and never come back. But he wasn't a coward. He knew what he had to do.

For several hours last night, Justin and Samuel had argued over the decision, but Justin's honor had prevailed. He couldn't run. Nor could he take the life of his best friend. His only option, if he couldn't somehow convince Peter that this was madness, was to die honorably.

Justin stepped into Peter's sight and called, "Peter, dear friend—"

"You take the life of my sister and then call me friend?" Peter replied, choking back a sob. "How dare you?"

"I call you friend because, whatever transpires here today, you will still be my friend." Justin walked closer, nodding to Peter's second, Henry Wardlaw. The crackling of a twig in the copse distracted him for a moment, but he couldn't allow his attention to be diverted for so much as a few seconds. "Let us discuss this reasonably. Why would I have—? Peter, I love

Alicia even now. We were to be married yesterday. Why...why would I have refused to marry her? You know it isn't so!"

Peter's hands trembled with rage. "I know that she took her own life so she didn't have to marry the man who got her with child and ruined her reputation."

Justin realized that further talk was useless. Peter simply couldn't see reason. "Peter, you know I'm a much better shot than you. You haven't a chance . . . if I shoot."

Peter bowed his head for a few seconds and then stared Justin straight in the eye. "I can do no less for my sister than to give my life defending her honor."

I, too, would defend her honor, Justin thought. He'd tried desperately for the past few days to discover the identity of the man who had ruined Alicia's life. His lack of success had enraged him nearly as much as her death. He felt so helpless. With dark eyes that spoke of love for his friend, Justin said, "So be it."

The pistols were selected. Henry took his place away from the line of fire, and the count began.

Justin strode apprehensively away from his friend, a myriad of thoughts whirling in his mind as the mist swirled about him. How had this happened? When had fate turned against him, and why? He thought of his family, of his father's pride, of his mother's gentle love, of Samuel's hero worship. How would this event affect them? Would they understand?

And Samuel . . . Would Justin's younger brother ever forgive him? Would the boy, still so young at fifteen, ever get over his disappointment at Justin's refusal to use his gun in a duel?

For those Justin loved, he grieved already. He knew their pain would be mixed with misunderstanding, humiliation, sadness.

At ten paces, Justin turned. From there he could hardly see Peter. Perhaps, if Peter fired and missed, his sense of honor would be satisfied and the matter would be put to rest. Justin's one hope was Peter's lack of skill with a pistol.

From that moment, everything became a blur. Justin never fired, but two shots rang out. Justin's cheek stung a bit and he heard the whisper of a bullet rushing past him. Peter fell, first to his knees and then face forward on the ground. Justin's pistol fell from his hand. Rushing to Peter's side, Justin swallowed back the bitter taste of bile that had surged forth when he saw Peter collapse. Gently he turned Peter over and cradled his friend's head in his arms. He was appalled by the rapidly spreading circle of scarlet on his friend's chest. Pain tore through Justin's heart as he felt the helplessness, the utter desolation, of watching his best friend die uselessly.

"Peter, speak to me," Justin pleaded, ripping Peter's shirt and swabbing at the flow of blood.

Peter's eyes fluttered open for a few seconds. "Justin, forgive me. Your face...the blood." Peter attempted a smile, but his pain ended it prematurely. "You're lucky... I'm a damnably poor shot. Why didn't you... Who shot me?"

"I don't know, but I'll find out." Justin rubbed his cheek and looked at his hand. Blood covered his fingers and palm, but he cared little for his own injuries. He glanced around. Henry Wardlaw stood in abject shock, the thickening mist making him almost invisible. "Henry, who fired that damned shot?"

Henry strode toward the two men and glared at Justin. "Who? With just the three of us here, you ask that question?"

"You can't think that I— Henry, I never fired!" Justin scanned the trees and saw nothing. Then he remembered Samuel. Justin knew, without doubt, that Samuel had fired the shot that killed Peter. If he showed Henry the unfired pistol, then Samuel would surely be accused of murder. Justin couldn't allow Samuel to hang because he had impulsively defended his older brother. He bowed his head in defeat. Now, his burden was heavier than before. His fiancée was dead, his best friend was dead, his brother could be hanged for murder—all because of a man from Charleston. Justin looked up at Henry pleadingly.

"I don't believe you and neither will anyone else." Henry stared at Justin with contempt for a few seconds longer. "I'm going for the sheriff."

Chapter One

Thalia Freemont sat astride her mare, Guinevere, and surveyed the cotton fields. Fluffy pods of white, almost ready for picking, jutted proudly toward the cornflower-blue sky from among the deep green leaves. The sea breeze whispered through the plants like a rumor spreading through a ballroom. It began on the edge of the field and ruffled the leaves like invisible waves until it reached the far side of the flat, sandy tract of land.

She could see Adam Woodsley, Misty Glade's overseer, making his way toward her, and she waved cheerfully to her friend. Adam was the only man who ever considered the possibility that she might be capable of thinking for herself. "Hello!" she called, and waved again.

"Ought not, just ought not..." Adam grumbled as he approached her. "Little hellion. She'll be a regular headache for the man fool enough to marry her."

Thalia stifled a laugh. She knew that he was talking either about her being astride her horse or her intense interest in farming, but she chose to ignore his scolding. "Good morning, Mr. Woodsley. How is everything this lovely day?"

Adam glanced at the sky, lifted his hat, exposing a shock of coppery red hair, wiped a grimy hand across his forehead and smiled. "Miss Freemont, this is the best crop of cotton I've seen since I was a boy. My daddy—and yours, too—would be proud of us."

Thalia flinched slightly at the mention of her father. He'd been dead a little less than two years, but she'd hardly known him while he was alive. Bethel Freemont had died giving birth to Thalia, and her father had never forgiven her. Immediately after his wife's funeral, he'd taken his tiny daughter to his childless sister, Molly Bishop, and her husband, Martin. She'd been reared at Sea Mist Plantation with her aunt, who had taught her to sew and run a household, and her uncle, who had taught her to farm. They had encouraged her skill with planting, and they had allowed her to be independent. Neither one could scold her or force her to become the lady her Aunt Molly was; they simply couldn't stifle her spirit.

Thalia offered Mr. Woodsley a smile and shook her head. "You're the best overseer on Edisto Island. Maybe the best in South Carolina."

Adam Woodsley grinned, and his blue eyes sparkled with energy and wit. "Well, I ain't never been one to be lie, and I guess you're mighty near right about that."

Smiling at his lack of modesty, Thalia nodded. Since her arrival at Misty Glade, she'd found Mr. Woodsley to be a good friend, one she could talk to without fear of reproach. It wasn't that he didn't scold her, but he always did it with a hint of admiration and friendship. "Mr. Woodsley—"

"I think you oughta call me Adam. I work for you and all." He smiled broadly, spat into the field, and waited for her answer.

Thalia returned his bright smile. "Mr. Woodsley, you know well and good that I shouldn't address you as Adam. A lady simply wouldn't do such a thing . . . Adam. Besides, you don't work for me, you work for my brother."

"Well, I ain't never noticed you being overly worried about being ladylike. It ain't no use you starting now." Grinning broadly, he pointed at the cotton bolls, pregnant with thick white fluff. "Ready to pick soon. Like I said, gonna be one of the best crops ever I saw."

He ignored her comment about working for her brother, as he always did. Her brother, Donald Freemont, made few friends among the hired help and the slaves.

Thalia scanned the field again and nodded proudly. She and Adam had planted this crop carefully, turning the soil until it was fine enough to pour freely through a sieve, fertilizing generously to ensure sturdy plants and dense growth, and guarding vigilantly against weed and pest infestations. Thalia and Adam—guided by Adam's keen sense of cotton propagation—had selected the finest bolls from last year's crop and kept the seeds for new plantings, gradually discarding the inferior strains. They secretly kept enough seed for Thalia's own plantation, Sea Mist, and Adam saw to it that both plantations were cared for equally.

Thalia had longed to return to Sea Mist from the moment she'd left the thriving plantation. During the few years after her aunt's and uncle's deaths, her father had kept her at various schools, never allowing her to return to her home. Then, a little more than two years ago, she'd come to Misty Glade. Her father had died shortly after her arrival, leaving Donald as her guardian. He steadfastly refused to allow her to visit Sea Mist, even for the day.

The overseer there was well chosen, but she didn't know how her property was faring without daily supervision. Since she couldn't supervise her own property, she did the next best thing: she made the farming at Misty Glade her first priority, hoping that someone would do the same at Sea Mist until she could return.

Before harvesting, Thalia and Adam would once again choose the best plants and take their bolls for seeds, ensuring a constantly improved crop. Cotton from Edisto Island plantations was already highly prized. French manufacturers demanded Edisto cotton and paid the highest prices for select fibers. Thalia knew that with a little more coddling this year's harvest would exceed their greatest expectations—and so would that of Sea Mist.

"Adam, when do you want to select the seed for next year's crop?" she asked, gazing proudly across the fields.

"Next week or so. Got to git this stuff picked purty soon, or we ain't gonna have nothing but mush." Adam pointed to the main field. "If you think it'll be all right, we'll start in the big field first. I think this'll hold off unless it looks like we're gonna have some rough weather."

"I agree. The sooner we get the cotton to market, the better off we'll be." Thalia turned to Adam. "Thanks for stopping to talk with me. I really appreciate the fine job you're doing—both here and at Sea Mist. I don't know what I'd do without you. I plan to go there to live soon, and if it weren't for you I'd have nothing but a patch of weeds to go home to."

Adam Woodsley beamed at her praise. "It's nice to work for somebody who cares about what goes on around here. Somebody who cares enough to come out and look at the fields."

Reining in Guinevere, Thalia nodded and rode off. She knew that Adam responded well to these little talks, even though she didn't know nearly as much about raising cotton as he did. From the little she could glean from Adam, her father had given up after her mother died, and had let Adam and his father run the plantation without benefit of supervision. Fortunately for Misty Glade and Sea Mist, Adam always did the best he could.

The past two years had been different. Under her brother Donald's lack of guidance, the plantation was sinking. Had it not been for Thalia's own money, there would have been no planting last spring. Thanks to Donald's gambling, Misty Glade couldn't even afford Adam Woodsley's salary. Donald simply didn't care. He gambled and caroused without ever stopping to consider where his money came from.

Thalia tried not to be too critical of her brother. After all, his childhood hadn't been very happy. Deprived of his mother's love at an early age, he'd grown up in a household where his father had grieved himself to death over a period of years. Donald had been on his own, seemingly without love from anyone. As a result, he'd grown up doing everything he could to gain his father's attention—but he'd never gotten it.

Thalia had, in many ways, been more fortunate. Though she'd been denied the love of both her mother and her father, she'd been reared across the island at Sea Mist Plantation by her childless aunt and uncle. Both of them loved her, doted on her, as they would have their own daughter. For that she was grateful.

By the time she reached the house she was in a somber, contemplative mood. And she didn't want to see her brother. She loved him and tried very hard to excuse his excesses, but these days she found herself impatient with him more often than not.

Leaving Guinevere with the stable boy, she decided to sit in the garden for a while. She changed her clothes quickly and found her paintbox. Her favorite pastime was painting the roses in the small formal garden behind the house. The garden had been her mother's, and her father had kept it groomed as a monument to her memory. Now Donald, too, maintained the garden, almost as a shrine to Bethel Freemont. As far as Thalia could tell, the rose garden was the one thing Donald really cared about, apart from gambling and drinking.

A few scattered blossoms had braved the summer heat and were now hanging heavy on their stems. She wanted to capture them on paper, particularly since Donald never allowed a single rose to be picked for the house. She selected a vibrant color and began to work.

Thalia didn't know how much time had passed. Wishing she could take but one single blossom to her room, she reached out and caressed the vivid red roses that perfumed the air around her. With such a seductive fragrance surrounding her, she could almost forget her problems. Almost, but not quite.

She mused that a woman who was surrounded by such beauty and tranquillity should have no troubles to distress her, but life had a way of mixing loveliness with adversity. Still, Thalia knew, she had a great deal for which to be grateful, and she said a prayer of thanks for all the blessings she'd received. Leaning over to examine the roses more closely, she noticed Clover, her personal servant, making her way across the expanse of lawn toward the garden. From the young black woman's hurried gait, Thalia could tell that something must be wrong.

Knowing that her presence would be required in the house, she packed away her paints and took a moment to study her work. Her watercolor rose, almost a duplicate of the one she had used as her model, was adequate, but she sighed wistfully, because she knew that she could never capture the real essence of the rose's beauty.

Smoothing a fold of the soft, cream-colored muslin of her skirt, Thalia gazed for a few seconds at the rosebush. She plucked a petal from a dying bloom and rubbed its velvety softness over her wrists, inhaling the fragrance that remained.

By that time, Clover had reached the rose garden and stopped beside the bench where Thalia was sitting. "Yes, Clover, what is it?"

"Miss Thalia, Mistah Donald say he wanna see you in the library right now," the young black woman said, gasping for air, and waited hesitantly, as if she hoped her mistress wouldn't send her back with a message.

Thalia understood Clover's trepidation. Under the best of circumstances, Donald Freemont was unpleasant to the servants, even those Thalia had brought with her from Sea Mist. If Thalia dared to refuse his summons, he'd take his revenge on the messenger.

"Thank you, Clover. If you'll collect my painting supplies, I'll go and see what he wants." Thalia arranged her skirts over her wide hoops, smiled to reassure the servant and then strode toward the house.

Though she loved Edisto Island, Thalia didn't feel truly at home at Misty Glade. In spite of her brother's vow that she would never live at Sea Mist again, she had decided to move to her own plantation as soon as possible. Her aunt and uncle had willed everything they owned to her, though it was currently being held in trust for her by Mr. Stevens at the bank—and Donald had been appointed her guardian.

Further delay would only make matters worse, so Thalia hurried across the lawn, up the wide steps to the veranda and over to the open window of the library. Pausing a moment to gather her courage, she inhaled deeply and then stepped through the window to confront her brother. He sat peering at a letter and didn't move until she walked over to the desk and asked, "What is it now, Donald?"

Donald Freemont slowly raised his eyes and gazed at his younger sister. She barely resembled him, because she was almost an exact duplicate of their mother. Thalia's silky blond hair crowned her head like a halo, while his own was closer to light brown than to blond. When Thalia looked at him, her deep blue eyes met his. His coloring was simply a faded version of her own—and Donald resented that as much as he resented everything else about his sister.

He'd tried very hard to love her, but had long ago given up. He'd learned to hate her from an early age, poisoned by his own father's resentment. She'd killed his mother. "Sit. Sit. Don't waste my time with your—"

"Donald, I—"

"Have that twit of a maid of yours pack your clothes. Your *pretty* clothes." Donald folded the letter, placed it in a drawer and then slammed the drawer shut. He gestured, indicating the leather-upholstered chair across from him.

Thalia could see that this was going to be an unpleasant conversation. "Donald, please, I don't want—"

"Damn!" he shouted, and leapt to his feet. "I can't be bothered by whatever you think you want. Do as I say."

Hesitating simply for the pleasure of defying her overbearing guardian, Thalia continued to stare for a few moments before seating herself in the chair opposite the one he indicated. "What is it this time?"

"Don't sass me, girl, or I'll wallop you," Donald threatened, seating himself once again. "You are to prepare for a trip to Charleston." He slapped his hand on the desk and leaned forward. "And don't think you can talk me out of this."

Thalia sat stiffly in the chair and stared. What could he be plotting now? For the past few months, Donald had paid so little attention to Misty Glade that Adam Woodsley, the overseer, now came directly to her for answers to his questions. "Donald, you can't mean to travel during the harvesting. How will . . ."

He sprang to his feet and swept around the desk so quickly that a stack of papers fluttered off the wooden surface and floated to the floor. Ignoring them, he leaned down until his face almost touched hers. "The harvesting can go to the devil for all I care. I'm ordering you to prepare for a journey. We're going to Charleston for a few weeks."

"But, Donald, think about the plantation," Thalia begged. Donald had already been drinking, and the dew on the lawn was hardly dry. No matter how hard she'd tried to stop it, his fondness for spirits overwhelmed them both. Instead of nagging him, she'd given up. Now the plantation was in danger. Knowing the trip would probably be the downfall of Misty Glade, she leaned away from him and tried to make him see reason. "Let me stay and see to the harvesting. You go on to Charleston and have a lovely time. You know I'll just be in your way."

"You may not remain here," Donald announced with a glare, and returned to his chair. "Now, before I drag you from here without any clothing at all, do as I say."

For a moment, Thalia felt as if she couldn't move. Further pleading would simply result in another fit of temper. Finally she rose, lifted her chin, and glared at him. "As you wish, Donald."

"Oh, and Thalia..." he began, drumming his fingers on the desk.

"Yes, Donald?" she replied, trying without success to keep the edge from her voice.

"I saw you in Mother's ... in the rose garden." Donald rose and walked toward her. "You didn't ... I mean, you know you're not supposed to pick the roses. You didn't ... you were careful not to damage any of the bushes?"

Thalia felt a little tug at her heart. Donald might have been a fine man if his mother hadn't died bearing her. His condition was, in truth, her own fault. She should learn to be more patient with him. "No, Donald, I didn't pick any roses, nor did I damage them. You keep them beautifully. Mother...Mother would be proud, I'm sure."

"'Mother would be proud.' How would you know?" he asked, inching closer, as if to gaze into her eyes and see the truth. "You never knew her."

With a swish of her skirts, Thalia left the room. When her brother was in such a state, there was little she could do other than obey. In the hallway, she met Clover, who was coming in with her painting supplies. Thalia shook her head sadly. "Clover, please pack my clothes. We're going to Charleston."

"Yes'm," Clover said, and headed up the stairs.

"Oh, Clover." Thalia smiled reassuringly at her servant. "Pack your things, too. You'll be coming along."

"*Yes'm,*" Clover agreed with a smile. "I'll do that."

As Thalia strode into the kitchen, she found Princess stirring a pot of soup. "Mmm, that smells wonderful. What is it?"

"Peas and ham hocks," came the terse reply. "An' jus' where you headin' in that purty dress?"

"I'm going out to see Mr. Woodsley." Thalia paused. "Princess, serve dinner early. We're going to Charleston. Have one of the girls clear the table while you pack your things."

"Now, Miss Thalia, you know I don't like ridin' in that boat, specially with Mistah Donald guiding it. You jes' let old Princess stay here this time." Princess continued stirring the soup as if she had nothing better to do.

Thalia reached down and hugged the woman's ample girth. "I would if I could, Princess, but you know Donald will want you along."

"That man is the burden of my life," Princess muttered, and checked the heavy skillet full of corn bread.

Thalia left the cook to her grumbling and went outside. She hadn't much time for her task. When she reached the stable, she found the stable boy had ordered him to saddle Guinevere.

"When you want her, Miss Thalia?" he asked, glancing pointedly at her attire.

Realizing that she'd likely ruin her gown, Thalia shook her head. She didn't want to take the time to explain. She was in too big a hurry. She glanced around, found an empty stall and hid there for a few seconds to remove her crinolines. She ran back to the stable boy and smiled wickedly. "Right now. And hurry, please."

When the saddle was in place and buckled down, the stable boy helped Thalia into the saddle. With a word of thanks and a smile, she rode out of the stable.

Thalia loved riding more than almost anything else in the world. Today, however, she had no time to enjoy the myriad trails through Misty Glade's live oaks, with their ghostly moss hanging like beards, or through the clattering palmettos, or through the cool glades where the cypress grew. She had a purpose. She had to find Adam Woodsley and give him last-minute instructions for the harvesting and slaughtering, or they'd have no food for the fall and winter.

After inquiring with one of the field hands, she rode across the neatly furrowed cotton field toward one of the barns. There she found Adam talking to one of the slaves. Both looked up as she rode closer.

"Mornin' again, Miss Thalia," Adam Woodsley called cheerfully. "What brings you into the fields in a fine gown like that?"

"Good morning, Mr. Woodsley...Adam," she replied, and allowed him to help her dismount. "My brother has planned a trip to Charleston and says that I must accompany him."

Adam's grin faded from a smile that lit his face to a narrow line. "As bad off as he was, Havelock Freemont would never have took himself off to Charleston with the harvesting to be done. My daddy before me served as overseer of this plantation, and these fields never saw the first of March without the plants in the ground, and the master was never away at harvesting time, even if he never helped."

"I know, Mr. Woodsley, and I'm sorry for the imposition. If I had any choice in the matter, I'd remain here and help." Thalia knew that her apology meant nothing. Adam Woodsley disliked Donald, and made no effort to hide his disdain for the younger man's weaknesses. "May I count on you, Mr. Woodsley?"

"Miss Thalia, if it weren't for you and the memory of your poor daddy, I'd walk off this place today with never a glance back." Adam picked up a piece of straw and stuck it between his teeth. "But don't you worry none. I'll take care of it for you."

"I appreciate your efforts, Mr. Woodsley. Please give my regards to Mrs. Woodsley." Thalia smiled and climbed into the saddle again. "I don't know how long we'll be gone, but if you encounter any problems, I'll be at the town house on Meeting Street."

"Don't you be a-worryin' none. You have yourself a grand time in Charleston." Adam grinned. "If you was a man, I'd tell you to swill down a pint of ale for me, but being as you ain't, I reckon I'll be content with tellin' you to buy yourself some pretty geegaws and have a good time."

"Thank you, Mr. Woodsley." Thalia flicked the reins, and Guinevere moved into a gentle trot.

Feeling a little obstinate, Thalia took the long way back to the house, even though she knew Donald would be waiting for her to join him for dinner. As she rode, she realized that she hadn't even asked when they were leaving. Donald seemed rather distressed about something, so they'd probably leave immediately after the noon meal. By the time they reached their town house, it would be too late for Princess to cook one of her wonderful suppers, so they'd have to plan for a cold plate of cheese, bread and fruit.

When she reached the stable, she dismounted and put her crinolines back on. Once in the house, she hurried up to her room to wash the dust off her face. Her room was directly above the dining room, and she could hear Donald bellowing something at Princess. Giving her hair a pat—it was in slight disarray from her ride—she sighed. He was probably angry, so she completed her task quickly and then ran lightly down the stairs.

Before rushing into the dining room, she smoothed her skirts and lifted her chin to a jaunty angle. "Ah, Donald, there you are."

Donald glared at his sister. He could see that she'd been riding, and it made him even angrier. "So, you would defy my orders and go for a ride."

Thalia had hoped that he would calm down once she arrived at the table. She took a moment to sip her milk while she decided how to answer him. Donald had to be handled carefully, or his anger would explode into violent rage. "Now, Donald, don't be angry with me. I was only out for a moment. I didn't realize you'd be ready to eat so soon."

Donald couldn't tell if she was being truthful or lying to him, which he thought she did quite frequently. "Well, now that you're here, don't waste any more of our time. I plan to leave immediately after dinner."

Hoping that she was disguising her disappointment, Thalia tried to smile. Agreeing with Donald was the easiest way to get along with him. Very frequently she agreed with him outwardly and then did what she thought was best. Today she could hardly do so, since she had no choice but to go with him.

The soup was delicious, and it put her in a better mood. Thalia complimented Princess on the excellent meal before retiring to her room. She found Clover closing the last trunk. "Finished?"

"Yes'm, all done," Clover announced, and crossed her arms. "I had to pack so fast, them dresses'll have wrinkles and take days to iron. That man don't never think of nobody but hisseif."

"Thank you for your help, Clover," Thalia said, and hugged her friend. "Why don't you run down to the kitchen and have a bowl of soup before we leave? It's still hot."

"I b'lieve I'll do jes' that," she said, and promptly left her mistress.

Thalia smiled and changed into the traveling gown Clover had laid out on the bed. Maybe she could order some new clothes while they were in Charleston. That always irritated Donald, since he had so little money of his own. Thank goodness her father had shown the good sense to leave her money in a trust administered by a banker instead of Donald. Life was troublesome enough with his being her guardian.

Thinking of her father, Thalia sank into a brocade chair by the cold hearth. This room, hers from the day she was born, had been lived in only for the past two years. Thalia hadn't visited Misty Glade until both her aunt and uncle had been killed in an accident while sailing to Charleston. Now she lived here, a stranger in her own home.

"Thalia!" Donald bellowed from the foot of the stairs.

Shaking off her sad memories, Thalia jumped to her feet and hurried into the hallway. She peered down the staircase at her brother's flushed face. "Yes, Donald?"

"We're leaving now."

"But, Donald, I need a moment to arrange my hair. You know—"

"Silence!" He turned to Ebenezer and motioned to him to go upstairs. "Bring her trunks, and don't dally a moment or I'll whip the hide off you."

"Donald, you can't speak to Ebenezer that way." Thalia strode halfway down the stairs. "In addition to your behavior being inexcusable, as always, please remember that Ebenezer belongs to me—as do Princess and Clover. If you wish one of my servants to do something for you, they will, of course, do it, as an accommodation. Not because you—"

"One more word and I'll thrash you, as well." Donald's face was as red as the sun that rose over the Atlantic on stormy mornings.

"Have I time to get my shawl?" Thalia asked, staring at Donald as if she were made of stone.

"If you continue to try my patience, I'll have you carried aboard without so much as a thought." Donald turned on his heels and strode to the front door. There he hesitated and glanced back at her. "I expect you on the dock in five minutes."

The trip from the island to Charleston was a harrowing one. Donald, even more inebriated than at dinner, insisted on taking the helm of the schooner despite Thalia's pleas to allow the captain to do his job. Even though the ocean was relatively calm, the boat tipped to one side and then the other with Donald's unsteady hand at the wheel, until nearly everyone felt ill. Water splashed over the sides of the ship, drenching the travelers thoroughly, and by the time they made port Thalia was furious and sticky from the salty residue.

She hailed a carriage without thinking of Donald's comfort and, with Clover and Princess, rode toward Meeting Street, leaving her brother at the dock to deal with the majority of the luggage. In the twilight, they rode a short distance down Bay Street and stopped at the public watering trough while the driver watered his horse.

Though she was eager to get to the town house, Thalia settled back to enjoy the sights of the bustling wharf. She realized that the animal needed a drink and that carriages frequently stopped there as they passed, and she waited patiently. She had so much to do when she arrived at the town house. She looked at the wharf. The last of the sunlight glimmered on the water of the Cooper River, sending shimmering ripples across the dark water as the gulls fished for their supper.

Thalia heard someone humming a jaunty tune and turned to see who was in such a jovial mood. She spotted a man strolling down the street as if he hadn't a care in the world. When he reached her carriage, he paused a moment and stopped humming. Roughly dressed in dark trousers and an open white shirt, he touched his hand to his forehead in salute and smiled warmly at her.

After her dousing on the trip from Edisto Island, Thalia didn't want to see anyone, nor did she want anyone to see her— least of all *this* ruggedly handsome man, who made her feel as if she looked like a field hand. His hair, dark and curling, barely touched his shoulders, and his eyes appeared to be gray, though she couldn't see them very well. Her gaze gravitated to a thin scar that traced the line of his square jaw, and she wondered what had caused it. She suspected that a woman must have been involved. She tried to smile, but knew that because of her wretched appearance she fell far short of her normally cheerful greeting.

"Good evening, miss," Justin Lionheart said, noticing the bright blue of her eyes. Even in the twilight they sparkled with a rich warmth.

"Good evening to you, sir," she replied, and felt a strong jab of Clover's elbow, deftly applied to her ribs. Thalia couldn't help it. Her innate friendliness always overcame her resolve to be ladylike.

Justin glanced at her and smiled again. She'd obviously arrived recently, and had, no doubt, experienced a difficult journey. Her disheveled appearance did little to diminish her beauty, softly enhanced by the golden twilight sky. "I had no idea the sea was as rough as your wet attire indicates."

Feeling a blush creep into her cheeks, Thalia prayed that the horse would soon have his fill of water. She could do nothing but reply. "I'm afraid, sir, that my brother lacks the necessary skills of a sea captain, but felt compelled to man the wheel."

"Ah, inexperience can cause disaster on the ocean. Please caution him against gambling with his lovely sister's life." Justin wondered what could make a man so inept that his passengers were drenched on a day when the sea was calm. "Should you have need to sail elsewhere, please come to me to see if I'm available. I promise you a more comfortable journey. I am Justin Lionheart, captain of the good ship *Blind Justice.*"

"Your kindness is unsurpassed, Captain Lionheart, but I'm afraid that would be impossible." Gambling with my life, she thought. Little does he know that Donald gambles with everything. Thalia was glad to see the horse finally lift his head from the watering trough. The driver glanced back at her. "I see my driver is ready to go on. Have a good evening."

Justin watched the carriage roll out of sight. She hadn't given him her name. She was a planter's daughter, no doubt, and had thought him beneath her notice. Well, it was good enough treatment for the likes of him. He knew better than to approach a young woman without a proper introduction. But she had spoken to him, risking a painful jab from her maid's elbow. This young woman showed more spirit than the usual planter's daughter.

Still, he didn't need a woman getting in the way of his business. The sooner he accomplished his task, the better off he'd be. He could get on with his life, such as it was.

When Thalia arrived at the town house, she set the two slaves to work, along with the housekeeper, Mrs. Hardy. Thalia, wanting nothing more than to wash off the salt, ordered a bath. While Thalia bathed, Princess prepared a cold supper and Clover unpacked the small trunk that contained Thalia's most essential items of clothing and toilette. She felt a little guilty for relaxing while everyone else was busy, but she couldn't stand the stickiness any longer.

The chill of evening was setting in, so Thalia built a fire and settled in front of it to warm herself for a moment. When the room seemed to be comfortable, she began to examine her wardrobe. Since her father's death, she and Donald had come to Charleston only infrequently, but Thalia still kept a few gowns at the town house. She selected a simple muslin dress, pulled it on and sat down to write a note to her old school friend, Lenore Calhoun.

When Clover finished unpacking the small trunk, she came to Thalia for further instructions. "What else, Miss Thalia? Supper ain't quite ready, and I'm done unpackin' our clothes till Mistah Donald get here with the big trunks."

Thalia looked at her servant sympathetically. There was always something to do. "Clover, I know you're tired, but would you feel like walking down to the Calhoun house and delivering a note to Miss Lenore? If you're too tired, I'll send Ebenezer when he arrives. And you can bathe, too. I know that salty feeling is horrible."

Clover grinned. "No'm, I ain't too tired. I'll bathe when I get back."

Watching her maid walk away with the note, Thalia settled back in front of the fire. She took off her slippers and stuck her feet out to warm them.

Without warning, the image of Justin Lionheart crept into her thoughts, and she smiled. Though his attire proclaimed him to be a common sailor—a sea captain, he'd said—his demeanor was that of a gentleman, even though he *had* spoken to her without an introduction. She wondered idly if he'd be in port for very long, and if she'd see him again.

Smiling, she decided that this trip to Charleston might not be as bad as she'd envisioned. Justin Lionheart might just put a spark into her life—if she ever saw him again.

Chapter Two

Thalia heard the front door open and walked down the stairs to see if Clover had returned with a response from Lenore Calhoun. When she reached the middle of the staircase, she found Lenore ready to bound up the stairs.

"Thalia!" Lenore cried, rushing up the steps and throwing her arms around Thalia.

She hugged Thalia so exuberantly that they almost lost their balance and toppled down the stairs. "Oh, Lenore, I'm so glad you came over. The only good thing about coming to town with Donald is seeing you. I'm sorry I didn't send you word in advance so you could've set aside some time for me."

"Oh, pooh. I always have time for you." Lenore linked her arm with Thalia's, and the two girls walked up the stairs to the morning room. "This house is so dark. Why don't you do a little redecorating while you're in town?"

"Redecorate?" Thalia glanced at the ornately patterned wallpaper. Its images were dark, almost unrecognizable, and the draperies were made of heavy velvet that was beginning to show its age. Change her father's home? Perhaps a change would be good for Donald. "Maybe I will. It depends on how long we're going to stay in town."

"Don't you know?" Lenore asked, settling herself on a rose-colored brocade chair. She looked around and smiled. "Now, *this* room looks fine. I wonder why the rest of the house looks so dreary?"

Thalia turned her head quickly to hide her pain. This room was the only one in the house that her mother had decorated.

The town house had been purchased shortly before Thalia's birth, and her mother had wanted this room to be her morning room. As things had turned out, it had become Thalia's mourning room. She'd seldom visited the town house before her father's death.

She could come here and think about her loneliness, about how it might have been if her mother had lived. Her aunt and uncle had been wonderful, but they could never completely obliterate the feeling of loss and rejection that Thalia felt when she had discovered the truth about her mother's death and her father's belief that Thalia was responsible for it.

The silence droned on for a moment, becoming almost unbearable to Thalia, and she brushed the sad memories aside. Usually the two women chattered like gulls fighting over a tasty tidbit, but Lenore's comments had taken the life out of Thalia's joy at seeing her friend again.

"Oh, I'm sorry, sweet," Lenore said, and leapt to her feet. She hurried to Thalia's side and embraced her. "Please forgive me. You know how my tongue wags. I'm always talking first and thinking later. What do I care about your father's decorator?"

Thalia smiled. She couldn't be angry with Lenore. Poor Lenore was one of those impulsive women who never learned to control their tongues, though with her it was usually a charming trait. Today it was a bit irritating. Thalia smiled at her best friend. "There's nothing to forgive. You know I'm just a little sensitive about my mother, particularly here."

Thalia motioned for Lenore to be seated and found a place for herself on the little brocade sofa that she had curled up on as a little girl during her infrequent visits here. "So, tell me all the news. What's happened since I last saw you? I seem to recall a certain gentleman by the name of John—"

"History, my dear, history. Where have you been? I've been in love at least four times since then. However, there's a certain man, a Mr. Nelson, who is new in town. He comes from a very wealthy Boston family and is simply the handsomest man I've ever met."

Unable to help herself, Thalia shook her head, the way Clover did when she pretended not to believe something Thalia said. "Lenore, dear friend, you're like a tonic to me. I never knew anyone who could fall in and out of love as quickly as you."

Lenore grinned and raised her eyebrows suggestively. "Well, my dear, some men don't deserve to be loved by wonderful me for very long. I mean, the idea of being devoted to one man is positively absurd—almost."

"I know, but it's about time you were getting serious." Thalia thought of her own predicament. "Isn't there *someone*?"

"As I said, Mr. Nelson is currently the most charming man in all of Charleston." Lenore leaned back, stretched luxuriously, and sighed. "Alas, he hasn't noticed that I'm exclusively devoted to him—at this moment."

"What a goose you are." Thalia shook her head and wagged her finger at her friend. "Mark my words, Miss Calhoun, a girl who chases after every man in trousers will find herself without a husband."

Lenore pouted prettily and fluttered her eyelashes. "Well, a girl can look around a little first, can't she? I mean, men do, don't they? Anyway, what's the harm in a little fun?"

"I suppose they do." Thalia leaned forward a little and smoothed an imaginary wrinkle. She thought of the way Justin Lionheart had smiled at her, and suddenly felt warm all over. She recalled his eyes, that wonderful gray in the twilight, and wondered if they were truly that color. "It doesn't seem fair, does it?"

"Not in the least." Lenore rose and strode to the window. "My mother acts as if I'm the last woman in the world who isn't married. She's terrified that I'll be an old maid, thereby humiliating her. You'd think I was twenty-five or something horrendous like that."

"Well, I don't have exactly the same situation, but Clover is bad enough, and Princess, too." Thalia joined her friend at the window, hoping to catch a glimpse of Captain Lionheart. "I think Charleston is beautiful at night, don't you?"

Lenore glanced at Thalia and scowled. "Changing the subject, are we?"

Surprised, Thalia looked at her friend. "Oh, I thought we were through discussing the horrors of old-maidhood that yawn before us like the gates of hell."

"We were," Lenore whispered, and then giggled. "But we weren't through discussing Mr. Nelson. You got us off the subject."

"Ah, yes, the mysterious Mr. Nelson," Thalia said teasingly, leading Lenore back to her seat. "Sit and tell me everything."

For more than an hour, Lenore regaled Thalia with the escapades and exploits of Mr. Edward Nelson. Thalia thought that Lenore must be exaggerating, as usual, when she continued raving about him. Mr. Nelson, it seemed, could do no wrong in Lenore's eyes.

Finally she laughed and held up her hand. "Gracious, Lenore, I do believe you're really in love this time."

Lenore glared at Thalia and said, "Whatever gave you that idea?"

"You did, you goose." Thalia moved to the sofa beside her friend and hugged her. "You certainly fall in and out of love as regularly as the tide, but I've never heard you carry on so about any man."

Before Lenore could answer, Thalia heard the front door open and close. "That must be Donald."

Lenore grimaced and crossed her arms. "I'd hoped that you'd come alone. I'm afraid I'm in entirely too good a mood to have your loathsome brother intrude. I don't know how you put up with him."

"Lenore," Thalia said softly, ready, as ever, to defend her brother. "He's my brother and I love him. I can't just pretend he doesn't exist, can I?"

"I would," Lenore retorted. She rose, shook out the hem of her gown and kissed Thalia on the cheek. "Goodbye, love. I'll see you in the morning. We'll go shopping together. Mrs. Kirkley has some new silks that are positively divine, according to Margaret Pickens."

"How is Margaret?" Thalia asked, tracing a finger along the dogwood blossoms carved into the banister.

"She's fine. You know Margaret, exceedingly practical." Lenore smiled fondly. "She's developed a liking for—do you remember Agatha Williams?"

"Yes, I remember her well. Why do you ask?" Thalia stopped and gazed at her friend. "Is something wrong with her?"

"Thalia, there's nothing wrong with Agatha that a good man wouldn't cure, stubborn though she is. I declare, that woman will never find a husband if she doesn't stop looking so hard— and trying to best every man that comes her way," Lenore prattled on. "Well, Margaret is sweet on Agatha's brother, Franklin. They've been together more than I can remember lately. They danced several dances together at the last Saint Cecilia's Ball."

Thalia nodded. "I'm happy for her. I hope something comes of this. Franklin is a good man, and Margaret is a delightful friend." Thalia thought for a moment. Lenore hadn't mentioned the last of the best friends from Mrs. Tallevande's School for Young Ladies. "Lenore, what ever happened to Pansy Monroe?"

Lenore hesitated, glancing around as if she were uncomfortable with the question. Finally she shrugged and shook her head gently from side to side. "I really don't know. Something awful happened. Her brother lost their plantation, and then she was gone. Nobody's seen her for the last few months."

"Nobody?" Thalia asked, astonished at her friend's revelation. "Lenore, hasn't someone tried to find her? I mean, she's our friend. She can't simply drop out of sight."

"Thalia, she had no money. She had no place to live." Lenore shifted restively again. "There was nothing anyone could do."

For a moment, Thalia felt her anger rising. There *was* something people could do. They could stop all that senseless gambling and close all the gambling clubs. That would help. But, even more, someone should have offered Pansy a place to live. "Didn't anyone think of giving her a home?"

"Gracious," Lenore said, tugging at the lace on her sleeve. "I suppose no one thought of that."

There was no sense in carrying the conversation any further. Lenore probably could do nothing if her parents didn't agree with her actions, though Thalia would have expected Mrs. Calhoun to be the first to offer Pansy a place to live. Thalia decided that while she was in town she'd try to find out what had happened to her friend.

Thalia placed her hand on Lenore's arm. "Lenore, do you...have you met Captain Justin Lionheart?"

"Yes, he's quite dashing. Why do you ask?" Lenore's eyes narrowed as she surveyed her friend. "What's going on here?"

Thalia knew that she shouldn't have mentioned Justin, but she couldn't help it. She'd thought of little else since she'd seen him. She'd done the wrong thing in bringing up his name; Lenore always made such an issue of things. Thalia tried to shrug off her query. "Nothing. I just met him this evening, and—"

"Aha!" Lenore cried, smiling maliciously. "You are certainly the one to scold me for falling in love so easily when you're practically swooning over a stranger."

"What a green goose you are. I declare, I never met anyone so apt to jump to conclusions as you." Thalia placed her hands on her hips and shook her head. "I just asked if you'd met him. That's all."

"*That's all?* He's the mystery man of the season. Nobody, but nobody, knows anything about him." Lenore eyed her friend suspiciously. "I doubt 'that's all,' but I can see that I'll get nothing more from you tonight, and I do need to run. Now, about tomorrow..." Lenore continued, returning to the subject of their proposed shopping trip.

The two women walked down the stairs, discussing the shops they intended to visit. When they reached the bottom, they found Donald staring up at them.

"Miss Calhoun, you certainly didn't waste any time." Donald's voice held a note of disapproval. He didn't like his sister's best friend, but he tried to smile. "How good to see you again. I do hope you're well, and your parents, too."

"How nice to see you, too, Mr. Freemont." Lenore continued walking. "I'm quite fine, as are my parents. Thank you for asking. I'll be sure to tell them you inquired."

Thalia and Lenore reached the door, opened it and walked onto the piazza. "Good night, Lenore," Thalia said, glancing at the street to see if someone might be walking past. "I'll be ready to go early in the morning."

She watched her friend walk down the steps and out through the wrought-iron gate. For a few seconds, she remained there, peering between the houses toward the harbor. From her vantage point, she could see the lanterns on the ships, swinging to and fro with the gentle motion of the waves. Their sails furled, the ships bobbed peacefully on the water, which glistened with a silvery trail of moonlight.

Was Justin Lionheart's ship among them? Mystery man, Lenore had called him. Instead of satisfying her curiosity, Thalia's inquiry had increased it.

After, Thalia realized that she was delaying going into the house, partly because she wanted to avoid Donald. She could, if she wanted, go to the back of the house and use the servants' stairs, but she knew that Donald would understand why she had gone that way. Instead, she lifted her chin and walked back into the foyer, where she found her brother waiting for her.

His face told her that he was already angry with her about something. She decided to ignore the obvious look of displeasure on his face and make an attempt at civilized conversation. "Ah, Donald, what entertainments have you planned for our visit this time?"

His lips, a little too large for his face, creased into an insincere smile. "Thalia, my dear, I hope that we can find some amusements to *our* liking. Charleston is a growing city. Why, only Boston compares with our culture, and I'm not at all sure that they can be considered as our equals."

"Having never been to Boston, I can't answer." Thalia thought for a moment, wondering if this was the time to bring up her ideas. "Donald, we do have some business to attend to. We need to speak with the French buyers. Our cotton is—"

"Cotton!" he shouted, glaring at her. "When are you going to realize that you're a lady? I won't have you hanging about the wharves like some . . . like some common woman."

Thalia knew immediately that she'd said the wrong thing. She'd have to visit the buyers herself, when Donald was otherwise occupied. She tried to smile. "As you wish, Donald. But I do want to do some shopping while I'm here, and maybe go to a play."

Thalia hoped that Donald wouldn't be too troublesome tonight. She crossed her fingers in the fold of her dress. "Do you think you can escort me? Us, I mean. Lenore will want to go along, I'm sure."

"A play?" Donald considered the idea. With a bit of luck, he could persuade his friend Randolph Taylor to accompany them. "I don't see why not." He patted his watch from his pocket and grimaced. "If I hurry, I can meet Randolph at the club. I hope you don't mind if I leave you alone on our first night in town? I do have pressing business."

Thalia almost sighed with relief. She could hardly believe that this was the same Donald she knew from Misty Glade. If his conduct continued to be so pleasant, their stay might not be quite as bad as she'd envisioned. "Of course not. Please enjoy yourself there while I complete our unpacking. You know I'll be busy here for hours, and there's no need for both of us to waste our first night in town."

Pressing business, indeed, she thought. His business dealt with gaming tables and spirits. She turned and went up to her room; there was really nothing for her to do this evening.

Seating herself in her rocking chair before the fire, she thought once again of Justin Lionheart. A smile teased her lips as she recalled his flamboyant gestures. His name seemed to fit him well. *Lionheart.* She'd never heard the name before, and she wondered idly if he'd made it up.

Realizing that she'd suddenly become sleepy, Thalia dressed for bed. She blew out her lamp and crawled between the crisp bed linens. Donald would be out until the wee hours of morning, so he wouldn't be likely to rise early enough to interfere with her day. She set about planning how she'd spend her time, wondering if she would see Justin Lionheart again. After a few minutes, she closed her eyes and nodded off to sleep.

Justin Lionheart sat in the tavern and downed another glass of rum. "Damn it, Edward, why didn't I ask her name? She is quite a beauty."

"Damned if I know, Justin. I wasn't there." Edward Nelson chuckled at his friend. He'd never seen Justin so upset over something so simple. "Perhaps, if you'd been less forward, the lady would have been more cooperative."

"By all that's holy, man, what else could I have done?" Justin signaled for more rum. He was in a fine state over his failure to discover the woman's name. "What if she's leaving? For all I know, she's already gone. I mean, she could have been coming in from one of the hammocks that dot the Carolina and Georgia coasts, only to leave immediately on another ship bound for Boston or England."

"Why do you say that?" Edward asked, tossing back his head and swallowing the last of his rum so that the tavern girl could refill it.

Justin shook his head sadly. "Her trunks were on top of the carriage, and I met her on the wharf. I know she'd just come in, but when I offered her my services if she should need a ship, she said it was quite impossible."

"But what could you have done?" Edward clapped his friend on the back. "I doubt you could have prevented her from leaving, if that was her intent."

"No," Justin admitted, drinking the last of his rum and rising. "But I just might have followed her."

"Followed her? How?"

"I *do* have a ship, you know." Justin pulled on his hat and headed for the door. "I'll find her. Just you wait and see."

"You're a fool, Justin Lionheart." Edward chuckled again and winked at the serving girl. "I guess I'm left to pay." He tossed a few coins on the table and followed Justin out the door. "I say, that was poor sport."

"What?" Justin asked, genuinely surprised. He considered himself an exceedingly sporting man.

For once, his exaggerated interest in a woman wasn't a lie. For once, he didn't have to pretend to be something he wasn't. He decided it was good to be himself. He liked the woman. She had caught his eye, and he'd admitted it to himself.

"Leaving me to settle our debt with the toothless serving girl." Edward pulled his cloak over his shoulders. "There's a nip in the air. Like we're to have an early fall."

Justin glanced at his friend and smiled. "Maybe, but if I'm right, this season may just be all the warmer for a certain miss I encountered this evening."

"If she didn't sail with the tide."

"If she didn't sail with the tide," Justin repeated, and launched into song about lost loves and the sea. He sang loudly and off-key, but he enjoyed the sound of his voice echoing off the wharves.

"God's blood, man, you're going to wake the city! The constable will have us in jail for instigating trouble. People will think war has broken out." Edward peered around, apparently looking for an officer who might really arrest them. "I've never seen you so taken with a woman before."

Justin stopped and stared at Edward. He considered Edward's remark for a moment and found it to be near the truth. "You may be right. Perhaps it would be better for me if she did sail away with the tide."

When Thalia awoke the next morning, she sensed that the day would be a wonderful one. She dressed in her nicest morning gown and hurried down the stairs. Clover was sitting at the table in the kitchen with Princess, and both servants rose when Thalia entered.

"Good morning," she said, and sat down with them. "I'll take my breakfast here with you, if you don't mind. I'll have ham and biscuits. Maybe a little molasses or honey."

"Miss Thalia, you ought to eat in the dining room," Princess said, setting a place for Thalia at the table. "Ladies don't eat in the kitchen with the help."

The three women ate while they discussed what needed to be done. Thalia licked some honey from her fingers and said, "Clover, I'm going shopping with Miss Calhoun. Would you be sure that all of Mr. Freemont's trunks are unpacked? I'm sure that he was out very late last night—"

"Last night?" Princess asked with a snort. "He didn't come in till after the widder Johnson's rooster crowed."

"Oh," Thalia said thoughtfully. "Well, maybe you'd better take care of our trunks first. Give him plenty of time to sleep without being disturbed."

"I ain't wakin' that man for no reason." Clover drank the remainder of her milk and stood. "I'll tippytoe around here like this was a wake and he was the guest of honor, all laid out in his best, ready to meet the Lord."

Thalia smiled. "You do that. And Princess—"

At that moment, Mrs. Hardy came in, and she seemed surprised to find Thalia sitting at the kitchen table. "Oh, Miss

Freemont, I didn't expect . . . I mean . . . you're up early this morning.''

Sopping up the last of the honey with her biscuit, Thalia grinned as Princess started to point out her bad manners. "Now, don't worry, Princess. I'd never do that before guests, but I wasn't about to waste that wonderful honey." She turned to Mrs. Hardy. "I'm an early riser, Mrs. Hardy. I realize that you've become accustomed to working by your own schedule, and I won't interfere. Please continue as is your custom, and ask me if you have any questions. I plan to be out for most of the morning."

The scarlet glow in Mrs. Hardy's face seemed to fade as she nodded in agreement with Thalia's remarks. "Yes, Miss Freemont, I'll be sure to ask."

"Clover will be unpacking my trunks. I understand that Mr. Freemont has only just returned from his club, so I'd appreciate it if you wouldn't disturb him. Oh, and one other thing . . . Would you make a list of your schedule for me? I promise not to interfere unnecessarily, but I do want to keep abreast of the household staff's work schedule. I'm here so infrequently, it's hard for me to keep up with your activities."

"I'll make a list today, Miss Freemont." Mrs. Hardy poured herself a goblet of fresh buttermilk and placed two biscuits on a plate. "Is there anything else?"

"No. Go on and enjoy your breakfast." Thalia rose and moved toward the door. "Clover, I need you to help me dress my hair, and then you can go about your business."

Thalia couldn't wait all morning for Lenore to get up and meander over at her own slow pace. With Clover's help, Thalia's hair was soon braided and twisted into a chignon low on her neck. Feeling happy about the day, she hurried down the stairs, wrapped her shawl about her shoulders and left. Since she hadn't encountered Donald this morning, she felt alive and pretty—almost sassy.

She walked jauntily down Meeting Street toward The Battery. Since Lenore wouldn't be ready for at least another hour, Thalia could enjoy the fresh breeze off the harbor and watch the big ships sail in and out.

When she reached the promenade, she strolled along slowly, peering out across the gently undulating juncture of the Ashley and Cooper Rivers. There were a few steamers, and several sailboats. While the steamers were faster, the sailboats were innately graceful, almost as if they were one with the sea.

She thought of Donald and his pitiful attempts at sailing. Why, she wondered for the hundredth time, did he refuse to assume the responsibility for his own life and for that of his plantation? Thalia wanted desperately to return to Sea Mist. She didn't know exactly how she'd arrange it, but she would. Nothing else meant anything to her. Sea Mist Plantation was the only true home she'd ever known.

The wind off the harbor ruffled her skirts, and she pulled her shawl more closely about her. There was a touch of autumn in the air, even though the end of September had yet to arrive. The sun, still young, scattered its rays like diamonds on the dimpled water and silhouetted the boats at anchor in the harbor. The smell of salt air was invigorating as she walked merrily along, pausing here and there to watch the gulls and pelicans fishing for their breakfasts.

Out in the harbor, Fort Sumter guarded Charleston from attack. What with all the quarreling about slavery and states' rights, she didn't know what the future held, but with the Federal army quartered at Fort Sumter she felt a little uncomfortable, as if it were a threat instead of protection. Uncle Martin had said that South Carolinians were prisoners in their own country, and many powerful men agreed with him.

Now, gazing out at the fort, she wondered where all the rhetoric would lead. "Stop it," she scolded herself. "It's much too beautiful a day to be pondering such weighty issues."

"You're much too beautiful a woman to be pondering such weighty issues," said a deep, masculine voice behind her.

She whirled around and found herself facing Justin Lionheart. Though she was at first a little embarrassed, her humor soon returned, and she found herself teasing him. "Mr. Lionheart, do you always sneak up on people like that?"

"Whenever I can, Miss . . ." Justin let his voice trail off in a questioning manner. He'd cursed himself all night for not finding out her name, and he'd decided that he'd find her first thing this morning if she was still in the city. The scent of some sweet flower perfumed the air around her, and he decided that it must be roses. He inhaled deeply, drawing the fragrance into his lungs and exhaling slowly to enjoy the full measure of its delight.

Thalia ignored his implied question. She knew she shouldn't be talking to him. They'd never been introduced, and somehow she felt that he was a temptation she would do well to avoid. She'd thought of him far too frequently since they'd met last evening. "I'm afraid I must be going, Mr. Lionheart."

"Oh, and where are you headed on such a bright morning?" he asked, hoping to keep her from leaving until he could find out more about her.

Feeling a bit abashed by his pointed questions, Thalia said nothing for a moment. She should never have spoken to him. Clover would raise a ruckus if she knew that Thalia was out here alone, talking to a strange man. But, as a rule, Thalia cared little for convention, and this morning—with this handsome man—was no exception. "I doubt you'd be interested in knowing, so I won't bore you," she said with a lilt in her voice, knowing that he could interpret her words as a challenge to try to learn more about her.

She turned and began to walk away, but he caught her by the arm. "Oh, you'd be surprised, miss, what I'm interested in."

Gasping, she stared at his hand on her arm. No man had ever touched her so familiarly, at least not a stranger. Thalia began to worry. She'd been flirting, but this man was altogether too forward, and she was too inexperienced to know how to rid herself of him. She wondered if he intended to harm her, but decided that he wouldn't be so foolish in full view of the citizenry of Charleston, several of whom were passing by. Thalia considered calling out to them, but knew she ought to be able to handle this situation without help. There was no doubt that she would be considered at fault here, since she was strolling about without an escort.

When she looked into his face again, his smile was captivating, not menacing. Thalia couldn't help smiling back at him, though she tried to look stern.

"Mr. Lionheart, be good enough to unhand me." Thalia lifted her chin defiantly and stared into his challenging gray eyes until he released her arm. "I regret that I'm going to be late for an appointment and have no further time to waste with you."

"I regret that far more than you, miss." Justin removed his hand from her arm, hoping she'd favor him with a smile before she left. The slight crinkle at the corners of her eyes, and the set of her somewhat pouty mouth, told him that she'd enjoyed their encounter, and he would have to settle for that—for now.

Thalia strode away. This time he didn't touch her; nor did he follow, at least not too closely. She sauntered along as if the event meant nothing to her, but she still felt uneasy. As she walked along, she nodded to several people who were familiar to her, but didn't stop. When she reached the end of the promenade, she glanced back to see if Justin Lionheart was nearby, and found him no more than a few feet away, talking with an acquaintance of her uncle Martin.

Talking, but watching her. Justin's gaze seemed to follow wherever she went. The breeze caught his black hair and ruffled it slightly; when he casually raked his fingers through it, unruly curls sprang forth.

Thalia smiled. He presented such an interesting picture, rugged but somehow cultured. His speech was that of an educated man, and his demeanor was relaxed and uninhibited, much like that of the young men she knew in Charleston. Justin's face, bronzed by the sun, was handsome in a powerful way, unlike Donald's. And the scar intrigued her. She found that she really wanted to know how he had come to have that narrow white line across his cheekbone.

"Ah, good morning, Miss Freemont," her uncle's friend called.

The two men had caught her staring. Color flooded Thalia's face. How could she ever explain what she was doing? Out alone this early in the morning, with no chaperon, gave scant testimony to her upbringing. She didn't care what Captain Lionheart thought, but her uncle's friend would be shocked.

Even worse, now Captain Lionheart knew her name. She'd prayed that nobody would say her name within Mr. Lionheart's hearing, but the answer to her prayer was apparently no. She smiled brightly, as if she had not a single care in the world and called, "Good morning, Mr. Saunders. How nice to see you this fine day. I'd like to come by your office soon to discuss the Sea Mist cotton. It's even finer this year than last."

"Certainly, my child," Caleb Saunders agreed. "But shouldn't I discuss plantation business with Donald? I mean, after all—"

"Sea Mist Plantation is mine, Mr. Saunders." Thalia tried not to sound bitter, but every man treated her the same way. She could hardly wait to take the reins of Sea Mist fully and show them what a woman could do when she chose to step out of the kitchen or nursery. "Donald has nothing, nothing whatsoever, to do with Sea Mist."

Beside Caleb Saunders, Justin grinned and touched his forehead in a salute. He admired her spunk. It was a rare woman who announced to the world that she was running a plantation without the assistance of a man. "Ah, Saunders, I'm afraid Miss Freemont and I haven't met. Would you be so kind?"

"Of course," Caleb Saunders answered, and the two men walked over to where Thalia was standing. "Miss Thalia Freemont, may I present Captain Justin Lionheart? Captain, Miss Freemont."

Thalia muttered the proper responses and stood for a moment while the men talked about the chill in the air. After a sufficient time, she gazed at Justin Lionheart and smiled. "Mr. Lionheart, I've enjoyed meeting you. This has certainly been an entertaining outing. I . . . I hope we meet again. Mr. Saunders, have a lovely day. I'll see you soon."

Turning on her heel, Thalia strode confidently away from the two men without waiting for their replies. *I hope we meet again.* How could she have said that? Did she mean it? Forcing Mr. Lionheart from her mind, she continued her journey and tried to concentrate on the day ahead.

She hurried up East Battery and ducked into the gate at Lenore's without looking back. She skipped up the steps and knocked at the door.

Lenore's servant, Mammy, opened the door, and Thalia rushed in without waiting to be asked. She threw her arms around Mammy's huge girth and then stood back to look at her. "Good morning, Mammy. You're just as pretty as ever. It's been so long since I've seen you."

"Lordy, Miss Thalia, you're a mess." Mammy hugged Thalia again. "I sho' missed you, chile."

"I've missed you, too. Is Lenore ready yet? We're going shopping." Thalia made her way into the parlor and sat on the chair nearest the window. She loved the view from Lenore's parlor.

Mammy trailed after her, shaking her head. "Now, you know, Miss Thalia, that girl ain't never been ready this early. I don't 'spect she'll be ready on time for her own funeral."

"I know, but I just couldn't stay at the town house." Thalia never could call it home. She still felt uncomfortable there, more so than anyplace else.

If Mammy was surprised, she didn't say anything about it. "Lordy, it's good to see you, Miss Thalia. You shore growed up to be a purty girl. I bet you has to fight the men off with a broom."

Thalia laughed as she imagined herself taking a broom to Justin Lionheart, but decided that she probably wouldn't. He certainly seemed interested, she had to give him that much. Perhaps it would take him longer than most men to discover that she didn't intend to marry.

Marriage caused too many problems. She'd seen that from an early age while visiting her friends' homes. Her brother told her she was too forward, and her father had reacted to that trait with such strength that he'd banned her forever from his sight. After seeing the cold, unhappy marriages of some of her friends, she had concluded that marriage wasn't for her. She planned to avoid the woes associated with the union. She could run her plantation alone. But, even though she didn't really want a husband, Justin Lionheart might prove to be entertaining while she was in town.

Chapter Three

Lenore burst into the room quickly and hugged Thalia. "Gracious, Thalia, but you do keep country hours. You must have been up before the roosters crowed this morning."

Thalia shook her head. "I suppose I was. I wanted to leave before Donald arose."

"Good plan," Lenore agreed. "Have you eaten?"

"Yes, have you?" Thalia asked, wondering how long it would take her friend to be ready to leave.

"Just barely," Lenore admitted. "Then we're ready to go."

After Lenore gave instructions to the housekeeper, the two women left. They walked back to Meeting Street and over to Tradd, where they went into Mrs. Kirkley's Shoppe, the most exclusive dressmaker's shop in Charleston.

Mrs. Kirkley's assistant seated the two women and offered them a cup of tea while they waited for the dressmaker. The tea never had a chance to cool, for Mrs. Kirkley entered the room a moment later; three young women trailed behind her, carrying fashion dolls and rolls of fabric. Like ducklings waddling after their mother, Thalia mused, trying desperately to hide her reaction. Mrs. Kirkley didn't cater to any but the finest of Charleston's families, and Thalia didn't want to fall from the good graces of her favorite seamstress.

"Good morning, Miss Calhoun and Miss Freemont." Mrs. Kirkley bustled about, as if to assure herself that the two women were being well taken care of. "I see that Miss Mac-Gregor has offered you our meager hospitality."

"Good morning, Mrs. Kirkley," the two women chorused.

They glanced at each other and giggled. Thalia thought they sounded rather as they had when they were children in Miss Tallevande's School for Young Ladies. Thalia reduced her girlish response to a more acceptable smile. "We've come to look at the new silks, Mrs. Kirkley, if they're available."

"Of course, they are, my dears. Follow me." She herded the three assistants ahead of her as she led Thalia and Lenore through the door and up a narrow staircase, all the while talking to them over her shoulder. "I'm sure you dear girls will find something lovely. You know I pride myself in acquiring only the best materials and employing the best seamstresses. What one wears is of critical importance these days."

Thalia listened to Mrs. Kirkley go on and on about the exclusivity of her shop and occasionally nodded or answered as indicated. One of the best reasons for going to Mrs. Kirkley's was the gossip. Although the seamstress swore her clients to secrecy as if they were the only ones she deigned to relate the latest tidbit to, she herself felt no such compulsion, and chattered about everyone with whom she came in contact.

By the time they reached the showing room, Thalia was hardly listening. Never one to gossip herself, she let the words flow over her as if she were a shell on the beach.

Lenore, apparently, felt no such compunctions. "What do you hear of that handsome Edward Nelson? Does he buy his shirts from you?"

"Mr. Nelson? Of course, he's a fine man." Mrs. Kirkley stared at Lenore for a moment. "Where *would* he purchase his shirts?"

"Uh, here, of course. I simply meant..." Lenore's voice trailed off. She clearly realized that she was caught in a ticklish situation.

Thalia realized that Lenore's interest in Mr. Nelson would soon be the topic of conversation between Mrs. Kirkley and other clients. She felt compelled to rescue her friend. "I came into town just last night, Mrs. Kirkley, and Lenore mentioned that Mr. Nelson was new in Charleston. She remarked that I might like to invite him to a small dinner party I'm planning next week, but she hasn't seen him lately."

Mrs. Kirkley's gaze shifted to Thalia. "I see. Well, he was here yesterday, ordering shirts, and as far as I can tell he's *ex-*

tremely fit." Enunciating her words carefully, she glanced back at Lenore. "An attractive man, without a doubt. Some young woman will be lucky to rescue him from the bachelor's block. His friend, that handsome Captain Lionheart, ordered shirts, as well. He's a thief of hearts, too, I'll bet."

Lenore winked at Thalia as if to say a silent "Thanks."

"I wouldn't know about that, Mrs. Kirkley." Lenore seemed to have recovered her composure. "I merely want to be assured that Charleston's society welcomes a gentleman like Mr. Nelson as is fitting. We wouldn't want to besmirch our reputation for hospitality, now would we?"

"Of course not." Mrs. Kirkley returned to her task. "If you ask me, which, of course, you didn't, I'd say that Captain Lionheart is much more interesting, although he's a bit devilish. A woman could never rest if she was married to him. Every shrew in a skirt would be after him. There's a story hidden somewhere behind that handsome face, and I, for one, would like to know what it is."

Trying to ignore the comments about Justin, Thalia moved to Mrs. Kirkley's side and began examining the rolls of silk and taffeta. She firmly pushed the captain out of her mind as she gazed at the rainbow of colors spread out before her, incredibly beautiful and delicate. Fingering the fabrics lovingly, Thalia shook her head. "I declare, I just don't know how I'll be able to choose from among all these colors. It gets more difficult every time I come in."

Mrs. Kirkley beamed at Thalia's praise. "Miss Freemont, will your brother be coming in for shirts?"

Thalia looked up, surprised by the question. "Why, I don't know, Mrs. Kirkley. Why do you ask?"

"Oh, no reason." Mrs. Kirkley smiled. "It's just that when Captain Lionheart was in to order *his* shirts, Miss Prentiss was with him. And I haven't seen your brother for some time."

Appalled that Mrs. Kirkley would relate such personal gossip about her customers, Thalia tried to smile. She shrugged casually as if the name meant nothing to her. Eugenia Prentiss was Donald's mistress. She had been chasing Donald for years, but so far he'd eluded her noose, as he called it. Was she using Captain Lionheart to make Donald jealous, or had she shifted her loyalty to the captain? Thalia felt a twinge that resembled jealousy, but cast it aside as nothing more than casual interest.

Lenore gazed steadily at Thalia. "My goodness, isn't that an odd turn of events?"

"Hardly, Lenore," Thalia answered evenly. "Miss Prentiss may associate with whomever she chooses. She's a lovely woman. And Captain Lionheart is certainly a handsome man. Who can blame her?"

"Well, well," Lenore said, smiling sweetly. "He's a handsome man, you say. How very interesting."

"Please try to quell your overactive imagination and concentrate on our purpose." Thalia spotted a sapphire-colored taffeta and lifted a rustling layer of the fabric to catch the light streaming in the windows. "Oh, how lovely."

"Thalia, you must have a gown made from that. It's exactly the color of your eyes." Lenore selected a piece of apple green but glanced wistfully at the blue. "I wish I could wear that color."

"Don't be silly, Lenore. This color would be fine on you," Thalia told her friend, privately hoping that Lenore would select the green. "Besides, that apple green will make you look like a vision."

Lenore grinned and raised her eyebrows a little as she held a piece of the fabric to her breast and peered into the mirror behind the table. "You're right, of course. This is perfect for me."

"I agree," Mrs. Kirkley said, and pulled a roll of violet-colored gauze from a covered wooden table that sat to one side of the room. "This is the latest thing from England."

Thalia stared at the color, marveling at its vibrancy. She'd never seen anything quite like it. "Where does the color come from?"

Mrs. Kirkley laid a fold of the cloth over her arm and let the sunlight caress the fabric for a moment before she spoke. "It's a wonderful new synthetic dye called mauvine. Can you imagine such a lush color? I was thrilled when I first saw it."

Lenore grimaced. "That's undoubtedly the most gorgeous piece of gauze I ever saw." She fingered a ringlet of her auburn hair. "Alas, I'll never wear it." She sighed wistfully and then looked at Thalia. "But you can."

"Me?" Thalia gazed longingly at the gauze. She would love to have a gown of this exquisite color. She held the gauze near her face and looked into the mirror. Her eyes changed mystically from their normal deep blue to a color that was almost as violet as the fabric. She glanced at Lenore, who bobbed her head approvingly. "All right. I'll take it. The blue taffeta, as well."

"Oh, how I envy you the ability to wear that violet gauze," Lenore said as they followed Mrs. Kirkley into the pattern room. "This must be a very special gown."

"It certainly will be," Mrs. Kirkley commented as she stepped over to her books. "Now, let's see . . ." She gazed at Thalia for a moment. "I have just the thing."

She proudly displayed a picture of an off-the-shoulder gown that came to a soft V at the bosom. "Exquisite. You'll never find anything that will suit you better."

Lenore glanced at a pattern with twelve flounces down the skirt. "This is quite the thing these days."

Mrs. Kirkley gave Lenore a withering stare. "Not in this luscious gauze. Its daring color will be greatly accented by a simpler gown, decorated with a shawl bertha of cream-colored Chantilly attached to the neckline and accented with dark violet satin roses. Around the bottom of the skirt, oh, say twelve inches from the floor, we'll put a shirred band of Chantilly and the same roses. Nobody in all of Charleston will have such an exquisite gown."

"Mrs. Kirkley is right, Lenore," Thalia agreed, fingering the gauze appreciatively. For a moment she allowed her mind to wander . . . to a man standing on the promenade, a man with laughing gray eyes. Would Justin Lionheart think her beautiful if he saw her in this gown? She shook herself slightly, hoping that Lenore and Mrs. Kirkley hadn't noticed her lapse. To cover her apparent daydreaming, she said quickly, "It needs a burnoose of the same satin as the roses to top it off perfectly."

At Thalia's words, Mrs. Kirkley beamed. "Precisely what I was thinking. Perhaps we'll close the burnoose with black frogs. Oh, Miss Freemont, this gown will be the talk of all Charleston. When will you wear it?"

Thalia thought carefully. This wasn't exactly the sort of gown she could wear to just any event. She had to choose the event carefully. "I...I don't know." She knew she sounded silly and indecisive, so she gazed at Mrs. Kirkley and smiled. "I arrived only last night. I'm sure that once I find out what social events are planned, I'll make the correct decision. Now, what about the blue?"

"I'd suggest something a little more fancy. The taffeta isn't nearly the equal of that divine gauze, and may need to be a little fussier." Mrs. Kirkley glanced through her patterns before stopping and pointing a long, gnarled finger at the one she thought most appropriate.

Thalia gazed at the drawing for a moment, but shook her head. "I believe all those ruffles will make me look silly." She shuffled through more patterns until she came to a simple gown with a single ruffle at the bottom of its wide skirt. "Here, this is what I want."

Mrs. Kirkley, apparently a little perturbed because Thalia disagreed with her choice of patterns, stared down her nose at the picture. "Well, I suppose..."

"Oh, Thalia, are you sure?" Lenore asked, as if to remind her that she had been out of touch with the world of fashion for some time. "Everyone is wearing simply dozens of ruffles this year."

Thalia shook her head. "The blue taffeta is quite lovely. I believe we can make it work without all those fussy ruffles. I'd simply die in that dress with... Never mind," she said and pointed once again to the pattern of her choice. "Mrs. Kirkley, do you think you and your girls could make this with a little inset of that embroidered pink lace at the bosom? Perhaps a ruffle of the darling pink lace and artificial roses around the hem would enhance the gown sufficiently so I wouldn't look so plain. I could wear a mantelet of the same pink lace."

The embroidered pink lace was quite a bit more expensive than the taffeta, and every bit as fashionable as the ruffles. Mrs. Kirkley glanced at the pattern Thalia had indicated, and nodded.

"If I could have a little of the lace made into a circle around a little spray of flowers, I could wear it in my hair." Thalia knew Mrs. Kirkley couldn't turn down the opportunity to make such a dress.

"Why, Miss Freemont, I never realized you . . ." Mrs. Kirkley paused for a moment, as if to gather her thoughts. "I never realized you possessed such a keen sense of color and fashion. Is there anything else?"

"I'd like several pairs of pantalets and new crinolines to wear with my new gowns." Thalia thought for a moment. She really needed a new riding costume. "What have you in the way of fabric for riding clothes?"

"I have just the thing. It comes in dark blue or black and is used primarily for riding clothes." Mrs. Kirkley left the room, and returned carrying two bolts of cloth. "Will either of these do?"

"Choose the blue, Thalia," Lenore urged her friend. "I just recently had a riding gown made of the black. It's wonderful."

Thalia assented quickly. She cared little what she wore riding, as long as it was serviceable. "I'll take a dressing gown, too. Oh, and I need a day dress. Something simple, in a light wool."

Nodding, Mrs. Kirkley laid the blue fabric alongside the two Thalia had already chosen and took the black back to the other room. She returned with several rolls of silk. "What about one of these?"

Gazing at the array of colored satins, Thalia could hardly decide. She finally selected a dark garnet color and chose lace and ribbons to adorn the dressing gown. "I believe that's all I need."

Lenore selected the materials for another gown, and then nodded. "Quite a successful shopping trip, wouldn't you say?"

"Certainly," Thalia agreed, gazing once more at the lovely violet gauze. Justin Lionheart's face swam before her eyes. For a few seconds, she could see herself in his arms, whirling around the dance floor while everyone watched. She could almost feel the touch of his arms around her, his face smiling down into hers. His lips—

"Ladies, if you'll come with me, I'll take your measurements." Mrs. Kirkley preceded them along the landing until they reached a more secluded room. They entered, followed by two of Mrs. Kirkley's assistants.

Mrs. Kirkley took Thalia's measurements first. Standing with her arms raised, she felt a little foolish. "When can you have these ready for fitting?"

"Thirty-six," Mrs. Kirkley called to one of the girls, and then stopped to think for a moment. "I believe we can have them ready for the first fitting in three days."

Thalia stared at Mrs. Kirkley for a moment. Such a short time span was unheard-of in Mrs. Kirkley's shop, because of her long list of clients. Thalia decided that there must be some event coming up soon that Mrs. Kirkley wanted to use as a showcase for the violet-colored gown. "Just send a note around, Mrs. Kirkley, and we'll come in for the fittings."

When Thalia left Mrs. Kirkley's shop, she felt excited. It had been a long time since she'd been to a real party. After her father's death, she'd worn mourning clothes, though she'd felt little grief. She had hardly known her father, and his death had affected her little.

She could still remember the heartache that had plagued her when her aunt and uncle had been killed several years before. Having lived with them since her mother's death, Thalia had loved them much more than she ever could her father. Her life at Sea Mist had been a happy one—one she regretted having lost since their deaths—but her father had insisted that she come to live at Misty Glade with him. She'd gradually forgiven him for refusing to see her all those years, but without knowing him she could hardly come to love him as a parent. The hurt in his eyes when he looked at her had almost crushed her, and Thalia had gradually come to avoid being with him whenever possible, hoping to alleviate the pain that nagged at each of them.

Now Thalia longed to go to a ball or party. She wanted to show off her glorious new gowns. "Lenore, did you think it odd that Mrs. Kirkley said we would have our fitting in three days' time?"

Lenore's eyes widened. "Gracious, I never would have guessed she'd rush like that. Why do you think she would?"

Thalia smiled conspiratorially. "I think she wants me to show off the violet-colored gown at some upcoming event, don't you?"

"Of course," Lenore gushed, squeezing Thalia's hand. "There's the Harvest Ball next week. The Saint Cecilia Society is giving it at the Hibernian Hall. Are you going?"

"I suppose," Thalia answered noncommittally. "Are you?"

"I wouldn't miss it if Queen Victoria were visiting my mother." Lenore looked at Thalia. "You're welcome to attend with us. I know you don't like to go to balls with Donald. Who would? He's such a snob."

"Lenore, that's not a nice thing to say. He's my brother." Thalia resented Lenore's comments about Donald, even though she agreed with her friend. She just didn't like hearing about how other people felt about Donald. "I'd love to attend the ball with you."

Her thoughts were on Justin Lionheart. Thalia could almost see herself in the beautiful new violet gown as she entered the ballroom. Would he be there to see her? Her heart pattered slightly, as if she were having palpitations, and she wondered if it could have anything to do with Justin. "How silly. You've just met the man."

"Who?" Lenore asked, stopping to stare at her friend. "What man?"

"Man?" Thalia hadn't realized she'd spoken out loud. She felt fresh color spring into her cheeks, and she scowled at Lenore. "Did I say man?"

"Yes, you did, and you'd better tell me everything about this man right now or I'm going to tell Clover you bought a red crinoline," Lenore threatened.

"You wouldn't." Thalia knew that Clover would ultimately believe the truth, but before she could be convinced there would be a bevy of questions to answer. Thalia had no choice but to tell Lenore about Justin—but without any apparent fuss or fanfare. "Just a man I met this morning on the way to your house. I mentioned him to you. Captain Lionheart is his name, I believe."

"'Just a man'?" Lenore repeated incredulously. "There's no such thing as 'just a man.' I knew you were evading my questions earlier. Tell me everything."

Thalia regretted having spoken aloud. Now she would never be able to stop the flood of questions, and she was discovering, to her dismay, that talking about Justin Lionheart made her uncomfortable, since she hadn't been able to decide how she really felt about him. Desperate to divert Lenore's attention, Thalia pointed to a stranger entering the tavern. "Is that Mr. Nelson?"

Lenore glanced around and then back at Thalia. "Where?"

Spotting the door closing at the tavern, Thalia shook her head sadly. "Over there.... Oh, no, he went into the tavern." Thalia started to walk ahead, hoping she'd diverted Lenore's attention long enough to keep her from remembering what they'd been talking about.

With a sassy grin, Lenore caught Thalia's arm, leaned over and whispered, "Let's go in."

Thalia turned to stare at her friend. "Lenore, have you gone daft?"

"Nobody will ever know." Lenore bit her bottom lip thoughtfully. "I dare you."

The words were dashed into Thalia's face like cold water from a well. "Now, Lenore, we're all grown up, and silly little games we played as girls are entirely inappropriate now, especially those like—"

"I said I dare you, and the dare stands," Lenore repeated, crossing her arms stubbornly.

Now Thalia was in a quandary. She'd never backed down from a dare—at least not yet. But she'd grown up a lot since the days when Lenore could talk her into things just by issuing a dare.

A shiver of excitement crept up her spine. Thalia really did want to go into the tavern. When they'd been at Mrs. Tallevande's School for Young Ladies, Lenore had always been able to convince Thalia to do anything with a dare—as long as it was something she really wanted to do. "What a little twit you are. We're not schoolgirls, putting pepper in Miss Abigail's tea. You're talking about going into a—a tavern."

"The gauntlet is thrown." Lenore held her ground, breaking eye contact only long enough to glance occasionally at the tavern door. "Will you or will you not accept my dare?"

"Lenore, you must see how preposterous this is. We are *ladies*. We can't go barging into a tavern. What would your mother think?" Thalia was scrambling for a good reason why they couldn't go into the tavern. Truthfully, she really couldn't think of one—except the one she'd given, and she didn't *really* care what Mrs. Calhoun, or anyone else, thought.

"She'll never know," Lenore answered, grabbing Thalia's arm and dragging her toward the tavern.

"You know that two ladies going into a tavern is nearly as bad as going into a—a brothel." Thalia knew she was using her last argument, but it didn't seem to hold any sway over Lenore, who kept marching toward the tavern door.

Lenore turned and whispered over her shoulder, "I'd follow him into a brothel, too. Don't you think that would be interesting? To see what they really do, I mean."

Feeling defeat enfold her like the cold mist from the harbor, Thalia straightened herself, shook Lenore's hand away and strode toward the tavern. Thalia knew this adventure would mean trouble, but she didn't really know how to avoid it. In fact, she didn't really know if she *wanted* to avoid it. She was as curious as Lenore—maybe more so. Though she could hardly know what Edward Nelson looked like, she had started the whole thing when she'd brought him up. Lenore should have seen through Thalia's ruse. She straightened her shoulders, touched the doorknob and wondered if she'd find a certain sea captain inside.

Justin Lionheart sat in a comfortable chair in the tavern and watched the other men enjoying their ale, although in truth there were few who could get away at this time of day. He felt frustrated that he'd been unsuccessful, thus far, in locating the man he'd come to Charleston to find, but he'd heard of a man who might be a good possibility. The man was a gambler, an uncaring aristocrat, but Justin had yet to meet him. He couldn't be sure, but he thought the woman he'd met this morning was the sister of the man he sought. If so, then a part of his revenge could involve her. A man was always protective of his sister, as Peter Kimball had been, and this Donald Freemont would be no different.

Justin was impatient with his lack of luck at finding his foe. He'd been here for several months, cultivating friendships, going to parties and suppers, gaining entry into the gambling clubs of the town as he searched for the mystery man who had ruined his life. To his surprise, he found that he liked Charleston a great deal. In fact, of late he'd considered making the port city his new home.

For a moment Justin's thoughts returned to Miss Thalia Freemont. As long as she'd thought there was no way of his discovering her name, she'd flirted with him; not as outrageously as some, but she flirted nonetheless. Women were so unpredictable. He wondered how she'd react when she discovered the true reason he was in Charleston. He didn't particularly like the idea of involving an innocent woman in his schemes, but then, this man had felt no such guilt when he'd destroyed Alicia's life. Justin had to remain committed to his revenge.

The serving girl placed a tankard of ale in front of him, and he glanced up at her. The slight earthy odor that emanated from her reminded him of how much he had enjoyed standing next to Miss Freemont. Her sweet fragrance—roses, he was now convinced—was as alluring to him as nectar to the bees of spring.

He smiled appreciatively, recalling her brilliant blue eyes. He'd seen that color but once before—on a bright summer afternoon in the Caribbean Sea. Justin surmised from his short association with her that she was an intelligent woman, one who would be interesting to know better. But he was in Charleston for another reason entirely, and until he'd met Miss Freemont he hadn't had the slightest inclination to become involved with one of the city's society ladies. Now, however, his quest might include her. He would have to pursue her until he discovered for sure if her brother was the man he sought.

Justin spied a man he hadn't yet questioned, and rose. He motioned to the serving girl to bring another glass of ale and strode to the man's table. He introduced himself and sat down at the man's invitation. Hoping his questions wouldn't put suspicion in the man's mind, Justin worded his query carefully. "I met a man from Charleston once. Can't recall his name, but he had a curious nickname. Dof, I believe it was. I thought I'd renew my acquaintance with him, but I can't seem to locate him. Could you help me? Maybe you know him."

The heavily bearded man nodded and took a long swig of the ale that Justin had bought him. The man wiped his mouth on his sleeve and peered at Justin through reddened eyes. "What did 'e look like?"

Here Justin was at a loss. He didn't know what the man looked like, only that he lacked morals. That description fit any number of men, here and everywhere else. "Average gentleman, I'd say."

"Charleston's full of 'em," the man replied, lifting the tankard again. "Don't know nobody with a nickname much. I just got 'ere meself."

Justin thanked the man and signaled for another bottle of ale. Leaving the drunken man, Justin threaded his way back to his own table and sat down. So far, his inquiries had been met with no useful information. But Justin knew his quarry was here; he had to be.

The door opened. He glanced up at his friend, Edward Nelson, who was making his way across the floor in the dim light. Justin's mood improved as he waved and smiled. "Well, if it isn't the sleepwalker himself. Did you awaken late today?"

Edward cursed good-naturedly and shook his head. "I swear, Justin, that I never met a man such as you. Here I was thinking I had arisen earlier than you, but your presence would seem to indicate the fault of my supposition. I'll go find two tankards while you congratulate yourself on winning this little bet."

"Maybe you'll win next time, Edward old man. Perhaps you should study the habits of sailors before you wager again on who will arise the earliest." Justin glanced around the room again as Edward walked away. They'd been at their club until the sun had risen over the harbor. Since they both had business to attend to, they'd promised to rest a while and then meet here. Edward had offered the wager, and Justin had been unable to refuse.

With Edward Nelson's help, Justin had eased into the fringes of society enough to gain entry into the gambling clubs and into the parlors of some of Charleston's society. He liked Edward a great deal—more, in fact, than anyone he'd known in a long time. Edward, a Boston native, had moved here to take possession of an inherited estate. He knew little about running a plantation and left most of the details to his overseer, giving him plenty of time to socialize.

Justin was sipping his ale slowly, scanning the room for newcomers, when he saw the door open. As usual, he was alert to the fact that he might encounter his nemesis at any time. He sat a little straighter, hoping that this man would be the one for whom he was searching. The search was becoming tiresome, and it weighed heavily on his mind most of the time, so badly that he could hardly sleep.

He was wrong about the newcomer. He was *very* wrong. Two women walked into the tavern, and a bit uncertainly, if he was any judge of demeanor. Justin couldn't be sure, because of the dim light, but he thought the two women were young ladies, probably planters' daughters, who were overcome with curiosity and very much out of place in this tavern full of ruffians and heavy drinkers.

Edward put the ale on the table with a thud and dropped into the seat next to Justin. "Here you are, old man. Drink in good health. Next time you won't be so lucky."

Ignoring the ale, Justin rose halfway out of his chair and touched his friend's shoulder. Pointing to the entrance, he whispered, "Look at that."

Thalia knew she was in trouble. Conversation stopped in the tavern when the door closed behind her. Silently cursing Lenore for talking her into this misbegotten adventure, and herself for really wanting to see the inside of a tavern, Thalia offered a silent prayer for protection against whatever kind of man haunted this sort of place. She included a prayer that she should try to be more like her Aunt Molly, but that addendum was halfhearted. The reason Thalia allowed herself to be talked into this kind of situation was that she *enjoyed* flouting society's traditions. In fact, entering a place so taboo intrigued her. So far, her escapades with Lenore had proven harmless, but this one might be the exception. It would certainly be more exciting than most.

Thalia hoped that Lenore would scan the room and decide that their mission was futile, that Thalia had been wrong. She wanted very much to be wrong, because she thought that Lenore would probably march herself over to Mr. Nelson's table and seat herself if he were indeed in the tavern. The odor of stale ale and perspiration permeated the air of the room, and she lifted her perfumed handkerchief to her nostrils in a vain attempt to ward off the nauseating smell.

"Isn't this exciting?" Lenore whispered, glancing around the room. "Ooh, you were right. There he is," she squealed under her breath. "Come on, Thalia."

Thalia cursed herself. Her diversion, intended to distract Lenore from pursuing their conversation about Justin Lionheart, had backfired right in her face, which she was sure was glowing like the flame of a gas lamp.

Her bravado failed when she saw the light in Lenore's eyes. Thalia had been right. Lenore wasn't content with merely looking around; she was already heading toward Edward Nelson's table.

"Oh, no," she whispered, feeling a little faint and wondering how fate could have played such a cruel trick on her. Justin Lionheart was the last person she would have expected to find in a tavern.

"Just act natural. We'll sit down and ask for a glass of—" Lenore glanced at Thalia and realized something was wrong. "What is it? What's wrong?"

Lenore's gaze followed Thalia's. Lenore didn't know who had upset her friend so much, but she saw Edward staring at them and smiled. She thought about waving, but decided that a smile would do just fine.

"Eh, look at the skirts what just wandered in, mate," a bearded man said, jabbing his elbow in his friend's ribs. He rose and began to stumble toward them. "I'll take that little tart with the golden hair for meself. Just help yourself to the other, laddie."

Oh, Lord, please allow me to faint before I die of embarrassment, Thalia prayed silently, and then lifted her chin proudly. Why should she be embarrassed? The rude man was at fault, not her. There was no law that said a lady couldn't go into a tavern for refreshment, just as a gentleman could. Glaring at the man with enough venom to still a galloping horse, she noticed some movement in her peripheral vision.

She could see Justin as he made his way across the room toward her. He must have heard the man's comments. While she would have fought for her right to enter the tavern, she would never have wanted Justin to hear the drunken man's remarks.

Justin hesitated and glowered at the drunk, but as he came closer a smile broke across his face. She could more easily have endured meeting her poor deceased aunt or Clover here than this man who made her feel so warm and tingly inside.

"My dear Miss Freemont, I apologize profusely for...for being so late." He placed his hand on her shoulders and deftly turned her around. Without a glance at her companion, Justin opened the door and ushered Thalia through. He didn't know what she was doing inside such a place, but he wanted to get her outside before the intoxicated Englishman reached her, never mind that he'd contributed greatly to the man's condition. "I intended for you to meet me outside the tavern, and I clearly forgot the time. You must be furious with me."

"Uh, no, Mr.... Captain Lionheart." Thalia could hardly speak. Where his fingers touched her shoulders, a warmth bloomed and spread in every direction, seemingly turning her bones to quivering jelly. She could hardly believe what was happening to her—and all from a single touch!

Back outside in the sunlight and fresh air, she wanted to kiss Justin Lionheart for not asking embarrassing questions. She looked up into his eyes, those wonderful gray teasing eyes, and found that it was hard to speak. "You are very kind. Thank you."

"I suppose it would be too much to presume that you were searching for me?" he asked, guiding her to a nearby tea-room. Justin couldn't fathom why a woman like Thalia Freemont would suddenly appear in a tavern doorway, but he was glad to see her. "May I buy you a cup of tea and a sweet cake?"

"No, Captain, you've done quite enough for one morning." Thalia wanted to escape from him as soon as possible, at least until she came up with a plausible story. She heard voices behind her and glanced back. Lenore was walking along, chatting with the man Thalia supposed was Edward Nelson, as if nothing out of the ordinary had happened.

"Then Thalia said that she thought she saw you going into the tavern. And then..." Lenore went on relating the story, giggling here and there as she spoke.

Thalia suppressed the urge to grab Lenore by the ear and drag her away for a good lecture on ladylike conduct. She could hardly scold her friend. Thalia had gone into the tavern with no more than the feeblest of arguments. "Lenore and I must get on... We have plans for... What I mean to say is—"

"Ooh, we'll be happy to have tea with you, Mr. Nelson," Lenore answered, loudly enough for Thalia—and Justin—to hear. "How good of you to ask us."

Thalia glowered at her friend and then turned to Captain Lionheart. Trying vainly to appear at ease with the rapidly shifting situation, she smiled bravely. "I suppose our plans have changed. Thank you, Captain Lionheart, for your most gracious invitation."

Chapter Four

Thalia sniffed the air. The tearoom smelled of sweet rolls, and she realized that she was hungry, having eaten so many hours earlier, before she and Lenore went shopping. She remembered the delicate violet gauze and glanced at Justin. He was gazing at her with a strange look on his face. What would he think if he could see her in that lovely gown? Would he think she was beautiful?

His gaze caught her eyes and held them for a moment. "You look lovely today, Miss Freemont."

A warm flush spread up Thalia's neck and into her cheeks. It was almost as if he'd read her mind. "Why, thank you, Captain Lionheart."

Thalia wished she could have thought of some witty remark with which to answer, but her mind was blank. Her quick sense of humor always seemed to be dormant when Justin Lionheart was around.

Thalia seldom cared what men thought of her, except for Adam Woodsley, with whom she shared a love for the land. But she'd discovered that she *did* want Justin to think well of her, and she'd probably destroyed any chance of that this morning, when she'd entered the tavern.

A portly man waddled across the floor, wiping his hands on his apron. "Good afternoon, ladies, gentlemen. Will ye be 'avin' tea and cakes?"

"Give us your best, Wilby." Justin continued to hold Thalia's arm until they reached the table the round man indicated. "Please sit here, Miss Freemont."

Thalia seated herself and straightened her gown as much as was possible beneath the narrow confines of the table. "Thank you, Captain Lionheart."

"Lionheart?" Lenore asked, staring openly at Justin for the first time. "You're the Captain Lionheart that we've been talking about all morning. Fancy that."

Fresh color sprang to Thalia's cheeks as she wondered how Lenore could act so foolishly. Wishing she could yank Lenore's hair, Thalia glowered at Lenore to quell any further revelations, and then smiled at Justin. "Yes, Captain, Mrs. Kirkley told us you had been in to order shirts."

Justin tried to hide his amusement. From the scarlet color of Thalia's face, he could tell that the conversation had entailed rather more than his shirts, but he didn't want to embarrass her further. "Oh, yes, Miss Freemont. She's an excellent seamstress. I've heard that everyone goes there."

Lenore bumbled on unabashedly. "Mrs. Kirkley said you had escorted Miss Prentiss there yesterday."

Now it was Justin's turn to be embarrassed. He would just as soon not have Thalia know that he'd been with Eugenia Prentiss in public—or private, for that matter. "Yes, I encountered Miss Prentiss outside Mrs. Kirkley's door. It seems we arrived at the same time."

Thalia noticed that Justin seemed to be squirming in his seat, and decided to test his interest in Donald's mistress. "You know Miss Prentiss well, I presume?"

"Well? Not really." Justin wanted to strangle whoever had told Thalia he'd escorted Eugenia to Mrs. Kirkley's. "We met at a supper recently."

"Only recently? Do you find her amusing?" Thalia asked, with a teasing lilt to her voice. She kicked Lenore's shin as a reminder to keep her from blurting out more questions, questions that might be as embarrassing to Thalia as to Justin.

"Mildly so," Justin admitted. "I find most women at least mildly amusing. Some I find intriguing."

Lenore had been listening to the conversation, and she turned now to Edward Nelson. "And you, Mr. Nelson? Do you find Miss Prentiss amusing?"

Edward laughed. "I find this conversation amusing. What is the fascination with Eugenia Prentiss?"

Lenore shrugged. "I'm not the least bit interested in her, but Thalia's brother is quite fascinated. In fact—"

"In fact," Thalia interrupted, glaring once again at her friend, "he sees her often when he's in Charleston."

Justin laced his fingers together and glanced from Lenore to Thalia. There was more to the story of Thalia's brother and Eugenia Prentiss than Thalia wanted Justin to know. Well, he decided, smiling at Thalia, everyone is entitled to have his or her own secrets—secrets he could better pursue later. "Is that right? Perhaps I know your brother."

"I doubt it," Thalia replied, shifting slightly to one side to allow Wilby to place a pot of tea on the table, along with a platter of sweet cakes and tiny cookies.

"Here ye be. The best cakes and cookies in the city." Wilby stood back proudly. He seemed to be waiting for them to eat.

Justin turned to him. "Thank you, Wilby. We'll call if we need anything else."

Lenore took two small cakes and passed the platter on. When everyone had been served, they ate in silence for a little while. Thalia hoped that everyone would be too busy eating the wonderful cakes to talk, but she was disappointed.

"Isn't it interesting the way we ran into you this morning?" Lenore asked, daintily wiping her mouth.

"Yes, it is," Justin agreed. "In fact, I'm sure the story of how you ladies came to be in the tavern is fascinating. Tell us about it."

Edward nodded. "Yes, please do."

At that moment, Thalia could easily have strangled Lenore without feeling the slightest remorse. But before she could say anything, Lenore prattled on.

"Oh, it was simple," Lenore said as she selected another small cake and placed it on her plate. "I dared her."

"Lenore!" Thalia exclaimed, leaping to her feet so quickly that her chair toppled over behind her.

Wilby, apparently startled by the sound of the chair crashing to the floor, rushed over. "Oh, dear lassie, what happened? Are ye hurt?"

Thalia thought that the earth must surely open up, and that she would be swallowed by that pit reserved for the sinful. Only Satan could be responsible for two perfectly respectable ladies having such a traumatic experience on a lovely day in Charleston. *Well,* she thought spontaneously, *mostly* respectable.

Before Thalia could answer Wilby, her problems increased. Mr. Stevens, her father's banker and the trustee of her estate, hurried over. "Miss Freemont? It *is* you! Are you injured?"

Her embarrassment now complete, Thalia decided that she needed only Donald's presence to add to her discomfort. "Good morning, Mr. Stevens. I apologize for interrupting your tea, but I'm quite fine."

Warren Stevens glanced at the others around the table. "Good morning, Miss Calhoun."

"Mr. Warren Stevens," Thalia began, wondering if her embarrassment would ever end. "You may be unacquainted with Mr. Nelson and Captain Lionheart. Please allow me to introduce them to you. Mr. Edward Nelson, Captain Justin Lionheart—"

"We're well acquainted, Miss Freemont," Justin replied, rising to take Warren Stevens's hand. "How good to see you again, sir."

"The feeling is quite mutual, Lionheart." Warren turned to Edward. "Nelson, happy to see you again. Looking to beat you at chess one day soon at the club."

"I look forward to playing the game with you, sir," Edward replied.

"Well, then, as nothing seems to be the matter, and Miss Freemont is unharmed, I'll be going back to my tea." Warren Stevens said his goodbyes and turned toward his table.

"Mr. Stevens, please wait," Thalia called as he started to walk away. "Have you seen or heard anything of Pansy Monroe? I'm trying to find out what happened to her."

Warren Stevens shook his head sadly. "I regret what happened. That young fool of a brother of hers lost everything. They were turned out of their house. He's still about, but she's nowhere to be found."

"Can you try to find out where she is?" Thalia asked, feeling kinship with her friend Pansy. If Thalia had had to depend on Donald for her security, she would probably have been joining Pansy soon. "I'd appreciate it. I'll be stopping by later."

"I'll do my best, Miss Freemont." Warren nodded his agreement. "I will begin the inquiry immediately." Saying his goodbyes, Warren left the tearoom.

Once Wilby righted her chair, Thalia placed her hand on the back of her seat and willed the color to drain from her face. "Please forgive me, but I must be getting home. I've plenty of unpacking yet to do, and I fear that the time has slipped by unnoticed. Thank you for your kindness, Captain Lionheart."

The disappointment on Lenore's face was obvious, but Thalia didn't care. She'd had enough excitement and embarrassment for one day—for many days, in fact.

Justin rose, placed a few coins on the table and smiled. "I'll be happy to walk you home. Edward can escort Miss Calhoun, if she wishes to remain and finish her tea."

"Oh, would you...Edward?" Lenore asked, batting her eyelashes at Edward Nelson.

Once again, Thalia fought the urge to wring Lenore's neck. The next time she encountered her best friend, Thalia planned to pound the truth out of her.

She turned to Justin. "Thank you, Captain Lionheart, but I know the way quite well and can make it alone. I don't want to cause you any inconvenience."

"No inconvenience at all. I shall be delighted to escort such a charming lady to her home." He glanced at the two people left at the table. "Happy to meet you, Miss Calhoun. Edward, I'll see you at the club."

"Captain Lionheart, I have two stops to make." Thalia smiled sweetly at Justin. "I'm sure you're far too busy to wait—"

"Not at all," Justin told her. "Not at all."

Leaving Justin outside, Thalia went first to see Warren Stevens, her banker. "Mr. Stevens, please make sure that Mr. Woodsley's wages are paid out of the money from Sea Mist. He's doing some good work for me, and I want to ensure that he's adequately paid."

"Fine, Miss Freemont," Warren said, beaming.

Thalia knew that Warren enjoyed handling her accounts because she wasn't much trouble. Her estate—while sizable enough to support her for the remainder of her life—was not by any means vast, but she made few demands. "Make sure that all of Sea Mist's expenses are paid the moment the bills arrive. I won't have my creditors waiting for their money."

When she had finished her business with Warren Stevens, she went to see the cotton buyer, Caleb Saunders. He was delighted to see her.

"Come in, Miss Freemont, come in." He ushered her to a chair. "May I order some tea?"

"No, thank you, Mr. Saunders." Thalia liked Mr. Saunders. When her Uncle Martin had been alive, Mr. Saunders had been a frequent visitor to Sea Mist. "I want to tell you that the cotton crop this year is the finest I've ever seen. Uncle Martin—and my father—would be proud. Adam will come in next week to discuss the particulars about transporting the cotton, but I wanted you to assure the French buyers that Sea Mist's cotton will exceed anything they've ever encountered."

"I'm happy to hear it," Caleb said. "It's always good to hear that the crops are well on their way to being picked, ginned and shipped. I can't tell you how delighted I am that we didn't have a hurricane this year. Why, I remember back in—"

"Thank you, Mr. Saunders." Thalia rose, having heard the stories of past hurricanes many times. "I must go. By the way, I'll soon be moving back to Sea Mist. You're welcome to visit when you think it would be beneficial. I'll contact you the moment I've moved home."

"Excellent, my dear," Caleb said, following her to the door. "Simply excellent."

He peered past her into his outer office. Justin was sitting there, reading the Charleston *Mercury*. "Captain Lionheart, are you here to see me?"

Justin looked up, shocked by the question. He glanced at Thalia and noticed the look of consternation on her face. "No... In fact, I encountered Miss Freemont at the tearoom. She was in quite a hurry to get here before you closed for the day, so I offered to escort her. Her friend, Miss Calhoun, couldn't accompany her."

"I see," Caleb smiled at Justin, and then at Thalia. "Tell Donald I said hello. I'm proud of the fine crop he's bringing in this year."

Thalia gritted her teeth. No matter what she said, Caleb Saunders would believe that the record crop was a result of Donald's supervision and not hers, so she remained silent. She and Justin left.

The walk to Thalia's town house wasn't as bad as she'd expected. Justin Lionheart was apparently sensitive to her feelings, and he didn't bring up the subject of the tavern again. She was exceedingly grateful for his tact. "Where are you from, Captain Lionheart?"

"Please call me Justin," he told her, taking her arm to help her avoid a puddle. "I'm from Virginia."

"Oh, where?"

"All over." Justin wasn't prepared to tell anyone exactly where he came from, especially the sister of the man he suspected of causing the deaths of his two best friends. He'd searched for more than two years for the man, and he couldn't chance giving away any information. For now, he wanted to observe without warning anyone who might sense the reason for his presence. The man he was searching for could easily run again.

"I see," Thalia replied, wondering why he had seemed to deliberately evade her question. "Do you plan to make Charleston your home, or are you visiting?"

Justin considered her question. In fact, he really liked Charleston, and had almost decided to make the city his home port—almost, but not quite. He wanted to be truthful with her, or at least as truthful as possible. "I'm thinking about it, but I haven't made the decision."

"Oh, that's too bad." Thalia didn't want to appear too let down, so she rushed on to say, "I think you'll learn to love our city, Captain."

"Justin. Please call me Justin." To Justin, Thalia appeared to be a little disappointed, and that made him feel a bit buoyant. "I already love Charleston—more and more."

They reached the Freemont town house, and Thalia hesitated outside the gate. "Well, here we are, Cap—Justin. Thank you for walking me home. It was very kind of you. I know you must be busy."

"Yes. In fact, I'm putting out to sea this very day." Justin watched her carefully, to gauge her reaction.

"Oh," Thalia said, her voice little more than a whisper. "Then you won't be here for the Harvest Ball or the Calhoun party."

Justin gazed into her eyes. They were the color of the Atlantic off the Bahamas, translucent azure with occasional glints of indigo. "I can't promise, but I'll try. Are you inviting me to escort you?"

Thalia stood as erect as possible and gazed up at him. He was nearly a foot taller than she, and had the carriage of a cultured man. "Captain Lionheart, I was doing no such thing. A lady doesn't ask a gentleman to escort her to parties."

Justin chuckled, opened the gate and took her arm. He guided her through and closed the iron gate behind them. Looking down again into the mysterious depths of her eyes, he smiled. "Neither does she walk into a tavern."

Anger rose in the usually even-tempered Thalia. She wanted to lash out at him, but before she could think of something sufficiently biting to say, he leaned down and kissed her forehead. Without saying another word, he turned and left her standing there gaping at him.

She stared at his back, wishing she could hurl some epithet after him, stared until she noticed how very broad his shoulders were and how very narrow his waist was where his coat nipped in. When he closed the gate, Justin winked at her. Thalia gasped, spun around and rushed up the steps. When she opened the front door, she ran right into Clover.

"Was that a man I saw you with? Who is he? How come you been prancin' 'round Charleston with a man and no escort? You ain't even been introduced to him." Clover wagged her finger in Thalia's face, then scowled, narrow-eyed, for a moment. "How come you actin' like a hussy first thing you come to town? I knows you had better raising than that!"

Thalia smiled. At least Clover hadn't seen the kiss. Hugging the servant, Thalia started humming and, leaving Clover with her mouth agape, hurried up the stairs, taking them two at a time.

"Miss Thalia Payton Freemont, don't you run up them stairs like you was a heathen. You better start actin' like a lady, or I'm gonna take a switch to you." Clover crossed her arms emphatically. "You ain't too old to be whupped."

Thalia looked back down the curved staircase and grinned. "No, but I'm too fast."

"Harrumph," came the reply. "Lord have mercy on that girl. Lord knows I done tried my best to teach her to act like a lady, and her bein' to that fine ladies' school and all. I never seen such a smart aleck."

Thalia left Clover to her grumbling and her petitions to heaven and went into the morning room. From here she could look down on Meeting Street and see everyone who walked by. She turned and danced around the room, wondering what in the world had happened to make her feel so good. It had to be the kiss. Captain Justin Lionheart had kissed her. Justin had kissed her.

She fell into her chair and hugged herself. He must like her. Suddenly Thalia sat up straight. Why did all this matter to her? She didn't care a whit about him. *Well,* she reasoned, *it never hurt to have admirers.* But he wasn't going to be in town for the dance or for Lenore's party.

That thought sobered her. She'd have a good time anyway. He acted far too familiar with her for her to be comfortable with him. Even though he behaved like one most of the time, Justin Lionheart couldn't be a gentleman. But then again, she seldom acted like a lady.

Donald Osgood Freemont rode his black stallion confidently up Meeting Street to Broad and then over to King Street. Since his arrival in Charleston last night, he'd done little but drink, gamble and nurse his throbbing head. Fortunately, Thalia had left earlier in the day, saving him from being chided for his indulgences. Not that he cared for her opinion, but he didn't relish the idea of her yammering at him when his head felt like the very devil.

To be perfectly fair, Thalia didn't frequently chastise him. However, she was very much a thorn in his side for other reasons. Her stubborn refusal to marry one of his friends was a constant irritant, and one he was determined to overcome. As her guardian, he had every right to select a husband for her. If it benefited him, well, all the better for his day's work.

But now his thoughts ran toward more tender affiliations. He arrived outside the home of Mrs. Eugenia Prentiss, his mistress, and tethered his horse to the fence. He counted himself lucky. Eugenia, a brilliant hostess, was a delightful woman adored by Charleston's society. Her house was frequently the site of the most amusing parties in the city, and she was included on all the guest lists of the city's matrons, who relished an invitation to one of Eugenia's affairs.

Donald was proud of his affiliation with Eugenia. The well-known link between their names prevented other men from trying to get too close; at least Donald hoped it did. Still, Eugenia's house was always bustling with activity.

As he entered the gate, he encountered a strange man leaving. The two men peered at each other for a few seconds before nodding their greetings and passing without speaking. Feeling the anger rising in him, Donald rushed up the steps to Eugenia's piazza and rapped sharply on the door.

As he was about to knock again, the door opened and Eugenia's butler, Higgins, greeted Donald. The unusually large man looked evenly at Donald and said, "Good evenin', sir. Miss Eugenia's retired for the day."

Never a patient man, Donald glared at Higgins and swore. "Damn it, man, wake her up, then. I've just come to town and I intend to—"

"Donald," Eugenia Prentiss interrupted from the staircase. "Always the diplomat, I see."

Donald took the stairs three at a time. When he reached her side, he slid his arm around her. "I've missed you, my dear."

Eugenia kissed his cheek and led him back down the stairs. "Higgins, please ask Cook to send in some coffee and pie."

Her elaborately decorated dressing gown swirling behind her, Eugenia went into the parlor and sat down on the little love seat near the fireplace. "Do be a good boy and lay a fire. There's a chill in the air tonight."

"Eugenia, darling," Donald said as he arranged the logs in the fireplace and lit them, "who was the man I met coming out of your house just now?"

"Oh, did you meet him?" she asked casually. "He's Captain Lionheart. He's new in town."

"Captain Lionheart?" Donald repeated, dusting off his hands and joining her on the love seat. "Whatever was he doing here?"

Eugenia smiled sweetly. "Paying a call, Donald. You know very well that my house is known for its hospitality."

"What kind of hospitality did you extend to Captain Lionheart?" Donald asked, unable to keep the edge from his voice.

"Jealous, darling?" she asked, curling her feet beneath her.

"Yes, Eugenia, my pet. What kind of hospitality?" Donald gazed at her for a moment. Her lovely eyes were somewhere between green and gray, her light brown hair lay in disarray about her shoulders. Donald did indeed feel jealous. "You are wearing a dressing gown."

"Oh, Donald. Forget Justin. He's a friend. Nothing more." Eugenia batted her eyes playfully. "Ah, here's our coffee."

Donald tried to determine whether she was lying or not. If Lionheart was just a friend, why was she wearing a dressing gown? It didn't ring true. "Did you, or did you not," Donald asked, waiting until Higgins had left the room and closed the door, "make love to that man?"

"Make love to Higgins?" she teased, sipping her coffee. "Donald, don't be tedious."

Jumping up, Donald almost upset the silver coffee service. "Tedious? Eugenia, what are you saying? Why are you treating me this way? You know exactly who I'm talking about."

"I'm treating you this way because you're acting like a child." Eugenia rose, put her coffee cup back on the tray and walked out of the room. "I'll see you when you can act like an adult."

Donald stood there a moment watching the door. Eugenia's tantrums were widely known in Charleston, and he expected her to return with a smile, acting as if nothing out of the ordinary had happened. When she didn't, he moved to the staircase, trying to decide whether to go after her or not. After all, he reasoned to himself, her bedroom was nearly as familiar to him as his own.

He took a step upward. Suddenly aware that he was being watched, he glanced behind him and saw Higgins standing there, his arms crossed and his face solemn as he held open the front door. Higgins's presence put Donald's dilemma in perspective. The servant's strength was well-known, and many a young man eager for Eugenia's more intimate affections had tested that strength, only to find it overwhelming. Donald had no wish to confront Higgins. Without a word, he strode back down the stairs and out the front door.

"Damn," he muttered as he mounted his horse and rode toward his club. This evening wasn't turning out to be as pleasant as he'd hoped.

When he reached his club, Randolph Taylor, who was leaving, called to him. "I say, Donald, are you coming along with us?"

Donald remained astride his horse, because it gave him a feeling of power to talk from such a superior position. "Coming? Where? I was coming to the club for—"

"A group of us are going over to the cockfights." Randolph mounted his own horse. "Come along—if you've a pocketful of money."

The gibe smarted, but Donald merely smiled as if Randolph had meant the words as a joke. "Sounds like a great idea. This evening my tastes are for the more exhilarating sports."

The two men rode to the edge of town and dismounted at the club where the cockfights were held. Donald felt the excitement begin to surge through him as he walked through the door and sat on one of the low benches nearest the pit. Those seats were reserved for the wealthier patrons, and Donald glanced smugly around to see who else had come. Seeing no one of importance, he settled back to enjoy himself.

Smoke filled the room, and the stench of dried blood mingled with the odor of the unwashed bodies of the more common men who frequented this particular club. The pit was fairly small, filled with blood and feathers. For a moment, the odor became stifling, but Donald soon became accustomed to it and relaxed.

Randolph nudged Donald. "That man Peterson has a sure winner."

"How do you know?" Donald asked, shifting from side to side to see the cock. Wagers would be placed shortly, and Donald wanted to know everything he could so that he could make a safe bet. After losing as much money as he had last evening, he could ill afford a second stretch of bad luck.

"Saw him fight last week." Randolph pulled out a cigar and lit it. He offered one to Donald. "He's a real champion, that bird is."

As Donald lit his cigar, he watched Peterson poking through the cage at his cock. The bird sure looked mean. The razor-sharp spurs on a gamecock could do considerable damage to man or beast, but if the bird wasn't mean enough the quality of his spurs meant little.

The room filled quickly. Several men taking wagers moved quickly through the crowd. Knowing he should be more conservative, Donald ignored reason and placed a sizable bet on Peterson's bird.

Before long, the fight began. Donald edged forward in his seat, clenching his fists together, as he shouted encouragement to the cock. The din gradually rose until the sound battered Donald's ears like continuous claps of thunder. The fierce clucking and crowing could hardly be heard in the roar that signaled the frenzy of the gamblers.

Peterson's bird raked across the other cock's shoulder, drawing blood early. The fight turned vicious. Blood splattered those closest to the pit, Donald included, and feathers began to fly in the mêlée.

The champion engineered a quick victory, and soon stood over the limp body of his enemy as his lifeblood seeped into the dirt. The heady pleasure of winning seduced Donald into making larger, riskier wagers. The evening was young, and his luck was good.

Thalia wandered about the house with nothing to do. Her paints were still packed, and the light was fading quickly. She was too restless to write poetry tonight, though she spent many delightful evenings composing sonnets in her journal. She sat in her room, wondering about what would happen at Lenore's party, until the sounds of the house gradually quieted. The only thing left for her to do was to go to bed.

As she lay there, trying to fall asleep, her mind was filled with memories of Justin Lionheart. His voice, his smile, his quick rescue of her at the tavern, all came back to her. No doubt he was sailing out of Charleston now, as he had told her he would. She really wanted him to be at Lenore's party, because the evening would be much more enjoyable if he came, but she doubted that he'd be back in time.

* * *

Donald wiped the perspiration from his brow. His luck had changed quickly after the first fight. Now he was indebted to several of his friends, and the evening wasn't nearly over. "Come, Randolph, old man. Give me a few dollars, just for the next match. I'm sure of the winner."

Randolph eyed him and shook his head. "For God's sake, man, give it up for the evening. You're already in debt to every decent man here."

Feeling the panic begin to rise, Donald caught his friend's arm. He had to wager on this next match. "I can win this time and pay everyone back. You know me, Randolph, I'm good for it."

Randolph studied him for a moment, and finally handed him a bill. "Look, Dof, I'll *give* you this, on condition that you help me win Thalia's favor. You know I've always wanted to marry her."

Donald ignored the use of his nickname, snatched the money from Randolph's hand and waved it at one of the men taking wagers. After placing his bet, he turned to Randolph again. Without a doubt, Thalia would be hard to convince, but Donald felt he could persuade—or coerce—her. His promise would at least ensure Randolph's continued goodwill. "I'll do what I can. In fact, I can almost guarantee that she'll marry you."

For the next few days, Thalia enjoyed renewing acquaintances with her friends, many of whom she hadn't seen in years. Margaret Pickens, Agatha Williams, and several of Thalia's aunt's old friends visited her and invited her to suppers or parties that were planned for the next few days. Like Lenore, they were all going to attend the Harvest Ball given by the Saint Cecilia Society, and Thalia admitted that she, too, was looking forward to the event.

She questioned everyone about Pansy Monroe, but could find no one who knew anything. It was almost as if Pansy had disappeared from the face of the earth. Thalia continued to worry, and decided that she would ask someone to help her locate her friend. If Pansy was in trouble, she wanted to help.

On the day of the fitting for her new clothes, Thalia could hardly wait to see her new dress. Once again she rose early and hurried over to Lenore's house to prod her friend.

She sat watching Lenore dress, and sighed. "I declare, Lenore, you take longer to dress than any woman I ever knew."

"I want to be beautiful." Lenore glanced at herself in the mirror. "Mammy," she said, pointing to one of her braids, "I think you need to do that one again. I believe it's braided more loosely than the other, and makes me look unbalanced."

Glancing around Mammy's wide girth, Thalia could see nothing wrong with the braid. Mammy had carefully made two braids and wound them into a bun at the nape of Lenore's neck. "Lenore, it's perfect. Why are you being so mean to Mammy?"

Mammy turned to Thalia and grinned. The large black woman rolled her eyes and shook her head slightly. "I don't know who you plans to see at Miz Kirkley's, but I don't recollect ever hearing about no man working there, and them girls doesn't care what you looks like."

"Well, I do," Lenore snapped, slapping her hand on the dressing table. "Please fix it."

"Maybe I should go on without you, Lenore," Thalia suggested, rising from her seat. "When you get ready, you can—"

Lenore jumped up and brushed Mammy aside. "No, no. I'm ready. I'll forget the braids for now."

Thalia winked at Mammy as Lenore led the way out the door. "I'm happy to have seen you again, Mammy," she called, and waved goodbye.

By the time Thalia and Lenore reached Mrs. Kirkley's, Thalia could hardly contain her excitement. The prospect of a new gown was one thing, but to have one that stood alone, a unique gown, was another. As they entered the shop, she inhaled deeply, cherishing the fragrance of fabrics that filled the rooms.

"Ah, ladies, how very prompt you are." Mrs. Kirkley opened the little swinging door and waved the two women through. "Come on up to the fitting rooms. We're quite excited about the new color, of course, but we feel that all your selections will be as satisfying."

Thalia and Lenore followed Mrs. Kirkley up the stairs, while her constant chatter flowed back over them like the wake behind a schooner. When they reached the fitting room, Mrs. Kirkley ushered them inside and hurried out to summon her assistants.

She returned, the assistants carrying mounds of dresses covered with the thinnest muslin. "Here we are, girls. Now, Miss Freemont, please allow Katherine to help you. Jane will assist you, Miss Calhoun."

Soon Thalia and Lenore were stripped down to their crinolines. Mrs. Kirkley directed Jane and Katherine to position the violet gown on four poles, lift it over Thalia's head like a gossamer canopy, and gently lower it onto her shoulders. Once the gown was safely over her head, they pulled it down until it hung like a violet cloud all around her.

When she looked into the mirror, Thalia was astonished at how well the gown looked on her. Maybe she wasn't as plain as Donald said she was. Lenore and Mrs. Kirkley had been right. Very few people could wear this color, and Thalia was one of the lucky ones who could.

Lenore shook her head sadly. "I really wish I could wear that gown. I never saw anything so fetching in my life."

"Oh, pooh, Lenore," Thalia scolded. "Your new gowns are just as pretty."

"I agree, Miss Freemont," Mrs. Kirkley said, standing back and tipping her head to see the gown's effects from a different angle. "That gown makes you look enchanting."

While Mrs. Kirkley and her assistants pinned and tucked, Thalia glanced at herself again. The color made her look prettier than she ever had. She wondered if Justin would return in time to see her wear this lovely gown. If he hadn't returned in time for the Harvest Ball, she decided, she'd simply wear the gown to every social event until he saw her in it.

Thalia couldn't understand why it was so important to her that Justin see her in this gown. In fact, she didn't understand why it was so important to her for him to think she was pretty. But, she decided, it *was* important.

After considerable fussing, the shopkeeper and her assistants removed the lovely gown. Thalia breathed a little more freely, and then tried on the blue gown and, true to Mrs. Kirkley's predictions, found it quite beautiful.

Lenore tried on her new frocks and chattered brightly. "I do believe this green looks quite splendid on me."

"It certainly does," Thalia agreed, watching her friend turn this way and that to see how the gown swished when she moved. "Don't swish around so, Lenore, you'll ruin that delicate fabric before you have a chance to wear the dress."

Mrs. Kirkley fidgeted with the waist of Lenore's dress, trying to make the little peak in front look right. When she was finally satisfied, she stood back. "Lovely. Perfectly lovely."

Thalia watched Lenore preen before the mirror and smiled. "Enchanting" was what Mrs. Kirkley had said about the violet gown. Thalia remembered compelling gray eyes, a stubborn square chin, and soft, warm lips caressing her cheek. Justin Lionheart.

Thalia closed her eyes and could almost feel Justin's presence. She suddenly wanted him to see her, to caress her with his eyes, and tell her how beautiful she was. Thalia bowed her head so that the other women wouldn't see her blush as she recalled his kiss. Would he kiss her again? A surge of excitement filled her, and Thalia smiled secretly. *I may just kiss him first.*

Chapter Five

While Clover arranged her hair, Thalia wondered where Justin Lionheart had gone. Lenore's party was no more than a few minutes away, and Thalia hadn't seen him since he'd escorted her home from the tearoom. She didn't have a new gown to wear, but nobody had seen the one she'd chosen for tonight.

Made of luscious cream-colored taffeta, the gown was edged with black Spanish lace, and she wore a shawl of the same lace to cover her bare shoulders. She looked pretty, and she knew it. She wasn't beautiful, but enough men were attracted to her to make parties interesting.

Donald would be escorting her this evening, but Thalia didn't even care about that. For the past few days he'd been quite agreeable, even though he kept mentioning Randolph Taylor to her, as if Randolph were about to be canonized. Thalia had little use for Randolph. He was nice enough, but he always seemed to be pushing her, and she didn't like that. Ever since she'd come to live with her father and Donald, Randolph had courted her as though she were the only single woman left in the state. She wondered sometimes if she was the reason for his friendship with Donald.

Randolph would be at Lenore's party tonight, but Thalia made up her mind that she didn't have to associate with him, even if he was Donald's best friend.

Clover placed an artificial rosebud in Thalia's hair and twined a string of pearls through the chignon. She grinned. "Purty is as purty does."

Examining her hair in the mirror, Thalia smiled in return. Without chastising her unnecessarily, Clover was reminding her that she was a lady and should act accordingly. "I agree." Thalia stood and hugged her friend. "Thank you, Clover. You've made me look almost beautiful."

"It ain't proper for a girl to think she's beautiful." Clover crossed her arms and shook her head. After a few seconds, she hugged Thalia in return, then looked her up and down and grinned. "But you is."

After pulling on long ivory kid gloves, Thalia hurried down the stairs. The cream-colored taffeta rustled dramatically, and after her solitude at the plantation she admitted that she enjoyed feeling like a princess rushing to meet her fairy-tale prince. That she probably wouldn't didn't matter. She simply liked feeling as if it were possible. The feeling was new to her.

She didn't want to risk Donald's wrath by keeping him waiting, and besides, she wanted to get there as quickly as possible herself. She composed herself and walked into the parlor.

"Donald, I..." she began and her voice dwindled away into silence.

Donald rose. Across from him, Randolph Taylor jumped to his feet and rushed across the room. "Miss Freemont—Thalia...how lovely you look this evening."

"Thank you, *Mr. Taylor.*" She turned to Donald and frowned. "I'm ready to leave now."

Thalia could hardly hold her tongue. Donald hadn't mentioned that Randolph would be going with them to Lenore's party. Though she allowed Randolph to help her into the carriage, she slid as far away from him as possible, hugging the door on the far side.

"This purports to be quite an evening, wouldn't you say...Thalia?" Randolph asked, and scooted a little closer to her.

Without turning to face him, Thalia replied, "Quite, *Mr. Taylor.*"

"Oh, do call me Randolph." Randolph patted Thalia's hand and grinned at her.

She drew her hand back and glared at him. How could she tell him, without being exceedingly rude, that such familiarity between them would never be permitted to develop? She was saved from having to embarrass herself by the lurching of the carriage. She was nearly thrown to the floor.

"Dear God, what's happened?" Randolph helped her back into her place and tucked his arm around her. "Have no fear, Thalia, I'll protect you."

"Whatever is going on out there?" Donald called to the driver. "You've dashed us all to the floor, man."

"Sorry, guv, but this nag's a mite skittish this evening," the driver answered, flicking the reins.

Thalia rearranged her skirts and concerned herself with examining the taffeta as best she could without touching Randolph. He sat happily beside her, puffed out like a proud rooster. "There seems to be no damage to my gown," she admitted finally.

Donald glanced at her and shouted to the driver, "I'll have your hide if you—"

"Donald, please," Thalia pleaded, placing her hand on his arm to restrain him. "The man can't help the condition of the road." Thalia felt that since none of them was hurt, no harm had been done, and the matter should be dropped. If Donald continued, he'd work himself into a rage before they ever reached the party.

"I'll handle this, Thalia," Donald answered, poking his head out the window again. He shouted once again to the driver, and then drew his head back inside. "That man is no more a driver than I'm a—"

"Sea captain?" Thalia supplied, smiling behind her fan.

Donald looked as if he were going to reply, but he didn't. He rode the remainder of the short distance in silence, occasionally peering out the window so that the driver would remember he was being watched.

When they arrived at the Calhoun home, other carriages were stopped out front. Donald insisted that they wait until their driver drew up in front of the gate before they got out. "It's the only respectable thing to do," he reminded Thalia. "And the Freemont name is a well-respected one."

Donald was always quick to point out what a good reputation the Freemont name enjoyed, but as far as Thalia could tell he did little to uphold that stature. She simply smiled and allowed Randolph to help her down. He took her arm as she walked along the brick path that led from the street to the steps of the Calhoun home, but she managed to extricate herself from his grasp when they reached the door.

Once inside, she hurried to greet Lenore. After speaking to Lenore's parents, she scanned the ballroom for Justin Lionheart. She felt a little let down when she didn't see him.

"You look lovely, my dear. I've missed seeing you," Wilhemina Calhoun said, kissing Thalia on the cheek. "You're enough like your dear mother, rest her soul, to be her twin. It's almost as if..." Mrs. Calhoun's voice dissolved into silence for a moment. "As if she gave her entire self to you when you were born."

Thalia tried to smile, but the thought of her mother giving herself up so that Thalia could live was a painful one. Mrs. Calhoun hugged her when she recognized her mistake.

"Oh, dear, I've said the wrong thing." She kissed Thalia again and held her close. "My dear little Thalia, she loved you from the moment she knew you were coming. I think she felt a special connection with you, as if she knew what a wonderful girl—lady—you would become." Wilhemina Calhoun blotted a tear that threatened to spill over her eyelid. "Looking back, I believe she knew what was in store for her."

"Mother, can't you see that—" Lenore began.

"Thalia, this is a party, and I'm acting such a fool. Can you ever forgive me?" Mrs. Calhoun asked, smiling once again.

"Of course, Mrs. Calhoun. I understand that you loved my mother very much." Thalia had heard most of this before, but not the part about Bethel Payton Freemont's suspecting that she would die in childbirth. "I just wish I could have known her."

"Well, dear child, go on and have a wonderful time." Mrs. Calhoun released Thalia. "You are darling in that gown. Every man here will be chasing after you."

Every man here? Did that include Justin Lionheart? She smiled at Mrs. Calhoun and went on into the room. The Calhouns had a wonderful ballroom. All around the dance floor was a balcony. It was a wonderful place for matrons to keep watch on their flock. She spotted her friends Margaret and Agatha downstairs on the dance floor across the room and headed their way. The crowd had gathered early, and knots of people were clutched together, hugging, kissing, talking, whispering, almost like a flock of gulls on the beach at The Battery.

Thalia glanced at the array of brightly colored gowns; they looked like so many gemstones scattered around the sides of a box. After making sure that no one else had a gown of the lovely violet that she planned to wear to the Harvest Ball, she walked slowly down the stairs, knowing that, with the help of her stiff crinolines, she almost appeared to be floating. As a child, she'd always thought that the ladies looked so beautiful, bobbing along as if they were afloat on the Ashley or the Cooper River, and she'd tried extra hard to emulate that elegance.

As she threaded her way across the dance floor, she glanced back and forth to make sure that Justin hadn't slipped in past Lenore unnoticed. Scolding herself for such wayward thoughts, she contented herself with talking to Margaret and Agatha, who'd arrived only moments before.

"You know, Thalia, that's probably the prettiest gown I've ever seen you wear." Agatha smiled sweetly. She tugged at the bodice of her own pink gown. "You look lovely."

"Oh, yes. You certainly do," Margaret agreed. "What have you been doing these past few days?"

Thalia spotted Randolph making his way across the room toward them. "Please, girls, let's get some punch. I declare, I'm positively dying of thirst. Must be the dust from the carriage ride over here."

"You only came four blocks, Thalia," Margaret reminded her, glancing around. She, too, saw Randolph, and she grinned. "But I'm thirsty, too."

Taking the two girls in tow, Thalia headed across the floor. When they reached the punch bowl she accepted a glass from the servant who offered it, and turned to see what had happened to Randolph. As she'd suspected, one of his cronies had stopped him. She smiled at her friends. She was glad Margaret hadn't made a fuss. All her friends knew how Thalia loathed Randolph and always helped her escape from him if possible. "Now, isn't this much better?"

"Why, it's fine, but why did we have to get our own punch? We could have gone to another corner of the room," Margaret said, looking around as if she hoped she'd spot a certain someone. "I believe Franklin—Mr. Williams—would have gotten it for us."

"Oh, pooh, Margaret. Everyone knows you're sweet on Franklin." Agatha grimaced and rolled her eyes. "Although I can't say why. That man is as dull-witted as a cow."

"He is not." Margaret was still peering at the crowd. "He's very smart."

Justin and his friend Eugenia Prentiss walked into the ballroom and greeted their host and hostess. He spoke briefly with Lenore. "How are you, Miss Calhoun? I'm happy to see you again."

"I'm quite well, Captain." Lenore smiled prettily, hoping her parents wouldn't ask where she'd met the captain. "It's nice to see you, as well."

"Is Tha—Miss Freemont . . . here this evening?" he asked, hoping Lenore wouldn't make more of his question than was intended.

"She is." Lenore glanced at her parents. Her mother was gazing at Captain Lionheart. Lenore turned to face him, hoping he'd take the hint and go on. "I'm delighted you could come this evening, Captain."

"Thank you, Miss Calhoun." Justin caught Lenore's mother's stare and smiled at her. "You've a charming home, Mrs. Calhoun. Thank you for inviting me to join you this evening."

"You're quite welcome, Captain Lionheart," Mrs. Calhoun answered, blushing profusely. "Please visit often."

"You are very kind." Justin hurried on. He didn't want to become involved with Mrs. Calhoun, and she looked like a woman who might seek him out for a casual afternoon's entertainment if he gave her the slightest indication he'd be willing. *Society women are all alike,* he thought as he moved on.

He turned to face the crowd of people milling about in the ballroom. The musicians were beginning to warm up, and he wanted to find Thalia to claim her for the first dance—if she hadn't already promised it to someone else. He paused. He'd never considered the possibility that she might be popular with the other men of Charleston. After all, she was a real beauty, and daring, too.

Then he spotted her. She was standing across the room, completely unaware that he was watching her. Her ivory gown and black lace shawl were perfect for her coloring, and he decided she was more beautiful than she'd been the last time he'd seen her. He had thought that was impossible.

Beneath the fat, flickering candles, she looked like a vision, an angel, perhaps, sent to earth to... What was he thinking? She was a woman, a planter's daughter. Any resemblance between her and an angel was purely superficial. Still, he wanted her.

Eugenia strode over to his side. She looked across the room and smiled when she saw who he was staring at. "Lovely, isn't she?"

"Yes, she is, Eugenia. Do you know her?" Justin asked, wondering how someone as innocent as Thalia seemed to be could be acquainted with a woman as worldly as Eugenia.

"Yes, I—"

"Uh—oh." Justin saw a man threading his way through the crowd toward Thalia and the two girls with whom she was standing.

At that moment, Thalia glanced his way and saw him. She stared across the room. Justin Lionheart had entered the room with Eugenia Prentiss on his arm. Glancing around, Thalia saw that Donald had spotted the newcomers, as well. She hoped he wouldn't cause trouble, but there was no telling. Donald liked Eugenia very much, though he never mentioned marriage.

As for Thalia, she felt a little tingle in her stomach. Disappointment surged through her. Why was Justin with Eugenia?

"Thalia!" Margaret cried, shaking her arm. "Are you listening? The music's beginning, and I asked who you plan to dance with."

Thalia wasn't listening. Justin had extricated himself from Eugenia's grasp and was making his way across the room. What should she do? she wondered. Should she pretend not to have noticed with whom he'd arrived? Or should she casually mention it?

"Uh—oh," she muttered. Randolph was coming toward her, too, and he was much closer than Justin. Thalia wanted to dance with Justin, especially the first dance. She had to find a way to evade Randolph long enough for Justin to reach her. She walked beneath an arbor of fall flowers and hid behind a tall man until she could decide what to do.

She mentally calculated the distances and decided that if she walked toward the orchestra she could meet Justin before Randolph got to her. Without speaking to Margaret and Agatha, she hurried toward the orchestra stand, praying that Randolph wouldn't cut her off.

Her calculations were wrong. Randolph saw her moving and caught her before she reached her goal. She tried very hard to appear unfazed by his arrival, but she really was quite disappointed.

"Thalia, my dear, may I—" Randolph began.

"Oh, how utterly clumsy of me, Miss Freemont, to be all the way across the room when our dance is beginning. I do hope I haven't—" Justin gazed pointedly at Randolph, and then back at Thalia "—caused any confusion."

"Oh, no, Captain Lionheart. On the contrary," she teased, smiling broadly at Justin. "You're just in time." She turned to Randolph. "I'm so sorry, Mr. Taylor, but I promised this dance to Captain Lionheart."

Before Randolph could answer, Justin took her in his arms and they waltzed away. Justin had seen Randolph before, and didn't like him. He was a heavy drinker and gambler who frequented the same club as Justin and Edward. Justin had no use for a man who couldn't hold his spirits.

"Miss Freemont, my dear, how good to see you," Justin said as he guided her skillfully around the dance floor. The feel of her, moving lightly in his arms and following his steps precisely, made him warm with anticipation.

"Captain, I wondered if you would return in time for this occasion." Thalia caught herself. She should never have indicated that she had missed him or wanted him here for her own purposes. It simply wasn't ladylike. "The Calhouns always have entertaining parties."

"So I've heard." Justin spun her around and skillfully pulled her closer into his arms.

Thalia felt color warm her cheeks, but she didn't resist. She rather liked the feeling of a man's arms around her. Suddenly the evening had taken on a fuzzy glow that had been missing earlier. All the candles seemed to be burning a little more softly, and the ballroom seemed much cozier, the music much sweeter. "Did you have a successful trip?"

"Yes. Quite." Justin smiled. She must have missed him. "May I hope that you missed me while I was gone?"

"Why, Captain Lionheart!" she protested, catching the slightest hint of a spicy scent clinging to Justin's lapels, mingled with the hearty fragrance of beeswax. "I hardly know you well enough to miss you."

Justin gazed into her eyes. The blue reflected the candlelight beautifully, invitingly. He'd missed her. The memory of her fragrance had tormented him much of the time he'd been away. "I seem to recall that we were well on our way to becoming friends, Thalia. Besides, what's there to know? I am but a lowly sea captain. I carry passengers on occasion. At other times I transport goods such as cotton, rice, wood, fabrics and materials for clothing, things like that. And I have a fast sailboat that I keep for fun."

His use of her given name sounded glorious to her, different from when anyone else said it. For a few seconds it echoed in her mind, sending shivers down her spine. She smiled and fluttered her eyelashes coquettishly. "Why, Captain, I do believe you're trying to confuse me. I'm just a simple country girl, and you're taking advantage of my unsophisticated nature."

"Unsophisticated?" Justin repeated, whirling her around and pulling her a little closer still. Her fragrance wafted up to his nostrils, that same luscious scent of roses that had kept him awake at night while the sea rocked his ship like a cradle. He grinned and raised an eyebrow. "I doubt that."

"How you do tease a girl!" Thalia tried to remember all the things she'd heard her friends say to their gentlemen callers, but her memory was limited to what she'd already said. She was on her own now. "You're much too...worldly for me."

"I suspect that you're a bit more worldly than you'd have me believe, Thalia." Justin glanced over her shoulder. The man he'd met when coming out of Eugenia's a few days earlier was now scowling at her. The man, he thought, must be more than a friend to Eugenia. Well, a little jealousy never hurt a man. He smiled at Thalia.

The waltz ended, and Justin took Thalia's arm and walked her back to the edge of the dance floor. He looked down at her, feeling once again the magnetism of her lovely eyes.

Several people gathered around them as they reached the edge of the dance floor. Thalia wondered if she'd get to dance with him again. A woman she didn't know linked her arm with Justin's and, to Thalia's amazement, kissed him lightly on the cheek.

She glanced around. She saw Donald standing with Eugenia, and the look on his face was horrible. He was livid. Thalia couldn't tell who he was angry with, whether it was Eugenia or Justin, but she knew he wouldn't be satisfied until he'd gained some sort of revenge for Eugenia's breach.

Poor Eugenia, Thalia thought. The woman was beautiful, and she knew it, but it didn't seem to affect her very much. She laughed easily and greeted everyone like her best friend. No wonder Donald was so jealous.

Randolph was dancing with Agatha. At least Thalia didn't have to worry about him—for now. She listened to the conversation swirling around her. Laughter erupted, but she couldn't understand what it was about, because she'd missed the beginning of the discussion.

Justin seemed to be the center of attention. Mrs. Calhoun joined the group and edged closer to Justin. Thalia was gradually pushed farther and farther away, until she was standing on the fringes of the group and watching the women clamor to get closer to Justin.

Franklin Williams asked her to dance, and she accepted. She liked Franklin well enough, but he'd never been more than a passing acquaintance. Conversation between them was a bit stilted, but perhaps that was because Thalia wasn't really paying attention. She kept looking back at the cluster of women around Justin.

Randolph finally caught up with her after Franklin took her back to the rows of chairs near the wall. She hardly had a chance to catch her breath before Randolph asked her to dance. Since she'd come with him and Donald, she couldn't refuse without seeming snobbish. She tried very hard to listen to him, but she found him as boring as ever. About halfway through the dance, she began to wonder if his own mother thought him boring, too.

"Thalia," he began, trying to pull her closer, "I'm quite fond—"

"Please, Randolph, I can't concentrate on my dance steps." Thalia didn't want to hear what she thought Randolph intended to say. Even if he wasn't going to ask her to marry him, she didn't want to listen to him.

"I'll speak with you later... after this dance..." He stumbled as he spoke.

Thalia grimaced as Randolph almost toppled them over on the dance floor. *What a clumsy oaf,* she thought, wondering how he ever managed to walk without tripping over his big feet. She endured the remainder of the dance, gritting her teeth to keep from telling him how awkward he was. When the music finally stopped, she hurried off the dance floor ahead of him.

She didn't know where she was going; she knew only that she wanted to get away from him. "Please excuse me for a moment, Randolph, I—I must... Please excuse me."

She left him standing there, gawking at her like a schoolboy. Thalia once again found herself in the group of women around Justin, but she couldn't stand that, either. She spotted the open windows and hurried toward them. Grateful that the windows of most Charleston homes opened from floor to ceiling, she stepped through the nearest one, crossed the piazza and strode into the Calhoun's garden.

Lenore's mother had a lovely rose garden, almost as beautiful as Thalia's mother's garden at Misty Glade. The two women had been friends as girls, and had remained close after their marriages. Mrs. Calhoun had often told Thalia stories of how happy Bethel Payton and Wilhemina Simms had been as girls. She'd recalled Bethel's wedding day, and how beautiful a bride Bethel had been. And now Lenore's mother was standing inside the ballroom, panting after Justin Lionheart, just like all the other women surrounding him.

Thalia didn't really care who Mrs. Calhoun chased after. In fact, the reputations of some of Charleston's matrons were highly questionable, but their status as married women or widows put them above reproach—almost. Unless they were caught in some flagrant affair that became public knowledge, nothing was really questioned. But for a young unmarried lady to act like the matrons was sure social suicide.

Thalia didn't much care for society's customs. If she really loved a man, she'd flout those stodgy traditions and do as her heart directed, but, because of her brother's insistence that she marry Randolph, she never expected that to happen. Thalia didn't ever get close enough to a man to fall in love. It wasn't worth it.

Men could be so foolish at times. Donald and Randolph spent endless hours at the gaming tables or wagering on nothing more significant than whether a beetle would cross a line they'd drawn in the dirt. All this came at the expense of Misty Glade and her own plantation, Sea Mist. If Donald would just let her go home to her own plantation, she wouldn't care if she ever married. She would be content to live the remainder of her life there, coming to town occasionally to conduct business and see friends.

She found a secluded bench, where she could be alone, and where she could hide from Randolph. After brushing her hand across the marble, she sat and arranged her voluminous skirts and crinolines around her. The hoops made it difficult to sit, but a lady learned early how to manage them.

Her thoughts drifted back to the dance she'd shared with Justin. He was a skillful dancer who seemed to take to it naturally, with an elegance of step that she would never have imagined a man capable of. His style certainly bested the other men she'd danced with in the short time she'd been going to parties and balls.

From nearby, the sound of footsteps distracted her from her delightful thoughts. She listened carefully, hoping that whoever was walking in the garden would go on past this little nook without coming to see if it was occupied. The footsteps drew closer, and Thalia realized that her hopes were in vain. Whoever was out there was headed her way. She decided it must be Donald, coming to scold her for leaving the ballroom unescorted. Bracing herself for a set-to, she watched the little path.

Hoping to avoid a confrontation, she started to rise, to head back to the ballroom, but then she decided that if she didn't make any noise she might not be discovered. For a few seconds she didn't even breathe, for fear the rustling of the taffeta would alert someone to her presence. Still, she couldn't hold her breath forever.

At the end of the little brick walkway, a man suddenly appeared out of the shadows. He was taller than Donald. Afraid that Randolph had come looking for her, she ducked when the man spoke.

"Ah, Miss Freemont," Justin said in a low, deep voice. He didn't want to draw attention to them, so he purposely kept as quiet as possible. "What a pleasant surprise."

Relief rushed out of Thalia like a flock of gulls startled at the beach. She couldn't contain her delight. "Why, Captain Lionheart, how happy I am it's you."

"Whom did you expect?" Justin didn't really need an answer. He'd seen her attempt to avoid Randolph Taylor, and he suspected that she'd come here to escape his clumsy, and evidently unwanted, attentions.

"Ran— No one in particular." Thalia didn't want to discuss Randolph Taylor with Justin—or anyone, for that matter. She simply wanted to forget that the obnoxious man existed.

Justin gazed at her. Light from the full moon cut a swath across the plants surrounding the little glade and illuminated her face with a halo of soft, translucent silver. Careful not to crush her gown, he sat beside her and inhaled the fresh, salty air that clung to this area, just across from The Battery. It was almost as good as being aboard his ship, especially since this lovely woman had said she was happy to see him.

They chatted about the party, about the people who were attending. Justin wanted to ask her about Randolph, but he didn't know exactly how to begin. He'd recognized the distress in her face as he'd approached her for the first dance, and he'd realized that she didn't like Randolph. Neither did Justin. He thought her dislike of the man exceedingly bright.

"Tell me about your family," Justin asked, hoping to discover something about the man he'd heard was her brother.

"There's not much to tell," Thalia said, recalling Mrs. Calhoun's earlier words and sighing deeply. "My brother Donald and I are all that's left."

"Donald?" Justin repeated, wondering why he hadn't met the man. "I don't believe I know him."

Thalia shook her head slightly. "You probably don't *want* to know him, either."

"Oh." Justin slid forward, eager now to hear what she had to say. "What's so awful about him that I wouldn't want to know him?"

"Donald is..." Thalia wondered how she could describe Donald without seeming too outspoken. "Well, he's... Could we change the subject? I don't really like talking about my disagreeable brother."

"I apologize." Justin took her hand in his and kissed it lightly. "I never meant to pry."

Thalia gazed at Justin through the fringe of her eyelashes. His profile was strong, emphasized by the radiant moonlight, and his eyes took on a silvery color that was vastly more beautiful in this light. His appearance was magnetic. Her hand was drawn to his face, as by a marionette's strings, and she found herself touching his cheek.

Justin dared not move. Thalia's hand brushed his cheek gently before she caught her breath and jerked it away. Why had she done that? Had she been as affected as he by the little kiss on her forehead that night at her gate?

Deciding to be brave, Justin slid his arm around her and gazed down into eyes that were glistening in the moonlight. He knew that if something didn't happen quickly he'd kiss her.

And what if he did? All she could do was slap him, since no one was around. He knew he was inching closer, but couldn't stop—didn't want to stop. He wanted to kiss her, maybe more than he'd ever wanted to kiss a woman.

Thalia felt the warmth of his breath on her cheeks. Behind him, the moon shimmered like a large pearl, opalescent, pregnant with its fullness. She'd never seen a lovelier moon, and she felt it had appeared especially for her and Justin. All around them the palmettos rustled in the cool breeze, and the scent of the roses surrounded them, mixed with the subtle fragrance of spice that emanated from Justin.

She knew he was going to kiss her. She welcomed it. Recalling her thoughts after he'd kissed her forehead that first time, she blushed, and was glad for the soft light. Feeling the strength of his magnetism, Thalia raised her chin and touched her lips to his.

Though she'd been kissed before, she wasn't prepared for the difference. Her body seemed to be jolted with a spellbinding force, as if his kiss were charged with some unknown power. The pressure was tender at first, and then the kiss grew into something infinitely more wonderful.

Thalia could hardly breathe. Justin's mouth covered hers hungrily, and she turned slightly in his arms to bring their bodies closer. What was she doing? She didn't care. She cared only that she felt more alive than she'd ever felt in her life. She instinctively knew that this moment was special and might never be repeated, and she was going to relish every second of this kiss.

Justin couldn't believe what was happening between them. He hadn't decided whether or not to chance kissing her, and then she'd made the decision for him. Now he pressed the point. His lips covered hers, devouring the soft nectar that reminded him of the sweet punch she'd been drinking earlier. He wanted his body next to hers, claiming as much as she was willing to give. Where was he heading? This spark between them was entirely unexpected, and he didn't know exactly how to deal with the feelings that flooded over the two of them like the gossamer softness of the moonlight caressing Thalia's lovely face.

Thalia's burning lungs begged for air. When Justin's lips left hers, she inhaled deeply, as if she'd been deprived of oxygen for hours. But she wanted the feel of his lips against hers again, the warmth that radiated from her mouth and illuminated every cell of her being.

Then she sat bolt upright. What was she doing? She'd kissed a perfect stranger. What must he think of her?

Jumping to her feet, she stared at him. What had he done to her to make her so pliable in his arms? "Captain... I... You must... Oh, dear..."

Knowing she would probably regret her actions, Thalia sat down again and thrust her arms around him. When she was as close as she could get to him, her bosom pressed against his chest, she kissed him again.

Then she snatched up the hem of her gown and darted out of the little nook. She jumped over the late beds of asters and chrysanthemums, and she didn't stop running until she reached the piazza. Breathless, she lowered her gown, smoothed it and waited by the steps until her chest stopped heaving.

Thalia glanced back to see if Justin had followed her. Hearing voices nearby, she pressed her body against the wall behind the chimney and remained very quiet for a moment. When the people passed by without noticing her, she watched until they were out of sight and then said, "Oh, dear God, what have I done now?"

Chapter Six

Thalia felt as if Justin's lips had branded hers for everyone to see. When she slipped back through the window into the ballroom, she believed that every eye turned to scrutinize her as she entered. Her heart was still pounding, and she knew that everyone would hear it. Scanning the room, she found Lenore talking with one of Charleston's matrons and hurried across the room to join them.

A young man she didn't know asked if she would dance with him, but she hardly looked up as she told him that she had promised Lenore she would assist her with some problem. Without glancing back, she threaded her way through the people milling about on the fringes of the dance floor until she reached Lenore. She really didn't know what she expected to do once she found her friend, but the impetus to find a barrier, some protection from Justin, drove her on.

By the time Thalia got to Lenore, her business with the matron was finished and she had turned to glance around. Thalia didn't know what to say. She knew her face was flushed with color—both from her quick escape from Justin and from the embarrassment she felt at returning to a room full of people who seemed to know where she had been and what she had been doing.

"My, my, what happened to you?" Lenore asked, linking her arm with Thalia's. "I think we need to go somewhere quiet to talk."

Thalia glanced around the room. She spotted Justin striding back through the window as if nothing had happened. Could he have kissed her as he had and feel nothing? To her, it was as if the palms and live oaks bowed and watched; the chrysanthemums and asters seemed to dip and sway to music that she alone heard.

Lenore was leading Thalia out through the back door and into the garden. This time, instead of seeking a bench in the rose garden, Lenore took her to a sheltered glade of live oaks beneath which the two girls had played house as children. They sat down on the well-worn marble bench.

"Now tell me what happened," Lenore demanded.

Realizing that little short of the truth would satisfy Lenore's concern, Thalia considered what she could safely say. She wasn't ready to discuss the emotions she'd felt when Justin had kissed her, but she wasn't sure that denying the event would work. Lenore could be quite shrewd at times.

"Lenore, you're making something of nothing. I simply went out for a breath of fresh air, and—"

"Aha!" Lenore exclaimed, clapping her hands together. "I knew you were up to something. I saw Captain Lionheart follow you into the garden. Do tell, and don't you dare leave out one word of this story, or I'll . . . I'll tell Randolph that you're interested in him."

"Lenore!" Thalia cried, leaping up from her seat. "You wouldn't! You know how that man irritates me, and if you give him the slightest bit of encouragement he'll never give up."

Lenore giggled and shook her head. "I can see you now, Mrs. Randolph Taylor . . ."

Thalia glowered at Lenore. This wasn't the first time Lenore had threatened to do such a terrible thing. Thalia was becoming more and more irritated with her oldest friend. Perhaps it was growing up without real parents, or having to manage Misty Glade, but somehow Thalia had matured and Lenore hadn't. Wanting to curb this foolish idea quickly, she sat down and crossed her arms. "Well, if you're more interested in discussing Randolph Taylor, I just won't tell you what really happened."

"If you think you're leaving this house—"

"All right." Thalia's plan had succeeded. She had diverted Lenore's attention from Randolph—for the moment, at least.

"I simply went into the garden for a breath of fresh air, and—"

"And, I joined her," Justin finished for Thalia. He'd heard Lenore's threat, and he didn't like it at all. Thalia didn't deserve such treatment from a friend.

"May I join the party, too?" Edward asked, stepping from behind Justin.

"Of course," Lenore gushed, pointing to another bench. "We'd love to have you."

Although she wasn't sure he could see her, Thalia smiled at Justin. She appreciated his rescuing her from Lenore's questions. But Lenore wouldn't be satisfied for long, especially not now that Justin had entered into the action more tangibly.

The two men sat on the bench that Lenore had indicated. Justin tried to gauge Thalia's reaction to his joining them, but couldn't, because the bower of trees blocked the moonlight. He wished Thalia had come here instead of the rose garden when he'd followed her. He would have had a more pronounced sense of privacy, and wouldn't have been so wary of being caught. He didn't plan to marry, especially after the fiasco that had precipitated his hurried departure from Richmond, so being discovered in a compromising situation was something he consciously avoided.

For the moment, he wished that Edward and Lenore would disappear. He wanted to kiss Thalia again. Something about kissing her was different from every other kiss he'd experienced, and he needed to know what it was. Maybe it was because she'd kissed him. That had surprised him a great deal. From the kind of kiss it had been, and her reaction, he knew she was a novice, but she certainly caught on quickly.

Thalia seemed to be different, and that very difference fascinated him. She didn't appear to be mired in the self-centeredness that trapped most of the women he knew, and he wanted to know why.

She had every reason to be like Lenore—and Alicia—but she wasn't. Thalia was a planter's daughter, wealthy, beautiful, and yet she seemed not to know it, or at least she didn't dwell on her appearance and her heredity. So far, every girl he'd met at Charleston had declared herself to be Miss So-and-So of the So-and-So family, who had lived in Charleston or the surrounding area for more than a hundred years. He could do without that sort of false sense of importance.

Edward nudged Justin in the ribs. He glanced at everyone and said, "Yes? Did I miss something?"

Lenore giggled and bowed her head. "Why, Captain Lionheart, were you daydreaming?"

Justin looked at Thalia, smiled, and shrugged. "Sorry, I suppose I was. Did you say something to me?"

"I asked how you like Charleston," Lenore repeated, glancing from Justin to Thalia.

"It's a beautiful city," Justin answered simply. He knew better than to expand on an answer when he didn't know the reason behind the question.

Edward smiled at Justin. "Ladies, if the two of you are going to be out shopping in the afternoon, we could perhaps meet for tea at Wilby's?"

Thalia's mouth opened in surprise. A gentleman *never* asked a lady to meet him without first asking her parents. Before she could reply, Lenore blurted out an answer.

"Oh, yes. With the Harvest Ball coming up, we simply must go down to the milliner's shop and look at the new ribbons and laces." Lenore caught Thalia's hand and held it as if defying her to refuse. "Thalia, what time will we be going?"

Knowing that she would have no choice but to accompany her friend on yet another escapade, Thalia decided that she could use the outing as an excuse to check to see if the Sea Mist and Misty Glade cotton had arrived at the wharves. She could also avoid spending time with Donald. With a steely look at Lenore, Thalia smiled through clenched teeth. "Whatever time you say, Lenore dear." Thalia punctuated her sentence with a squeeze that brought a gasp from her friend. She rose and faced the men. "Gentlemen, I'm sorry, but I'm feeling the chill of the night air and would like to return to the ballroom."

Justin stifled a chuckle. He could imagine what had happened. "Yes, dear ladies, do please join us for tea at Wilby's." He stood, walked over to Thalia and offered her his arm.

She placed her hand on his arm, and they walked down the winding brick path toward the gaily lit house. Thalia could feel a surging of her emotions as she trod along with Justin, as if her blood were pulsing rhythmically with the heat of his gaze.

Leaning down so that only Thalia could hear, he whispered, "Of course, if you'd rather, we could meet again at the tavern."

Thalia tried to pull her hand away, but Justin caught it in his. Chuckling as they walked along, he glanced at her face. As they came into the full moonlight, he could see a rosy sheen that seemed to emanate from within her.

Thalia couldn't extricate her hand from Justin's grasp without embarrassing herself, but she could inflict a bit of punishment for his presumption. Walking a little closer to him, she smiled sweetly at him, edged her fingers beneath his waistcoat, caught several hairs on his arm and jerked with all her might.

"Agh!" he cried, pulling his arm free from her malicious grip. He looked down into her impish face and grinned. She'd managed to put him in his place rather quickly without saying a single word. What a woman!

"What was that?" Edward asked, leaning closer.

"Eh," Justin muttered, wondering where Miss Freemont's audacity would end. He gazed down at her sweet smile of concern. "Just stumbled, old man. Nothing serious."

Thalia linked her arm with his once again and fluttered her eyelashes. "I'm so sorry, Captain," she said with sickening sweetness, smiling brightly up at Justin as they walked into the circular glow of the lamps on the piazza. Fluttering her fan daintily, she continued, "Please allow me to help you. I'd hate for something to happen to you. I declare, I never saw a sea captain who was so clumsy."

Justin stared at her for a moment, and then bellowed with laughter. Thalia Freemont was like no other woman.

All the way home, Thalia sang one of the tunes the orchestra had played, her voice trilling over the clopping of the horses' hooves.

Because Eugenia had shown up escorted by Captain Lionheart, Donald was in a foul humor. Jealousy had tainted his entire evening. "Shut up, will you? You sound like a ninny."

In the darkness, Thalia stuck her tongue out at her brother. Her mood was much too good for him to spoil with his moping. As she considered the situation, she decided that she could well be in a mood as foul as Donald's, but then, Justin had paid her a great deal of attention. He must have escorted Eugenia to the party merely because he was a gentleman.

Eugenia, on the other hand, had practically ignored Donald. Though Thalia didn't know how, she suspected that Donald must have brought Eugenia's wrath on himself. *Poor Donald,* she thought. He probably won't get married, and all because of our parents. He's probably afraid, way down deep, that Eugenia might die in childbirth, or something dreadful like that. Then he'd end up just like Father.

Thalia peered at Donald's silhouette as they rode along in silence. His lips formed a straight line, and she feared that his temper would flare again before the evening was over. Vowing to scurry out of his way as soon as possible, she prayed that he wouldn't take his vengeance on her or the servants.

When they arrived home, Thalia hurried up the stairs and closed her door. She knew that if Donald sent for her she'd have to go, to protect the servants from his temper, but for now, getting out of his way was paramount in her mind.

For once, Donald bore his anger in silence. He settled into a chair in the parlor and drank two more glasses of port. The ride home with Thalia had been trying, but except for one outburst he'd remained quiet. If it hadn't been for her damnably cheerful attitude and her joyful singing, he could have kept his peace with her.

Donald was angry for more than one reason. First of all, his mistress had arrived escorted by that damnable Captain Lionheart. *Who ever heard of such a ridiculous name?* Donald wondered. And, secondly, Thalia had conveniently evaded Randolph's attempt to ask her to marry him. And, as if that weren't enough, she had then disappeared, only to return followed by Lionheart.

About to burst into a fit of rage, Donald had sought out the men's smoking room and downed a goodly amount of port. The libation had done little to calm his temper, but he had used the time alone to begin developing a plan. Thalia must marry. She must marry Randolph. Together, he and Randolph would find a way to convince her that no other course of action was open to her.

Donald's pockets were empty. He owed nearly all his friends money, and most particularly Randolph. And he had promised Randolph that Thalia would marry him.

Donald took a bottle of brandy from the serving tray and made his way up stairs. Outside Thalia's door, he paused, listening to see if she was still awake. He heard nothing, so he crossed the hall to his room. He sat in his chair and pondered his situation until the sun rose. He knew his problems would be solved if he could simply convince Thalia to marry Randolph. Then poor Randolph wouldn't have the nerve to dun him for the money he owed. He would surely settle some small amount on Donald after the wedding.

For Thalia to marry Randolph was the only answer. If he couldn't manage to convince her soon, he would be in deep trouble. Though his friends were tolerant, they wouldn't overlook the mounting balances he owed them.

Donald thought again about Eugenia. He would marry her if he had to, but he didn't want to be tied down, at least not until he'd regained his fortune. He'd have to work doubly hard. Maybe there would soon be a high-stakes game at the club, wherein he could win a large sum of money. With a little capital, he'd be in a better position to improve his fortunes. Every gambler lost occasionally and needed a bit of a reserve.

He thought of Justin. There was something odd about that man, almost familiar to Donald. He tried to remember if he'd seen him before, but couldn't. Randolph had been no help on that score, but Donald wouldn't rest until he knew.

For a few minutes, he tried valiantly to think, but his mind was addled by vast quantities of drink. *Tomorrow,* he decided, *I'll find an investigator. Then I'll know exactly who this man is.* Donald practically sucked the last few drops from the crystal brandy decanter and then threw it into the fireplace, where it erupted into a million glittering shards of glass.

Whistling a jaunty tune, Justin marched steadily along the few blocks from the Calhoun home to his lodgings. Though he couldn't fathom why, he felt particularly happy with the way the evening had turned out. He hadn't intended to attend the Calhoun party until he'd discovered that Thalia would be there.

In fact, he'd rushed his trip to Savannah simply to go to this party.

He had tomorrow—today, this afternoon—to look forward to, as well. Recalling Thalia's reaction to the events beneath the live oak, he chuckled aloud. What a woman she was.

Donald Freemont. Justin contemplated the name. Was Donald Freemont the man for whom he was looking? If so, exacting his revenge on the man might prove difficult, especially in light of the fact that Justin was very interested in Thalia Freemont. But he might possibly use Thalia as a way to get to Donald.

In spite of going to bed so late, Thalia rose early, pulled on a pink lace-and-silk dressing gown and draped herself across a Grecian couch to continue thinking about Justin. She knew she should be thinking about the plantation, about planting greens, cabbages and onions for winter harvest. But, somehow, she found it difficult to think of onions when her heart kept forcing her to remember Justin.

She hardly slept all night, dreaming of Justin and his kisses. Thoroughly ashamed of herself for acting like such a light-skirt, she promised herself that she would remain quite aloof. Captain Lionheart would simply have to accustom himself to keeping his hands away.

But you kissed him first, you green goose, she told herself. *Ah, and what a kiss it was.*

Thalia grew warm all over as she recalled that exquisitely romantic moment. The moon had been perfect. The fragrance of flowers and of Justin's soap had combined to make the atmosphere unforgettable. *You're acting like you never kissed a man before,* she scolded. *Remember who you are.* As Donald always said, the Freemonts of Edisto Island enjoyed an excellent reputation.

The door opened, and Clover peeked inside. She poked her head in farther to look for Thalia. "What you doin' over there? How come you still layin' around here like a hog in a mud puddle?"

"Don't you remember, Clover? The Calhoun party was last night." Thalia rose and whirled around the room, hugging herself. "And what a gala event it was. I don't ever recall having so much fun."

Clover crossed her arms and watched Thalia dancing around. "Uh-huh. Just what is you up to, Miss Dancin' Queen?"

Thalia hugged and kissed Clover and then continued to dance around. "Nothing, absolutely nothing this glorious morning. Did I miss the sunrise? I know it must have been lovely."

"If you don't stop actin' like a child's top, spinnin' and whirlin' round me, I's gonna send for the doctor." Clover pulled Thalia's petticoats from the wardrobe. "Mistah Donald still asleep. You get yourself ready for the day. Ain't no reason for you to be wallerin' in the bed this time o' mornin'."

Thalia fell back on the bed with an exhausted sigh. "Why not? Why should I— What time is it?" Thalia became suddenly alert and looked at the shelf clock. "Oh, dear, it's after eleven."

Dressing as quickly as she could, Thalia pushed aside her thoughts of Justin. She would see him in little more than two hours. After selecting an afternoon gown of sprigged muslin, she pulled it on and settled in front of her dressing table. "Fix my hair nicely this morning, Clover, I'm going out immediately. Lenore says there's a new milliner and lady's shop in town. I want to buy some ribbons and artificial flowers."

Clover brushed Thalia's hair until it shone and then wove it into braids that formed a neat chignon at the base of her neck. "I don't reckon you want pearls and roses in your hair this mornin', do you, Miss Dancin' Queen?"

"Oh, Clover, hush up. Can't you see I'm just happy?" Thalia slipped on her gloves and slid the loop of cord attached to her fan over her wrist.

"Well, you won't be near so happy if you wakes up Mistah Donald after he been up drinkin' all night." Clover hung Thalia's dressing gown in the wardrobe and closed the door. "Ebenezer done found one of your daddy's favorite brandy bottles busted in the fireplace. Glass everywhere."

"That doesn't sound good." Thalia tiptoed to the door and peeked out. She smiled sheepishly back at Clover. "I think I'll slip out before he wakes up."

Donald's condition could do little to destroy Thalia's good mood this morning. Not even the weather could hamper her spirits as she strode out of her house. Cool mist touched her face, leaving a kiss of moisture on her cheeks. Above her, a sky as gray and delicate as the silk of a spider's web threatened to further dampen the day's activities, but for now the silken web held back the rain.

She hurried along Meeting Street toward Lenore's house. Lenore probably wouldn't want to linger long this morning, either, since the party hadn't ended until very late. She'd more than likely have to help supervise the cleaning if Thalia didn't get there before Mrs. Calhoun arose.

Thalia skipped up the steps of the Calhoun house and tapped on the door. She didn't want to awaken the elder Calhoun unless she absolutely had to. Mrs. Calhoun would surely talk long enough to take up the time Thalia had set aside to check on the arrival of the cotton.

Wilhemina Calhoun answered the door. "Thalia, darling, do come in."

Trying to disguise her disappointment, Thalia stepped inside. She glanced at the cleanup going on in the large ballroom as they passed. If she closed her eyes briefly, she could almost see herself whirling about the room with Justin. "Good morning, Mrs. Calhoun. Your party was the most elegant I've ever attended."

Wilhemina noticed the dreamy look on Thalia's face. *Only a man could cause a look like that,* she mused. She chuckled and dropped a kiss on Thalia's forehead. "You're a sweet child, Thalia. Lenore's getting ready."

"Did she tell you we were going shopping?" Thalia asked, hoping that her friend had already prepared her mother for the outing.

"Yes, so you don't have to worry about finding a way to convince me that you must go. You're both naughty girls, running off like this when there's so much to be done." Wilhemina reverted to the term she'd used when Thalia and Lenore were children. Taking Thalia's hand, Wilhemina led her to the dining room. "Was it raining when you came in?"

Thalia glanced out the window and saw the rain beginning to fall. She could just see the rose garden from there, and she smiled. *What a wonderful evening it was,* she thought. Thalia hoped that Mrs. Calhoun wouldn't try to postpone their shopping trip, because she really wanted to see Justin again, and there was no other way. If it continued to rain, she'd have to wait until it stopped to see the warehouses at the wharves. It was just too muddy when it rained.

She smiled innocently at Mrs. Calhoun. "No, ma'am. It just started. It doesn't look like it will rain long. The sun will probably come out any minute."

"I see." Wilhemina Calhoun gazed at the window and then at Thalia. "I don't know about that. But you're not going anywhere until you've eaten dinner."

"Oh, Mrs. Calhoun, I couldn't eat a thing. I'm so ex—" She stopped and thought about what she was saying. "I'm not very hungry this morning."

"No food, no shopping." Wilhemina settled into a chair and directed Thalia to do the same. "I won't discuss it further."

"Yes, ma'am." Thalia sat on the chair Mrs. Calhoun indicated and opened her eyes wide when Mammy placed a steaming plate of vegetables and corn bread on the table.

Wilhemina watched Thalia for a moment. The girl was obviously excited about something, and that something, Wilhemina knew, must be a man. "Thalia, dear, didn't I see you walking in the garden last night with that handsome Captain Lionheart?"

Thalia almost choked on her corn bread. After a few seconds of trying to regain her composure, she smiled. "Why, yes, you did. We... I mean, we didn't do anything wrong. We were just enjoying the last few roses of summer. You know, we're likely to have frost any time now."

So, I was right, Wilhemina thought. "Thalia, if Molly were alive, I know she'd caution you about this. As a relative outsider, I can see that you're a levelheaded girl and won't do anything foolish. But please, be careful. Nobody really knows anything about Justin Lionheart."

Thalia considered Mrs. Calhoun's words. She appreciated them. True enough, Aunt Molly would have scolded her—not to mention Clover—but she was old enough to know her own mind, wasn't she? "Thank you for having faith in me, Mrs. Calhoun. I... I'll try to behave like a lady."

"I know you will, my dear." Wilhemina smiled gently and shook her head. "I just wish Lenore had some of your common sense. I can't imagine how the two of you became best friends."

"We've been friends for a long time, and old friendships are lasting," Thalia said finally. "It's true, Lenore and I are different now, but I still love her, even if she acts like a green goose every now and then."

"You're right, and I'm glad you're her friend." Wilhemina placed her napkin in her lap. "Maybe you can keep her out of trouble. Now, eat your dinner."

Thalia felt a little guilty. She hadn't exactly lied to Mrs. Calhoun, but she hadn't told her all the truth. As to keeping Lenore out of trouble, Thalia was having enough trouble staying out of trouble herself. She looked at the plate again and groaned. "Heavens, I declare I simply can't eat all of that."

"Well, give it a try." Wilhemina glanced at the clock. "Mammy, go tell Lenore that if she doesn't come down immediately there'll be no dinner, and if there's no dinner there'll be no shopping."

"I'm here." Lenore raced into the room as if she were being chased by a pack of wild boars. She kissed her mother's cheek and winked at Thalia. "Mother, I can't eat all of this. I'll be as fat as Mrs. Rutledge."

"Don't be disrespectful, Lenore," Wilhemina said in a chiding tone. "And don't slouch."

"Yes, ma'am," Lenore said deferentially, and seated herself.

"You'd think I'd reared her with the animals." Wilhemina signaled for Lenore's dinner to be brought to her.

Thalia could hardly eat. Everything concerning Justin seemed to be moving too quickly, as if she were standing by and watching her life being played by some actress she didn't know. Without stuffing herself, she dutifully ate enough to please Mrs. Calhoun, who continued to eye the girls suspiciously.

Wilhemina dabbed at the corners of her mouth and placed her napkin on the table. "Now, ladies, I'd like an explanation of where you were for so long last night."

Lenore's fork clattered to her plate. "We, uh . . . we weren't gone long."

Realizing that Mrs. Calhoun had probably timed their absence, Thalia set her glass of milk on the table, deliberately wiped the residue from her lips, and grinned sheepishly. "I'm sorry, Mrs. Calhoun. It's probably my fault."

"Really?" Wilhemina's gaze moved from her daughter to Thalia. "Please tell me what happened, my dear, that you found it necessary to stay in the garden for more than half an hour, keeping Lenore from her duties as hostess."

"Please forgive me. You know how quickly time passes when Lenore and I get together." Thalia's thoughts raced. Mrs. Calhoun was no schoolgirl, so her story needed to be plausible. "May I confide in you, Mrs. Calhoun? Confidentially, of course."

"I'm appalled that you think a word of what you say to me would be repeated," Wilhemina answered, shaking her head sadly. "I thought you trusted me."

"Oh, I do," Thalia amended hastily. "It's just that this matter is so... delicate."

"Delicate?" Wilhemina rose abruptly. "You aren't— What I mean to say is, you... your reputation hasn't been compromised by some blundering—"

"Oh, no, ma'am," Thalia assured her, wondering how she'd gotten herself into such a situation. "Please, sit, and I'll tell you."

Mrs. Calhoun sat and drew her chair closer to the table. She signaled to Mammy to leave. "All right, my dear, what's troubling you?"

Thalia prayed that Lenore wouldn't blurt out something silly, and a glance showed that she was as confused as her mother. "Well, Mrs. Calhoun, it's Randolph Taylor."

"Randolph? What's he done? He didn't—"

"No, ma'am. It's just that—I declare, that man can't seem to understand that I've no interest in him." Thalia could see that Lenore was breathing again. No doubt the dear little twit had thought that Thalia was going to say something about Edward and Justin. "I've done everything Aunt Molly told me to do, but he keeps coming around and making a nuisance of himself."

"I see," Wilhemina replied, leaning back as if to consider the situation. After a moment, she continued, "Well, Thalia, my dear, you can't offend the Taylor family. They've been in Charleston for ages. Why, one of Mr. Taylor's ancestors was one of the original settlers here."

"I realize that, Mrs. Calhoun. So you can see the delicate predicament in which I find myself." Thalia buried her head in her hands, as if the situation were very grave. "Can you advise me?"

Wilhemina rose, fairly floated around the table and embraced Thalia. "Come, we'll take a moment in the ladies' parlor."

The two young women trailed after Mrs. Calhoun as she swept from the room, walked down the wide hallway and entered the ladies' parlor. She ensconced herself in a wine-colored brocade chair near a large window and artfully arranged her skirts. "All right. Now, a lady would handle Mr. Taylor very carefully. Men don't like to be turned down when they propose, and, I suspect, Mr. Taylor is no different."

Following along, Thalia perched on the edge of the sofa and listened more carefully. While she had merely been trying to divert Mrs. Calhoun's attention from a potentially touchy subject, she had miraculously blundered onto a subject that might save her some embarrassment. "I suppose not. Please, go on."

"Evade his proposals for as long as you can. Unfortunately, most men have no more sense than mosquitoes, and keep pestering you until they catch you unawares." Wilhemina eyed Thalia suspiciously. "You aren't playing games with him, are you?"

"Oh, no, ma'am." Thalia frowned. She hoped that her sincerity could be conveyed by the look on her face. "It's not that at all. I just don't like him."

"Quite understandable, although I'm forced to say this, Thalia, my dear, since your own dear mother isn't here to advise you in this matter." Wilhemina stood, gazed at her daughter's best friend for a moment, crossed the room and sat on the sofa beside her. She placed her arm around Thalia's shoulders. "Thalia, dearest, you should consider Mr. Taylor's offer carefully when he makes it, and make it he will. Men . . . well, they seldom realize that ladies have any intelligence at all. He probably believes you don't know your own mind, and that once he proposes you'll fall immediately into his arms."

"I assure you," Thalia said vehemently, "that will never happen."

"As I said, you must consider his offer. You know he's considered quite a catch," Wilhemina told her. "But if you're sure you won't change your mind, you must avoid him whenever possible." Glancing from Thalia to Lenore and back again, Wilhemina returned to the original subject. "But you should never again leave a party for so long a time without a proper chaperon. I saw you two girls return with Mr. Nelson and Captain Lionheart."

Thalia prayed the expression on her face didn't change. The mention of Justin's name brought a slight quiver to her body, and she hoped that Mrs. Calhoun didn't notice.

"I'll not have your reputations ruined," Wilhemina continued, looking at Thalia with new interest. "You're shivering. Are you cold?"

"Uh, yes, ma'am. Just a bit." Thalia crossed her fingers and said a little prayer, asking forgiveness for the lie.

"Well, if you're going out soon there's no need to start a fire in here." Wilhemina hugged Thalia closer to her. "Now, back to the two gentlemen. Tread carefully, girls. These are men of the world, and I won't have you acting foolishly. Now, be on your way."

"Thank you very much, Mrs. Calhoun." Thalia kissed Wilhemina on the cheek and rose.

She hurried from the room, Lenore following in her wake. Without hesitating a moment, they pulled on their cloaks and hastened out the door. Thalia didn't stop rushing until they were a block away. "Gracious, Lenore, that woman must have spies everywhere. How did she know we came back with Edward and Justin? They didn't even enter the ballroom with us."

"I've always thought my mother had spies. It's like she's everywhere, especially when I'm doing something I shouldn't." Lenore peered around cautiously, taking extra care to look behind them to see if they were being followed. "I hope she doesn't find out about today."

"It's too late to worry about that now," Thalia reminded her friend. "You should have thought of that last night when you were making all these plans."

"Oh, hush up, Thalia." Lenore stopped, placed her arms on her hips and glared at her friend. "You didn't protest too much. You are just as eager to see Captain Lionheart as I am to see Mr. Nelson. Don't be a hypocrite."

"Acting like a lady isn't hypocritical," Thalia retorted, though she secretly agreed with Lenore. Thalia had never been one to follow traditions too closely, nor was she overly concerned about besmirching the family name. After all, Donald seemed to be doing enough of that all by himself.

"Thalia, you never cared one whit for acting like a lady. The only thing that interested you in school was learning to dance and to write poetry." Lenore's tone was mildly accusing. "Besides, ladies have no fun."

Thalia couldn't help smiling. The prospect of becoming a lady had taken on different implications for them as they'd grown up. As little girls, Thalia and Lenore had wanted to be exactly like Wilhemina Calhoun and Molly Bishop. When they'd reached the exciting adolescent years, their outlook had changed somewhat. They'd seen the older women as leading hard, dull lives, and they'd wanted nothing to do with becoming a lady. Though Thalia's feelings had tempered somewhat, she was still resisting the yoke of becoming a lady.

The cool wind whipped around Thalia, and she pulled her cloak more closely about her. She glanced up and down the street. They were nearing the little shop where they planned to buy ribbons and flowers. "I hope we're not too late. And I'm so full I don't think I can eat another bite."

"What? Those wonderful little cakes?" Lenore asked, as if she were surprised. "I could eat a dozen."

They found the little notions shop and went inside. For a moment Thalia stood and took in everything. She didn't know which way to go first. There were colorful ribbons, bright buttons, fancy laces, lovely hats, pretty artificial flowers and neat stacks of handkerchiefs.

"What were you and my mother discussing when I came down?" Lenore asked, glancing at Thalia.

Thalia smiled conspiratorially. "She asked about Justin."

"She didn't!" Lenore exclaimed. "You didn't tell her where we were going, did you?"

"Shh!" Thalia said, pointing to the shop clerk. "Do you want everyone to know? We'll talk later."

Thalia looked first through the handkerchiefs and selected several edged with tatting. "Goodness," she said as she handed her choices to the clerk. "Everything is so pretty that I simply don't know what I want."

Lenore was looking at bonnets. "I think I'll try on a couple of these."

"Go ahead. I'm going to look at the flowers and ribbons." Thalia moved to the ribbon counter. She chose several and asked the clerk to cut appropriate lengths. From there she went to the flower counter and looked at the sprigs of artificial flowers. "Oh, aren't these lovely?"

She held up a tiny nosegay of violets for Lenore to see. She could already see them on her new violet dress. Thinking of the dress brought Justin to mind. She'd hardly slept because of her anticipation, and now she was standing in a shop whiling away the time as if she had nowhere to go. But then, Justin wasn't expecting her yet. She glanced at Lenore and smiled. "Don't you think these would look pretty with my new dress?"

"Oh, yes." Lenore turned to the mirror again and studied her face. She shifted the hat on her head, a little forward and to the right. "What about this one?"

Thalia looked at the scarlet hat. With Lenore's auburn hair, the hat made her look a little silly. Thalia glanced at the other hats. "I think the green one. Or maybe that light blue, with the pretty lace. You know, I believe Edward prefers green. Don't you think?"

"Do you really think he does?" Lenore removed the red hat and put the green one on. "How about this? Do you think he'll like this one?"

The lime-green taffeta complemented Lenore's coloring perfectly. "Lenore, that looks wonderful. It's perfect for you. I declare, I don't know anyone else who could wear it. And Edward will love it."

Lenore preened in front of the mirror, tilting her head first one way and then the other. "I believe you're right. It *is* perfect for me. May I wear it? You can put my old bonnet in a box.''

The two women made several purchases and then left the shop. They were excitedly discussing their finds and walking toward the tea shop when they encountered Justin and Edward.

"Ah, I suspected that you might have need of a strong arm to carry your packages." Justin took Thalia's parcels and offered her his arm. "We came to escort you to tea."

"Thank you. What a gentleman you are, Captain Lionheart," Thalia said, happy to be relieved of the cumbersome boxes.

"And you, Miss Freemont, are a delightful wonder to me." Justin turned Thalia around, and they began walking toward the tearoom.

Lenore handed her purchases to Edward and took his arm. "Why, thank you, Mr. Nelson."

Justin looked down into Thalia's alert blue eyes. "Miss Freemont, you look lovely this afternoon."

"Now, Captain, you're just being kind." Thalia smiled, secretly happy that her extra time dressing had resulted in a compliment. She sincerely hoped that he meant it. "Do you think it will rain?"

"I most certainly do." Justin caught her eye and let his gaze linger, memorizing the brilliant glitter of blue. Feeling a little abashed for staring, he glanced up at the sky. Low clouds, pregnant with the promise of rain, hung over the Charleston peninsula. "I believe that rain is inevitable."

"Oh, dear." Thalia gazed up, wishing she'd brought her parasol. "I hope it doesn't, at least until I get home."

"Whether it rains or not, Miss Freemont," Justin said, peering deeply into her eyes, "means little. When I'm with you, the sun seems to follow and warm me all over."

Chapter Seven

Raindrops began to fall as they neared the tea shop, but Thalia didn't really mind. She thought that the cotton crop back at Edisto should be in the barns by now, ready to be ginned and packed for shipment. Adam Woodsley had sent word that the cotton for sale had been harvested and the seed cotton was ready to be picked. Even that job should be done by now.

Lightning streaked across the sky overhead, and thunder rumbled long and low over the harbor. As the rain fell harder, the four began to walk faster. Justin handed her the packages for a moment while he removed his cloak. Making a shelter over both of them, he grinned. "Isn't this wonderful? It's almost like a storm at sea. Wild and beautiful, treacherous and sensual. Like a woman."

"Wonderful? Like a woman? I'm not sure I would characterize a rainstorm either way, but I do like the fresh aroma of a good rain." Thalia snuggled closer beneath the cloak, telling herself that she was merely trying to protect her clothing.

They soon reached the tearoom and rushed up the steps. As they opened the door and walked in, a deluge of rain began. "Gracious," Thalia exclaimed, shaking the raindrops off her gown. "We arrived just in time to avoid being thoroughly drenched."

Wilby hurried over to the foursome, wiping his hands on his apron as he crossed the room. "Aye, but it's a turrible bad storm we be 'avin' this day, don't you know? It's glad I am ye stopped in to see old Wilby. Come in, come in."

Thalia smiled at Wilby and followed him to a table near the window. Justin pulled out her chair and waited for her to be seated. "Thank you, Justin."

Lenore launched into a giggling report on her mother's lecture about a lady's decorum, but Thalia remained quiet. She was thinking of Justin as she listened and gazed out the windows. Everything about him intrigued her. *Mysterious*, she thought again. *Yes, he's certainly mysterious.*

Thalia watched rivulets suddenly forming into brooks where the walkways had once been. She and Lenore would have to hire a carriage to take them home, even if the rain stopped soon, or their gowns would be ruined. The time to leave was quickly approaching, and she didn't really want to leave Justin. Nor did she want to listen to Lenore's prattle. She would prefer to sit down with Justin and talk about whatever interested him, what he loved, what he hated. She wanted to know everything about him.

She reached for her cup and accidentally touched his hand. Her body seemed to sizzle from his warm touch on her cold skin. She understood now why ladies wore gloves; it was to prevent the intimate feeling that touching a man could generate. Thalia looked into his eyes and felt as if she could happily drown in their depths. She was definitely in over her head with this man. He was, she suspected, far more sophisticated than she would ever be.

The chill of her damp garments sent a shiver down her spine, or at least that was what she told herself. Thalia was glad for the steaming cup of tea and the warm pastries, though she could hardly eat after the platter of vegetables she'd had at the Calhoun home.

"Are you cold, Thalia?" Justin asked, reaching for her arm. "Let me ask Wilby to put another log on the fire."

Justin disappeared for a moment and then returned. "He's on the way. My cloak is too wet to be placed over that lovely gown, so we'll have to depend on the fire."

"I—I'll be fine." She'd hoped he hadn't noticed her shivering, and she wondered now if he felt the same way. Did his fingers tingle where they'd brushed hers? She had to stop thinking about Justin. This wasn't like her at all.

She watched Edward for a moment and decided that Lenore enchanted him. Well, she thought, smiling at Lenore, they seem to be well suited for each other.

And Justin? How would he fit into her life? He'd compared the storm to a woman, wild and beautiful, treacherous and sensual. Did that mean he'd had a bad experience with a woman? Were all his romances stormy? She glanced at Justin and found him staring at her. When their eyes met, there seemed to be a current—a wild and treacherous current—between them that threatened to sweep her away. Thalia didn't want to become involved with Justin, but she always felt so alive when she was with him. It was as if she could really be herself with him, without putting on the artificial manners and restrictions that went with being a planter's daughter.

"My cotton is in," she said, catching his gaze on her. "I raise cotton at Misty Glade."

"*You* raise cotton at Misty Glade?" Justin asked, surprised by the turn of the conversation, and astonished by her revelation. "Surely you mean that cotton is raised at your plantation."

"No," she replied, realizing she'd made a mistake. She'd thought he was different, but he wasn't. He assumed that because she was a woman her mind was always on pretty clothes. Well, Thalia did like pretty clothes, but she loved farming. "I mean exactly what I said. My brother—he owns Misty Glade—isn't the least bit interested in farming. Along with my overseer, I run two plantations, though I never get to see my own."

Justin looked at her with new respect. "You know, I've never met a woman like you. I'd like to see your plantation someday."

"So would I." Thalia smiled, happy that he didn't disapprove of her for taking on a man's job. "I haven't seen Sea Mist Plantation—which I own—in several years."

"Oh? Why not?"

Thalia looked away. She'd opened the subject, and now she could hardly say she didn't want to talk about it. "My... I lived with an aunt and uncle on Sea Mist. They're dead, and now it's mine. But my brother doesn't think it's proper for me to live there alone, and he's my guardian. I don't have much choice, but I'm moving back soon. I promised myself."

"I hope you do," Justin said sincerely. "Let me know if you need my help."

Thalia wanted to get off the touchy subject of her exile from Sea Mist. "I must say, Captain—"

"Justin."

"Justin," she repeated, feeling a sudden fluttering in her stomach. "I'm awfully glad you were able to return from your journey in time for the Calhoun party." Thalia smiled and raised her eyebrows playfully. "I'm afraid the evening would have become quite dull without your quick wit."

"I must admit to having rushed my trip," Justin replied, all the while wondering why he was confessing such a thing to a planter's daughter. "I didn't want to miss the party."

"How fortunate for us. And was your trip a business trip?" Thalia asked.

"Yes, quite successful." Justin felt a little safer discussing business, rather than more personal issues. He was glad Thalia didn't press him. Though he was skilled at diverting potentially embarrassing questions, he didn't really want to have to do that with her. "I made a quick trip to Bermuda for a local merchant."

Thalia nodded her head. "I see. You said you hire your ship for cargo?"

"Sometimes cargo," he replied, leaning closer to her. He could just barely catch the fragrance of roses that seemed always to surround her. He realized in that moment that he would, most probably, never smell a rose again without thinking of her. "Sometimes ... sometimes passengers. I take almost anything. I love to feel the ocean beneath my feet. I'll do anything—almost—to take her out. Except slaves. I don't carry slaves."

"Oh," Thalia said simply. A curl of black hair, damp from the rain, fell across his forehead, and he brushed it back casually. The unruly lock sprang back, and he shrugged, apparently having decided to ignore it.

Justin watched Thalia closely. She was a lovely woman with no artifice—at least, none that he could see. But his experiences in the past had left him cautious and wary of beautiful women, particularly wealthy, beautiful women. "Would you like to see my ship? She's the gamest vessel on the sea."

"Gamest?" Thalia asked, noticing how reverently he spoke of his ship. Justin Lionheart was clearly a man who loved his life at sea. Gazing at his eyes, which seemed to reflect the colors of the mist that hovered over the harbor most mornings, she decided that he belonged with the ocean, that he was a part of that great undulating power that both welcomed and threatened unwary travelers. The woman who married Justin would have to share that love for the sea, or she would seldom see him at all.

"She's quick and proud. Many a man has tried to match her in races, but so far she's been the gamest." Justin spoke proudly. He loved his ship, the *Blind Justice*. It had become his home.

Games, Thalia mused. *Do all men think of nothing but gaming? Is Justin yet another man like my brother, who will stop at nothing until he's wagered his fortune away?* She remembered Mrs. Calhoun's warning about Justin, about the mystery surrounding him. "Are you a gambling man, Captain...Justin?"

"Who among us isn't? We gamble every day of our lives," Justin answered wryly.

"Many do, I suppose," Thalia conceded, sipping her tea. Here was another reason to avoid Justin, and yet she still felt his magnetism. Did he affect all women this way? She glanced at Lenore, who seemed to notice no one other than Edward Nelson. Thalia suddenly felt confused by her emotions. She needed to get away from Justin, to think about why she was so attracted to him, and so soon.

The rain continued to pour, as if it were determined to trap her with both Justin and her own troubling feelings. For a few seconds she listened to the raindrops spattering the windows. Justin, as if he had caught the slightest hint of her mood, fell silent and signaled for more tea.

Justin watched Thalia carefully. He suddenly felt as though the mood of the afternoon had changed slightly, and he didn't know the reason. He thought back over the conversation, and could remember nothing that should have precipitated such a change. Thalia wasn't exactly sullen or sulking, but her demeanor was more guarded; her lips straightened into a line that replaced the lovely smile that had been there.

Her blue eyes, usually filled with the warmth of sunlight, were now an ice blue and shaded. Despite the rain, the day had seemed cheerful and warm enough, but since the change in her it had become a normal dull and dreary rainy afternoon.

Justin had weathered storms of temperament before, and he would weather this one, as well. He wondered if the alteration in her mood was the result of a petulance he hadn't detected in her. She was, after all, the daughter of a wealthy planter. In his experience, such women were prone to such unpredictable behavior.

It was, he decided, a good thing for him to have found out now how similar she was to his preconceived ideas of society women. So far he'd put her above such pettiness. Now he knew better. She was no different from all the rest.

The rain began to slacken. Justin waffled. Should he escort her home or allow her to get there as best she could? True, their afternoon had been spoiled by something indefinable—to him, at least—but he would remain a gentleman regardless of her behavior. He continued to watch her for a few minutes.

Thalia gazed out the window. How could she have been so taken in by his easy manner? Justin was no different from Donald. *He is different,* she told herself, acknowledging that she had perhaps jumped to conclusions. *But,* she reminded herself, *he admits to being a gambler.*

"May I escort you home, Miss Freemont? The rain seems to be slackening," Justin finally asked. "I doubt whether the respite will last long, though."

"Home?" Thalia looked at him, puzzled by his sudden mention of taking her home. The silence had droned on for a little while while she'd been thinking, but it hadn't seemed all that long. Had she bored him that quickly? "Oh no, Jus—Captain Lionheart, I'm perfectly capable of—"

"I know you're capable. However, I am a gentleman, and I refuse to allow you to go home unescorted." Justin motioned toward Edward and Lenore. "They don't appear ready to go just yet, so why don't we leave them here?"

"Well, if you think... You're right," she replied after glancing at Lenore. Poor Lenore seemed oblivious of everything going on around her. In fact, Lenore would probably prefer to be left alone with Edward. In this public place, they'd probably need no chaperon. She just hoped that Lenore didn't do anything foolish. "But, I can—"

"I insist." Justin stood and helped Thalia from her chair. "Good afternoon, Lenore and Edward. I'm escorting Miss Freemont back to her town house."

Thalia nodded goodbye to the two. They hardly seemed to notice that she was leaving. She and Justin moved quietly to the door.

"Wait here a moment," he said, and walked down the steps. He saw a for-hire carriage coming down the street. It wasn't as well kept as he would have liked, but it would keep them dry. He called to the driver, who pulled to a halt in front of the tea shop. Justin gave the driver the address and went back to fetch Thalia.

"Captain, you mustn't feel obligated to—"

"Get in, Miss Freemont." Justin opened the door and lifted her without waiting for her answer. He deposited her on the seat and climbed in after her.

As the carriage lumbered off, the rain started to fall again. "My goodness, but it looks as if we made the right decision," Thalia said, staring out the window on her side of the carriage.

"Yes, it does." Justin was very aware of Thalia. Her fragrance clung to her and perfumed the damp air around the two of them. "Miss Freemont, I...Thalia, I don't know why I said that..." Justin's voice dwindled off. Thus far, he'd made it his policy not to apologize for some indiscretion *imagined* by a woman. Since he hadn't said or done anything offensive, he assumed that she had imagined some infraction of the unwritten rules of Charleston society. "I'm sorry if—"

"Don't apologize...Justin." Thalia turned to look at him. She knew she had been unfair to him, classifying him with Donald and his friends simply at the mention of gambling. She didn't usually pass judgment so quickly, but gambling was a tender spot, since Donald couldn't seem to refrain from it. "The fault is mine."

Justin opened his mouth, but nothing came out. No woman had ever apologized to him, not for any reason. He was taken aback for a moment. "I'm sure, Thalia, that the fault lies with the damp weather. It's enough to make everyone a little moody, wouldn't you say?''

"Yes," she agreed, glad that he didn't hold the uncomfortable moments against her. She liked him too much. Being with him lifted her spirits considerably. Curtains of rain began to fall, shutting them off from civilization, almost as if they were the only two people in all of Charleston. "I like rain, usually, but . . ."

Thalia couldn't finish her sentence. Justin's eyes seemed to take her breath away. Once again they were like the gentle mist that rose from the rivers at dawn, suffusing the light with a vague warmth that penetrated everything. He was so close to her, his face so near that she could see the beginnings of his afternoon stubble. "I—I . . . We need the rain," she finally stammered.

Justin was enchanted. Her face had softened into the gentle beauty that always touched his heart. He couldn't seem to draw away from her, though he knew that he should. Justin didn't remember moving, but his lips caressed hers, or maybe hers caressed his. For a moment, he didn't breathe, afraid that she would flutter away as the butterfly kiss she'd placed on his mouth had disappeared.

He could no longer hold back. Whether she had initiated the contact or whether he had, Justin now had to pursue the action. He slid his arms around her, drawing her close as he gazed down into the loveliest sapphire eyes he'd ever seen. They glistened from within, illuminating an inner depth that he hadn't noticed before.

Thalia felt the power in his embrace and breathlessly allowed the feeling to capture her. Seconds passed like minutes until his lips touched hers again. This time, the kiss wasn't as gentle, but it was filled with want. His tongue slipped between her lips, and Thalia caught her breath as he gently explored the hidden recesses of her mouth.

Warmth suffused her, passing through her body, inch by inch, until she felt as if her entire body were glowing from within. Her eyes closed, and she felt as if she'd been swept away from herself, as if she were being carried aloft by a powerful storm that cuddled and protected her while it demonstrated its strength.

The carriage jolted over a hole in the road, jostling them apart. Thalia felt as if she were coming out of a daze as she gazed into his eyes once again. "I—I... We're almost there."

Thalia stared out the window, afraid to look at Justin again. The power of the emotion that their embrace had engendered was too strong for her to deal with now. She knew too little about the feelings between a man and a woman, untutored as she was in the ways of love.

The carriage drew to a halt. Justin stared at her for a moment and then opened the door. Rain fell in sheets, spattering mud onto everything as it carved tiny rivulets in the dirt and whisked leaves and twigs along in its path. "Don't get out," she whispered as she stood. Without waiting for his answer, she crossed in front of him and jumped to the ground.

Water surged up over her boots, but she didn't care. She knew she had to get away from Justin. His presence was too overpowering. Lifting her skirts as best she could, she ran through the gate, across the sidewalk and up the steps. Not until she reached the piazza could she look back. From there she could barely see Justin inside the coach. Seconds before the carriage lurched into its lumbering roll, he raised his fingers to his head as if in a salute.

Thalia smiled and lifted her hand as he drove away. For a moment, she stood there staring after the carriage in wonder. Then she shook as much water as she could from her skirts and entered the house. She met Clover coming down the stairs.

"Lawsy, if you ain't a sight. I never seen so much water on a lady in my life. Ain't you got sense enough to carry a parasol?" Clover crossed her arms and shook her head. "Ebenezer!" she called, coming down the stairs.

"What you want, woman?" he asked, poking his head through a narrow opening in the door that led to the back of the house. "I's busy."

"Well, you ain't too busy to bring some hot water up for Miss Thalia's bath. That child done went and got herself soaked like a yard dog. Now git." Clover turned to Thalia. "And you just march yourself right up these stairs and get off them wet clothes. I ain't never gonna git all them rain spots off that dress."

Thalia watched as Clover ambled off toward the kitchen, still muttering. As she started up the stairs, she heard the ongoing tirade. "Ain't got sense God gave a banny hen. Took off in all her fine clothes and come back here lookin' like a mangy dog, that's what."

Thalia, shivering, strode across the hallway and headed up the stairs. When she reached her room, she began to remove her wet clothes. After taking off her gown and crinolines, she pulled on her dressing gown and sat down to wait for her bath water. She was glad that Clover was taking care of that matter before the inevitable scolding for getting a good gown wet.

Before she had much time to think about the afternoon's entertainment, Clover came in with the first pail of hot water. Ebenezer stood in the hallway with two others while he waited for Clover to pour. He brought up one more load before the tub was filled.

"Now just git yourself in there before you catches your death of cold. I ain't never seen a lady act like such as you." Clover gathered up the gown and crinolines. "I'll have to scrub them crinolines and the hem of that dress to git all that mud out."

Thalia ladled in a silver spoon full of rose-scented bath flakes, settled herself into the tub and drizzled hot water over her body. The steaming water relaxed her, and she bathed quickly. After drying herself completely, she brushed her hair and pulled on her nightgown. She wanted to take a nap before supper—if she could sleep for thinking about Justin.

Donald went into his club. He hoped that some of his friends would be there playing cards. After glancing around the room, he found no one he knew, and he cursed silently. Then he spotted Captain Justin Lionheart.

Being new in town, Justin wouldn't know anything about Donald and might be willing to lend him money should his luck run bad this evening. Donald walked over and introduced himself.

"Freemont?" Justin asked, gazing at Donald. "I believe I'm acquainted with your lovely sister, Thalia."

"Yes. Thalia's my sister." Donald stared at his new acquaintance. "How would you know her?"

"A mutual friend introduced us. Caleb Saunders and I were talking the other morning when Miss Freemont was walking on the promenade at The Battery." Justin began to feel a rush of excitement. Could this be the man for whom he was searching? He certainly looked like the description Alicia's friend had provided, sketchy though it was. And the name Donald Freemont was interesting. The man he sought was nicknamed Dof. Justin instinctively felt he was nearing the end of his search.

"Indeed? Well, then, I'm happy to meet you." Donald looked around the room. None of his friends were there. "I'd hoped to find my friend Randolph Taylor here this evening. We spend a great many hours here together. Could I interest you in a game of cards?"

Justin smiled pleasantly. He wanted to get to know this man better. "I'd be delighted."

"Let me order us a bottle of port." Donald signaled for a bottle and two glasses. "Nothing quite like a glass of port after supper."

"No, you're right," Justin agreed.

Before the first hand was completed, Justin knew that Donald knew nothing about gambling. He lost very quickly and very stupidly. Drinking as fast as he could pour, Donald soon began to show signs of drunkenness. After a few hands, Donald seemed reluctant to continue. "Is there something wrong? I'm happy to give you a chance to win back some of your money."

"No, no. That's not it." Donald peered around, searching the room for Randolph. Donald's pockets were empty, and he knew that no one else in the club would lend him money tonight. He poured himself the last of the port and drank it in one gulp. "I was hoping my friend Randolph would arrive. He owes me a sum of money, and . . ."

So that's it, Justin thought. Donald Freemont's out of funds and is looking for someone who will lend him gambling money. "If you're a bit short, I'd be happy to make you a small loan."

Donald turned back to Justin. "Could you? That would be capital. I really expected to collect—"

"Think nothing of it." Justin removed some bills from his purse and handed them to Donald. "Don't be in a hurry to return the money. I've just returned from a good run in my ship, and have plenty for the time being."

"What's the name of your ship?" Donald asked, pretending to be friendly. After all, the man had lent him some money.

"She's the *Blind Justice*. A real beauty." Justin could hardly contain his pride. "She's the fastest ship around. I keep a schooner here, too."

"Really? I'm known as a first-rate captain, myself," Donald said with a smile. "My ship is pretty fast. Maybe we can have a race someday."

Justin could hardly keep from laughing. He remembered how wet Thalia had been on her arrival in Charleston. She'd told him then that her brother had captained the ship that brought them from Edisto Island. He nodded. "Someday soon. For now, I'm afraid I have business elsewhere."

"Fine meeting you. I hope we can play again sometime." Donald stood and grinned broadly. "Maybe then my luck will change and I'll win back some of my money."

"Whenever you choose," Justin said, rising and nodding goodbye. He peered at Donald for a few seconds. "I have this odd feeling that we've met before, sometime in the past."

"Met before?" Donald repeated, staring at Justin. The man didn't look at all familiar to him, at least not that he could recall. "Don't think so."

Justin couldn't risk mentioning his home or the Kimballs, not until he had something more to go on. He shrugged. "Guess not, then. Well, we'll race soon. You name the time. You never know about Lady Luck. She's a fickle mistress."

Donald thought of Eugenia and her connection with this man. Why would he mention mistresses? It seemed an odd reference. *Oh, well,* he thought. *Maybe he means nothing by it.*

Justin left as quickly as he could. He wanted Donald to think well of him; otherwise he would never have lent Donald any money. Lending money to gamblers was bad business, but Justin had an ulterior motive. He wanted to get to know Donald better, and this seemed to be the quickest way. Justin had plenty of money, and if it took every penny of it he intended to find his man—and he thought Donald Freemont might just be his man.

He stood in the hallway watching Donald for a few minutes. Donald signaled for another bottle and settled in his chair. A man swaggered past Justin and headed toward Donald's table. When the man sat down, Justin recognized him as Randolph Taylor. He stumbled a bit and fell headlong into the chair opposite Donald.

Suppressing a laugh, Justin watched the two men. Donald handed a few bills to Randolph, beaming with pride. Justin had surmised as much. So Donald Freemont was a man who loved to gamble but couldn't afford to lose.

Justin considered that idea for a few moments. Maybe that was why Thalia had grown so silent this afternoon. He had mentioned gambling. Perhaps she knew of her brother's gambling excesses and disliked any man who shared his taste for the gaming tables. If Justin was any judge of character, she had good reason to dislike gamblers. Donald had probably gambled away every penny of their money.

He could stand the stale smell of liquor and tobacco no longer, and he headed out the door. He had thought that Edward would be here tonight, but perhaps he'd found a way to get himself invited to the Calhoun house for supper. Justin chuckled at the foolish way Edward had fallen for Lenore Calhoun. She was pretty enough, but completely unsophisticated and girlish.

Thalia. Now there was a woman. She could hold her tongue, match wits with him easily, and maintain her dignity.

What of her relationship with Donald? Justin felt that he might be treading on quicksand. He enjoyed his time with Thalia and wanted to continue seeing her, but if he did so how could he, in good conscience, pursue her brother as he planned to?

Walking down the street toward the Charleston Hotel, where he maintained a room these days, Justin felt his excitement rise. After all these years of searching, could he really have found the man? Justin thought back to the reason for his search and became angry all over again.

The man Justin was searching for had caused two deaths, the deaths of people he had loved. Unable to return to his own home because one of the deaths was blamed on him, Justin had started his search, all the time plotting his revenge. If Donald was that man, Justin planned to destroy him. He could feel victory within his grasp, and he didn't plan to let Donald Freemont slip away again.

Chapter Eight

Thalia stood on the piazza and watched the sun rise over the juncture of the Ashley and Cooper Rivers. Despite the chill that curled around her, she had been there for more than an hour, staring between the houses at the undulating water. A gray mist rose, a mist the color of Justin's eyes, and embraced the live oaks with their gnarled trunks and limbs while the swordlike fronds of the palmetto trees sliced through the gray moisture with every shift of the wind.

Though she had spent most of the night thinking of Justin, she had reached no conclusions. Thalia enjoyed every moment they spent together—well, almost—but he'd admitted to being a gambler like her brother. And yet he was different. What a dilemma! What else did she need to know about this enigmatic man?

"Everything," she whispered to the gulls taking early flight. "I want to know everything about him."

His kisses had been exciting. Their second kiss had been so very thrilling. She closed her eyes and imagined Justin's lips on hers, felt once again the surging and pounding of her blood as he embraced her.

She had to find a way to avoid another occasion when they would be alone. Thalia knew that she couldn't combat the betrayal of her own body. When Justin looked at her the way he did, something began to melt within her and she felt like a dab of butter on a bowl of grits, slowly dissolving into a pile of mush.

Thalia knew that such feelings were dangerous to her. Aunt Molly had warned her against intimate contact many times, but Thalia hadn't known the power of the attraction that could exist between a man and a woman, even when the two didn't know each other very well.

Since she hadn't seen him for several days, she wondered if today would bring another exciting encounter with Justin Lionheart. "Lionheart. Such a strong, unusual name," she whispered to the stillness of the early morning. *Thalia Lionheart,* her heart echoed.

What was she thinking of? For months she'd discouraged every suitor who'd gotten close enough to court her, and now she was mentally linking her name with Justin's. Such prattle was a sign of weakness, she decided, and went back into her bedroom.

Justin lay awake in his bed, wondering about Thalia Freemont. Though he knew full well that she was a planter's daughter, he kept forgetting that fact when he was with her. Something about Thalia was different. He'd been reared near Richmond, Virginia, and knew many such girls, but none compared to Thalia.

Their simpering smiles and their treacherous games belied their ladylike bearing, making them dangerous participants in the never-ending battle that raged between unmarried men and unmarried—and sometimes married—women. Alicia Kimball had taught him that lesson well. Her deceitful nature had cost him his inheritance and the life of his best friend. Justin refused to allow such a thing to happen again.

He rose and dressed for the day. He had several errands to run before the Harvest Ball this evening, and, though he couldn't really understand why, he was exceedingly happy at the prospect of seeing Thalia again.

Donald and Randolph rode silently toward Meeting Street in the Taylor carriage. Neither man could have ridden after consuming as much brandy as they had at the cockfight.

Randolph looked over at Donald. "You know, Donald old man, we don't have to go out there every night. I mean, there are other, more . . . tender entertainments to be had in Charleston, if you know what I mean."

Donald knew what Randolph meant. But, for some reason, Eugenia had been strangely cool toward him since his return to Charleston. "The cocks are exciting, more exciting than anything I know of, except, of course, the horses at Washington Race Course."

"Well, I expect if you don't find some money soon you needn't attend the races next year." Randolph leaned his aching head against the back of the carriage. "I don't know anyone who's willing to advance you so much as one more dollar, except me, of course. And I can't afford it much longer."

"You're a capital fellow, Randolph. As I told you, my father's estate is in somewhat of an unsettled state right now," Donald lied. He tried to remember what he'd told Randolph before, but couldn't. "Some trivial clause about Thalia is holding everything up."

"A beautiful girl, that Thalia." Randolph turned to watch his friend. "Donald, does she ever speak of me?"

Donald could recall many conversations with Thalia about Randolph. Thalia despised him, but Donald couldn't tell his friend that. He needed his money too much. "She speaks of you frequently, Randolph, my friend. You know, I believe she's quite fond of you."

Randolph's eyes widened. "Dof, old friend, you really mean that? I never realized it, but...I mean, I'm seldom around her. Does she really like me?"

"Certainly. Why would you think otherwise?" Donald asked. He didn't want to lie to Randolph, but for the present he had no real choice. He needed money too badly.

"Do you think... I mean, do I... Oh, hell, should I ask her to marry me?" Randolph asked, leaning forward once again. "I mean, she's so skittish when I'm around her."

"You know women. Play hard to get." Donald held his aching head and wished he'd rejected that last bottle of brandy instead of swilling it down. Suddenly filled with inspiration, he patted Randolph's arm. "You know, the more they like you, the more they try to hide it. Makes the game more interesting."

Randolph thought about that for a moment. "You're right, Donald. I've heard that said more than once."

"You know, Randolph—" Donald was thinking about how to relate his plan so that it would seem proper "—I could assist you in your endeavor to obtain her hand."

"You've said that before," Randolph observed dryly. "More than once."

"Yes, but I have an idea that might prod her along. Never mind the details." Donald studied his friend for a few seconds. "She has a rather large dowry, and I need the money so badly. Misty Glade is in poor shape. You know Thalia has an independent income, but won't give me a cent."

"Well, I'd heard something of the sort," Randolph admitted, lacing his fingers together around his knees. "But what has that to do with me?"

"Well, you don't need money, and I do. As I see it, she owes me for the years of misery she put me through," Donald said, trying to gauge his friend's reaction. For his plan to work, the suggestion had to come from Randolph. "Not to mention the expense of all these new gowns. She sends the bills to me. One of the reasons I have so little money is that it took every bit for the planting this year. She wouldn't lend me a dime. Not one dime."

"Do tell," Randolph said. "She's so sweet, I'd have never thought it."

"I don't know what she did to my father, but during the last few months of his life he changed his will." Donald slapped his knee and grimaced. "That money is rightly mine. I need it if my plantation is to continue to thrive. I work in the fields from sunup to sunset, trying to bring in a decent crop."

"It's not easy." Randolph seemed to be considering the matter. "You know, Donald, if you were to help convince Thalia to marry me, I'd be happy to give that dowry to you."

"Oh, no, Randolph. I couldn't accept it." Donald licked his lips, almost as if he could already taste victory. They were nearly to his house, and he wanted this deal concluded before they arrived. "I'll struggle on somehow."

"Oh, come on, man. You know my father left me quite fit in the pocketbook." Randolph laughed and shook his head. "He had a lot of money. And I don't have a sister to spend it all. Say you'll help me, and it's yours."

Donald tried to appear as if he were considering the suggestion for the first time. "I don't know—"

"Come on, it's rightfully yours anyway."

"Well," Donald finally said. "If you insist."

Donald Freemont staggered into bed. His gambling losses were mounting, and he didn't know how to change his luck. It was Thalia, he knew. She stood between him and the chance of a secure future. Somehow he'd have to convince her to accept Randolph's proposal.

"Damn Father for willing Sea Mist to her." Donald didn't bother to remove his clothes before pulling the covers up over himself. "Father should have left her money under my guardianship and I wouldn't be in this predicament. Thank God Randolph's brain is dulled with brandy."

These thoughts were not new to Donald. He frequently cursed his father for leaving a plantation to Thalia. But, more, he condemned his father for leaving such a large sum of money as a dowry and another sum for her to live on. With that money Donald could pay off his creditors and live as he had always lived. He knew his luck would change if he could just find a way to get his hands on her money.

Unable to think or plot any longer, Donald fell into a drunken stupor.

Thalia had been excited all day about the Harvest Ball. Though she knew she'd be dressed far too early, she had eaten a bite and now urged her servants to help her dress.

She stood impatiently while Clover, Princess and Mrs. Hardy lowered the violet-colored gown. When the gown was in place over the hoops, Thalia peered at herself in the mirror. "How does it look?"

"I ain't never seen no dress that color, but it shore does look purty." Clover tilted her head from one side to the other, gazing at the gown. "I just know you'll be the purtiest girl there."

"Do you really think so?" Thalia asked, a little breathlessly. "Do you think it's too daring? The color, I mean? Maybe I should change."

Clover stared at Thalia. "Just 'cause you the purtiest don't mean you got to act like one of them little hussies— What they name? Chandler? If you goes to this party actin' like them, I won't never let you go—"

"Clover!" Thalia exclaimed, trying to hide her smile. "You know you shouldn't speak ill of others." Thalia's smile broke through, and she hugged her friend. "But you're right about them. I'll behave myself."

Mrs. Hardy and Princess added their compliments before they left. Clover braided Thalia's hair carefully, threading a strand of pearls through the loops and tucking tiny artificial flowers into the chignon. "There you is. I ain't never seen nobody no purtier."

Thalia looked at herself in the mirror. She did look pretty, prettier than she'd ever looked. It seemed that the color of her gown changed the color of eyes to a deep violet-blue. "Oh, Clover, you're masterful."

Unable to contain her excitement any longer, Thalia hurried down the stairs, her violet skirts floating about her like a soft cloud. She hoped Donald would be ready to go. Even if they were the first to arrive, Thalia didn't care. She didn't want to miss one moment of one of the biggest affairs of the year in Charleston.

She reached the foyer and rushed into the parlor. "Donald, I simply— Mr. Taylor, how good to see you," she stammered, glancing around for Donald. He hadn't mentioned that Randolph would be attending the ball with them. "I'm sorry. Donald must not be ready yet. I'll go and—"

"No, Miss Freemont," Randolph interrupted, catching her arm. "I'm afraid that Donald isn't feeling well. He said that he would rest a while longer and then join us."

Disappointment surged through Thalia like a swelling river during a flood. What could she say? She didn't want to go alone with Randolph, but she didn't want to miss the ball, either. "I'm sorry, Mr. Taylor. I'll remain here with Donald until he feels well enough to attend. Please go along without us."

"No, no. He gave very specific instructions that I was to see that you arrived safely at the ball." Randolph smiled and waved with his free hand. "So you see, it's all arranged."

"I see." Thalia could do nothing to extricate herself from Randolph's grasp without appearing foolish, and she was equally unable to avoid attending the ball with Randolph. "Allow me to get my cloak."

Randolph walked with Thalia to the foyer, where Clover met them with the lovely deep violet cape that matched the little satin flowers embellishing her dress. Clover's eyes met Thalia's. Both women were thinking the same thing. Neither of them liked Randolph, but with Donald's temperament, little could be done except to go along with his arrangement.

"Good night, Clover. Thank you," Thalia said, moving gracefully toward the door.

"Mistah Taylor, you better take good care of my missy." Clover wagged her finger threateningly. "I don't take good to folk mistreatin' her."

"Clover!" Thalia exclaimed, turning to stare at her servant.

Randolph smiled cheerfully. "Fear not, Clover, I'll protect her from every scoundrel there."

"Harrumph," Clover grunted as she watched them leave.

For the first time in her life, Thalia hoped that she would be among the first to arrive at a major ball. Perhaps, once she reached the Hibernian Hall, she could slip away from Randolph, and no one would realize that she had come with him. She glanced up, wished upon the first star she saw and left her fate in the hands of the gods.

The silence between them was irritating, and grated on Thalia's nerves. "Isn't it a lovely night for a ball?"

"Quite the thing," Randolph agreed, gazing at her. "Miss Freemont, may I say that I've never seen you look lovelier. In fact, your beauty has given me courage. Would—"

"What a beautiful moon," Thalia continued, trying to ignore Randolph's compliment, and knowing what he intended to say next. Somehow she had to divert his attention until they could reach the St. Cecilia's Harvest Ball. "I declare, I believe that's a harvest moon. Do you think it is?"

Randolph glanced at the moon. "Lovely. Miss—"

"Mr. Taylor, are you superstitious?" she asked, praying that he'd continue to answer her questions instead of asking the one he obviously wanted to ask.

"What? Superstitious?"

"Yes. Are you afraid of witches?"

"Witches?" he repeated dumbly, as if he couldn't follow the conversation.

"Yes, you know witches are said to fly on nights like this. I recall reading that on nights with a full moon—"

"Miss Freemont, I . . . It cannot have escaped your—"

"Oh, look, Randolph," she interrupted, pointing out the window of the carriage. "Isn't that the Calhoun carriage?"

Randolph sighed and looked where she was pointing.

Thalia's luck failed her. The gods, in their infinite wisdom, ignored her wish to arrive at the ball before everyone else. The street in front of the Hibernian Hall was crowded with carriages of every description. There was no way she could enter the hall without being seen with Randolph.

"Thalia!" Lenore exclaimed when she spotted Thalia getting from the carriage. Rushing over, she began chatting amiably after nodding a greeting to Randolph. "You simply must see Mother's new dress. Come along. You don't mind, do you, Mr. Taylor?"

Thalia almost laughed. She allowed Lenore to continue chattering until they were well away from Randolph. "Thank you, Lenore. I can't believe that Donald would do such a thing to me. Imagine, making me ride over here in that addlepated Randolph's carriage alone."

"Mother spotted you right away and almost chased me over to rescue you." Lenore gazed at Thalia for a few seconds. "What did you tell her?"

"Remember the other day when we were sneaking off to have tea with Justin and Edward?" Thalia asked, glancing all around to see if anyone could hear them.

"Yes, I remember. What happened?"

"Well, your mother mentioned seeing us leave your party and reminded me that a lady doesn't do such things, particularly when she's the hostess or with the hostess." Thalia looked around once again and saw Donald alighting from Eugenia's carriage. "The nerve of him. I declare, I may never speak to him again. Look, Lenore, Donald isn't sick at all. He's with Eugenia."

Lenore stared at Donald and Eugenia as they headed up the steps, pausing here and there to speak to people they knew.

"Doesn't he know that a lady doesn't ride alone in a closed carriage with a man after dark? What's wrong with him? Your reputation should be important enough for him to realize that."

"I think he's plotting something. This afternoon he seemed rather cheerful for having been out all night with Randolph." Thalia saw Randolph rush over to Donald. "Uh-oh. Let's get inside. I don't want Donald to catch me out here. At least he'll hold his tongue if we're inside where people can hear us."

Thalia and Lenore hurried into the hall and found Mrs. Calhoun. "Oh, my, what a lovely dress, Mrs. Calhoun." Thalia kissed Wilhemina Calhoun on the cheek. "Thank you for sending Lenore to rescue me," Thalia whispered, and then said aloud, "How nice to see you again."

"Gracious, dear, what a stunning gown." Wilhemina held Thalia at arm's length and looked up and down the dress. "I can't say that I've ever seen a more beautiful gown... or a lovelier girl."

When they entered the ballroom, Thalia glanced around, her gaze pausing on every man with dark hair. She was clutching her dance card so tightly, she was afraid she would ruin it. Several young men she knew came over and asked for dances, and she graciously accepted several, writing their names in quickly. So far, Justin wasn't here. *Stop it,* she told herself sternly. *Justin Lionheart is not for you.*

Nevertheless, every time someone entered the ballroom, she automatically looked to see who it was. She was saving the first and last dances for Justin, as well as several in between—if he asked for them. The orchestra was beginning to tune up. Dissonant sounds filtered through the chatter as people milled around beneath chandeliers and sconces filled with tall white candles. The golden glow bathed the room in a soft light that flattered the people greeting friends below. Thalia noticed the refreshments table at one end and motioned for Lenore to follow.

Thalia threaded her way through the throng of people and finally arrived at the linen-covered table. A portly man ladled punch from an ornate silver punch bowl and handed her a cup. "Thank you, sir," she said, and turned to see what had happened to Lenore.

"Gracious," Lenore complained as she reached Thalia. "I thought I would never get away from some old cow who wanted to ask who you were."

"Who was she?" Thalia asked, peering across the ballroom to see who Lenore could be talking about.

"Some cousin of Mother's. Irene Baker or something." Lenore tapped Thalia's shoulder. "Don't worry. She's just nosy."

The orchestra began to play. Thalia was a little disappointed, because she wanted to dance the first dance of the evening with Justin. "Oh, no. Randolph is looking for me."

Thalia ducked down behind a tall man and, dragging Lenore with her, scooted past the refreshment table to a row of chairs that lined the walls. She sat down in the first of two empty chairs.

She and Lenore leaned to one side and then the other as they watched the dancers begin to whirl about the floor. "Isn't it beautiful, Lenore?"

"Oh, yes. It certainly—" Lenore stopped in midsentence. "Oh, look. There's Edward."

"Well, don't act like a goose. Wait until..." Thalia's voice dwindled off. Justin had entered the ballroom with Edward. "Justin's with him."

Lenore glanced from side to side. "How are they ever going to find us if we're hiding behind all these people?"

"I don't know." Thalia tried to think of a plan, but every time she came up with something she saw Randolph still searching for her. If she stood at all, he'd find her. "Maybe if you casually walk around the edge of the dance floor you can reach Edward and Justin and lead them back here."

Lenore nodded and rose. Thalia watched as Lenore made her way along the fringe of dancers until she'd almost reached the two men. They saw her coming and strode toward her. Thalia gave a quick sigh of relief as Lenore pointed back to the refreshment table. Justin gazed in Thalia's direction until finally she caught his eye.

"There you are!" Randolph exclaimed, sitting in the empty chair beside her. "I've been looking everywhere for you."

"Have you?" Thalia could have cursed, but smiled instead. "I was so thirsty that I came directly to get some punch."

"May I have this dance, Miss Freemont?" Randolph asked, rising once again.

Thalia's heart sank. Justin was too far away to help her this time, and she couldn't very well refuse to dance with Randolph after allowing him to drive her over in his carriage. "Of course."

She rose and took his arm. They joined the dancers on the ballroom floor. Every time she turned around, Thalia glanced at Justin. He looked a bit perturbed. She wondered if his mood was a result of her dancing with Randolph, and secretly hoped it was. She had never before made a man jealous.

Randolph did his usual masterful job of crushing Thalia's new kid slippers—and her toes—but she smiled dutifully and said nothing. She simply wanted the dance to end. When the music finally, thankfully stopped, Thalia almost ran from the dance floor, with Randolph trailing after her like a reluctant child. She knew that if she hadn't rushed away he would have insisted on a second dance. Neither she—nor her slippers and toes—could stand another such beating.

Thalia hoped that Franklin Williams, her friend Agatha's brother, would forget that he'd asked her to dance the second set with him. Unfortunately, Franklin moved to her side as she left the dance floor.

"Miss Freemont? I believe this is my dance." Franklin reached down shyly and took her hand.

Thalia could do nothing but smile. Since she'd planned on dancing the first and last dance with Justin, she'd filled in her card for most of the other dances. She wouldn't get to talk to him for at least one more dance.

Franklin, a passable dancer, said little while he danced. He concentrated so hard on avoiding her toes that he lacked the timing and rhythm necessary to look graceful. Thalia tolerated his attempts with a smile. At least he didn't ruin her shoes as Randolph probably had.

Over his shoulder she could see Lenore and Justin dancing together, and she resented it more than she would have believed possible. Reason told her that he would dance with other women, but she had wanted to dance with him first.

Justin caught Thalia's eye and smiled. He didn't like seeing her in another man's arms, but he could do little about it. In fact, he really wanted to believe that he was more concerned with his own emotions than with her dancing with another man. He tried, but he wasn't very successful. He knew he couldn't dance every set with her without attracting more attention than he was willing to draw upon himself; his apparent jealousy over the matter, however, was most disconcerting.

Acknowledging his jealousy, Justin began to plot a way to claim her as he danced. For the next few sets, she danced with a variety of partners, never the same man more than once. Quite proper, he thought, nearly tripping over his own feet as he executed a particularly difficult step. The dance finally ended, and he escorted his partner back to her doting mother.

Finally he decided that enough was enough and moved toward Thalia. He intended to dance with her, whether her dance card was full or not. Justin strode to where Edward and Lenore were standing. "Damn," he interrupted, scowling back at the dancers. "I can't seem to find her long enough to place my name on her dance card."

Lenore giggled and then chewed her lip. "Well, I think she probably saved at least one dance for you," she said finally. She didn't know exactly what Thalia would want her to say, so, for perhaps the first time in her life, she said as little as possible.

Thalia finished her last dance and excused herself without allowing her partner to escort her off the floor. She headed straight for Justin, Lenore and Edward. Nothing would stop her this time, she thought. And then she saw Randolph. He caught up with her before she could reach Justin.

Randolph grabbed her arm and turned her around to face him. "Miss Freemont—Thalia . . . it's rather stuffy in here this evening. Wouldn't you like to stroll outside for a few moments?"

Thalia thought for a moment that she would become physically ill, but decided that ruining her dress was too high a price to pay for ridding herself of Randolph Taylor. "I'm so sorry, but—"

"But Miss Freemont has promised to dance with me." Justin swung her away before Randolph could voice his objections. He smiled down at Thalia, drinking in the fragrance that surrounded her like a fine mist. Gazing deeply into her eyes, he enunciated his next words very clearly, speaking loudly enough for Randolph to hear. "Thalia . . . my darling, how could you have forgotten your promise so quickly?"

Holding back a smile, Thalia tried to look as enraptured with Justin as possible. "Justin . . . dearest . . . please forgive me. I tried . . ."

As Justin spun her around, she could see the rage painting Randolph's face the vivid oranges and reds of fire. She smiled sweetly at Justin, and when his back was to the fringe of the dance floor he winked at her.

"I'm afraid we've truly enraged Mr. Taylor." Thalia could hardly keep from laughing. But to laugh would destroy the little scene she and Justin had enacted for Randolph's benefit.

Catching a glimpse of Randolph pushing aside people in order to get to Donald, she realized that she would have to face her brother's anger, as well. Fine. It was time Donald realized that she had no intention of marrying Randolph. For now, she didn't care what Donald thought. The Harvest Ball was the grandest she'd ever attended, and she knew she was among the prettiest of the unmarried girls present. Her card had filled quickly. Since she'd already danced with Randolph, she didn't have to worry about suffering with him again. She could honestly tell him that all her dances were taken.

She glanced around. Of all the men in the ballroom, Justin was easily the handsomest. His skin, gently bronzed by the sun, was accented by dark hair that threatened to curl at any moment. His eyes, a pale blue-gray, were intense and alert, taking in everything around them. His black trousers and coat were stylish, yet they hugged muscles more accustomed to shipboard chores than to the gentler art of dancing.

Yet she sensed that he would be comfortable in any environment. She could easily imagine him sitting on the back steps with Ebenezer and the other servants, talking over the day's events with them.

Justin would be at home with the ladies taking tea in the afternoon; he'd fit in quite well with the gentlemen who retired after supper with their brandy and cigars; and he danced as if the steps had been invented for him, gracefully, passionately, adroitly. Thalia, always the best dancer in her class, felt as if she were a schoolgirl, whirling about the floor with the dancing master.

"Where are you, Miss Freemont?" Justin asked, squeezing her hand slightly. "Is there room in your private world for me?"

"Private world?" Color sprang to Thalia's cheeks. "I'm sorry. I was concentrating on my dance steps. You're such a wonderful dancer, I was afraid you might think me cloddish."

"You dance divinely, Thalia." Justin pulled her a little closer, fighting the urge to rest his cheek against her shining golden hair. "You're teasing me again."

"You, sir, are mocking my deplorable lack of grace and skill," she retorted, secretly happy that he'd commented on her ability.

"I? Mock? Never, Miss Freemont." Justin smiled down at her, fascinated by the glow reflected in those large eyes of hers that seemed to change in mere moments from a vibrant blue to a rich indigo. "You're lovely tonight, Miss Freemont. Could I escort you outside for a breath of air?"

Chapter Nine

Thalia inhaled deeply, hoping to still her rampaging heart. Justin tucked her arm into his, and they walked silently across the piazza.

Charleston is the most beautiful city in the world, she decided, glancing up at Justin. Silhouetted against the moon, he looked far handsomer than she remembered. He looked down at her, and in the soft gray shadows of his face she could see his reassuring smile.

The murmurs of muffled conversation drifted toward them as they sauntered along through the intricate garden that adjoined the Hibernian Hall. Others, apparently also seeking the seclusion of darkness, had left the ball earlier and already discovered the intoxicating effect of the Carolina moon.

Neither Thalia nor Justin said anything as they walked, but she thought he knew where he was heading. He seemed to be directing their steps here in the garden as he had on the dance floor. Her aunt's words echoed somewhere deep inside her head, but she curtained off that part of her memory and concentrated on memorizing everything around her. She didn't know how long Donald intended to stay in Charleston, and she never wanted to forget this night.

As the muffled conversation faded away, Justin leaned down and kissed her lightly on the forehead. "Have I told you how lovely you look this evening, Miss Freemont? That gown is positively spectacular."

Thalia's heart nearly leapt from her chest. "Why, I don't recall it if you have, Captain Lionheart. Thank you, most graciously, for noticing."

Justin glanced back and then suddenly pulled Thalia into an alcove nestled deep in a grove of live oaks. He kissed her, full on the mouth, his tongue searching and probing until he felt sure she would detect the response of his body. He removed his coat and placed it on a marble bench. As they sat down, he drew her close and whispered, "Why are we so formal, Thalia?"

Words could hardly form, she was breathing so shallowly as she slid her arms around his neck. "Formal? I—I don't know what you mean."

"I think," he said, relishing her willing response, "I think that we're beyond the formality of titles and surnames. I seem to recall hearing your lovely voice speak my name no more than a few days ago."

Thalia knew he was right, but somehow the rapid progress, the depth of their relationship, made her shy. "You began by calling me Miss Freemont."

"True," he agreed. "And I asked, 'Why are *we* so formal?'"

"Justin," she whispered, leaning against his broad chest and nestling her head in the crook of his neck. "Why do you call yourself by the name Lionheart?"

Nothing she might have said could have surprised him any more than that particular question. "What makes you think that Lionheart is not my name?"

"I don't know," she answered plainly, not moving from the warmth of his embrace. "I just know that your name isn't Lionheart."

When Justin had chosen the name Lionheart, he'd done so knowing people might question its authenticity. To him, the name had become his badge of honor, a constant reminder of his quest for the man who'd deprived him of his birthright, of his dignity, of his future. Now he questioned his judgment. Had he selected a less ostentatious name, he might be better off. Not that he cared one whit whether or not people believed him when he gave them his name, but now that he believed his prey was within his grasp he felt that the curiosity of people like Thalia could damage his chances to confirm his suspicions.

"My dear, I have more important things in mind than discussing what we call each other," he finally said, and closed the distance between his lips and hers.

Thalia forgot her question. Justin's kiss branded her lips forever, leaving a scorching imprint for all to see—or so she thought. She wanted the kiss never to end. The moon glowed more brightly; the stars glittered more brilliantly; her heart nearly burst with wanting. Though she didn't know exactly what she wanted, Thalia knew for a certainty, that Justin either had it—or simply was it—whatever *it* was.

No matter how hard she tried, she couldn't get close enough to him. Her gown, made of the most delicate of fabrics, seemed a prison to her breasts. His arms completely encircled her; his lips brushed her eyelids, her cheek, her earlobes, her shoulder. Each spot ignited, shooting sparks to other parts of her body until she thought she would burn from the inside out.

Certain that her gown would be scorched by his touch, she nonetheless allowed him to lift her into his lap. For a moment, the new closeness seemed much better. Then Thalia found herself nearly reclining across his lap. "Justin," she whispered, thrilling to the sound of his name.

"What, dearest?" he asked, nibbling on the tenderest flesh of her neck. His thumb rubbed against the swell of her breast, and he hesitated. What was he doing? For the past few minutes, he'd had little on his mind other than making love to this lovely innocent.

Justin pulled her erect and slid her off his lap. "Thalia, I can't... You mustn't hate me. I assure you that..."

Bewildered, Thalia tried to see his eyes, those wonderful gray eyes that seemed to see into her soul. Why was he apologizing? He hadn't really done anything wrong. Maybe she wasn't... Wasn't what? Her mind raced as she tried to understand his apology. Her breast, nipple still taut against the fabric of her gown, felt oddly abandoned after the provocative touch of his thumb.

"Justin, I don't know what to say." Cool air swept over her, and she shivered.

Glancing at her delicately boned bare shoulders, Justin rose and began to pace, but he couldn't keep from gazing at her. Why hadn't she given him a proper dressing-down? He knew from the past few days that she liked a little excitement and wasn't above flirting—within the limits of ladylike conduct—but he felt confident that she was as pure as the fluffy white clouds that adorned the Carolina skies.

And then he had a sobering thought. Donald Freemont was indebted to nearly every decent man in Charleston. Was Thalia selling herself to the highest bidder? If so, why had she selected him? Only Thalia could answer those questions, and Justin Lionheart wasn't about to ask them; nor was he about to bid unknowingly. For all he knew, Donald could be lurking nearby, waiting for an appropriate moment to "discover" the crime about to be perpetrated upon his innocent sister.

He grabbed her hand and jerked her to her feet. "Come, Thalia. Let's go back to the ball."

Thalia allowed him to nearly drag her back to the ballroom. When they reached the piazza, he stopped. "I believe that, to guard your reputation, you should enter alone."

Hurt and confused, she didn't answer. Thalia stepped through the open window and into the glare of a thousand candles. The lovely glow, the opulent decorations, her stunning gown, now meant less than nothing to her. Without speaking to anyone, she stepped back through the window. Justin was nowhere to be seen, and for that she was grateful.

She hurried around to the front and found the doorman. Stopping momentarily, she told him to find Donald Freemont and tell him she wasn't well and had gone home.

Even the Carolina moon had slid hastily behind a threatening cloud of black gossamer. Instead of being the most wonderful evening of her life, tonight had turned out to be one of the most miserable.

Donald burst through Thalia's door so hard that it slammed against the wall and bounced back into his face. "Damn it, Thalia! What is the meaning of this?"

Thalia sat up in bed, astonished by his presence and by his tone. He apparently did not believe she was ill. "I . . . Donald, I'm not feeling well. Can't you have a little—"

"Not feeling well?" He strode across the room and jerked her out of bed. "How dare you leave the ball without telling me?"

Rage replaced the hurt she'd felt at Justin's rejection. Donald was just the person she needed to vent her feelings upon. "How dare I? How dare you? You sent me off alone in that carriage with that mutton-headed Randolph Taylor, knowing how I abhor him. You were ill, if you recall. I probably have the same illness as you. In fact, I probably caught it from you."

Donald stood there listening to her tirade. He'd never seen her so angry. For a moment he was taken aback, but then he recovered. "Pack your things. We're leaving in the morning for the island."

Thalia endured the rough trip back to Edisto in silence. Donald's face was contorted with anger left over from last night, and she didn't want to tempt fate. After he'd stalked from her room, she'd lain there for hours, wondering where she'd gotten the courage to say the things she'd said.

Genius, she thought, mentally praising herself for her raging retort. For one long, wonderful moment, he'd been speechless. She chuckled. "Probably got it from you," she muttered, still smiling at his reaction.

"You say somethin'?" Clover asked, eyeing Thalia suspiciously.

"Me? No," Thalia lied. "It must have been the ocean."

Clover didn't reply, but Thalia knew that her lie hadn't been convincing. At the moment, she didn't care. Thalia wanted to get home and see to her crops.

Home? Where was home?

The only real home she'd ever known was Sea Mist. She thought longingly of the beautiful plantation, with its fertile fields, its freshwater lake, its cool live-oak glades, where she could sit alone for hours and watch the birds play. She was homesick.

In the time she'd been forced to live at Misty Glade, she'd kept busy, so busy that after the first few days the homesickness had left her. Nobody had really managed the house since her mother's death. Nobody, except Adam Woodsley, managed the plantation.

Her father, though well enough physically, had been dead mentally. After years of all but denying her existence, Havelock Freemont had sent for his daughter. Her aunt and uncle had been killed in a boating accident, and, though it hurt him deeply to see her, he wanted to try to make up for the pain he somehow knew he'd inflicted on her by almost denying her existence.

At the funeral, for the first time in her life, Thalia had come face-to-face with her father. She could see the pain etched in his eyes when he looked at her. When she looked at her brother, she saw anger and distrust. At first, she thought that time would heal that pain and anger, but it didn't. And no matter how hard she tried to be a loving daughter and sister, to bridge the eighteen-year gap that yawned between them, she failed.

After a few weeks, Havelock Freemont started to avoid her. He never said anything overtly, but she sensed it. After his death, when she entered his bedroom for the first time, she could see the reason. It seemed like yesterday; the memories were so vivid, too vivid.

He'd been dead but one day, had not even been buried. Thalia went to his room to look for a gold watch that he had always worn on special occasions.

The room was cool when she walked in, dark and cool. She hesitated at the threshold, peering into the darkness until her eyes adjusted. She spotted a lamp on the table by the bed, strode across the room and lit the wick.

As she turned around, she allowed her gaze to scan the room in an attempt to understand the man who was her father. And then she saw it. The painting. The lamp nearly fell from her hand as she gasped aloud.

Thalia was almost an exact double for her mother. For several minutes, she stood there staring. This was the first time she'd ever seen a picture of her mother, and the shock stunned her. It was as though she were staring at a portrait of herself. No wonder her father found it difficult to look at her. If she'd only known sooner, maybe . . .

But she hadn't known. Even if she had, nothing would have changed. Havelock Freemont had died inside when his wife did, and Thalia had been powerless to breathe life into him again.

Too much time had passed; too much damage had been done by his heartache.

She tried to share Donald's grief, but he only became more distant. His eyes now accused her of having caused his father's death, as well as his mother's. Thalia was alone, so alone. And she was hurt and scared and lonely.

After a few days, she walked out to her father and mother's graves and stood there for several minutes. Then she sat down between them. As she attempted to make some sense of the life she'd been fated to live, she began to cry. Her tears were for a young woman who had died in childbirth, and for the daughter who had never known her mother. Her tears were for an old man, a man made old by his grief, and for the daughter he had spurned. Her tears were for a young man who had lost both his parents, and for his sister, a young woman who wanted only to be loved and accepted.

Thalia looked out over the ocean. Tears threatened to fall once again, not for the loss of a man whom she'd known but a few days, but for that same young woman, who had been rejected yet again. And, still, she didn't know why.

Justin gazed across the harbor. It was golden and still in the twilight. He still couldn't believe he'd fled the ball like a pubescent young man confronted by sexual intimacy for the first time. *Hellfire,* he cursed inwardly, *Thalia should have been the one to run instead of me. She has more to lose than I do.* Or did she?

What had she to lose? What had she to gain? The two questions had plagued his sleep all night, and he still had no answers. He decided he owed Thalia some explanation. Clearly, she didn't understand his reactions.

Feeling somewhat buoyed by his decision, Justin left The Battery and walked up Meeting Street. His spirits improved with each step as he anticipated seeing her again. He strode confidently up the steps to her house and rapped on the door.

A woman opened the door and asked, "May I help you, sir?"

"Yes," he answered, peering past her into the foyer. "Captain Justin Lionheart here to see Miss Freemont."

"I'm sorry, Captain, but Miss Freemont isn't in."

"I see." Justin considered the situation for a few seconds. Then, as the woman began to close the door, he reached out and stopped her. "I beg your pardon, but when do you expect her?"

The woman gazed at him for a few moments, as if sizing him up or assessing his worth. "Captain . . . Lionheart, is it? Yes, well, I can't say when Miss Freemont will return. Now, if you'll excuse me, I have duties to attend to."

Justin nodded and stepped back. He'd irritated Thalia to the point that she was refusing to see him. Maybe Lenore Calhoun could help him.

A decisive man, Justin returned to the street and made his way to the Calhoun home. When he arrived, a servant informed him that Miss Calhoun would see him shortly. After waiting nearly an hour, Justin decided to leave. But Lenore arrived just as he arose from his chair.

"Ah, Captain Lionheart, how good to see you again," she said, and held out her hand to him. "Please be seated."

Lenore indicated a chair and seated herself. Justin paced for a moment and then stared at Lenore. "Lenore, I don't know exactly what I came here for. In fact, I'm not sure about anything that's happened—"

The doors opened, and Wilhemina Calhoun swept into the room. Justin leapt to his feet. "Lenore, dear, why didn't you tell me we had a guest?" Wilhemina gazed for a few seconds at Justin and then smiled graciously. "Captain Lionheart. Welcome to our home."

"Thank you, Mrs. Calhoun. I hope I'm not disturbing you." Justin waited for Wilhemina to be seated and then sat down again. "I really came to see Len—Miss Calhoun."

"Oh?" Wilhemina gazed at her daughter. "And you know my daughter well enough to call upon her, I presume."

"Yes, ma'am," he answered, and then amended his response. "Well, not exactly, ma'am, and I beg your pardon, but this is very important. You see, last night at the ball, I . . ."

Could Justin explain the situation to Mrs. Calhoun? No, he couldn't. No matter how badly he wanted to see Thalia—to explain the situation to her—he couldn't risk her reputation by relating the details of the incident to a woman of Mrs. Calhoun's stature in Charleston. He didn't know whether she would spread the story about or not, and he didn't want to take the chance.

"Yes, Captain?" Wilhemina was intrigued by this man's visit. She'd seen the look on Thalia's face when she'd danced with him last night. The fact that he was visiting Lenore, Thalia's best friend, puzzled her. "Please go on."

Justin felt like a child who'd been naughty and was being forced to publicly acknowledge his misdeed. The only answer was to simply say what he had to say. Mrs. Calhoun wasn't an ogre, or at least he hadn't seen any evidence of it. "Mrs. Calhoun, my business actually concerns Tha—Miss Freemont. I came here to ask Lenore—Miss Calhoun—if she knew why..."

Justin was stammering like a witless fool. He wasn't usually shy around matrons, but the subject of his inquiry was extremely delicate. He simply didn't know whether to trust Wilhemina Calhoun or not.

"Captain, I assure you that any questions you may have about Thalia may be directed to me." Wilhemina smiled, recognizing that Justin was wrestling with himself about how much to tell her. "Thalia Freemont is like a daughter to me."

A daughter? That made matters even worse. He could hardly address his question to a woman who claimed to be as close as a mother to Thalia.

Lenore glanced from her mother to Justin and back again. The two of them were sparring silently. She began to giggle. The whole situation was ridiculous.

Wilhemina gave Lenore a withering stare. "Lenore, dear, would you like to excuse yourself?"

"No, ma'am. I'm sorry." Lenore folded her hands primly in her lap and tried to compose herself.

"Now, Captain, what do you wish to know?"

Justin decided that he'd never learn anything unless he said something. "Well, Mrs. Calhoun, last evening Miss Freemont and I were...walking in the garden. We had somewhat of a misunderstanding, and—"

Wilhemina's eyes widened, and she rose, staring accusingly at Justin. "Young man, are you saying that you...that you— Did you harm Thalia in any way?"

For a moment, Justin didn't know how to answer. He'd done Thalia no physical harm, but he still remembered that haunting look in her eyes. He couldn't know if he'd harmed her emotionally until he talked with her in person. He realized that Wilhemina Calhoun was standing over him, glowering at him with all the force of the mother of a wronged woman. "Oh, no, Mrs. Calhoun, be assured that I didn't harm her in any way. I just wanted to talk to her, and—"

Lenore interrupted him. "Thalia's gone."

"Gone?" Wilhemina and Justin repeated in unison.

"Where has she gone, dear?" Wilhemina asked, taking her seat again.

"She's gone back to Misty Glade."

"How do you know?" Justin asked, feeling let down. Where the hell was Misty Glade? He hadn't even thought to inquire before.

"She sent Clover over this morning to tell me." Lenore glanced at her mother. "She said she was sorry that she had to leave without coming by to see you."

Justin felt as if he'd been hit by a wave that had washed over the side of his boat. She'd left town. She'd gone back to Misty Glade. He looked up and smiled at Mrs. Calhoun. "I'll just bet she's going to Sea Mist."

Thalia stood in her mother's rose garden, staring at nothing. Since her arrival, she'd done little. There was little to do now that the cotton had been picked. Adam and the slaves would take care of it from now on.

Justin Lionheart's image had constantly obstructed her vision, stolen her thoughts and disrupted her life for the past few weeks. Nothing had changed since she'd arrived at Misty Glade. The homesickness she'd felt on the trip home was something else that still plagued her.

Edisto Island was only forty miles southwest of Charleston, but she might as well be in China. Thalia wanted to see Justin. She wanted to return to Sea Mist. She wanted to be free of the mysterious turbulence with which fate had tormented her all her life. If the solitude of Sea Mist was the answer, then she wanted to be there.

"Miss Thalia?" Clover spoke quietly to avoid giving Thalia a start.

"Yes, Clover?" Thalia turned around slowly, trying to compose her face to hide her feelings.

"Mistah Donald wants to see you right now." Clover gazed at Thalia for a long moment. "What ails you, Miss Thalia? You been just like your pappy ever since you came home from Charleston."

Just like her father. Thalia rose. The words stung. She knew the helpless feeling of watching someone wither away and die because of a lost love. Justin wasn't even a lost love. She'd never loved him. But the rejection hurt, all the same. "I'm fine, Clover. Don't worry."

Thalia sauntered up the brick walkway as if she hadn't a care in the world. Let Donald wait, she thought. *What can he do to me?*

Donald stood when she entered the room. "Sit down, Thalia. We have to discuss a delicate situation."

Delicate situation? Was Donald with child? That was the only delicate situation she knew about. Men seldom thought any situation was delicate. "Yes, Donald?"

He paced around the desk a few times before sitting down and threading his fingers together. "I overlooked your conduct on the night of the Harvest Ball because I felt that you were overwrought. You've had time to regain your normal good sense, so we'll discuss this now."

"This, Donald," she said, rising, "is not something I wish to discuss with you. If you have anything further to say—"

"We *will* discuss this," Donald roared, slamming his fist down on the desk.

A half-empty bottle on the desk toppled over, and amber liquid began to pour from it onto the lush carpet below. Thalia leapt to her feet, ran to the door and called for Clover to bring some towels to absorb the spill.

"Really, Donald," she said when Clover had left the room. She knelt by the desk and patted the carpet with the towels.

"See what you made me do?" Donald asked. "This would never have happened if you weren't so stubborn and willful."

"My fault?" Thalia couldn't believe what she was hearing. "What a ridiculous notion."

"Your fault!" Donald sat down and bowed his head for a few moments, as if to gather his strength. When he looked up again, the venom in his eyes was readily apparent. "Thalia, we must discuss your future."

For a few seconds, Thalia was too stunned to speak. Certain that he wanted to talk about her leaving the party and the row they'd had afterward, she had been prepared to defend herself against the attack. She sank back into her chair. "I don't understand. What are you talking about, Donald?"

"I'm referring to a conversation I recently had with Randolph." Donald tried to smile. He wanted Thalia to think that he was acting solely as her guardian, with her best interests in mind. "Randolph, may I remind you, is a wealthy man. You would do well to treat him more . . . kindly."

"Randolph is a boring—"

"Stop, Thalia. I won't hear any such talk." Donald stood and moved around the desk. He sat down just opposite her, staring deeply into her eyes. "I'm telling you . . . no, I'm ordering you, to treat Randolph well. He wishes to offer for your hand in marriage. I'm inclined to accept his proposal."

"Go ahead, then. The two of you will make a handsome couple." Thalia stood and glared at Donald. "But leave me out of your negotiations. I shall never marry that fool."

"Your impertinence is exactly why I'm having such difficulty marrying you off." Donald waved his hands before him as if in desperation. "A willful woman is undesirable. Please learn to act more ladylike. Perhaps I should summon Eugenia—Miss Prentiss—to teach you the ways of a woman."

For a moment Thalia said nothing. The shocking idea of Donald bringing his mistress to Misty Glade to teach her to be more ladylike was as ludicrous as that of Donald marrying Randolph. "If you bring that . . . that fancy woman into my house with the intention of her teaching me manners, I shall walk out that front door and never return."

"Preposterous." Donald grinned maliciously. "You will live here with me until you marry Randolph. If I choose to bring Miss Prentiss here, you will treat her with the utmost courtesy."

"Go ahead, if you dare." Thalia turned and walked toward the door. She stopped and looked back at him. "I'm leaving for Sea Mist in the morning."

"You will not!" Donald screamed, lunging across the room and snatching her shoulders. He shook her with such ferocity that her head wobbled back and forth like a rag doll's. "You will cease your impertinence. You will conduct yourself like a lady. You will marry Randolph."

Thalia could only stare at her brother and wonder how such hatred could have flourished within him without tainting everything he did. She wondered why his prized roses did not die from his slightest touch. She said nothing. Nothing could penetrate the steely visage that he presented to her.

Donald released her, allowing her to fall to the floor in a heap. Without stopping to see if she was hurt, he stepped over her and ran from the room. In such a rage that he hardly knew where he was going, he found himself in the small rose garden that had been his mother's. He paced for a few minutes, until the fragrance of the few remaining blooms had calmed him, and then he sat on the bench.

His mother had always smelled of roses. As a child, he had climbed into her lap, nestling his head against her bosom, and hidden there from whatever demon had been pursuing him. He remembered the sweet songs she'd sung to calm him, the gentle touch of her hand on his forehead as she'd brushed away an errant curl of his downy blond hair.

Donald thought of the lilting laughter that always accompanied their playful moments. How she'd loved to scamper about the garden with him, playing hide-and-seek. How his heart ached with wanting to see her again. How his hatred welled inside him for the sister who had deprived him of his mother's love.

Thalia hadn't killed Bethel Freemont intentionally. Donald knew that. The rational man inside him knew that. But the scared child who had watched his mother placed in a box that was nailed shut and then placed in the cold, dark earth didn't know, couldn't accept that truth. No matter how hard he tried to like his sister, everything about her reminded him of his mother. Even down to the fragrance of roses.

Donald opened the little metal box that he kept in the rose garden. Hoping to regain his composure and eradicate the haunting memories of his mother, he began to clip dead leaves and spent flowers. The work softened his rage, and he began to regret the harsh words, and the force, he had turned upon his only sister.

It was her own fault. If she weren't such a stubborn girl, he would be kinder to her. He could do nothing with her. She refused even his least offensive suggestions. Her outbursts were enough to try the patience of any man. "Well," he said to the rosebushes as he caressed a particularly lovely bloom, "she'll regret her actions. When she's married to Randolph, I'll have plenty of money, and she'll have another man to try and tame her."

Justin's ship was too big for the little harbor at Edisto Island, even though he'd sailed over in the small schooner that he kept for entertainment rather than for business. The trip, while a short one, had heightened his need to see Thalia again. All during the past few days, he'd thought of little else.

Her image haunted his sleep, and her memory haunted his waking hours. He kept remembering that expression on her face, that sad rejected look that seemed so foreign to such lovely features.

Usually he would have forgotten the incident after a few days. Women, he knew from experience, were prone to use any tool, including pity and sympathy, to ensnare an unwary man. And Justin Lionheart was anything but an unwary man.

But Thalia was different. And it was *he* who had instigated the incident, not she. He had sought her out. He had asked her to the garden. He had kissed her.

When he'd taken care of his ship, he asked directions to Misty Glade. He hired a horse from a stable near the docks and headed toward the plantation.

He planned to use his acquaintance with Donald to gain entry into the house. The islanders were renowned for their hospitality, and Justin intended to make the most of their reputation.

As he rode up the lane that led to the main house, he was surprised by the size of the plantation. The house itself should have been an imposing structure, but, with peeling Doric columns and a whitewashed facade that attested to its owner's lack of interest in its upkeep, it merely looked sad.

Justin grimaced at such waste. Donald apparently gambled away all the profits from his cotton and rice crops without any thought of maintaining his plantation.

So much the better—if Donald was truly the man Justin was searching for. The revenge might not be as sweet, but it would come more quickly.

As Justin dismounted, he thought again of Thalia. Where did she fit into this scheme of revenge? He knew then that his relationship with Thalia would have to be a guarded one, for he couldn't allow himself to become involved with the sister of his victim.

Chapter Ten

"Rider out front, Miss Thalia!" Ebenezer called from the hallway.

Thalia extricated herself from the basket of beans she was snapping and dusted her hands on her apron. "Who is it, Ebenezer?" she asked, poking her head out the kitchen door.

"Don't rightly know, Miss Thalia." Ebenezer scratched his chin thoughtfully. "I don't recollect ever seeing him."

Thalia removed her apron and turned to Princess. "Finish these beans while I go see what's going on."

Walking along the sheltered walkway, she soon reached the house. She paused in front of the mirror in the hallway and tucked a loose curl back into her bun. Though she would have preferred to change her dress before greeting a guest, Thalia didn't want to keep him waiting. Her attire could be excused, but rudeness could not.

Ebenezer was huddled by the parlor door. "I sent him in there, Miss Thalia."

"Thank you, Ebenezer." Thalia smiled at the old butler. She'd brought him, along with Clover and Princess, from Sea Mist. The three of them kept her from being too homesick, at least most of the time. "Tell Donald we have a guest."

"It's right late in the day, Miss Thalia," Ebenezer said, frowning slightly. "I believe Mistah Donald... He ain't feeling too good."

Thalia immediately understood. Donald had been drinking again and was, in all likelihood, too intoxicated to be pleasant company. "Then don't mention our guest. I'll talk with Donald later, if there's a need."

Ebenezer accepted the reprieve with a smile. Thalia wished again that she could return to Sea Mist and take her servants with her. None of them was happy at Misty Glade.

With a quick look at her dress to reassure herself that it wasn't stained, she opened the door to the parlor. Justin Lionheart was standing at the hearth, looking at the picture of her mother. He apparently hadn't heard her come in.

"Captain," she said, crossing the room to join him. "I must say that I didn't expect to see you, but I'm happy you've come."

"Thank you, Miss Freemont." Justin turned from the remarkable portrait to look at its subject. "This likeness is incredible. Who is the artist?"

Thalia glanced at the woman in the portrait and could almost imagine she was looking into a mirror. "I...I don't know. My mother died when I was born."

Justin whirled around, staring for a few seconds at the portrait and then at Thalia again. "Are you saying that this isn't you?"

"Yes. She was my mother." Thalia turned and walked toward the settee. "Please, make yourself at home. Can I get you anything? You must be hungry or thirsty after your journey."

Thalia knew she was chattering, but she didn't know what to expect from Justin. After their last meeting, she'd been sure she'd never see him again.

"I'm . . . No, thank you. Perhaps later." Justin sat down beside her. "Thalia, I've come—"

"We'd be pleased to have you spend a few days with us. We have a lovely plantation." Thalia twisted the folds of her skirt between her fingers. What did he want? Why was he here? "Please, I—"

"Thalia, hush." Justin wanted to stay; he wanted to go. But first he had to find out if she was angry with him about his abrupt departure. He folded her hand in his.

The sudden touch of his hand again sent shivers of excitement through her body, and all the memories of his kisses returned in full force. "Yes, Justin?" she whispered, her voice quivering with anticipation.

Justin took a deep breath and began, "I want to talk to you about the Harvest Ball."

Thalia jerked her hand away, rose, and walked to the window. From there she could see a vast expanse of lawn that had once been immaculately kept. Now weeds had overtaken the flower beds, the shrubs were spindly and sparse, and the buildings were in a state of disrepair. She saw all of that and none of that. She simply stared for a moment. "I'm sorry about that evening, Justin." She turned to face him again. "But it's past. I recommend that you forget it. I'll try to do the same."

"Look, Thalia, I—"

"I'll send Ebenezer to show you to a room." She crossed to the door and rested her hand on the knob. "It's too late to go back to Charleston. Supper will be in about an hour. Please rest, or feel free to walk about the grounds."

She opened the door and walked into the foyer. Her heart, she believed, was pounding loudly enough for Adam to hear down at the cotton sheds. When she was sure that Justin wasn't following her, she directed Ebenezer to see Justin to a guest room, after which she skipped up the stairs and ran into her room. She slammed the door and leaned back against it for a moment, knowing that her wobbly legs wouldn't carry her any farther.

After a few minutes, she went to the bellpull and rang for Clover. It was time to dress for supper, and, since they had such a special guest, Thalia wanted to look her best.

She gave instructions for a bath and, while Clover was gone, went to Donald's room to tell him about their visitor. Finding him passed out on the bed, she shook him gently to see if he would wake easily. After a couple of sound shakes, she decided that he wouldn't wake until morning and would be in a foul mood for the day.

At least she didn't have to tolerate him at supper. But she did have Justin to contend with. If Donald were awake and sober, entertaining her guest would be much easier.

When she was finally ready, she lifted her chin and walked calmly down the stairs. She'd chosen the gown of blue taffeta trimmed with an inset of embroidered pink lace at the bosom. It had turned out to be nearly as pretty as the violet gown. She had looped a mantelet of the same pink lace across her shoulders, and she felt as fashionable as any woman could possibly expect to feel.

The look on Justin's face told her that she'd succeeded. She smiled as if she didn't know what his expression meant and sat down opposite where he had been sitting. "I'm sorry if I kept you waiting."

Justin gazed at her for a moment and then took his seat again. "I must say that it was well worth the wait. You look lovely tonight."

"Why, thank you, Captain, for your compliment." Thalia smoothed her skirts and smiled again. "I'm sorry that my brother won't be joining us for supper. I'm afraid he's...indisposed."

Justin interpreted her comment to mean that Donald was drunk again. In the past few weeks, Justin had seen Donald Freemont drink far more than he should. The man just couldn't hold his liquor. Nor could he gamble. "I'm sorry to hear that. He and I are members of the same club. One evening a short time ago, he and I—"

What was he saying? Justin recalled, almost too late, her evident dislike of gambling. With a brother who gambled as often and badly as Donald Freemont, she couldn't be blamed for disliking the sport. He smiled and shrugged. "I'm sure you aren't interested in the boring activities of your brother and me."

"On the contrary, Justin." The name just slipped out, and she felt color rising in her cheeks. "I'm naturally interested in anything that...my brother does."

"Never mind. I'd rather hear about your plantation." Justin recalled the way her eyes had sparkled that day on the promenade at The Battery, when she'd been talking to Caleb Saunders. She evidently loved Sea Mist Plantation, and that puzzled him. If she loved it as much as he suspected, why was she here with her brother? "Tell me everything."

Thalia couldn't help smiling as she recalled Sea Mist, which lay but a few miles south of Misty Glade. "Oh, I think it's the most wonderful place on earth." She settled back in her chair and tilted her head thoughtfully. "The grass is green, so green that it's hard to believe. And the sky is so much bluer there, as if the vast expanse of sky over Sea Mist had its own special, vibrant color. The sunrises and sunsets are spectacular. And the best cotton in the world grows there."

"What makes you say that?" he asked, intrigued by her description of her plantation. He'd never seen a woman who loved the land enough to talk about it in such glowing terms.

"Because we demand—and receive—the highest prices for our cotton. French manufacturers refuse to buy any but Edisto Island cotton, and of all the cotton here, mine is the best. Adam and I see to that."

Adam? Justin hadn't considered the possibility that Thalia might have a partner—or, perhaps, a lover. "Who is Adam?"

Thalia smiled as she recalled the floppy hat Adam always wore, and how he removed it to wipe his forehead. "Adam Woodsley's the hardest-working overseer in the state."

"And he works for you at Sea Mist?" Justin didn't know whether to be relieved or jealous. It was readily apparent that Adam had garnered a place of importance in Thalia's heart. Justin found that he really wanted to know how deep her feelings went for this man, but he could hardly ask her if she and Adam were lovers. He said nothing. Better to let her explain herself than to confuse the issue with speculation.

"Not exactly," she admitted. How could she explain the relationship she shared with Adam? It almost defied definition. In reality, he did work for her, since she paid his salary, but he was officially employed by Donald. "He actually works for my brother. But he's very good."

Justin nodded. Her hesitation puzzled him a little. Time would have to tell him about the true nature of her relationship with Adam Woodsley. "Tell me more."

"We grow rice, a little indigo, a few food crops. Primarily the same type of things we grow here at Misty Glade." Thalia thought for a moment, remembering the vitality that belonged to Sea Mist that was lacking at Misty Glade. "Only better."

Justin smiled. The undercurrent he caught was that she was homesick. He was, too, but he could never go home. At least she could ride across the island to her home if she really wanted to.

"Tell me about your home, Justin," Thalia said, turning the conversation to him. He knew far more about her than she thought she'd ever find out about him.

"My home?" Justin considered the question. He rose and strode to the window, peering out across a wide expanse of lawn and formal gardens. The gardens were now overgrown, except for one that appeared to be well tended. Justin didn't really want to talk about himself. He knew he might give away some bit of information that could tip Donald off, if indeed he was the man he was seeking. "The *Blind Justice* is my home. I've lived there for several years. So long that my real home is but a misty memory."

Thalia heard the yearning in his voice and knew that he was evading the truth. For some reason she didn't understand, Justin Lionheart couldn't go home. She suddenly felt sad. Sad, and lonely for Sea Mist. "I'm sorry to hear that. Everyone needs someplace to call home."

"You're right." Justin turned to face her. "But home isn't necessarily a beautiful white house with pretty flowers. Sometimes it's sad. Sometimes it's a terrible place to be. Sometimes," he said, hesitating for a moment before giving voice to his thoughts, "sometimes home is in the heart."

"'Scuse me, Miss Thalia, but supper's ready." Ebenezer bowed slightly and left the room.

"Come, Justin. My cook, Princess, is the best around." Thalia stood and waited for Justin to join her. She linked her arm with his, thrilling at the little jolt she felt when they touched.

"Better than the cook at Sea Mist?" he asked, willing his heart to stop pounding.

Thalia stopped and looked at him. With a smile that touched her lips and extended to her eyes, she nodded vigorously. "She *is* from Sea Mist."

"I see. Am I, then, to believe that everything on or about Sea Mist is better than anywhere else in the world?" he asked, pulling out her chair for her.

"Exactly." Thalia looked at the table settings. The long table was set with two places—one at each end. Conversation might prove difficult, but, more than that, she disliked having him so far away. Still, it couldn't be helped. The servants had set the table properly.

Justin glanced at the table. He was happy to see only two settings, but he was unhappy with their placement. Since he was a guest, he could hardly recommend a different arrangement. *I'll be damned if I can't,* he swore to himself. Without further thought or discussion of the subject, he walked to his end of the table, picked up as much of his place setting as he could safely carry, and took it down to the end nearest Thalia.

He sat down, put his napkin in his lap and smiled. "Now, isn't that better?"

Thalia laughed. When Justin was around, *everything* seemed so much better. "I believe it is."

Supper was delicious. They had a spicy gumbo, a delicately seasoned flounder, and sweet potatoes from the garden. Thalia ate little. With Justin sitting at her right, she could hardly concentrate on her food.

"Thalia, you must eat more of this wonderful supper," Justin urged her. "I've eaten several meals with you, and you never eat more than a few bites of anything, not even those delicious little cakes at Wilby's."

She felt as if she'd explode if she ate any more. It wasn't how much she ate, but that the food had to compete for space with all those wretched butterflies that were constantly taking flight whenever Justin smiled at her or touched her. "No, thanks. I'm not really hungry. We had a large dinner."

Justin could readily believe that Sea Mist was the best of all possible worlds if everything else measured up to the food Princess cooked. "Well, then, how about a turn about the grounds to aid our digestion."

"That sounds lovely." Thalia rose, and they were soon walking out the front door. She noticed the dingy whitewash and wished Donald had taken care of the appearance of Misty Glade. "Let me show you my mother's rose garden first. Donald keeps it just as it was when she . . . when I was born."

What had she started to say? Justin wondered. He knew that Bethel Freemont had died when Thalia was born. Wilhemina Calhoun had told him that tragic story. In fact, Wilhemina had said several interesting things to him that afternoon when Lenore had told him that Thalia had returned with Donald to Misty Glade.

They walked without speaking until they reached the little garden, with its scores of rosebushes. Only a few brave roses remained, but the fragrance reminded him of Thalia's own scent. Did her choice of scent have anything to do with her mother's obvious love for roses? That was a question he couldn't ask, not now, maybe never.

The grounds were in bad shape. They moved from the rose garden into a little garden of flowering shrubs. Bordered by asters and chrysanthemums, the shrubs were laden with blooms. "What are these?"

"Camellias," Thalia replied. "They'll start blooming in late November or early December and stay beautiful through the winter."

"I think my mother has some of these." Justin looked at the tightly wound buds and felt a pang of homesickness. But he couldn't let his feelings stop him from what he must do. "Tell me, why does Donald tend only the roses and let everything else go to weeds?"

Thalia gazed at the weeds filtering up through the asters and chrysanthemums. "I try to weed the gardens myself, but I don't have time. What with the planting and harvesting, preparing for ginning and market, my time is taken up by the cotton and rice we produce."

"You mean you handle all of that?" Justin asked, stopping to stare at her. He couldn't believe that this petite woman, little more than five feet tall, really ran the entire plantation. "I can't believe—"

She interrupted him. "I didn't think so. Nobody else believes it, either."

"Well," he backtracked, trying to salvage her feelings, "I didn't mean that I really don't believe what you say. It's just that there's so much to do here, and, well, you do have a brother who could—"

"Donald isn't interested in crops." Thalia sat down on a bench and stared at the camellia bush across from her. Its buds were fat, and would produce a beautiful bloom in a few weeks. Such beauty seemed to be wasted here in the eroded glory that had once been Misty Glade Plantation. She hoped her own plantation and gardens were being better cared for. "He has other, more interesting pursuits."

"But his plantation. Surely he . . ." Justin's voice trailed off. He knew a great deal more about Donald Freemont than he'd ever thought possible. The man was an idle aristocrat, very much as Justin had envisioned. "Tell me about your childhood."

"I grew up at Sea Mist with my aunt and uncle." Thalia didn't know how much to tell Justin. People who were getting to know each other asked questions, and his weren't particularly the prying kind. "My mother died . . . when I was born. My father couldn't . . . he couldn't take care of a baby, so he took me to his sister's plantation."

"But what about Donald?" Justin asked, getting to the point of his line of questioning. "Did he go with you to Sea Mist?"

"No. He stayed here." Thalia didn't want to elaborate any further on the question of Donald's childhood. After all, she could only speculate herself, since she hadn't been here to witness it.

Ah, Justin thought, *the picture becomes clearer.* Donald had grown up without a mother—and, most probably, without a father, even though his father had lived here. "I guess you only got to see your father on special occasions. Christmas. Your birthday."

Thalia winced. She'd hoped that Justin wouldn't ask that question at all. How could she tell him that her father had hated to look at her? The idea hurt too much for her to even give voice to it. "No. I saw him . . . Well, he was a busy man, having to run the plantation all alone. I almost never got to see him."

Pain sliced through Justin. How cruel to have a father who lived no more than a few miles away, and yet never get to see him. The idea that Justin had caused her such apparent discomfort made him feel worse than he'd felt in a long time. Thalia didn't deserve such treatment from him. Justin resolved to think more carefully before he asked any more questions. "My father was always busy, too."

"Let's move down by the ocean. There's a little copse of trees there that we can sit under. It's a lovely view." Thalia stood and waited for Justin to follow suit.

Justin and Thalia sauntered down the long path that led from the gardens to the ocean. As they came closer to the beach, he could hear the screeching of gulls and the whispering of breakers. With each step, the whispering became louder, until it finally became a roar.

There was no bench here, and Justin wondered where they would sit. When he decided that they'd just walk, Thalia surprised him by pulling a large piece of canvas from the scrubby palms that grew beneath the stately palmettos and live oaks. He helped her spread the fabric out, and then they sat down.

Thalia looked across the waves. The moon was just rising, a golden crescent that would soon turn to silver. A few stars were peeking out, just beginning their night's show of glitter and sparkle. The sky was a deep azure, mottled with violets and mauves.

"I've never seen a more beautiful sky," Justin finally said, prying his gaze away from the spectacular scenery to look at Thalia. In the time that he'd known her, he'd never really realized how complex she was. Maybe it was because she was always with that twit of a girl, Lenore, who was more typical of the girls of marriageable age Justin knew.

"I agree." Thalia didn't know why, but the sky *was* lovelier than she'd ever seen it.

Justin was inches away from her, and she was very aware of his body. She could almost feel the warmth he radiated. Could the simple fact that she was with an interesting man have changed the way she saw the sky? If so, then love must be a potent force. It wasn't that she was in love with him, or anything like that, but that emotion must surely be very powerful.

Then Justin's arms were around her, and the world seemed a soft and gentle place, a place with no hard edges and no sharp points to injure a tender spirit. After a moment, she relaxed against him and stared out to sea.

The Atlantic, crashing restlessly against the shore, almost begged them to splash and play. Thalia didn't have a bathing costume, but she'd sneaked off once to swim in her chemise and pantalets. Clover would have had fits if she'd found out, but Thalia hadn't cared. The experience had been wonderful.

"What are you thinking about?" Justin asked, his voice low and raspy.

Thalia couldn't tell him exactly what she'd been thinking, but she could come close. "I was thinking about how wonderfully warm and comforting the ocean must be to those who chance to swim or wade."

"It is. I've done it many times," Justin admitted, inhaling deeply of the scent of roses mingled with the slightly salty air. He found the two fragrances vitalizing, almost intoxicating. Justin wanted to kiss her, to feel the softness of her lips. "We could, if you like, go swimming—"

"Justin!" she exclaimed, rearing back to look at him. "How can you suggest such a thing?"

He chuckled at her indignation at his suggestion when she'd practically invited him to ask her. "Now, don't be too upset. I didn't mean now."

"When do you mean?" Thalia asked, and then realized it didn't matter when he meant. She still didn't have a bathing costume, and she couldn't swim with him in any case. He was closer now, breathing gently into her hair. The sensation almost drove her insane with its intense warmth. "Forget it. It's impossible."

"Someday, Thalia my dear, we'll swim together," he whispered against her hair. God, but he wanted to kiss her. Something about the way she looked here in the moonlight drew him like iron filings to a magnet.

Justin reached up and tilted her head slightly so that he could see the full beauty of her face. It was almost like looking at the moon. Every phase of the moon had its own beauty, but none compared to the full moon—or her full lips. Her delicate skin, now bathed in the soft golden glow provided by the crescent moon, was, if anything, lovelier than he'd ever seen it. He could no longer fight the impulse to kiss her, and he gave in with a soft intake of breath.

If Justin hadn't kissed her when he did, Thalia would surely have kissed him. She couldn't recall wanting anything as badly as she wanted to taste his lips on hers. For a few seconds, the kiss was sweet, almost chaste, and then it blossomed like the swell of a wave as it reached shallow water.

Justin's tongue parted her lips as he cupped her chin in his hand. He gently pressed her back onto the canvas and caressed her face, marveling at the silky texture of her skin. He brushed against her breast and heard her gasp. He knew that what he was doing was wrong, but he felt compelled to go on. Something about her, some force, drew him closer and closer to her, almost willing him to kiss her.

No woman had ever affected Justin this way, and he didn't want it to happen. He wanted to be near her, to hear a soft sigh escape her as he pressed his lips against hers. He wanted to feel the gentle rise and fall of her chest as she breathed.

Deep water, he thought. *You're diving into deep water, Justin old boy.*

He drew away from her and stared down into the glittering depths of her indigo eyes. What could he say to her that would tell her how strongly he felt about what he was doing without lying to her? There was nothing he could say. There could be nothing between them. "Thalia," he whispered, nuzzling against her neck. "I . . . We must stop this."

Thalia felt jarred by his words. He had reached a certain point and had stopped, the way the waves receded from the beach as the tide ebbed. "Justin, what's wrong?" she asked breathlessly. "Have I done something to . . . repulse you?" She had to know.

"Nothing's wrong with you, my sweet." Justin cradled her head in his arms and gazed down at her. Her innocent face, her questioning eyes, disturbed him far more than he cared to admit, even to himself. "This isn't proper. We're not married."

Married? What could he mean? Thalia struggled to a sitting position, her face flaming with color. Their kisses, sweet and exciting to her, meant much more to him. They were leading to . . . to a place that she wasn't ready to go just yet. "Justin, I'm sorry. I didn't mean—"

"Shh!" Justin placed a finger over her lips. "Don't say anything. Let's just walk back to the house."

He stood and helped her to her feet. For a moment, Thalia wasn't sure she could walk. As they strolled, hand in hand, back to the house, Thalia felt the heat their kisses had generated gradually subside. An odd sensation pulsed deep in the pit of her stomach, and she wondered if it had anything to do with the joining of a man and a woman.

Gazing at Justin surreptitiously through her lashes, she decided that she wanted to experience that moment, that joining of man and woman. Justin, obviously seasoned in the art of making love, was the man she wanted to initiate her into that mysterious realm of adulthood. "Justin," she purred, looping her arm in his, "someday soon I won't let you stop."

Chapter Eleven

Justin could hardly believe what he'd heard—or thought he heard. Thalia had actually said that she wanted him to make love to her. They walked across the piazza, and she removed her arm from the crook of his. "Thalia," he asked, opening the door for her, "did I hear—"

"Shh!" she whispered, smiling coquettishly. "I'm not sure what you heard. Perhaps you should listen more carefully." She walked to the stairs. "Now, if you'll excuse me, I've had a long day and need my rest."

Standing at the foot of the stairs, he watched until she was out of sight. What was she up to? She had very nearly invited him to make love to her. Did she mean now? She'd said "someday soon." He'd heard her quite distinctly, but he couldn't believe she meant what she'd said.

Now, after that flirtatious smile, he knew she meant every word. His only question now was, when? Soon. Someday soon. Then he thought of another question. Why?

Justin stared out across the lawn. The sun was rising, a glorious scarlet that seemed to burst through the indigo sky. For no more than a few seconds, the brilliance was breathtaking, and then the view began to fade into softer tones, more subdued hues, that seemed lifeless after that former splendor.

He didn't know how long he'd been standing there when he saw a furtive movement on the lawn. What—or who—was about this early at Misty Glade? Probably a servant or a slave, he decided, watching the gray shadow almost floating as it advanced toward the beach. *Hell,* he swore to himself. *Maybe it's a ghost.*

Justin had never seen a ghost, though he firmly believed in them. His grandmother had told stories often enough. This time, however, he didn't think the shadow moving across the lawn was an apparition. He was almost sure he recognized the gentle swaying of the wide skirt. Without waiting for any further sign that he was right, Justin hurried down the stairs and followed Thalia.

Though he trotted along at first, he finally had to slow down without having overtaken her. Where could she have gone? He glanced around. Where was he?

There was nothing for him to do but return the way he'd come. Maybe she'd cut across somewhere. He walked up until the sand met the sea oats, climbed a dune and peered all around. From his vantage point, he could just see her, riding out of the stable, directly away from him.

Running once again, he reached the stable. There he found a stable boy, asked for a mount and was soon heading after Thalia again. By the time he reached her, she'd dismounted and walked a short distance into a cotton field. She and a man wearing a floppy hat were bending over some of the plants. Justin watched for a few minutes with interest. The man, Justin decided as he dismounted, must be Adam Woodsley.

They were deep in concentration over a cotton boll when he walked up. "Good morning, folks."

Thalia whirled around and almost fell. Adam caught her before she took a tumble in the soft dirt. "Justin! What are you doing out here this early?"

"I just thought I'd have a look around." Justin glanced from her to Adam. They didn't act like lovers, but he could see that there was some bond between them. "I'm not disturbing anything, am I?"

"No, no." Thalia looked from one man to the other. It was clear that they were sizing each other up. Men were so foolish, she thought. "Captain Justin Lionheart, this is Adam Woodsley. Adam, Justin."

The two men shook hands, and, for a few minutes, the conversation turned to polite introductory questions and answers.

Justin finally looked at the two fluffs of white, one in Thalia's hand and one in Adam's. "What are you looking for?"

"We're looking at the cotton bolls we're saving for seed," Adam answered, holding out the cotton boll in his hand for Justin to see. "Have a look. It's the finest cotton you'll ever see."

Justin knew little about cotton. He fingered the fibers and handed it back to Adam. "I don't know much about cotton. We raised tobacco, primarily."

Thalia gazed steadily at Justin for a moment. He'd never said he'd been raised on a plantation. She'd assumed, because he was a sea captain, that sailing was his family's trade as well. Justin Lionheart was proving to be more and more of an enigma. She'd have to listen closely from now on to determine exactly who he was, because, she felt instinctively, there was a lot to learn about this handsome man with the sliver of a scar on his cheek and the flash of silver-gray in his eyes.

Suddenly Justin knew he'd revealed something about his past that he hadn't planned on saying. He didn't really believe that by indicating that he'd grown up on a plantation his plans would be jeopardized, but he still hadn't intended divulging anything about his past. No matter what he said, Adam wouldn't be affected, nor could he interfere, but Thalia might possibly prove to be an obstacle if she figured out what was happening before his revenge was complete. He'd simply have to make sure he didn't let any other information slip.

Randolph Taylor appeared at Misty Glade early that morning. He'd caught the ferry over, hoping to discuss his futile attempts to ask Thalia to marry him. Ebenezer announced his presence during breakfast.

"Gracious!" Thalia said, wiping her mouth daintily. "He must have slept on the ferry dock."

Donald glared at her. His head felt the size of a hogshead of molasses, and it was pounding like a drum of the same proportions. "Ebenezer, please send him in and ask Princess to set another place at the table."

Thalia's enjoyment of the day vanished. Randolph's appearance at Misty Glade would mean that she would have to find places to hide from him. He would, no doubt, be more persistent here than he had been in Charleston.

She smiled at Justin. Last night on the beach had been wonderful, maybe the most exciting thing ever to happen to her. Randolph entered the dining room, and she said, "Justin, are you acquainted with Mr. Taylor?"

Justin rose and nodded. "Certainly. Randolph and I frequent the same clubs."

Thalia heard his words with regret. She'd wanted to believe that Justin wasn't a gambler. Almost every man in Charleston was, and particularly the young men. Uncle Martin had said many times that the youngsters of Charleston were more dissolute than the Romans at the height of their degeneracy.

As the conversation about the clubs picked up among the men, Thalia wondered why the young men of Charleston hadn't emulated their fathers' and grandfathers' hardworking way of life. It was as if the younger men thought that, when they were thrust into the position of having to run a plantation, the skills necessary to do so would simply envelop them. Donald, for instance, knew nothing about growing cotton. He wouldn't know a fine, promising strain of cotton from a dead plant unless the leaves and bolls had fallen off.

Justin listened to the conversation for a moment. He felt very strongly that the man for whom he was searching was Donald Freemont, but he couldn't be sure until he heard the nickname. The only way he was likely to hear the name was to be with Donald and his friends as much as possible.

Donald sipped his coffee and looked around the table. Justin's presence had surprised Donald this morning, but a man who liked a wager was always a welcome addition at Misty Glade. Donald studied his guest for a moment. "Say, Justin, didn't you mention a race? A boat race? What sort of ship do you have?"

Justin smiled, as if the mention of a wager were important to him. "Oh, yes, I do recall discussing a race. In fact, I sailed over here. Of course, my sailboat isn't very fancy, but she is sleek and fast."

Donald's lips curled slightly as he sensed that the bait had been taken. "Well, then, maybe we can have a little race before your return to Charleston. How long do you plan to be here with us?''

Justin glanced quickly at Thalia. Donald's question had caught her attention, and she was listening for his answer. "I don't know exactly. Perhaps a day or two. Your hospitality is excellent, and I wouldn't want to stay longer—"

Donald interrupted him. "Stay, old man. Stay as long as you wish. We're happy to have you. Isn't that right, Thalia?"

Thalia was taken by surprise. She would never have suspected that Donald liked Justin well enough to ask him to stay longer. She wasn't sure whether she wanted Justin to stay or not. He represented a quality of uncertainty that she didn't understand, particularly after last night. "Of course, Donald. Please, Captain Lionheart, stay as long as you wish. Though I wonder if you might find our country living a little less exciting than that to which you're accustomed."

"I sincerely doubt that," Justin said with a smile. He knew she was thinking of the time they'd shared down at the beach. He, too, had spent a great deal of time thinking about that. Her words had haunted his sleep, making him so restless that he had been awake to watch the sunrise this morning. He gazed directly at her. "I find country living most . . . stimulating."

Randolph smiled at Thalia. He didn't understand the undercurrent that seemed to flow between Justin and Thalia, but he didn't like it at all. He suspected that it threatened the relationship Donald had promised would develop when Thalia knew him better. "Miss Freemont, will you show me the grounds after breakfast?"

Thalia tried very hard not to grimace, but she wasn't sure whether or not she succeeded. Donald's eyes were fixed on her, and she knew that if she declined she risked a demonstration of his rage. "Why, of course, Mr. Taylor. But you've been here many times before. You know our grounds are less than spectacular."

"Except for the rose garden," Donald interjected. "Mother's rose garden is exceptional. We even have a few roses still blooming, due to my coddling, of course."

"I might even like to see them myself," Justin said, smiling at everyone. He didn't like the idea of Thalia being alone with Randolph Taylor. The man was as bad as Donald, maybe worse. "I think it's a grand idea. Won't you come with us, Donald?"

"Er, why not?" Donald said. He couldn't very well say that Justin couldn't see the grounds if he wished to. After all, he wanted to make sure he kept Justin's friendship. Nobody else in Charleston would lend him any money, and he needed money badly. "Then we'll have a look at your boat."

Justin caught Thalia's eye. She looked lovely this morning, as fresh as the dew that still dotted the lawn. Apparently their meeting hadn't caused her any sleeplessness. He smiled. He liked a woman who knew what she wanted. "Then it's settled. We'll all go."

For Thalia, the trek about the grounds was almost unbearable, but she dutifully went along, listening to the conversation and making appropriate remarks here and there. Donald, Randolph, and Justin were making plans for a sailboat race. She wasn't interested, and she didn't care for the idea. Donald had no money to wager, yet he seemed to have overlooked that small problem. He and the other two men had made substantial bets concerning the outcome of the race. Donald wagered rather heavily on his boat, and Thalia knew what a poor sailor he was. She didn't know about Justin, but she could hardly imagine that he would be anything less than an excellent seaman.

Randolph placed his money on Donald. *What a foolish man you are, Randolph,* she thought. Loyalty is admirable, but not when you're betting on a man who sails no better than Donald.

Justin kept watching her as she walked along, and she felt a little abashed at his response to her words the previous night. She'd said them in haste, in the moments when the fresh memory of his lips on hers had made her want more than he'd offered.

She hoped he'd understood exactly what she'd meant, that someday soon she wanted him to make a woman of her. Someday soon. A day of her choosing. Thalia knew she had little chance of marrying a man who loved the sea. She also knew that she'd yet to meet a man she really wanted to marry. She was perfectly willing never to marry, but she didn't intend to go through the rest of her life speculating about what she'd missed.

Justin studied Thalia. He couldn't get what she'd said off his mind. As he walked along with the group, it seemed that his feet moved in time with the strumming of her words in his mind. *Someday soon. Someday soon.* He felt himself stiffening in anticipation and tried to think of something else. But everything here made him very aware of Thalia. The fragrance of roses surrounded him with a sweet innocence that reminded him of her, made him look her way.

He watched the soft swish of her gown from side to side. The way her dress fell just off the shoulders, exposing a creamy expanse of the swell of her bosom, enticing and yet innocent. Justin thought he was going mad. He was. Mad with desire for Thalia.

How had it happened? He thought he'd steeled his heart against women, that none would ever touch him. But, somehow, Thalia had found a way to break through the barriers he'd erected to protect himself. He didn't love her, not yet. He couldn't. She had become the means to an end. She was the key to his revenge. As long as he forced himself to think of her that way, then he would be fine.

The trouble is, he thought as they sauntered along the beach where he'd almost made love to Thalia the night before, *it just isn't that simple. Nothing is that simple.*

Thalia felt the color rising in her cheeks. She'd made sure, early this morning when she'd walked alone on the beach, that the canvas was hidden away in the scrub palms. She hadn't considered that she and Justin—along with her brother and Randolph—would be strolling along this very part of the beach together.

Justin wished he could think of some way to get Thalia alone. He wanted to talk to her. *For God's sake,* he swore, glaring at the back of Randolph's head, *the woman's making me crazy. Saying something so provocative one minute and then acting as though nothing had happened the next.*

Justin knew now that he had nothing to fear from Adam Woodsley, but Randolph Taylor was a different matter. Though a fairly nice-looking man, to Justin's way of thinking Randolph suffered from the same lack of discipline as many of

Charleston's fashionable men. Justin couldn't imagine Thalia falling in love with a man like Randolph. She had, he thought, much more sense than that. In fact, Thalia had more sense than her brother and Randolph combined.

When they'd made the rounds of Misty Glade's grounds, Thalia excused herself. She had to meet with Adam Woodsley this morning, and she had already wasted far too much of her time strolling around the plantation and accomplishing nothing.

Randolph, as always, had made a nuisance of himself. He tagged along after Thalia like a puppy following its mother. Thalia found his crestfallen look so amusing that she finally gave in and allowed him to accompany her to see Adam. Justin, she noted happily, watched her and Randolph leave with a puzzled look in his eye. A good feeling washed over her. Justin was jealous. She had decided she liked the feeling.

She and Randolph went to the stable, mounted and rode out to the cotton barns. There she saw Adam talking to one of the slaves.

Thalia dismounted and walked toward Adam. He finished giving instructions to the slave and turned to greet her. She introduced Adam to Randolph and saw the amused look in the overseer's eyes. She knew he was thinking that her beaux were coming out here to see her because she rarely visited in town. She hoped that he wouldn't say anything awkward, though she realized that Adam was too intelligent for that.

After listening to his report on the progress of loading the ship with cotton, she nodded and smiled. She could hardly contain herself. As she and Adam had surmised that day when they'd last surveyed the fields before she went to Charleston, both Misty Glade and Sea Mist had produced record crops.

When she glanced at Randolph, she saw the puzzled look on his face and couldn't stifle a laugh. "I'm sorry, Randolph. I realize all this must be boring, but I warned you."

"Oh, no, Miss Freemont. Nothing could be boring with you around," he exclaimed.

He doesn't know how true that is, Thalia mused, thinking back to the day she'd walked into the tavern with Lenore.

Poor Lenore. Even though the two of them had been close friends for years, Thalia had outgrown Lenore. Whereas Lenore had remained basically the same, Thalia had matured, become more aware of the complexities of life. Lenore, on the other hand, simply moved from day to day, never noticing how life affected her nor how things changed. Until the past few weeks, Thalia had thought that Lenore was simply young for her age. But she would never really grow up; of that, Thalia was now certain.

Lenore was destined to become the pampered little wife of some wealthy man, someone who expected his wife to do almost no thinking of her own. Sadly, Lenore fit the bill perfectly. *Sadly, yes,* Thalia thought, *sadly, because she could be so much more than she's willing to become.*

Edward Nelson might like a woman like that—and evidently he did. During the weeks that Thalia had been in Charleston, he'd hovered around Lenore almost constantly. He had the air of a man who would treasure a delicate woman who needed protecting from the world.

Thalia wanted to face the world head-on, on her own terms. She wanted to run her own plantation as she saw fit, without the interference of a man who would rather gamble than see to his crops. Thalia, with Adam at her side, would make Sea Mist the best plantation it could possibly be. She would go to Sea Mist today. She didn't care about getting Donald's permission, or anyone's help. She could do it on her own.

Thalia stared at Randolph. She couldn't tell Adam what she wanted with Randolph around. She'd have to come back later. "Adam, I need to speak with you again today. Will you be available?"

Adam gazed speculatively at her and nodded. "Yes, I'll be around these barns all afternoon, seeing to the loading of the wagons. I just sent Willie to make sure everything's all right at the dock."

"I'll be back after dinner, then." Thalia turned and let Adam help her mount.

She and Randolph rode back by way of the beach and then the docks. There, for the first time, she saw Justin's sailboat, the *Spirit of Justice*. She wondered why the word *Justice* appeared in the names of both his ships, and decided that she'd discovered, accidentally, another clue about him.

Justin and Donald spotted her and Randolph and waved. Justin and Donald were aboard the *Spirit of Justice,* but came ashore to meet the two riders.

"Well, Randolph," Donald asked, striding toward them, "what do you think of my plantation? It's been a while since you've been out here."

Randolph nodded his head vigorously. "You've got a fine overseer. Now I know how you have all this free time to play around instead of working. When my father passes along, I'll not have it so good."

Thalia burned with anger. Randolph and Donald were chatting about the plantation and how well it was managed. Neither of them seemed to think she had anything to do with it, even though Randolph had seen her giving instructions to Adam. She was beyond caring. As soon as she could manage it, she'd be back at her own plantation, and Misty Glade be damned. She was taking Adam with her.

"I'm sorry, gentlemen, but I have to see about dinner." Thalia smiled sweetly, knowing that they expected no more of her than the planning of meals. "Please take your time and enjoy yourselves."

Without waiting for a reply, she turned Guinevere toward home and coaxed her into a gallop. By the time she reached Misty Glade, her hair had come free of its restraining pins and was flying in the wind like a cloud around her head. She didn't care. She loved the feeling of the cool ocean breeze in her hair.

When she arrived at the stable, she dismounted and hurried up the path toward the house. Once inside, she took the stairs two at the time, ran along the landing to her room and closed the door. She pulled the bell for Clover and began to undress.

Clover opened the door and entered. "Yas'm?"

"Pack our trunks, Clover," Thalia said, pouring some water into the washbowl. "We're going home."

"Home?" Clover repeated, dropping into a chair. "You mean we going back to Sea Mist?"

"That's right. Don't tell anyone but Ebenezer and Princess." Thalia washed her face quickly and brushed her hair. "Here, help me put on a gown. Nobody must suspect a thing, or we'll run into trouble. By the time Donald awakens tomorrow, we'll be home."

"*Yes, ma'am,*" Clover said. "We'll be ready. When we gonna leave?"

"We'll leave at daybreak." Thalia sat down and let Clover rebraid her errant curls. "Make sure Ebenezer understands. He's to take a wagon, hitch Guinevere and Lancelot to it and have our trunks aboard."

Clover finished the chignon and stood back. "Looks good, Miss Thalia. We'll have a good homecoming, too. Just you wait."

The decision made, Thalia set about to plan the smallest of details. She couldn't afford for anything to go wrong. Randolph and Donald would most assuredly sleep late—they always did—but, Justin was another matter. She didn't know his sleeping habits. Even if he saw her leave, he wouldn't say anything, she felt sure.

She wondered if he might follow her. That might prove interesting. If he could figure out where she was going, then he was welcome to follow her.

After dinner, Thalia slipped away from the men. She hurried out to the stable and then waited long enough to see if anyone came looking for her. When no one did, she rode out to see Adam.

"Adam," she called as she approached the cotton barns.

He poked his head out from behind a bale of cotton. "Back so soon?"

"Yes, I'm rather in a hurry." Thalia glanced back the way she'd come and dismounted. "Adam, I'm going home."

"Home, Miss Thalia?" he asked, removing his hat and scratching his head.

"Yes, Adam, I'm going home to Sea Mist." Thalia sat down on some planks that the men used for a table. "I want you to go with me. Will you?"

Adam grinned widely and plopped his hat back on his head. "When do we leave?"

"There's the catch." Thalia poked at a rock with the toe of her shoe. "I don't want Donald—or anyone else—to know we've gone. Clover, Princess and Ebenezer are going, too. Do you have a wagon?"

"Don't need much, the missus and me." Adam looked across the fields and sighed. "Been here all my life. Never thought I'd see the day that I'd ride away from here and never want to come back."

Thalia followed his gaze. The fields, now being turned under in preparation for winter, were going to be fallow next year. Donald wouldn't care enough to find a new foreman. She felt sad. *Well, you can't be his nursemaid forever,* she chided herself. "Is there a place for you and Mrs. Woodsley to live at Sea Mist? It's been so long since I was there, I don't even remember."

Adam studied her for a moment. "Yes, ma'am. It'll all come back, Miss Thalia. It won't take long, either. Anybody who loves that place as much as you do won't have any trouble adjusting."

She reached out and hugged him impulsively. "I'm lucky to have you," she said, and stood again. "Well, I've been gone long enough. Be ready to leave at daybreak."

Justin saw Thalia hug Adam. "Well, old boy," he muttered, stopping to see what else happened, "it looks like you were wrong."

He didn't want Thalia to know he'd seen her embrace the overseer, so he turned his horse and went in a different direction. When she was well away from the barns, he slanted toward her and caught up. "Where have you been? I've been looking everywhere."

"Oh, uh...I had to go back to check on the progress of loading the wagons. This is an important time for the plantation." Thalia studied Justin for a few seconds. "The cotton should all be loaded and gone today."

They rode companionably back to the stable. Justin helped her to dismount and allowed his hands to linger an extra moment or two on her waist. He could hardly control the urge to kiss her, even though the stable boy was there watching. He sensed Thalia's excitement, and knew that she felt the same way he did.

Leaving the stable, they walked in silence for a short distance and then sat down on a bench. There were a thousand questions Justin wanted to ask her, but he could voice none of them, not until he decided what her relationship with Adam was. He finally screwed up the courage to bring up her promise, as he now called it. "Thalia, about the other night. You said—"

"Oh, there you are," Randolph called, walking into view.

Thalia didn't know whether to be happy or sad. She wasn't ready to talk to Justin about the other night, but she didn't want Randolph around, either. "Oh, hello, Randolph."

Randolph sat down across from them on the grass. "Where have you two been?"

"I've been down to speak to Adam." Thalia didn't want Randolph to place too much significance on the fact that she was sitting on the bench with Justin. On the other hand, it might discourage him from proposing to her.

"And I've been out riding." Justin watched the expression on Randolph's face change. He was clearly jealous.

"Mr. Lionheart and I met as we were coming toward the stable. What have you been doing?" Thalia asked pointedly.

"Nothing. Donald and I were . . ." His voice faded away, as if he had just realized he shouldn't tell them what they'd been doing.

Thalia knew that Donald and Randolph were up to no good. Neither of them was worth the time it would take to walk away from them. "Well, gentlemen, if you'll excuse me, I've chores to attend to before supper."

Even though she wanted to run all the way back to the house, she paced herself carefully. When she reached the piazza, she hurried inside and ran up the stairs. Once she got to her room, she let herself inside, closed the door behind her and locked herself in. She didn't usually have to worry about Donald, but since this evening was to be of particular importance, she didn't want to take any chances.

Supper dragged on and on. The three men at the table seemed intent on outdoing each other. The bragging got so ridiculous that Thalia finally decided not to listen any longer. Her mind was elsewhere, anyway.

Clover had reported that all the trunks were packed. She and Ebenezer had taken them down the servants' stairs and left them in a storeroom that Donald seldom entered. Everything was ready.

Thalia hardly slept a wink. The night droned on, with the frogs groaning and the wind whistling eerily. Rain threatened to postpone her departure, and she prayed that the storm would hold off long enough for them to ride across the island to Sea Mist without getting wet. Before dawn, she rose and dressed.

Tiptoeing down the servants' stairs, she cringed at each creaking sound. Donald and Randolph were probably too inebriated to hear, but she felt sure that Justin wasn't. She continued until she reached the first-floor landing. There she found Clover and Ebenezer ready to go.

"I'm glad you're up," Thalia whispered, and hugged Clover. "I couldn't wait much longer."

"Everything ready, Miss Thalia," Ebenezer said. "I sho' am glad to be goin' home."

"Me too," she admitted as she hurried out the back door.

There she found a wagon already loaded. The wagon belonged to Misty Glade, but she didn't care. She'd send it back in a few days. In reality, she decided, she should keep it. After all, she'd spent a great deal of money on this plantation since her father's death.

Ebenezer took the reins, and Thalia sat on the seat with him. Clover and Princess sat in the back of the wagon. When Thalia looked back at them, she realized that they couldn't have taken anything else.

As they rode past the stable, Adam and his family joined them in another wagon. She could tell from their muffled conversation that they were as excited as she was. When they reached the highest point on Misty Glade's grounds, she turned and gazed back at the house.

There, on the piazza, silhouetted against the light from a lamp inside his room, Justin stood watching her. She didn't know if he could see her or not, but she smiled. Then, impulsively, she blew him a kiss. She couldn't tell for sure, but she thought she saw him return her gesture. She knew Justin wouldn't tell.

Chapter Twelve

Justin watched the wagons roll over the hill. He had to admire Thalia. She had guts. Not many young women would take charge of their own lives as she was doing. He had no doubts as to where she was going. Sea Mist Plantation had been calling her as if it had a voice all its own—and, from the way she talked, it did.

She'd blown him a kiss, or at least he thought she had. He could hardly tell in the gray light of daybreak. In case she could see him, he'd returned her gesture. He thought of Clover. If the slave had seen her, then Thalia was in for a lecture.

Justin went back into his room. In case someone else was awake, he didn't want to be seen standing there watching Thalia leave. That would be difficult to explain to Donald. Justin suspected that the day would bring a hefty display of temper. He'd almost decided to follow after Thalia, but the idea of listening to Donald rant and rave persuaded him to stay. Donald might say something Justin desperately needed to hear. For now, Thalia would have to come second.

Thalia's arrival at Sea Mist was a joyous one. The ride hadn't taken very long, but to her it had seemed to go on for days. The sun had risen and spread its warm glow to dispel the mists of daybreak. She peered intently ahead, praying that she would see her house soon. When she could finally see the large white house and its array of barns and stables, she almost leapt from the wagon. Tears rimmed her eyes and finally streaked down her cheeks as the realization of her dream for the past few years rose to life out of the mists.

"Hold on there, Miss Thalia." Ebenezer grabbed her arm. "You can't go runnin' off up to the house by yo'self. Just you sit here and wait."

She knew he was right, but that didn't make the wait any easier. After what seemed an interminable time, the wagons stopped in front of the house and she jumped down. As she reached the door, she hesitated. Who was she expecting? For the past few minutes, she'd forgotten that Aunt Molly and Uncle Martin were dead. This was her first trip home since the boating accident that had killed them both.

It occurred to her that she didn't know who lived in the house now. Nobody was supposed to be there except the housekeeper, but Thalia didn't even know who the housekeeper was—or even if she had one. Gathering her courage, she rapped smartly on the door and listened for the approach of footsteps.

Ebenezer and Adam vaulted up the steps. Adam drew her aside and pounded on the door. "I'll make sure everything is all right, Miss Freemont."

Adam tried the door, but found it locked. He pounded harder. They heard the sound of footsteps, and a voice called, "Coming, coming."

"Who is it?" she asked Adam. "Do you know?"

Before Adam could answer, the door opened, and the muzzle of a gun poked through. "Who's there?" a man's voice asked from inside.

Thalia's eyebrows raised. Nobody was supposed to be living here. She brushed Adam and Ebenezer aside. "I'll tell you who's here," she shouted, pushing the door open wider. "The owner of this house is here, and I demand to know who you are and why you're in my home."

"Thalia, don't be so hasty," Adam cautioned, trying to protect her as best he could.

The door opened even wider, and a man dressed in nothing but a pair of trousers gaped at them. "How do I know you's the owner of this house? What makes you think I'm not?"

Rage rose in Thalia. This was her home, and it was being violated by this man's presence. "You, sir!" she exclaimed, jerking her uncle Martin's rifle from the man's hand and passing it on to the astonished Adam. "If you're not out of my home within two minutes, Mr. Woodsley will shoot you and I'll tell the sheriff you broke into my home and threatened to kill us."

"But what about my things?" he asked, walking barefoot onto the porch.

"I don't know what things you're referring to, but I assure you that my servants will locate them and send them to you wherever you go." Thalia brushed past the man and into the hallway. "Adam, tell the others to begin unloading. We have a lot to do here."

Adam chuckled and shook his head. "I ain't never seen a woman like you, Miss Thalia."

As Adam motioned to his wife and the slaves to unload the wagons, Thalia marched from room to room and examined the damage. She started up the stairs and suddenly stopped short, causing Adam to run right into her back. A woman was peeking over the banister at them.

"Darlin'," she called down the stairs, "who's these folks?"

Thalia's face clouded with anger. "Darlin'," she mocked, rushing up the remainder of the stairs, "if you don't remove your reprehensible self from my home immediately—"

Thalia staggered back and grabbed the handrail for support. She knew this woman. They'd gone to Miss Tallevande's School for Young Ladies together when they were little girls. "Pansy? Pansy Monroe? Is that you?"

"I'm Pansy Monroe," she answered, squinting at Thalia. "Lord have mercy, I can't believe—"

"It is you!" Thalia cried, starting toward her old friend.

"Oh, no!" Pansy turned and ran back down the hallway.

"Adam," Thalia called, pausing a moment before going after her friend. She'd ordered the man off her land, but now she needed to know what he meant to Pansy before she enforced that verdict. "Keep that man here if you can. Find something decent for him to wear. I'm going to talk to my friend. I'll let you know what to do with him after I talk to her. There's something odd going on here. Oh, look around and make sure nothing's missing. Be sure to look in the gun room. Uncle Martin had a beautiful collection of pistols and rifles."

Thalia didn't wait for Adam's answer. She knew him well enough to know he'd do what she asked if it was in any way possible. She'd watched the door slam and knew where Pansy had gone. She followed as quickly as possible. Courtesy demanded that she knock on the door, but she didn't hesitate before going in. She found Pansy lying in the dark room across an unmade bed, sobbing as if her life were over.

Walking softly across the carpet, Thalia opened the draperies. A cool breeze filled the room almost as quickly as the sunlight did. For a few seconds, she didn't know what to do. Pansy had obviously encountered some terrible luck, or she wouldn't be here with that wretched man lurking downstairs. Thalia didn't think the man was Pansy's father.

"Pansy," Thalia said softly, sitting down on the plush feather mattress with her friend. "Tell me what you're doing here."

"Oh, Thalia, I'm just mortified for you to find me here like this." The sobs subsided a little, and soon Pansy's crying had stopped altogether. "I never thought you'd find us."

"Who is that man?" Thalia asked, stroking Pansy's black hair as gently as she could. "Come on. It can't be as bad as all that."

"I didn't have anywhere to go." Pansy peered up at Thalia with big, wet brown eyes. "I didn't mean to—to just take your house like this, but I didn't—I mean, you remember my brother, Tom?"

"Yes, I remember him." Thalia had seen him fairly recently, but she couldn't recall where it was. It had to be while she was in Charleston. Maybe she'd seen him on the street. "Tell me all about it."

Clover peered in the door. "Miss Thalia, you need me for something?"

"Yes, Clover, I do. See if you can find some coffee and bring it here." Thalia continued to stroke Pansy's hair soothingly. "And tell Princess to make sure that everyone here, including Mr.... What's his name, Pansy?"

"Rice. He's Walter Rice."

"That everyone, including Mr. Rice, has a good breakfast." Thalia returned her attention to Pansy. She held her out at arm's length as Clover closed the door. "Now, Pansy, tell me everything. You have nothing to be ashamed of. I'm here now."

"You're... You don't hate me?" Pansy asked, wiping her eyes on the sleeve of her gown.

"Of course not. How could I hate you?" Thalia hugged her old friend and wondered what could have caused such a change in her. "Now, tell me. I won't bite."

A knock sounded at the door. Thalia grimaced, thinking that she'd never get to hear Pansy's story. "Come in."

Adam poked his head into the room. "Sorry to intrude, but I need to know where your trunks go."

"Oh, of course. My room is at the front of the house. Just across the hall." Thalia glanced at Pansy and then back at Adam. "Oh, one other thing. Treat Mr. Rice courteously, but don't let him leave."

"He won't." Adam chuckled and raised his eyebrows wryly. "He's unloading trunks and mumbling something about how he never saw no woman could do what this one done. I believe those were his words."

Thalia laughed. She still didn't know what sort of relationship Pansy had with Mr. Rice, but he obviously knew his place. "Well, keep an eye on him and keep him working. I need some time alone with my friend."

Before long, Pansy explained how her brother had lost a lot of money and as a result had had to sell their plantation. Thalia could sympathize with her friend on that score. Donald would probably end up doing the same thing.

"I didn't have anywhere to go." Pansy hung her head. "Then I heard Lenore tell Agatha something about your brother keeping you at his place and never letting you go back home to Sea Mist. I checked around and found it was pretty empty, except for the slaves who did the farming. I was going to come out here alone, and then I found Walter. Or, rather, he found me."

"What do you mean by that?" Thalia could feel her temper returning. She didn't think Mr. Rice could have been Pansy's savior, but she was open-minded and would listen to the story. "Go on."

"Well, he said he'd bring me out here." Pansy looked at Thalia. "Honestly, Thalia, I've always been a good girl. You know that. He just... I mean, I owed him and—"

"Adam!" Thalia roared, jumping to her feet. She ran to the door and flung it open just as Adam appeared at the top of the stairs. "Make sure that…that man—" She whirled about and looked at Pansy. "Do you love that man? Are you … are you in the family way?"

The astonished look on Pansy's face made her seem like a statue for a moment. "Love? No. We just— I mean, he— No. I'm not in the family way."

"Do you want him to stay here with you?" Thalia asked, holding her breath. If Pansy said yes, then Thalia would invite them both to remain as her guests. She prayed that Pansy would say no.

"No. I don't know, Thalia." Tears were streaming down Pansy's face again. "I'm so ashamed. It's my fault, really."

"No, it isn't. No man should take advantage of a helpless woman." Thalia turned back to Adam. "Take Uncle Martin's rifle and make sure that Walter Rice leaves my property this instant. I don't care what you have to do. We'll send for the sheriff if he lingers longer than it takes to walk off my land. Give him enough money for the ferry. I want him off Edisto Island. Tell him if I ever see his sorry face around here again, I'll shoot his … I'll shoot him."

Adam left, and Thalia glanced about the room. This room had been her aunt and uncle's room. She recalled coming here as a child for comforting when she'd been scared by storms or the myriad other things that frighten children. Nothing much had changed. The "tenants" had done little to the rest of the house, and this room was at least neat. The cobwebs had been cleared away, and the furniture dusted.

"Pansy, you're welcome to stay here as long as you need to." Thalia rose and straightened a cuff that had formed in the hem of her gown. "I need to get everyone busy cleaning up, so you just go back to bed and rest for now. We'll talk later."

Her brown eyes wide and glistening with tears, Pansy stood and faced Thalia. "I'll help. If I'm going to stay here, I can at least help to make the place habitable."

Thalia shook her head. "No, Pansy. You're a guest, not a servant. You won't be treated like a poor relation here."

"I know you'd never do that, Thalia, but I'd feel better if I could help." Pansy looked around the room. "I suppose you'll want this room."

"No, I'll take my old room." Thalia glanced at the fixtures, the painting of the horse and hounds, the pitcher and bowl, the rocking chair by the hearth where her aunt had rocked her as a child. Aunt Molly and Uncle Martin were gone now. A house as beautiful as this was for the living. "Do whatever you like to make it yours."

"Thank you, Thalia. I'm so grateful for what you're doing." Pansy touched Thalia's arm tentatively. "I don't know what I'd do if you threw me out with . . . with Walter."

"Nonsense. We're friends, Pansy. Nothing can change that." Thalia left the room to check on the progress the others were making.

She wandered from room to room, assessing what needed to be done and trying to establish a routine that would accomplish the most the quickest. Thalia finally worked her way back down to the lower floor, where she found Adam talking with his wife. "Ah, there you are, Adam."

"Were you looking for me?" Adam asked as she walked over to his side.

Thalia smiled at Adam's wife. Though Thalia had met Mrs. Woodsley, they weren't well acquainted. She turned to Adam. "Yes, I need to find out who's living in the overseer's house. Can you check on that, or do you already know?"

"I know. The foreman is there. He's been living there since the Bishops died. Why do you ask?" Adam glanced around the house when a loud noise sounded from the back. "I'll go check on that, Thalia."

"Fine," Thalia said, and then touched Adam's arm. "For the present, why don't you and Mrs. Woodsley live in the guest cottage?"

"Oh, miss, that's much too grand a place—"

"Nonsense," Thalia said, interrupting him. "I brought you here, and now I'm providing a place for you to live. I'll probably have no use for it, anyway."

"Oh, thank you, miss—and my name's Irene." Adam's wife smiled broadly and then added, "If I may be so bold as to say so, miss, I believe you'll be needing a housekeeper. I'd be happy to oblige if you'll take me."

"You're very kind, Irene." Thalia looked at the cobwebs and the thick dust and grinned. "I accept. But I think for the next few days this house will have several housekeepers. It seems there's enough dust here to fill the Atlantic."

"I'll agree with that." Irene began to look around. "Miss, I'll take our trunks down to the cottage and find an apron. Within the time it takes to snap a bean, I'll be on the job. If you'll forgive me for suggesting it, I'll clear your room first, while the servants take on the kitchen and dining room. Once those rooms are in tip-top shape, we can discuss plans for the rest of the house."

"That's fine, Irene." Thalia decided that she'd done the right thing by accepting Irene's offer to become the housekeeper. Irene and Adam had no children, and Irene seemed to be an energetic young woman. Thalia had no doubt that Sea Mist Plantation would regain its glittering personality very soon.

Justin waited until he was sure that Donald and Randolph had been downstairs for a good thirty minutes. He had wanted the discovery of Thalia's absence to take place before he made his entrance. He had been hearing loud cursing and banging for half an hour now. Donald was angrier than Justin had expected, surprisingly so.

When he knew he could no longer reasonably delay going downstairs, Justin walked slowly down the stairs and into the dining room as if he'd heard nothing. He wanted to be sure that Donald wouldn't suspect that Justin had had anything to do with Thalia's sudden departure.

"I'm ravenous," Justin said as he sat down at the table. He grinned at his two obviously irritated companions. "When's breakfast?"

"There will be no breakfast," Donald said between clenched teeth. "The bitch has gone, and taken the servants with her."

Justin almost jumped to his feet. He didn't like hearing Thalia referred to in such degrading terms, and he had to quell his rising temper before he spoke again. He looked around in mock surprise. "Thalia? Gone? Nonsense! Where would she go?"

Donald glared at Justin through glazed-over eyes that spoke of heavy drinking. "Gone? Where else? She's gone back to Sea Mist."

"Sea Mist? I don't believe I know the place." Justin glanced around and tilted his head so that he could see through the doorway that led to the back of the house. "There must be food somewhere. What are we to eat?"

He rose and walked to the door. "Hello! Is anybody back there?"

Donald chortled and then clutched his head. "I told you, she's taken the servants."

Randolph scowled and finally stood. "Well, I'm for going back to Charleston. We know we can find food there."

Justin choked back a laugh. Neither of these men had considered the idea of finding food and making breakfast for themselves. "I suppose that's an idea. What do you say, we'll race to Charleston?"

For a moment, Donald looked livid, but then his expression gradually softened. "Sounds fine to me. I'll have to arrange to hire a cook, I suppose."

"Then we're on for the race?" Justin asked, hoping that Donald would agree. He wanted to keep Donald away from Thalia for as long as possible. The preparations for the race would take the better part of the day, and Donald had to hire a cook somewhere.

"Say, Donald, doesn't that foreman of yours have a wife? I'll bet she can cook," Randolph suggested, glumly propping his elbows on the table. "I'm hungry."

"Right. I'll go get her." Donald stood and hurried out of the dining room.

Justin didn't stay around to entertain Randolph. Without doubt, Randolph was not the man for whom he was searching, and he didn't like the man at all. But he didn't go too far away. He suspected that Woodsley had gone with Thalia, as well as the house servants, but he said nothing.

In about ten minutes, Donald came roaring back into the house, and Justin almost ran back to the dining room. "What is it?" he asked, trying not to laugh at Donald's face, which was contorted with rage.

"He's gone. Damn it all to hell, he's gone, too." Donald swept his arm across the sideboard, and several pieces of china and porcelain flew off the top and crashed against the wall. One serving dish even went through the window.

"I'll kill her, that haughty bitch." Donald paced around, knocking over chairs and sending whatever was light enough into the wall to be smashed.

"Now, hold on, Donald," Justin said, trying to soothe Donald's anger. "The man's probably just down at the barns, or in the fields, doing his job."

"The bastard's gone. Everything. I checked." Donald fell into his chair. "I can't believe this is happening to me. Why, I've given that man the run of the place. Never interfered with his job. Let him have his own way. Paid him a good wage."

"I say, that's ungrateful of the man." Randolph, who'd hidden behind the door when Donald started throwing things, peeked out. "Come, chums, let's be off to Charleston. Things are dreadfully dreary here, anyway."

Justin went upstairs to pack, leaving the other two men alone. When he was gone, Randolph stared at Donald. "Well? What have you to say now?"

"About what? What are you talking about, man?" Donald was wondering how he was going to get along without servants. He couldn't afford to hire anyone. He'd just have to bring one of the slaves from the field in to keep house and cook.

"About Thalia. You promised me that she'd be mine, that she and I would marry," Randolph said, trying to hold his temper. "Now she's gone."

Donald gaped at Randolph. Good Lord, but he had enough to worry about. Still, he couldn't afford to anger Randolph. "Don't worry, Randolph. She'll be back." Donald secretly prayed, prayed for the first time in years, that Thalia would return. He had nowhere else to turn.

Thalia took one last look at her beautiful home. Sea Mist Plantation—the house, anyway—was restored to its former shine and polish. Aunt Molly would have been proud. She hated to leave, but she had business in Charleston that wouldn't wait.

When she reached the ferry dock, she noticed that Donald's schooner was gone—along with Justin's. For the past few days, she'd had little time during the day to think about Justin, but his memory had caused the nights to be as restless as ever. She dreamed of him when she was asleep, and she thought of him when she lay in bed trying to sleep.

Since Donald's schooner was gone, she assumed he'd gone to Charleston. Thalia didn't want to see him—or Randolph—if she could help it, so she planned to take a room at the Charleston Hotel. Clover would serve as her chaperon.

The trip to Charleston was a smooth one. When she arrived, she hired a carriage and reached the Charleston Hotel without incident. She and Clover spent about an hour unpacking and getting everything in order. While Clover pressed the few gowns she had brought, Thalia conducted her business.

She went first to see Warren Stevens at the bank. When she entered his office, she smiled cheerfully and sat down. "Mr. Stevens, I have several requests, some of an odd nature. First, please settle a sum of two hundred dollars on my brother and say that it is for the time I spent at Misty Glade. Call it rent, or whatever you choose."

"But, Miss Freemont, you can't mean that Donald is charging—"

"No, Mr. Stevens, I'm *giving* the money to him." Thalia chose her next words carefully. "My residence—my permanent residence—is now Sea Mist Plantation. Please forward any correspondence to me there."

"I see." Stevens rounded his desk, sat down and began making notes. "I know you're happy to be home."

"True, I'm delighted." Thalia smiled, remembering the homey smell of beeswax and candles as Irene had polished the furniture to a high shine. "Next, I'd like to settle a yearly sum on Mrs. Irene Woodsley as my housekeeper. I think the same as Mrs. Hardy's income will be sufficient— No, make it more. Say, three hundred dollars more."

Stevens continued to write, nodding his head occasionally. "You certainly know your own mind, Miss Freemont."

"Now, let's see. Mr. Woodsley will be permanently transferred to my plantation. Give him a raise of three hundred dollars per year." Thalia mentally marked off the items she'd come to discuss with Mr. Stevens. "Oh, yes, about Pansy Monroe—"

"I'm sorry, Miss Freemont, but I've been unable to discover anything about her. She seems to have disappeared from the area." Stevens raised his hands in defeat. "But I'll keep looking."

"Never mind, Mr. Stevens." Thalia was pleased that Mr. Stevens had nothing to report, for it meant that he had not discovered her friend's shame. She smiled and added, "She's with me at Sea Mist."

"With you? But how?" Stevens asked, puzzled by the new turn of events.

"She . . . she came there looking for me." Thalia hoped nobody would ever find out what had really happened. "If you should have any correspondence for her, send it in care of Sea Mist."

"Certainly." Stevens scribbled a few more notes and then leaned back in his chair.

"I want you to settle a sum of money on her. She's with me as my friend, and I can't stand to see her penniless." Thalia considered the question for a few seconds. "Do you think one thousand dollars would be sufficient? Yes, that will do. One thousand dollars per year until she marries, but I don't want her—or anyone else—to know where it comes from. Not ever."

Stevens gulped and made a quick note. "Is that all?"

"No. I want to hire a few free blacks to help work my plantation. The grounds are in deplorable shape, and I'll need a few to work in the house." Thalia thought for a moment. "I want two for the house, and four for the fields and grounds."

"But, Miss Freemont, why not buy slaves?" Stevens asked, gazing directly at her. "There's an ad in the *Mercury* this very day announcing a sale."

"I'm not interested in acquiring more slaves, Mr. Stevens." Thalia enunciated her words very carefully. "In fact, I want you to arrange to free Clover, Ebenezer and Princess. If you'll then establish a wage for each of them, I'll be happy and won't trouble you any more today."

For a few seconds, Stevens just stared. Freeing slaves was not unheard-of, but it was highly unconventional. "Miss Freemont, I suggest that you wait until you're married to make such a radical—"

"I want it done now, Mr. Stevens." Thalia rose and met his open stare. "In fact, I want it done before I leave Charleston at the end of the week."

Once she'd concluded her business, Thalia felt better. Christmas was coming, and she'd give her favorite slaves their freedom then. She would leave it to them to decide whether they wanted to stay with her or to go. She whispered a silent prayer that they'd stay.

As she walked down the streets of Charleston, she kept looking for Justin. She'd secretly hoped that she'd see him on this trip, but had stopped short of openly inquiring after him. Still, she could look while she shopped.

Christmas was coming, and she wanted to surprise every one of her servants and slaves with special gifts. This was to be the finest Christmas ever witnessed at Sea Mist. Everyone would sing carols and drink eggnog and open presents. Nobody, not one single person, would be left out.

She went into a little shop that specialized in women's ready-made clothing. Thalia bought pretty shawls for Irene, Clover and Princess. She found a lovely lace-and-ivory fan for Pansy, and then discovered a shawl that matched it perfectly. After looking at the nice caps, she bought enough for all the house and kitchen servants. She had such fun that she almost forgot the time. She quickly finished purchasing the things she would need to have some little gift for everyone. Her days would be happily spent between now and Christmas, with her fingers busy sewing and knitting.

She stopped in the notions shop and purchased several spools of red ribbon for decorating. She found tiny sprigs of artificial red flowers and bought a bolt of red lace. After leaving the notions shop, she stopped at a market and bought a bag full of apples and enough cloves to make pomanders for several rooms. There were no cranberries, but she found a basket of crab apples and asked the merchant to send them back to the hotel with her other purchases. She could hardly wait until Christmas.

Thalia thought of Justin. Would she see him at Christmas-time? Hoping that she would, she looked for a gift, but found

none that she wanted for him. She'd simply have to make
something.

She couldn't resist Mrs. Kirkley's shop. She went in, and
Mrs. Kirkley immediately ushered her upstairs to the fabric
rooms. "Mrs. Kirkley, I'm looking for something spectacular.
I realize that you probably won't have anything as wonderful
as that violet gauze, but I need something for a Christmas ball.
Can you help me?"

Mrs. Kirkley smiled and beckoned Thalia to a table with
gauzes. "I have this lovely sapphire gauze that changes color
slightly when you look at it from different angles. It's not truly
the changeable type of fabric, like the taffeta, but it's even
lovelier. Especially with your eyes."

Thalia watched as Mrs. Kirkley removed a protective cloth
from a roll of the filmiest blue gauze she had ever seen. Its
color, a true sapphire, seemed to shimmer with a little azure,
though the difference was hard to discern. "Oh, Mrs. Kirkley.
It's truly wonderful."

Mrs. Kirkley beamed with satisfaction. "I knew you'd like
it. I don't know of anyone else who could wear it as well. With
your coloring, well . . . it's perfect for you."

They took the gauze into the pattern room, and Thalia
looked at some sketches. "Mrs. Kirkley, you know I like simpler patterns, without all the flounces. I think that fabric would
show much better with a long, flowing skirt, don't you?"

"I think, Miss Freemont," Mrs. Kirkley said, so excited that
she could hardly sit still, "I think that if we combine this with
a few selected rhinestones, we could achieve the effect of ici-
cles. Oh, what a lovely gown that would make."

Thalia nodded excitedly. "You have my measurements already. I'm leaving town quite soon, so could you send it to my
plantation? Sea Mist on Edisto Island."

"Oh, you're there now," Mrs. Kirkley said, as if she were
thinking of the gossip value of such knowledge. "Will there be
anything else?"

Thalia thought of Pansy. "You still have Pansy Monroe's
measurements, I believe. She would like a gown, as well."

Mrs. Kirkley's eyebrows rose sharply, as if she knew Pansy
couldn't pay for an expensive gown. "Well, I suppose I do,
but—"

"Wonderful. She's my guest, and she asked me to select a gown for her." Thalia smiled sweetly. "It's so lonely out there. Nobody to talk to."

"I imagine so," Mrs. Kirkley said slowly, and then she smiled. This little bit of gossip might prove interesting. "What does Miss Monroe want?"

Pausing a moment to remember Pansy's exotic coloring, Thalia moved back to the fabric room. "I think something in a daring shade, maybe Christmas red or holly green. No, red is more festive."

Thalia looked at the gauzes. There she found a deep red, somewhere between a true red and a burgundy. "This, I think, will be perfect."

"I believe you're right." Mrs. Kirkley took the roll of fabric. "Now, how shall we make it? It is too bad Miss Monroe isn't here to select her own gown. I wonder why she would ask you—"

"She's so busy, Mrs. Kirkley," Thalia said, interrupting her. She didn't want anyone speculating on why Pansy hadn't come to town. "She's helping me to prepare for Christmas, and we just moved back to Sea Mist. I declare, there isn't enough time in the day for all we have to do."

Mrs. Kirkley smiled. "You mean she's working for you?"

"No," Thalia said emphatically. "She's my guest. And my friend. Though I appreciate everything she does for me, she's certainly not at Sea Mist as a hired servant. I value her company, and *you* should value her business."

"Oh, I do," Mrs. Kirkley explained quickly. "It's just that I haven't seen her around for a while, and—"

"Good. I wouldn't want any rumors to start here." Thalia gazed squarely into Mrs. Kirkley's eyes. "I can't abide gossips and rumors. I'd simply have to take my business elsewhere."

"Heavens, Miss Freemont, have I ever given you cause to believe that I might repeat—"

"Yes, you have." Thalia continued to stare at Mrs. Kirkley. "And I won't stand for it where Pansy is concerned. Do I make myself perfectly clear?"

"Perfectly," Mrs. Kirkley said. "Now, er, what shall we do to make Miss Monroe's gown special?"

"I think perhaps a little gold lace, or maybe some gold satin embroidered with holly or little red roses." Thalia glanced at the patterns. "Yes, some of the gold satin set into a bodice embroidered with the roses. Maybe a few gold satin roses scattered about the ruffle at the hem."

"Oh, that will be lovely. Miss Monroe will be happy she asked you to choose for her." Mrs. Kirkley smiled and gazed at the expensive fabric. "Where shall I send the bill?"

Thalia thought for a moment. If Mrs. Kirkley sent the bill to Thalia, then the seamstress would assume that Thalia was paying for it. "Oh, I think she has an account with Mr. Stevens at the bank. Send the bill to him."

As she left the store, she ran into Justin. "Justin!" she exclaimed, feeling a thrill slither down her spine. "What are you . . . How nice to see you."

"How nice to see you, Thalia." Justin smiled widely. He'd missed her, and would have gone out to Sea Mist as soon as he completed his most recent trip. He'd planned to leave the following morning. "What are you doing in town?"

"I have business to attend to." Thalia's voice was hardly above a whisper. She'd missed him more than she would ever have thought possible. "How have you been?"

"I've been fine." Justin looked around. "Where were you headed?"

"Back to my hotel." Thalia glanced nervously at a man standing across the street. Thank goodness she didn't know him. "I'm in a bit of a hurry."

"Where are you staying?"

"The Charleston Hotel." Thalia fidgeted with her reticule. She knew that Donald would see her if she made herself too visible. "I'm afraid I must go."

"I'll walk you." Justin fell into step with her as she started down the street. "I'm staying there, too."

Thalia wanted desperately to ask Justin how Donald had reacted to her abrupt departure, but she was hesitant. She didn't know how friendly her brother and Justin were. For all she knew, they might have become best friends by now. She'd just have to wait until she could find out some other way. Randolph would probably blurt out everything she wanted to know when next she saw him.

She remembered her words to Justin. "Someday soon I won't let you stop," she'd said.

Her life was changing. She'd broken her ties with her brother, or at least the most binding ones. And now she was on her own, a woman in charge of her own destiny. Had the time come to take that step from girlhood to womanhood? She bit her lip. How could she be sure?

As they neared the hotel, Justin gazed down at her. She had an odd look on her face, as if she were embroiled in some dilemma. He couldn't deny the pounding of his heart, nor the racing of his pulse. "I'd like to mention that your brother was exceedingly—" Justin refrained from speaking until they'd passed a man who'd been watching them on the street. "Exceedingly angry."

Thalia smiled. She'd known he would be. "I can imagine that he made your day miserable."

Justin followed her through the front door of the hotel. "Actually, it was amusing."

"I'd like to discuss this further, but—"

"But we've arrived at the hotel," he finished for her. "You could . . . come to my room. We could order tea."

Color flooded Thalia's face. She'd been thinking the same thing. Ever since she'd seen him, she'd wondered what it would be like to make love to him. Maybe if they talked a bit longer, she'd know what to do. But she couldn't go to his room. She just couldn't. "I'm sorry, Justin, I can't. But you can come to my room."

They walked farther down the hall and turned. Thalia's heart was pounding with every step. She hoped that Clover wouldn't make a nuisance of herself, but, after all, she couldn't possibly go to Justin's room . . . not yet.

"Here we are," she said, opening the door to a room a short distance from the lobby.

She looked up and down the hallway. "Won't you come in? Maybe for just a moment."

With as much dignity as she could muster, Thalia walked into her room, with Justin trailing after her. Nothing seemed to be out of place as she glanced quickly around the dimly lit room.

Justin followed her in and turned up a lamp. "Nice place, isn't it?"

"It's fine." Thalia's rooms were much larger than most in the hotel. Her suite provided a tiny room for Clover, as well as a parlor and bedroom for Thalia.

Justin glanced around. His parlor was not much larger than the tiniest servant's room, but he liked it that way. Thalia belonged in a place like this one, ornately decorated and large. She seemed at home here.

Thalia removed her gloves and cloak and sat down. "Will you have tea, or perhaps a glass of wine?"

"Nothing, please," Justin said, looking around. He was sure Clover was lurking about someplace, just waiting for him to do something wrong.

Thalia was beginning to question the wisdom of bringing Justin into her room. She had no one to blame for this but herself. She often blamed Lenore's taunts and dares for the things she did, but, in fact, she did nothing she didn't really want to do. "You were telling me about Donald."

"Ah, yes." Justin sat down next to her on the sofa. Her fragrance enveloped him, and he had to think chilling thoughts to keep his physically developing interest in her disguised. "I knew when I saw you going over that rise that Donald would be furious."

"And he was?" Thalia asked, smiling at the idea of Donald's ire. "I'm sorry you had to be there to witness it."

"It was a sight to behold." Justin shifted so that he actually slid closer to her. "He threw things, knocked things off tables. Made quite a mess. Even broke the window in the dining room."

Thalia chuckled and fiddled with the seam of her skirt. She wanted to reach out and touch Justin, but carefully commanded her hands to stay firmly placed on her lap. She didn't know where Clover was. She might well be watching them at this very moment. "I've seen him have such fits frequently. That's why he can't keep a hired servant."

"Well, he and Randolph didn't know what to do with themselves. They finally gave up and came back to Charleston." Justin grinned wickedly. "We raced, and I won."

"I suppose there was a hefty wager on the race," Thalia offered dryly. Justin seemed like such a wonderful man, but he kept revealing that he was no different from all the rest. Didn't men ever understand what they were doing? Pansy was without a place to live because of her brother's gambling, and Thalia would be, too, if she didn't have money and a plantation that Donald couldn't touch.

Justin regretted mentioning the race. He knew how she felt about gambling, and had tried very hard to avoid the subject. "Does he know you're in town?"

"No," Thalia admitted, gazing into Justin's eyes. For a moment, just a fleeting moment, she let herself be carried away into their depths, and she caught a hint of what he might really be like. "I . . . Please don't tell him."

"I wouldn't," Justin answered, remembering how furious Donald was with Thalia. Donald might do something drastic. Justin found that idea entirely within the realm of reality, and he wanted to prepare Thalia in case Donald did try to harm her. "Thalia, I don't believe Donald thinks rationally all the time. I want you to be careful. He could . . . What I mean to say is, I don't trust him."

Thalia was happy to hear that Justin didn't trust Donald, but she was nonetheless frightened by his warning. "Did he . . . did he say anything that sounded like a threat?"

"Not exactly," Justin said, but he couldn't ever forget hearing Donald say he could kill her. It had been in the heat of the moment, when he was at his most irate. He hoped that Donald had calmed down since that morning. "But I want you to be careful. I just don't think he's entirely stable right now."

Their eyes met. Thalia wanted to turn away from him, to avert her eyes, but she couldn't. Justin's silvery-gray eyes were almost magnetic, drawing her gaze constantly to meet his. He was going to kiss her. She tilted her head back slightly to accept his kiss.

This time, their kiss started out with a pent-up passion that neither of them truly wanted to recognize. Thalia slid her arms around his neck and turned slightly to press her body against his. Was this the moment? Would she allow Justin to make love to her?

Justin drew away, as if he'd heard her thoughts and wanted to know the answer to her question. She still couldn't decide, and her indecision somehow translated itself to him. Clover was probably watching them from some dark corner.

"I think it's time I returned to my room, Thalia." Justin kissed her lightly, savoring the satiny touch of her lips. "If I remain here much longer, I won't promise to behave like a gentleman."

For a few seconds more, Thalia was plagued by indecision. She relished the power of his embrace, of his lips crushing hers again, but drew back. This wasn't the time. Nor was the Charleston Hotel the place.

When Thalia Payton Freemont became a woman, she wanted that spectacular event to occur at Sea Mist, at home, in her own bed. She smiled, pressed her lips to his once more and whispered, "Good night, Justin. Soon...soon."

Chapter Thirteen

Justin knew he'd said more than he should have to Thalia about her brother, but he couldn't help it. Something about Donald's behavior lately had made Justin think that the man really was up to no good. Randolph had seemed awfully cheerful last night, intimating that an announcement was to be made shortly.

Thalia didn't seem to know that her brother was innately evil, and Justin wasn't about to tell her. She still represented his best chance of exacting his revenge against Donald—if he was right.

He couldn't get her out of his mind. Randolph Taylor was giving a party tonight, but Justin didn't know whether or not he would attend. Thalia most probably wouldn't be there, and, for Justin, a party didn't mean much these days if she wasn't there to provide an amusing distraction. He'd have to find out somehow whether or not she planned to attend. Then he'd make his decision.

"She did what?" Donald asked, incredulous. "When?"

Warren Stevens didn't like Donald Freemont, but he had to follow Thalia's instructions. "Just yesterday."

"Was she here? In your office?" Donald asked, pacing back and forth impatiently.

"Yes, she was here." Stevens knew that Thalia didn't want Donald to know she was in town, so he added, "But I think she's already gone back to Sea Mist."

"Sea Mist!" Donald slammed his fist against Stevens's desk. "Where's she staying here?" He looked at Stevens and realized that the man wouldn't tell him. "Never mind. I'll find out."

Donald left immediately. He strode over to Randolph's and told him the story he'd just heard from Stevens. "She's still here," he said. "I know she is. I'm going to bring her to your party tonight."

Thalia left for Sea Mist that very morning. She'd been afraid that Donald would discover her presence in Charleston and come to find her. She'd be eternally grateful to Justin for telling her how Donald had reacted to her leaving Misty Glade, but she thought his warnings were unnecessary. Donald would be angry for a while, but he'd never do anything to hurt her. He was her brother.

The plantation was running smoothly by the time she and Clover returned. Over the next few days, Adam supervised the slaughter of hogs and steers for the coming winter's food, while she and the women worked outside in the cold making lard for cooking, lye soap and candles. Then they took some of the corn the men had harvested and made hominy out of it. Her hands looked like a slave's hands, but she felt good about what she was doing. She was mistress—and master—of her own land.

By day's end, she was coughing, freezing and worn-out. Her hands and feet ached, and she fell gratefully into bed each night, hardly caring if she warmed up or not. She didn't want to think about Justin, but she did. She couldn't get him off her mind. While she was stirring the fat, rendering it into lard, she would often stop completely and prop herself on the oar they used to mix and cook the raw fat. The pungent odor would frequently bring her back to the present, but sometimes one of the other women had to speak to her.

Clover eyed Thalia suspiciously. "I don't know what's come over you. You actin' like a chicken with his head cut off. Ain't got a lick of sense."

"Oh, Clover, don't be silly. I . . ." Thalia knew she'd better come up with a logical excuse or Clover might just dose her with one of Princess's potions for "what ails you." Having tasted those concoctions before, Thalia wanted to avoid them at all cost. "I'm just tired. We've been working awfully hard."

"Something ain't right. I knows it ain't." Clover kept watching Thalia all day.

About midafternoon a slave Thalia recognized as Andy—he was one of Donald's—arrived. "Miss Thalia," he said, breathing heavily, "Mistah Donald want me to come and give you this letter."

For a few seconds, Thalia could hardly breathe. She knew that Donald hadn't had time to forgive her for leaving, and she didn't want to face him until he had. She took the letter from the boy. "Run on up to the house. Prineess is cooking supper. Tell her to give you something to eat."

Thalia watched the boy run across the lawn and in the back door to the kitchen. She gave the oar to Irene. "Here, I suppose I'd better read this to see if I need to send an answer."

As she opened the letter, Thalia's fingers trembled slightly. She recognized Donald's tight little script.

Dear Thalia,
I hope this missive finds you well. We miss you here at Misty Glade and wish you would return, but I understand your commitment to your plantation. In any event, I want you to come over to discuss a problem with me. I'll look for your return with Andy.

With love,
Donald Osgood Freemont

Thalia could hardly believe what she was reading. Had Donald truly said he loved her? If so, it was the first time. Perhaps living alone had sobered him up a bit and he was ready to assume responsibility for his life. She doubted it, but couldn't shake the feeling that Donald had really changed. Something was different.

She considered her task. All the soap and candles were made, the hominy was made and stored, and the lard was almost ready, too. She could leave without causing a real problem, if she returned immediately.

"Clover," she said, looking at her friend. "I'm going to ride over to Misty Glade to see Donald. I'll be back shortly."

"Miss Thalia," Clover said, crossing her arms defiantly, "you ain't going over there by yo'self. If I don't go, you ain't going."

"Now, Clover…" Thalia began, but Clover interrupted her.

"I mean it." Clover dropped her lard bucket. "We going together."

Thalia knew she was beaten. "Ask Ebenezer to bring the carriage around. We'll be back tonight."

The trip to Misty Glade went smoothly enough, even though Thalia still had a vague feeling that she didn't want to return to a house that would bring back so many bad memories. When they arrived, Donald greeted them at the front door.

"I haven't found a good housekeeper yet," he explained. "Come in." He kissed Thalia on the cheek and then turned to Clover. "Clover, how good to see you, too."

Clover crossed her arms. "Harrumph."

Thalia ignored Clover's reaction and stepped into the parlor. "What is it, Donald? What's so urgent that I had to come tonight?"

"Christmas, Thalia." Donald smiled broadly and sat down. "I'm going to have a large Christmas ball, and you must be my hostess."

"Why me?" Thalia asked, noticing that her throat was a little sore. "Why not bring Eugenia over? She's a wonderful hostess, from what I hear."

"She is, but I want you." Donald edged forward on his chair. "This is to be the grandest gala ever held on Edisto Island. Spare no expense."

Thalia eyed him suspiciously. Had he truly changed? He must have, if he had the money to give this ball. "All right, Donald. I'll help you this time. When do you want to have it?"

For a few minutes, they discussed possible dates, settling on the Saturday before Christmas.

Donald asked her to remain with him during the holidays. "Nobody should be alone at Christmas, Thalia, not even me."

Her heart went out to him. She knew that, in some respects, he'd always been alone. She couldn't let that happen this Christmas. Though she'd been looking forward to having her first Christmas as mistress of Sea Mist, she could do that next year. She held back a cough as long as she could, but finally gave in to it. When the spasm was over, she smiled and said, "Well, I'll spend this Christmas with you, if you'll spend next Christmas with me."

"Splendid!" Donald exclaimed, jumping up. "What a tradition we'll start."

Thalia left shortly after their conversation. By the time she arrived at Sea Mist, the sun had set. She ate a ham biscuit and drank a glass of milk. Within ten minutes after she drained her glass, Thalia was in bed. For a little while, she thought of things she could do to make Donald's party special. She thought wistfully of how lovely Sea Mist would be at Christmas, all decorated with holly and ivy and with a large tree surrounded by all the presents she'd been making in her spare time.

If Donald was to have a good showing at his Christmas ball, then she'd have to start sending invitations immediately. As she fell asleep, she thought once again of Justin. What would she give him for Christmas?

All night she dreamed of him. In her dream, she couldn't decide what to give him for Christmas and, when Christmas Day arrived, she had to face him empty-handed. As hard as she'd searched, she'd come up with nothing. He gave her a little heart-shaped locket. It was the most beautiful locket she'd ever seen, but she could see that he was angry with her. He swore to get revenge, but she didn't understand why. The locket disappeared. Apparently he hadn't given her anything, either.

Thalia awoke bathed in sweat. Something was wrong. At first, she thought that the house was on fire, but she couldn't smell smoke. She got up and walked toward the door. When she got near enough to reach the bellpull, she fell forward and jerked it completely down.

"Lawsy mercy, what happened to my baby?" Clover knelt beside Thalia and touched her forehead. Heat seemed to radiate from Thalia's body. Clover jumped up and ran for the stairs. "Ebenezer, Ebenezer, wake up your useless self and go for the doctor! Miss Thalia's sick!"

Pansy opened her door and ran into the hallway. "What is it, Clover?"

"Miss Thalia's sick." Clover returned to Thalia's room.

By this time, Thalia had risen to a sitting position. "Clover, what's all the fuss about? What happened?"

"You's just worked yo'self half to death, that's what. Working out there, stirring all that mess." Clover helped Thalia back into bed. "It's a wonder you ain't dead." Clover ran back to the door. "Princess, get down here."

In a few minutes, Princess ambled into Thalia's room. "Oh, Lordy, what happened here?"

"Miss Thalia's sick." Clover crossed her arms. "You got a potion to get rid of that cold?"

"I do. Stay put."

Princess moved faster than Thalia had ever seen the cook move. Thalia was freezing. "Clover, I'm f-f-freezing. Put a log on the fire."

"You ain't freezing, you got a chill." Clover tossed another log on the fire and stoked the ashes until flames licked at the new log. "Miss Pansy, you stay with her, and if she get out of that bed, whomp her with this hot poker."

Pansy laughed and sat down beside Thalia's bed. "Thalia, I'm worried about you. You've been working like the least important slave on the place. You've got to consider your health. You weren't meant to work like that."

A cough wracked Thalia's body. After a moment, she offered Pansy a wan smile. "Pansy, I can't ask them to do something I wouldn't do, now can I?"

"You can and you should. My mother, God rest her soul, never did anything like you're doing." Pansy curled her feet beneath her and started to rock. "She supervised, but I never saw her stirring fat or dipping candles or anything like that."

"I know you're right, Pansy," Thalia said, coughing again. "But you don't know how I feel. This is *my* home. These are *my* people. I must take care of them."

"You can't take care of them if you're sick yourself." Pansy reached over and tucked the covers beneath Thalia's chin. "You're going to stay right there for the next few days. I'll make sure everything gets done properly."

"I've got to plan for Donald's Christmas ball. There are too many things to do for me to lie in bed all day." Thalia shivered again and wished Clover would hurry back with some more quilts.

"You ain't gonna move from that bed till I says you is." Clover entered the room with an armful of quilts. "You ain't too big for me to take a switch to. If Mistah Donald wants a party, let him get that painted woman of his to make the party. You ain't getting up till you're better, and that's that.''

For the next several days, Thalia slept, coughed, drank plenty of water and wrote invitations for Donald's party. She spent much of her waking time either thinking of diversions for the few days when people would be staying at Misty Glade or thinking of Justin. She wondered what he was doing, who he was spending his time with, but one thing kept coming back into her mind to interrupt everything else—his kisses and embraces.

She had something else to consider, as well. He'd told her very little about his background, but she'd gleaned enough from remarks here and there to decide that his childhood had been happy. He'd grown up on a plantation in Virginia, so he knew a little about the life of a planter.

Why had he left? From what she could understand, his parents were well-to-do. Was he a second son? Or had something else precipitated his departure from his family? A disagreement? A crime? *He could even be a murderer,* she thought, and then decided that he'd never intentionally hurt anyone. He just wasn't the type. Thalia didn't know why he'd left, couldn't know unless she asked him directly, and she wouldn't do that— not yet. She wouldn't pry into his past. He'd have to tell her in his own good time.

Princess plied her with potions and liniments, salves and smelly things that Thalia didn't even care to discover the origins of. And, in a few days, she felt much better and resumed control of her household.

In her spare moments—which were few—she took her paints down to the beach and began to paint. She did several small watercolors of the ocean, the dunes and the palmettos. She tried to remember what Justin's sailboat, the *Spirit of Justice,* looked like, and painted it as well as she could recall. Then she started an oil painting, not knowing what she wanted to paint. As she stroked the canvas, she chose sepia tones, and gradually the shape of a face came into focus. She stepped back and looked. It was Justin.

Thalia wasn't a portrait painter, but the likeness was remarkable. She mixed colors and dabbed here and there, wiping away paint, putting it back, blending, defining, refining. She recalled that little twitch around his mouth when he laughed, the lines that radiated from his eyes. His image swam before her, and she painted as if her hand were being held by an angel who'd memorized Justin's features. His eyes gave her the most trouble. Sometimes—that silvery-gray, sometimes that gentle blue-gray, their definition was elusive. She settled on the blue-gray that almost always appeared when he was happiest—or when he kissed her.

After a few minutes, she sat back and stared. The portrait was complete. She'd hardly noticed the time. Her watercolors were dry. She selected one for Justin, the one of the *Spirit of Justice*, with sailboats dotting the harbor and gulls diving for their dinner. Since he was a sea captain, she thought, he'd like that best.

As she gathered her supplies, she began to consider decorations for Sea Mist. She wanted a large tree in the parlor.

One cold, crisp morning, she donned her heaviest boots and her oldest dress. The time had come to select the Sea Mist Christmas tree. She woke Pansy early and told her to dress warmly.

After breakfast, she went looking for Adam. He would have to go along and cut the tree. He told her he'd bring a couple of young slaves to help carry the tree and boughs of cedar. As they were preparing to leave, they heard a horse galloping up the road.

"Who can that be?" Pansy asked, squinting to see who was coming.

"I don't know." Thalia frowned. She hoped that whoever the visitor was, he wouldn't keep her from her task for very long. She stared harder. The rider looked like Justin. "It's Justin!" she shouted, hugging Pansy happily.

When he got close enough to recognize her, he waved his hat above his head. "Hello!" he called as he rode into the yard and dismounted.

Thalia could hardly keep from leaping into his arms. She smiled pleasantly and hoped that the sound of her heart wasn't audible to everyone in the area. "Welcome to Sea Mist Plantation, Justin."

Justin grinned, fixed his eyes on Thalia for a moment and then looked at the little group. "Happy to be here. I brought over some packages for you. Something from Mrs. Kirkley. I hired a wagon to bring them." He glanced around and noticed that everyone was dressed warmly. "Were you going somewhere?"

"You're just in time," Adam said, shaking hands with Justin. "We're off to find a Christmas tree."

"Great. May I come along?" Justin asked, noticing the woman with Thalia for the first time. "I don't believe we've met."

"No," Thalia answered, unable to turn away from Justin. She hadn't realized how much she enjoyed just looking at him. Her excitement was doubled by his remark about the packages from Mrs. Kirkley. "Allow me to introduce you."

She made the introductions quickly, and noticed how Pansy blushed when Justin looked at her. Thalia wondered if it was because Pansy felt like a soiled woman, but she said nothing. Justin didn't know anything about Pansy, and Thalia wouldn't tell him, at least not now. She felt that, somehow, he'd understand.

"I need to speak to Clover for a moment," Thalia said, and hurried back into the house. "Clover!" She waited for the servant to appear. "I'm expecting some packages from Mrs. Kirkley. Take them to my room and open them. Press the gowns. I fear they'll be frightfully wrinkled."

"Yes, Miss Thalia, I'll do it first thing."

Thalia returned to the group outside. "Well," she said finally, "let's go."

The little band walked into the forest at the back of Sea Mist. Here and there, someone would point out one of the little pines that grew in the woods, but they all wanted to wait. It seemed that everyone wanted an extraordinary tree, one far more beautiful than any they'd seen so far.

They walked back and forth, traversing the thick forest, until they reached a small glade. There they found a stately cedar that seemed perfect. After many oohs and ahs, Thalia, Justin, Adam and Pansy launched into a discussion of where the tree should be cut. The place was decided, and Adam told one of the slaves to chop down the tree. Adam tied a large piece of burlap around the tree and then sent a boy home with it while everyone else continued to search for boughs of holly and cedar.

Thalia remembered a thicket of holly trees, and they found it without too much trouble. Fortunately, Adam had brought another burlap bag that made transporting the prickly holly and cedar much easier.

On the way back to the house, the little group sang Christmas carols. "Joy to the World" and "The First Noel" were among Thalia's favorites, and she sang along happily, noticing that Justin was a little off-key, though he seemed to enjoy the singing every bit as much as the rest of them. When the house came into view, they were finishing the last chorus.

"I love to sing," Justin confessed sheepishly. "I come from a family of people who love to sing. The problem is that everyone else in my family is gifted, and I'm...well, less than talented."

Adam chortled and clapped Justin on the back. "Keeping a tune means nothing if the words are heartfelt. Keep singing, my friend."

"Adam," Justin said with a broad smile, "I appreciate your appreciation of my music. Shall I sing some more?"

"No," the others in the group chorused. They joined in Justin's laughter as they hurried up the front steps of the house.

The Christmas tree was nowhere in sight, so Adam said, "I'll find out where the tree is and make sure the cut is level. I'll fill a bucket with rocks to anchor the tree securely and bring it in as quickly as possible."

Thalia watched Adam leave. Then she turned to the three young black men who were whitewashing the thick columns and the facade of the house. She smiled proudly as she thought of Sea Mist being returned to its original splendor in time for the holidays.

"Dressing her up for Christmas," Thalia said by way of explanation. "The place is going to shine like a pearl."

Justin looked at the columns and nodded. "I believe you're right."

"What are your plans for Christmas, Justin?" Thalia asked, as if she could read the sad look in his eyes.

"Me?" Justin hesitated. He didn't want her to think he had absolutely nothing to do but sit in his room and watch the fire crackle. "Oh, I don't know yet."

"You mean you aren't going home?" she asked incredulously. She couldn't believe that he wasn't going to spend the holidays with his family. Christmas meant a lot to her. Aunt Molly and Uncle Martin always found the biggest tree on the plantation and cut it for the parlor. Weeks before the holiday, everyone would mysteriously disappear, making gifts for everyone else. When Justin didn't answer, she hugged him. "You're going to stay out here and spend Christmas with us."

"Now, Thalia, I don't want to intrude on—"

"Intrude? What a ridiculous thing to say." Thalia turned to Pansy and winked. "Saint Nicholas already plans to leave your Christmas goodies here—that is, if you've been a good little boy."

Justin smiled, though his spirits were a little dampened. He couldn't go home for Christmas. His family always made much of the holiday season, and that was one part of his exile that he really hated. Spending the holidays with Thalia might prove interesting. "Well, if you put it that way. I'd hate to miss out on Christmas simply because Saint Nicholas didn't know where to find me."

"Then it's settled." Thalia felt happier than she'd been in a long time. The chill of the day seemed to disappear when Justin was around, and he would help make her first Christmas since her return to Sea Mist even more special.

Clover opened the front door. "What you standin' out here for? Don't you know you gonna catch your death o' cold again? I done nursed you through one batch of bein' sick, and I b'lieve if you get sick again you'll plumb die on me. I ain't havin' it. Get yo'self in here. An' the rest o' you folks, too. I b'lieve Princess done made some hot choc'late."

Justin eyed Thalia speculatively. She did look a little paler than usual. As they walked through the door behind Clover, he caught her arm and asked, "Have you been ill?"

"Just a cold," Thalia answered, shaking her head and pointing at Clover. "She's just like an old mother hen."

"I think she's right." Justin hooked her arm through his. "You should be more careful, particularly if you've been ill."

"Don't worry about me. I'm fine," Thalia protested, leading the way into the parlor.

Justin waited until Thalia sat on the sofa and Pansy sat opposite her before choosing a seat beside Thalia. "I do worry."

Pansy watched the exchange between Thalia and Justin for a moment. She could see that an undercurrent ran between the two of them, and she smiled. Justin seemed to be a fine man, just right for Thalia. A sea captain. They looked as if they belonged together. A touch of nostalgia caught Pansy, and she remembered what a flirt she used to be. She had had beaux everywhere. Now she was of little use to any man, soiled as she was. Not so with Thalia and her sea captain. Pansy thought that might prove an interesting match. Maybe she could nudge it along. "My goodness, Captain Lionheart, you must meet a lot of interesting people and visit a lot of interesting places."

Justin turned to face Pansy. He detected a note of sadness about her, though she'd seemed cheerful enough when he'd first met her. "I do, Miss Monroe, but I find that I'm increasingly drawn to Charleston."

"Oh, how nice," Pansy said, wondering how she could maneuver the conversation around to Thalia without embarrassing her. "Thalia Freemont is one of the most interesting women I've ever known."

"Pansy!" Thalia exclaimed, astonished at the turn of the conversation.

"Well, it's true. You are interesting," Pansy said. "How many women do you know, Captain Lionheart—"

"Call me Justin."

"Thank you, Justin," Pansy said. "Just how many women do you know who're capable of running a big plantation like this? Why, this is one of the largest on the island."

Before Justin could answer, Thalia glared at her friend and said, "Pansy, I'm sure Justin isn't the least bit interested in—"

"As I told you once before, Thalia—" Justin grinned "—you'd be surprised what I'm interested in."

"See, Thalia?" Pansy asked. She knew that if she pursued the subject much further, Thalia would probably get angry. "I think I'll go see what's keeping Clover. I could use a cup of chocolate about now.'' She walked slowly out and closed the door firmly behind her.

Thalia watched Pansy leave. For a few seconds, she was unsure of being alone with Justin again—until he slipped his arms around her and kissed her soundly.

When he moved away, he brushed his lips against her forehead and whispered, ''I've been wanting to do that all day.''

Thalia caught her breath and willed her heart to return to its normal cadence. She looked up into Justin's face and smiled. ''No more than I.''

A clatter came from the hallway. ''Goodness. How clumsy of me,'' Pansy warbled. She picked up the spoons she'd dropped intentionally to alert the two in the parlor to her presence and called back to Clover, ''Bring some more spoons.''

Justin chuckled. ''Quite a thoughtful woman. I can't wait for you to tell me all about her.''

He rose and walked to the door. ''I'm so sorry, Pansy. If you'd warned me, I could have opened the door and kept you from spilling the spoons.'' He reached down and picked them up.

''Thank you, Justin. You're so kind,'' Pansy cooed, as if she'd dropped them by accident. ''You don't have a brother, do you?''

Justin stiffened. He did have a brother, only one. Pansy was asking playfully, and wasn't aware that she'd struck a nerve in Justin. There was no harm in answering honestly. ''Yes. I have a brother, but he's eleven years younger. Would you be interested in a man who's hardly begun to shave?''

Sensing the playfulness of his question, Pansy winked at Justin. ''Maybe I'll wait for him.''

They went back into the parlor to join Thalia. Pansy placed the silver tray laden with cookies and cups of hot chocolate on the low table by the sofa. ''Mighty festive,'' she remarked, and handed everyone a cup.

Thalia watched Pansy thoughtfully. In her innocence, she'd gotten Justin to answer a question about his past. Maybe he just didn't like to talk about himself and his family. Maybe he didn't have such a dark past, after all. Thalia had been imagining all sorts of reasons that he'd taken to the sea—including murder.

"Here we are," Adam called as he stepped into the parlor. Two young black men followed him, one carrying the tree and the other a bucket of stones. "Where do we put it?"

Thalia surveyed the room. She'd been thinking of the best place all day. "I've decided that we should stand it in front of the double windows in the corner. That way, it can be seen from the front of the house, and from the side."

Adam and the boys placed the Christmas tree where she'd indicated. Thalia went to the young men and smiled. "Go back to the kitchen and have some hot chocolate and cookies. You deserve it. Adam, go and find Irene. She needs to be here, too."

Thalia went to the kitchen to give instructions to Princess. She wanted everyone in the house to have some chocolate. "Princess, please make sufficient chocolate for everyone. Oh, and after dinner, make plenty of popcorn for stringing. This is going to be a beautiful tree. By the way, when will dinner be ready?"

"Soon as you can set yo'self down at the table." Princess grinned a toothless grin. "I knowed you'd be hungry. And I done took the kernels off the cob for popping."

"Splendid. Set places at the table for Pansy, Captain Lion-heart, Adam, Irene and me." Thalia returned to the parlor. "Dinner is ready."

Adam returned with Irene and Thalia ushered them into the dining room. "We all need to be together. Justin, will you say the blessing?"

Justin did. When he was finished, Princess ladled hearty bowls of gumbo over rice for everyone. The spicy aroma filled the room and Thalia could hardly wait to eat. The meal couldn't have been better—unless, of course, she were eating alone with Justin, and he had pulled his chair up next to hers. But it was a lighthearted hour filled with laughter.

After dinner, everyone strung popcorn for the Christmas tree. Since Thalia didn't have any cranberries to string, she'd made sure they had some dried red beans in their place. They made garlands of colored paper, looped together to form long chains, and draped them from the limbs. She made ribbon loops to attach to the tiny crab apples she'd bought in Charleston and hung them from several limbs. She cut some of the ta-pers she'd made from marsh myrtle berries into short pieces and whittled away the wax at one end so that there would be enough of a wick exposed to light. Then she fit them into tiny holders that could be clipped to the tree. Lastly, she took a little angel she'd made from corn husks and a little lace, and asked Justin to place it atop the tree.

When he'd finished, Thalia stood back and exclaimed, "Oh, how lovely. It's the best tree ever."

"I don't think I've ever seen a prettier tree. When do we light the candles?" Pansy asked, stepping back beside Thalia to assess their work.

"Not until Christmas Eve," Thalia answered. She and Pansy stuck cloves into the crab apples and attached more of the red ribbon. They hung the pomanders in the dining room, the parlor, the library, her morning room, and each bedroom.

"Now, Pansy, I have a surprise for you." Thalia took her friend's hand and led her up the stairs. "Close your eyes."

When Pansy's eyes were closed, Thalia led her into her bedroom. The two gowns were hanging side by side. They were stunning. "All right, you may open your eyes."

Pansy opened her eyes, and for a few seconds she blinked in astonishment. "Why, Thalia, I never saw two prettier gowns in my life. Where are you going to wear them?"

"I'm not. Well, I'm going to wear the blue." Thalia couldn't resist. She went over and fingered the delicate fabric. The rhinestones had been set at intervals, and the entire dress glittered. "The red is yours."

"Mine?" Pansy asked and rushed over. "How? Who?" Pansy stuttered and then looked at Thalia. "Thalia, I can't take charity. The gown is more beautiful than anything I've ever seen, and..."

"Mr. Stevens tells me you have money in the bank." Thalia crossed her fingers behind her back. She didn't like lying to Pansy, but she couldn't hurt her feelings, either. "I'm sorry if I overstepped my bounds, but I naturally assumed that you'd want a new dress for the ball, and, since you weren't coming into town, I decided that I could order for you. After all, Mrs. Kirkley has your measurements."

Pansy stared at Thalia in disbelief. "Thalia, I have no money. There must be some mistake."

Thalia shook her head. "No, Mr. Stevens said most particularly that you should contact him directly if you have any needs. He would have told you sooner, but you'd disappeared."

Pansy dropped into the rocker and gazed straight ahead. "Then everything I did . . . I didn't have to . . . How much do I have?"

"Well, I don't know exactly, but I think he said something about an annual deposit or something. You know I don't understand anything about finances," she lied again. *God, forgive me, but I'm just trying to salvage my friend's life the best way I can,* she prayed silently. "I presume that since he now knows where you are, he'll be sending you an accounting or something."

The girls tried on the dresses, each helping the other into and out of the lovely gowns. Thalia smiled. "Pansy, I don't know when I've seen you look lovelier."

Pansy giggled and then clapped her hand over her mouth. "I know. Don't I sound like Lenore?"

"Yes, you do, Miss Gigglebox," Thalia said, wagging her finger at Pansy. "And you'd better stop it right now. I know you've got better sense than she does, though I sometimes believe it's all a pretense with her."

Pansy nodded. "You may be right."

The two women changed back into gowns that were more suitable for supper. Thalia could hardly wait to get downstairs again. When she did, she found Justin standing back and admiring the decorations.

She studied Justin for a few moments. He hadn't really said how long he intended to stay, but he had said he'd be at Sea Mist for Christmas. For now, that was enough.

Thalia finished placing boughs of holly and cedar and cassina tied with red ribbon on the mantels all through the house until the fragrance filled every room. She positioned candles in all the windows and spread holly or cedar around them. On Christmas Eve the house would be visible from a great distance, and everyone would know that Sea Mist was in its glory again.

She then tied a few boughs of holly, cassina—or Christmas berry—and cedar together with a big red bow and asked Justin to hang it on the front door. Then she hung branches of mistletoe tied with red satin ribbon in the wide archways that led to the parlor, the dining room and the ballroom. Now, at last, she felt that her home was ready for Christmas. All it needed was the aromatic smells of Christmas spices and baking for her to be content, and she could already catch the fragrance coming from the back of the house. Since Justin was here, everything was perfect, better than she had ever thought possible.

She turned to Justin. "We're going to Donald's for a few days, and you're invited to go with us. He's having a huge ball, and I need to go over pretty soon to decorate the house. I sent you an invitation, but I suppose you'd already left your hotel. Will you come with me?"

Justin couldn't hide his anticipation. He wanted more than anything to spend a little more time with Donald—not to mention Thalia. "I'd love to. When do we leave?"

"Tomorrow," she said, smiling with happiness. She noticed a change in his face, a sure sign that he wanted to be with her. And she desperately wanted to be with him. "We'll have a wonderful time. The ball is one night, and we have lots of other festivities planned." She smiled, a little coyly, and continued, "Then we'll come back here in time for Christmas Eve."

Chapter Fourteen

Thalia couldn't sleep. She tossed and turned for about an hour before rising and pulling on her dressing gown. She didn't know exactly what she intended to do, but she wanted to see her Christmas tree alone. Taking a lamp, she tiptoed down the stairs and into the parlor.

She placed the lamp on a table near the tree and turned the flame down low so that the light barely dispelled the darkness. She stepped back and finally sat down on the sofa, listening to the sounds of the house settling and to the crackle of the almost-burned log. For a long time, she just stared. She thought of her aunt and uncle, of all the joyful Christmases she'd shared with them. Though they weren't here any longer, she felt that they would be here in spirit, approving of what she'd done.

Then her thoughts turned to Justin. If ever she could love a man, she thought, it might be Justin. He seemed so different, so understanding. She enjoyed his sense of humor, the way his eyes sort of crinkled up when he laughed.

She remembered the way she felt when he kissed her, the way her body kept moving closer of its own accord. Aunt Molly had told her that such behavior was unladylike, and Thalia agreed, but then, she did little that could be considered ladylike these days. She wondered if Aunt Molly had felt the same sensations when Uncle Martin kissed her.

Several times, Thalia had walked into a room and seen them quickly separate. She suspected that they'd been kissing, or maybe even more. She also suspected that, even though Aunt Molly had said that kissing and fondling were unladylike, she would have understood Thalia's feelings. But Aunt Molly had died before she could really talk to Thalia about the relationship between a man and a woman.

Thalia rose and walked about the dimly lit room for a few minutes. How she longed for someone to talk to, someone who would listen and not judge. She could always talk to Pansy, but her relationship with that awful Mr. Rice hadn't been one of love.

"Oh, Aunt Molly," she whispered to the stillness of the room. "What should I do?"

She continued to pace, stopping occasionally to rearrange the cedar boughs or to straighten a tilted candle. "I have these . . . these odd feelings . . . I can't explain. I want him to kiss me, to touch me, to—"

A noise stopped her where she stood and silenced her. Somehow she knew that she wasn't alone in the room. Who could have crept in without her hearing? Could it be the ghost of Aunt Molly? She gathered her courage and asked, "Who's there?"

For a few seconds, the silence lingered like the curtain of mist that hovered around her in the early mornings when she rode out to the fields. Then she heard another sound, a footstep.

Thalia whirled around and found herself facing a man— Justin Lionheart. "You . . . How did you get in here?"

He said nothing for a moment, then strode to her side. He took her in his arms and kissed her, bringing her to a higher state of desire than she had ever known. Thalia broke away and stared at him, unable to think clearly, or to speak.

"I heard something and came down to see if we had an intruder." Justin dropped his hands to his side. "I didn't mean to eavesdrop on you. In fact, I only slipped into the room because I heard footsteps in here."

Thalia felt the color spring into her cheeks. He must have heard her when she'd spoken aloud. What had she said? She'd been talking about him, about the way she felt when he kissed her.

Now was her chance. She'd told him that someday, someday soon . . . If she ever could love a man, that man was Justin; she knew that instinctively. *Of course, you don't love him,* she chided herself. *You're too sensible to fall in love with a sea captain. A man who'd be gone most of the time. Besides, she didn't really want to fall in love, anyway.* But she didn't want to go through life without knowing about physical love. Now was her chance, maybe her only chance.

She smiled, hoping he would interpret it as a sign of consent. For a long moment, he did nothing, and Thalia thought she might have misjudged him. What if he didn't want to make love to her?

Justin stood there, studying her, for a few seconds. Her smile was inviting, as if she was giving herself to him. He considered that. He wanted nothing more than to sweep her off her feet, carry her up the stairs to his room, and spend the night making love to her, teaching her the art of love.

From her kisses, he knew she'd be a good pupil. She'd quickly learned how to accept his kisses, how to respond. But was he willing to take the one thing that was truly hers? Even if she thought she wanted to give him her virginity—and he was certain that she was a virgin—did she really know what she was doing?

Justin had never given so much thought to making love before. In fact, he'd never thought so much about making love to one woman before. Ever since he'd met her, that first evening in Charleston, when she'd been so bedraggled and wet, he'd wanted her. But was it fair to her?

Her smile began to waver, and he thought for a moment that she might cry. He could stand a lot of things, but not that. And he couldn't keep staring at her, dressed in that light dressing gown and looking so damnably beautiful that he could fairly taste her kisses.

He didn't love her. He couldn't. She was just another woman offering her body to him. She was a vehicle for obtaining revenge against the man who'd caused the deaths of Peter Kimball, his best friend, and Alicia Kimball, the girl he had been engaged to.

Enough time had passed for him to get over Alicia's death. He realized that he hadn't really loved her, either. They'd simply been engaged because everyone had thought it was the thing to do. They'd grown up together. The engagement had just seemed right. Now he knew he could never have been happy

with her. They had been too different. And she must have realized it, too, because she'd had an affair.

Justin gazed back at Thalia. The lamp shone behind her, and
a halo of light seemed to surround her. Was she truly different
from Alicia, and from all the other women he'd known? Or
would she betray him at the first opportunity? No, he didn't
love her. He'd never love a woman again—at least, that was
what he kept telling himself. And he found that he was telling
himself that more and more often when he was around Thalia.

He took the few steps that separated them. Without saying
a word, he lifted her into his arms, walked out of the parlor and
carried her up the stairs to his room. Opening the door wasn't
easy, but he managed. He placed her on the center of the bed
and then locked the door. He wasn't taking any chances that
someone might interrupt them.

The fire in his room had died down until it hardly gave any
glow that told of warmth, but it cast a shimmer of golden light
over Thalia as she lay there, expectant, where he'd placed her.
He knew that she would be curious but frightened, and he
suddenly wanted this experience to be wonderful for her.

Fully clothed, he lay down beside her and started kissing her.
He covered her face and neck with light, sweet kisses that were
like the promises he didn't want to make but knew she wanted
to hear.

Desire raged in him and burned, warning him of the pent-up
emotions that threatened to supersede his better intentions and
ruin this splendid moment. Justin knew he could control himself for only so long, but he kept thinking of Thalia's feelings.
There would be pain—of that he was certain—but if he could
do anything to ensure that the pain was lessened, he would.

Thalia clung to him. What was she doing here in Justin's
bedroom, letting him touch her this way? Her mind urged her
to leap from the bed and leave at once, but her body rebelled,
compelling her to stay and sample the pleasures of the unknown.

Justin was a stranger to her. She knew nothing about him,
she reasoned. *It doesn't matter,* her body replied, arching to
meet his fingertips as they touched her breasts, first one and
then the other. Thalia gasped. Before, when his thumb had
brushed against her breast, she'd known that a mere touch

could send waves of pleasure through her, but she'd never even guessed how strong those waves could be.

The dressing gown, a thin summer silk, was like a barrier between them. She wanted to rip it off, to shred the filmy fabric so that she could experience Justin's touch without interference. As if he could read her mind, he unbuttoned the offending gown, lifted her and slipped it off her body.

Naked now, she lay exposed to the chilly air, but she didn't care, because his fingers had begun a slow massage of her breasts again. Her nipples, usually large and rosy, tightened into tiny rosebuds of sensation that seemed to shimmer throughout her, leaving no part of her body untouched. His kisses deepened as his fingers played along her stomach, sending ripples of intense feeling in circles, until every inch of her screamed for more.

Justin took his time, hoping that his slow pace would dispel some of Thalia's natural inhibitions and prepare her for what was to come. Thalia's breathing told him that she was willing, eager for him to make love to her, but he wanted to savor these precious moments. He gazed down at her, her golden hair spread around her head like a velvety crown. Her eyes, open wide with passion, invited him, urged him, begged him to continue.

The time for Justin to undress had come. Thalia had reached a state of desire that would continue to simmer for a few seconds until he could resume his deliberate lovemaking. He stripped as quickly as possible, tossing his shirt and trousers without a thought for where they landed.

Now his body was as bare as hers, and pressed against that silken skin that quivered beneath his touch. Though he wanted to gaze at her, to memorize every luscious curve and swell of her body, he realized she must be getting cold, and pulled the covers over them.

Thalia had thought she knew what to expect, but her expectations had, so far, been surpassed so dramatically that she had stopped trying to guess what would happen next and was simply cherishing the experience. Justin's kisses and embraces had promised much, and his fingers were now fulfilling those promises.

Thalia was wild with passion, yearning for him to claim her in that sweetest of acts, when a man and a woman were joined as one. She silently willed him to continue, yet feared that the consummation would fall short of her imaginings. Her inexperience stifled her expectations, but not her pleasure. Filled with desire, she writhed beneath his touch, moaning softly occasionally, when she could no longer withhold her responses to his caresses.

For Justin, this extended prelude was both exquisite torture and sensual madness. His lips captured a pebble-hard nipple and he sucked gently, thrilling at her guttural groan when he did so. He slid his fingers into that moist spot between her legs and knew she was ready for him. Her fingers were laced through his hair, pulling him closer, and he wanted her as much as she wanted him—maybe more.

Rock hard against her, he could no longer rein in his own desires. Justin slowly slid over her, kissing her and coddling her, murmuring sweet words of love as he moved. "Thalia," he whispered, nibbling on her earlobe, "I'll try not to hurt you, love, but—"

"Shh!" Thalia murmured, raising her hips to meet his.

Justin could delay no longer. He positioned himself above that damp warmth, kissed her deeply, and entered her as slowly and gently as possible. His mouth caught her gasp and silenced it. For a few seconds, he held himself still, waiting for some sign that the pain had subsided. When her hips shifted again, Justin began a smooth motion that she could easily follow.

Driven by an animal force, Thalia parried his thrusts and felt her frenzy magnify with each passing moment. She felt the swell of a wave within her, growing heavier, until at last it surged forth and broke, sending sensations over her like sea foam until her entire body quivered with satisfaction.

Justin recognized her release and quickly found his own. He cradled her head between his arms and kissed her, long and hard. Still holding her, he slid to one side and drew her into his embrace, savoring the feeling of her silky skin and hair against his body.

For long minutes, neither of them spoke. Justin didn't trust his voice, and he didn't like the words that were clamoring to be spoken. Many of the words were superlatives; many were love words. There was too much at stake. He couldn't allow himself to become emotionally embroiled with Thalia—no matter how much he loved her.

Cool air swept over Thalia when Justin moved to one side. The moisture that gave evidence of their joining was sticky over the most sensitive part of her, and her breasts ached. She had been thoroughly loved by Justin, and she thoroughly loved him.

The time of her opposition to marriage had come to an end. She could now freely admit that she loved Justin. Listening breathlessly for the words that were sure to come, the proposal of marriage, the confession of loving, she lay there breathless. Several moments passed, and she turned over slightly to look at him.

Where were the love words? Why wasn't he talking to her? Realization took but a few more seconds. The words she ached to hear weren't coming. Justin didn't love her; he'd accommodated her. She'd thrown herself at him, and he had taken what she'd freely given. Nothing, not even the act just consummated between them, bound them together.

Thalia rose slowly, looked around for her dressing gown, glanced back at Justin and returned to her room without speaking. There was nothing she could say.

Puzzled, Justin watched her go. The woman who had given him such pleasure had left without a word, and he had let her go. He needed to think, to decide about his future.

He climbed out of bed and went to sit by the dying embers that had cast such a lovely glow on Thalia's perfect skin. For a few minutes he thought of her, of the pleasure they could share together.

And then he remembered. He remembered why he'd come to Charleston. He remembered that Christmas was coming, and that he was exiled from those he loved. He remembered the waxen face of Alicia as she had lain on her bier, waiting to be buried with her unborn child, a child probably fathered by Donald Freemont. Justin remembered his best friend, dying in his arms. He remembered the agony that had carved such horror into Samuel's face that day on the dueling field. He remembered a young boy, thrust suddenly into an adulthood filled with guilt and pain that could never be erased.

He had to remain strong, committed. With regret, he put his experience with Thalia behind him. He couldn't allow himself to think of it, or his resolve would weaken. He thought of Donald, smugly accepting money from him time and again. Then a new thought occurred to him. Donald might not be the man for whom he was searching. If so, then Justin might have a future with Thalia.

The idea was so farfetched that Justin quickly dismissed it. He'd learned too many things about Donald that pointed to his guilt. He needed but one more clue to prove beyond doubt that Donald had fathered Alicia's child and set in motion a string of events that had torn the lives of the Lee and Kimball families asunder.

His fingers traced the scar across his cheek. Time had healed his external wound, but would never mend the internal injuries he had suffered. Thalia, sweet, dear Thalia, came close. For the first time since Alicia's death, Justin had completely forgotten all that had transpired in that short time.

Thalia, innocent Thalia, was among Donald's victims, too. She just didn't know it yet.

Standing with her back pressed to the bedroom door, Thalia breathed deeply. What had she done?

Her fingers traced down her stomach to the moisture between her legs. The residue was partly hers, partly Justin's. She'd wanted the union, had asked for it. Now she had the consequences to consider. Had their joining produced a child?

She wanted to talk to someone, but who? Who could answer her questions without passing judgment? Pansy could, but Thalia didn't want to burden her friend now, just as she was trying to recover from her own traumatic experiences. Thalia would have to face this situation alone, as she had faced everything for the past few years. There was nobody to confide in.

Justin. A mysterious man, a secretive man, he'd made love to her. Those few minutes had been the most splendid of her life, and she couldn't really regret her actions. She was truly a woman now, in every sense. That had been her aim.

In making love to Justin, she'd destroyed any chance of marriage with anyone else. Justin didn't want to get married, or he would have asked her during those precious moments of lovely afterglow. And she would have nobody else.

Thalia was strong enough to face facts. She'd done what she intended. Now she had to find a way to live with it. If there was a child, she would give it the happiest of homes—somewhere else. She'd tell it about its father, about how he'd died tragically at sea.

But, because she'd given herself to Justin, she faced losing the one thing that she'd worked to regain for these past few years. Sea Mist Plantation.

The next morning, Thalia got up and watched the sunrise. Its steel gray reminded her of the bleak feeling that had accompanied her as she lay down to sleep. Nothing could change what she'd done.

The gray day promised to be busy. She and Justin and Pansy were riding over to Misty Glade, followed by Princess, Clover and Ebenezer, in the wagons. They stopped along the way and chopped down a cedar that would serve as Donald's Christmas tree. Thalia could muster little enthusiasm for the project, but tried hard to smile at everyone and spread a little cheer among them, despite the cold wind that knifed through her cloak and numbed her body until it felt as lifeless as her heart.

With a desolate feeling, Justin watched Thalia mechanically go through a task that had been the source of so much joy the previous day. He knew the fault lay with him. He could have returned to his room without her ever knowing he'd heard her words, and nothing would have changed between them. Or he could have told her he loved her. He wondered how she would react if he told her tonight. Would she fling herself into his arms, abandoning herself to his lovemaking as she did last night? He suspected so, but the words refused to be voiced until he knew what his future—and Donald's—held.

They reached Misty Glade as a cold rain began to fall. The servants scurried back and forth, unloading the wagon and bringing in all the supplies Thalia had packed to make Donald's party wonderful.

Donald poked his head out of the library when he heard the noises of their entry. "Thalia, dear sister, how good to see you back home." He kissed her on the cheek and drew her close.

"Hello, Donald." Thalia chose to ignore his reference to Misty Glade as her home. "We're here to decorate and prepare for the ball and parties."

"Excellent." Donald nodded his head approvingly as Princess brought in a box of cakes and pies. "Good to have you home again, Princess."

Princess appeared not to hear him, for she marched straight past him and out back to the kitchen. Clover, too, followed without speaking.

Pansy came in, carrying a carton of ribbon and assorted items Thalia intended to use for decorating. "Oh, Donald—" Thalia caught his arm "—you remember Pansy Monroe, don't you?"

Donald turned and smiled at Pansy. "I believe so. I think I know your brother, but—"

"Donald!" Thalia glared at him until he closed his gaping mouth. "Pansy is staying with me. You know how I've always complained that I have no one to talk with, no close friends on the island. Well, now I have Pansy."

Donald stared at Thalia for a moment before the explanation dawned on Donald. He knew her brother well, frequented the same clubs. He knew, too, that Tom Monroe had lost a great deal of money, enough to force the sale of the family plantation to pay his gambling debts. "How nice to see you again, Miss Monroe. I'm delighted that Thalia now has a friend close by."

Pansy blushed. Donald knew about her brother and the seemingly hopeless situation she was in. She just hoped that he didn't know about Walter Rice. If she remembered correctly, there had been some breach between Thalia and her brother. That being the case, Pansy thought that Thalia probably wouldn't tell Donald the truth. For that, she was grateful. "Thank you, Mr. Freemont, for inviting me to your party."

Justin appeared at the door with the cedar tree. "Where shall I put this?"

"Justin, old friend," Donald exclaimed, clapping Justin on the back. "What a surprise. I didn't expect you until tomorrow."

"Tomorrow?" Justin asked and propped the tree against the staircase. "Why tomorrow?"

"I thought you'd arrive with the other guests." Donald studied the tree for a moment. "But come on in. How about the ballroom?"

"Fine with me. Lead the way." Justin followed Donald into the ballroom and placed the tree in a corner. "We'll need a bucket with stones to anchor this tree."

"Right. I'll put Nat on it." Donald ushered Justin into the hallway again. "Randolph is already here, Thalia. I'll find him. I know he'll want to say hello the moment he discovers you're here." Donald gazed pointedly at Justin. "Randolph simply adores Thalia."

"Donald! Please!" Thalia retorted, hoping Donald wouldn't embarrass her further.

Randolph almost tumbled down the stairs trying to reach Thalia as quickly as possible. She looked on him pityingly for the first time. He was besotted with her. No matter how she snubbed him, he would adore her. After her night of lovemaking and rejection, she knew how Randolph felt. But after that same night of lovemaking and rejection she knew that she could never marry anyone but Justin.

"Hello, Randolph," she said, casting a glance at Justin to see his reaction to Donald's words. If she expected something obvious, she was disappointed. The only indication that Justin had heard Donald at all was a slight pulsing of a muscle in his jaw. "How nice to see you."

"Oh, Thalia, you're looking lovelier than ever." Randolph bent over and kissed Thalia's hand. He lingered there for a few seconds before straightening himself. Then he noticed Pansy. "Miss Monroe...what a...pleasant surprise."

Pansy smiled as Randolph kissed her hand. "Good to see you, Mr. Taylor."

Justin and Randolph shook hands, but said little. Thalia almost giggled at the hostility that seemed to bristle between them. They were acting like tomcats, preening and posing, each trying to show the other who was the stronger.

With a huge ball scheduled for the following evening, Thalia had little time to observe the two men. She set about decorating Misty Glade so that it would be as beautiful as Sea Mist—or would be if it were in the same excellent condition.

The time flew, and soon every room looked as festive as she could possibly make it.

Randolph and Justin both hovered around, under the pretext of being helpful. In truth, they were more in the way than helpful, but Thalia said nothing.

Pansy fluttered about, taking as much pressure off Thalia as possible. While Thalia strung garlands of popcorn, Pansy arranged boughs of cedar on the mantel and made pretty bows of red satin and lace ribbons. She tied small bows on the Christmas tree and put large ones on the mantel and the windowsills.

Thalia studied Justin, who was holding the ladder for Randolph as he positioned candles on the tree. The two men appeared to be trying desperately to get along in order to impress her and each other. Before the week was out, Thalia feared, they might well come to blows.

Donald put in an occasional appearance. He excused himself by saying that he had urgent plantation business and couldn't put it off. Thalia was glad of that. She didn't want to spend any more time with him than was absolutely necessary. She just wished he'd taken Randolph with him.

To her dismay, Donald took Justin instead, leaving Thalia alone in the ballroom with Randolph. He smiled and came to sit beside her. Randolph tried very hard to make pleasant conversation, but Thalia wasn't really interested in hearing it. Most of his talk concerned news of friends in Charleston, and there was the occasional bit of the local gossip.

"You know, Thalia, my dear—" he licked his lips before continuing "—Miss Monroe is reputed to have left Charleston with a man of questionable heritage."

Doing her best to control her temper, Thalia dropped her needle in the popcorn bowl and stared at Randolph. "I'm sure you don't believe such a thing is possible, Randolph, so I'd suggest that you put an end to such rumors when you hear them. Miss Monroe is at Sea Mist at my invitation. If she hired a man to bring her belongings, then I see nothing wrong. I do, however," she said, emphasizing her words so that he couldn't mistake her meaning, "dislike hearing idle gossip about a subject nobody could possibly know the straight of—particularly you."

"Please, don't mistake my meaning," he declared, taking her idle hand in his. "I never implied that I believed any of that rubbish. I just thought you might want to...to make Miss Monroe aware of what is being said."

Thalia slipped her hand from his and started stringing popcorn again. "If that is the case," she said finally, "then I appreciate it. But I hope never to hear that you passed on this vicious lie to anyone else. I would be...irrevocably disappointed in you, because that would be to imply that I am also at fault."

"Miss—Thalia," Randolph implored, plainly aghast that she would think such a thing, "I shall endeavor to squelch any rumors which might possibly reflect upon you. Why, I'd...I'd call out a man who said anything to besmirch your reputation."

Justin walked into the room as Randolph spoke. Randolph Taylor was in love with Thalia. There could be no doubt of that. Justin doubted that Thalia returned the feeling—in fact, he knew she didn't—but he felt responsible for arresting the possibility of such a relationship before it could ever come to fruition.

Thalia smiled at Justin. She hoped he hadn't heard Randolph's words. She didn't want to have to defend Pansy to anyone, and least of all to Justin. Nor did she want to hear any gossip spread in this house during Donald's party. She'd have to find a way to make sure it simply didn't occur.

At bedtime, Thalia struggled up to her old room. She'd avoided the room all day, hoping to stave off all the bad memories until she was so tired she could hardly think. As she crept into bed, her thoughts turned to Justin. He was sleeping just down the hall, and she wanted desperately to join him in his bed. But to do so would result in further hurt, a deeper hurt that would take years to heal. She punched her down pillow and curled it beneath her head.

Thalia didn't want to think about Justin. She resisted the urge to give in to her desires and sneak down to his room. She suppressed the gnawing inside that told her of the pleasure and comfort awaiting her there.

What did she want from him? What did he want from her? Who was he? Who was she? Questions and more questions, none with easy answers.

The night was long. She tossed and turned, but didn't sleep. She listened to the sounds of the house settling, of the wind rustling through the eaves and the shutters. Every sound seemed to urge her, to beckon to her to leave her bed and go to Justin.

She braved the storm that welled within her, raging and blustering, fueled by indecision and desire. She didn't give in. But somehow, when the sun rose the next morning and the rooster crowed to announce the end of night, her victory seemed hollow, even more of a defeat than she'd ever imagined possible.

Chapter Fifteen

Thalia patted cold water on her puffy eyes. Her pale face and swollen eyes made her look like a child who had been crying all night. Her head ached from lack of sleep, but today would be too busy to allow her much respite.

After spending a morning watching Justin and Randolph try to outdo each other, Thalia decided that a nap following dinner would be appropriate. Her room was the only place she could escape them.

As she went upstairs, Ebenezer opened the door, and a strange man asked for Donald. Thalia wondered what the man could want, but dismissed him as just another of her brother's cronies and went up to her room.

Donald sat across from the investigator. "Well? What have you learned? Come on, man. I'm paying you a fortune for this information, and you have the audacity to sit there smugly and tantalize me with innuendo? I won't stand for it."

The investigator stared at Donald as if he'd underestimated his client. "I'm dreadful sorry, Mr. Freemont. I'll give it to you straightaway."

"That's much better." Donald settled back in his chair while the man read from a sheaf of papers.

"Traced Lionheart back to Richmond, Virginia." He smiled at Donald, as if he were waiting for congratulations on a job well done.

"Well, man, is that it?" Donald leapt from his chair. "Hellfire, I already knew that. He makes no—"

"That ain't all, chum." The dark-haired man continued, "Lost track, but discovered a missing person wanted for murder. Name of Justin Lee. Comes from a good family."

"Justin Lee?" Donald repeated, savoring the name for a moment. It struck no chord of alarm, but touched a vague memory. He could have heard the name anywhere. He couldn't remember exactly where. But the murder incident might just come in handy if Donald got too indebted to Justin, if Justin decided to force him to pay up. "Go on. Is there more?"

"You bet yer life there is." The man grinned, exposing an expanse of toothless mouth. "The bloke's one and the same. Killed some rich gentry, name of…" He searched his notes for a moment. "Oh, yeah, name of Kimball. Peter Kimball."

The name Kimball cleared the cobwebs of his mind. Donald conjured the image of a woman, hardly more than a girl—Alicia Kimball. Why had Justin killed Alicia's brother? "Go on," he finally said.

"Well, 'ere's the good bit." The man licked his lips again, savoring the moment when he'd reveal the most interesting item. "The man Justin Lee—your Justin Lionheart—was engaged to this Kimball wench. Seems he got her in the family way and then refused to marry her. She killed herself, and then her brother called him out. Lee shot Kimball and left. Tore his family up, the story I get."

Donald sank back in his chair. Did Justin know about his relationship with Alicia? Was it possible that Justin had come here searching for him? No, he decided. That was too farfetched. Nobody had known about him, nobody except Alicia. And she'd never have told, because the little twit had fallen in love with him.

"Ahem." The investigator was rising from his chair. "Will there be anything else?"

"Anything—? Er, no." Donald stood and moved around his desk. He escorted the man to the door, wanting to be rid of him before Justin found out that he had hired an investigator. If Justin was suspicious of him, then something would have to be done.

"Then there's the matter of my compensation. I incurred a bit of expense during—"

"Send me a bill." Donald ushered the man out of the library and into the foyer. When they reached the front door, Donald repeated, "Send me a bill." Then he closed the door.

What should I do? he wondered, trying to think of all the implications. *Suppose Justin does know about my relationship with Alicia?* Donald strode quickly back to the library and sat down. He leaned back in the chair and peered out the window, his mind whirling with possibilities. *For now, while Justin is in a lending mood, I'll do nothing. But,* he concluded, *I foresee a time when Mr. Justin Lee—Captain Justin Lionheart—will become expendable.*

Justin and Randolph walked down the stairs together. "Say, Randolph, how long have you known our friend Donald?"

"Oh, all my life, I suppose." Randolph studied Justin for a moment. "He's all right, you know, just a bit unlucky."

"I know. It's too bad." Justin didn't want to raise Randolph's suspicions, but the time had come to find out for sure whether or not Donald was the man for whom he had been searching for so long. As they reached the landing, Justin glanced down the stairs. He didn't see Thalia. He wanted to escort her downstairs, if possible. "Oh, I need to go back to my room for a moment. If you'll excuse me."

"Certainly," Randolph said, and continued walking down the stairs.

Justin waited at the top of the stairs until he heard Randolph greet Pansy. Then he turned and strode to Thalia's door. He listened for a few seconds, hoping to hear a sound that would indicate that she was still there. He raised his hand to knock, but at that very instant, as if by magic, the door opened.

"Oh, Justin," she said, surprised to find him standing outside her door. "Were you looking for me?"

Justin held out his arm. "I was hoping to escort you downstairs."

Thalia, dressed in her newest ball gown, placed her gloved hand on his arm. His trousers, a midnight blue, hugged his thighs, accentuating every ripple of muscle there. His hair, neatly combed, threatened to curl, but for now he looked immaculate—and more desirable than ever. She thought they must make a handsome couple.

Justin stared down at her. He'd never seen her look lovelier. Once, he'd thought she'd never look prettier than she had the night when she'd worn that purplish gown, whatever the name of the color was. Now, dressed in this gown that was the color of the water off Bermuda, a sort of azure blue, she was even more beautiful. It set off her eyes perfectly. The silver stones glittered and glistened as she walked with assurance toward the stairs.

Before he let her take the first step to go down to the foyer, where she would belong to everyone, as the hostess should, he wanted a few moments alone with her. He placed a hand on each of her bare shoulders and stared directly into her eyes. After their magical night of lovemaking, she'd tried to avoid him. Though he knew why, he wanted to call a silent truce for the Christmas season. He didn't like the idea of her hating him—if she did—during the most enchanting time of the year. "Thalia," he began, but he couldn't go on. He leaned down and kissed her gently on the lips.

Thalia didn't want Justin to kiss her. She needed no reminders of the spellbinding night they'd spent together. Every touch, every nuance, of that experience was etched in her memory, to haunt her dreams every night for the rest of her life. There was no way to erase that memory, and she knew she wouldn't even if she could.

Her eyes closed, and he kissed her again. This time, the caress was more forceful, more demanding, and she responded, not of her own volition, but because her body betrayed her. She was powerless to stop him; even if he carried her back to his room and ravished her, she wouldn't try to stay his desires. Hers were every bit as great as his—and she would never have another chance to satisfy the longing that had been growing within her ever since his first caress.

The din of conversation rose from the foyer, and Justin drew away. He knew that he was leaving something unfinished between them, but the time hadn't come—not yet—when he could honestly tell her that he wanted her with him always. No matter how badly Justin wanted to exact his revenge for the deaths of his friends and the havoc wreaked in his life, he didn't want to hurt Thalia. Separating the two was becoming a dilemma he felt he might be inadequate to deal with.

He chose to avoid thinking of a permanent relationship with Thalia, though he craved it more than he had ever coveted anyone or anything in his life. Perhaps their time would come soon.

Guests were already arriving. Justin could delay Thalia no longer without causing Donald to come searching for her. As hostess, she needed to be downstairs greeting the guests. But to let her go downstairs meant he would have to share her, and he wasn't quite ready for that. He closed the distance between them again. This time his kiss promised passion, promised a future of sorts. He wanted to make love to Thalia again—and soon. That was the one thing he knew for certain.

Thalia walked down the stairs. She knew how her dress glittered in the soft light, and was delighted that she'd decided to use the rhinestones. She felt sure that nobody else at the ball would have a gown this pretty.

As she reached the bottom of the stairs, she saw Pansy laughing at something Randolph had said. Thalia noticed that the two of them looked nice together, as if they really belonged. She thought about it for a minute. Randolph really needed someone, and so did Pansy. Maybe, just maybe, if Thalia was completely out of the way, the two of them would discover each other.

Thalia thought about Randolph. He was certainly the loyal sort. He'd remained friends with Donald through the hardest of times—when Donald had owed him money. Randolph had been pursuing Thalia relentlessly ever since she'd come of marriageable age. His loyalty would be perfect for Pansy, whose sweet spirit needed undemanding love. Thalia resolved to work on the relationship. Maybe she'd take Pansy with her to Charleston for Race Week in February.

Donald's guests were arriving in large numbers now. The ferry Thalia had chartered must have arrived. She'd sent every carriage and wagon she could find down to the docks to pick up their guests.

For the next hour, she did little except smile and hug and kiss—or be kissed by—the hundred or so guests. Not all of them were staying all night, but a good many of them were. Thalia, Pansy, Lenore, Margaret and Agatha would be sleeping together. They wouldn't get much sleep, but it would be fun to have all her friends together again.

Lenore caught Thalia's attention and dragged her into the small library. "Look!" she exclaimed, thrusting her finger out for Thalia to see.

"A ring! Oh, Lenore, I'm so happy for you." Thalia hugged her best friend. She was glad that Lenore was getting married. "Who's the lucky man?"

"Edward Nelson, of course." Lenore was fairly dancing about the room. "We're getting married in June. Mother absolutely refuses to consider an earlier date."

"She's right, Lenore," Thalia said. "There are so many things to do before a wedding. And now Margaret is engaged to that Franklin Williams. I declare, I don't know how she can put up with him, he's so dull-witted."

"Dull-witted, but rich, Thalia," Lenore reminded her. "Besides, Margaret isn't exactly considered clever."

"Neither are you," Thalia told her teasingly. "But I love you anyway."

The two women linked arms and returned to the ball. Edward met them at the door to the ballroom. Thalia looked up at him and smiled. "Congratulations, Edward. Take good care of my friend."

"I shall, Thalia." Edward beamed at Lenore, taking her hand and leading her onto the dance floor.

Every time Thalia looked up, she caught Justin staring at her. She wondered why, but couldn't ask. When her duties in the receiving line were completed, she went to the ballroom. Justin almost leapt on her as she walked through the door.

He leaned down and kissed her chastely on the cheek. "Merry Christmas, Miss Freemont."

"Merry Christmas to you, Captain Lionheart." She gazed up at him. His blue-gray eyes were glittering in the soft candlelight, and tiny lines radiated from the corners of his eyes. He looked happier than she'd ever seen him. "Has something happened? You look so happy."

Justin whirled her onto the dance floor without answering. After a turn around the fringes of the floor, he smiled. "I was determined to dance the first dance with the hostess. That's all." He grinned, a little wickedly. "I could see that the eloquent Mr. Taylor had set his sights on you, so I perched beside the door until you walked through.''

"How perfectly devious of you," Thalia scolded him with a teasing lilt to her voice. "And my toes thank you very much.''

"Toes?'' he asked, allowing his gaze to sweep down her body. "What about the rest of you?''

Color rose in Thalia's cheeks. How could she answer such a question without appearing foolish? She decided she couldn't, so she smiled sweetly and batted her eyelashes. She'd seen other girls practice that coquettish maneuver until their eyelids fluttered like a hummingbird's wings; she thought she did fairly well.

"No answer? Well, I understand.'' Justin drew her a little closer.

Thalia could hardly breathe. Her body kept remembering the gentle caress of Justin's hand as it had played down her naked flesh, his lips as they had tugged and teased at her breasts. Just thinking about it, Thalia felt her nipples harden into little pebbles. She wondered if Justin could see them, but didn't look down. She didn't want to draw his attention there if he hadn't already noticed.

Justin's body sizzled with want of her. Every movement they made caused some inadvertent touch and sent waves of heat through him. If this dance didn't end soon, he—and Thalia, as well—would be embarrassed by his physical display. He drew Thalia a little closer, hoping to block everyone else's view of the front of his body. And that, he discovered quickly, was a mistake. With her body close to his, the agony of wanting her increased a thousandfold.

He was in danger now of looking like a schoolboy who couldn't control his own body. Justin willed the dance to be over, but the orchestra played on. They whirled about the floor, their bodies touching occasionally to add fuel to the already raging fire inside him. He maneuvered them toward the door, hoping that when the dance was over he could escape without being noticed.

Lord, will this dance never end? Thalia wondered. She could feel Justin's arousal, and her own must be equally obvious to him. Somehow, she thought, she had to end this dance and quickly. Then she heard the end of the music. Gratefully she darted from the floor, with Justin on her heels. Before she could speak, Randolph tapped her arm.

Randolph quickly claimed her for the next dance. While they were dancing, she talked about Pansy. She raved about Pansy, about everything she could think of that would attract a man to a woman, but Randolph had eyes only for her. He hardly commented about Pansy. Still, the evening was young.

Donald claimed Thalia for the next dance. "Thalia, my dear, I've told Randolph that he has my permission to ask for your hand. I hope you'll do the sensible thing and accept."

Thalia glowered at Donald. "How foolish of you. I've told you before that I won't marry Randolph, no matter what you say."

"You'll be a spinster. Old and decrepit, with no one to look after you," Donald warned her, turning her expertly about the floor. "You're going to marry Randolph, and that's that. I won't listen to your childish whining."

"I am not whining, nor am I marrying that dunderhead." Thalia bit her lower lip to keep from shouting. She had no idea that Donald had gone so far. "You tell him that I'm committed to remaining unwed."

"I'll do no such thing. I'm setting a date for the wedding." Donald squeezed her hand until Thalia almost cried out. "He's planning to ask you this evening. Thalia, this is important to me. Very important. Don't you dare do anything to risk losing him. I've got to have the money from—"

"Money? What money?" she asked, knowing she didn't want to hear what her brother would say next.

Donald tried to smile. "It's nothing that concerns you."

"Tell me this instant, Donald. I demand to know what you've done." Thalia felt a burning in her chest, as if a fire had caught there and was consuming her from within.

Donald had let something slip that he shouldn't have. *But*, he reasoned, *what difference did it make?* She'd find out sooner or later. "Randolph and I have this arrangement. After you're married, he's going to give me Sea—" He'd almost said that Randolph was going to give him Sea Mist, and he knew Thalia would go wild if he related that little secret. "Uh, he's going to give me some money."

Thalia stopped dancing. She stared up at her brother with contempt. If she replied now, she knew, she'd regret her words. She did the only thing she could possibly do—she walked off the dance floor and left Donald standing there. He'd done nothing less than auction her off to the highest bidder. And the price was Sea Mist. Though he'd gone on to say "some money," she knew he was lying.

She almost ran out onto the piazza. The night was cool, and she hadn't stopped to pick up her shawl or cloak. She wanted to get away, from Donald, from Randolph, from everyone. She wanted to return to Sea Mist, where none of these awful, upsetting things ever happened. Why wouldn't Donald listen to reason? Why didn't Randolph understand that she wanted nothing to do with him?

Justin watched Thalia run out the door. His first impulse was to go after her, but he hesitated. He spotted Donald and Randolph standing by the punch bowl and sauntered over as if he'd seen nothing out of the ordinary. As he approached, he heard something about an exchange. Thalia for Sea Mist. He felt sick. He knew how much she loved her plantation, and he knew for a certainty that she would never willingly allow Donald to do such a thing.

"Justin," Donald said, looking pensively at his guest, "I understand you're from around Richmond, Virginia."

"Yes, that's right." Justin wondered where Donald had gotten his information. Not many people knew he was from Richmond. But this was just the opening he needed. He had to pursue this conversation. "Why do you ask?"

"Oh, I visited there once." Donald watched Justin's eyes for some sign of recognition, but there was none.

Justin carefully schooled his features, holding his muscles rigid to keep from showing emotion. He wanted to attack Donald right there, but knew he couldn't. The time wasn't right; nor was a physical attack the way to hurt Donald. Humiliation was the only way. Donald would have to lose his plantation and see his sister disgraced.

Justin had gambled frequently with Donald, allowing him to sink further and further in debt. In a few weeks' time, he would hold enough of Donald's markers to demand payment in full.

Donald's only recourse would be to sell his property, or give it to Justin in exchange for forgiving the debts.

"Say, Dof, where did Thalia go?" Randolph asked, peering first at the dancers and then at the people standing around the dance floor.

Dof. The name struck Justin like a kettleful of molten lead. Rage burned in him as he watched Donald look around casually for his sister.

Justin edged away from Donald and slipped out the door to find Thalia. He knew, with as much certainty as a man could have, that she'd gone down to the beach. Her canvas would still be tucked away where they'd left it the last time.

Justin loped along like a lion that had spotted its victim, like the huge, bloodthirsty cat that had provided the inspiration for his name. Justin Lionheart. The fiercest of all predators. And this predator had spotted his prey.

Revenge. Revenge. Revenge. The words pounded in his mind as he ran along and finally caught up with Thalia. His feelings for her, those that he had tried so hard to deny, had confused him for a time, had delayed his search for Dof. The search was over. Justin's path was clear. Humiliate and destroy. That was his task. To humiliate and destroy Donald Freemont.

"Thalia," Justin called as he approached her. "Wait up."

Justin caught up with her and slid his arm around her waist. "What's wrong? I saw you leave the ballroom as if you were upset."

Anger had filtered through Thalia's body until every part of her rebelled at Donald's unmitigated gall. The nerve of him, promising her to Randolph in exchange for Sea Mist. "Nothing. I . . . I just wanted some fresh air, to be alone."

Justin could understand why. With such a bastard for a brother, her life must be awfully hard to take. "I hope you don't mind if I come along."

"No, I don't mind."

They walked along, with Justin's arm tucked around her waist, until they reached the beach. There, Justin stopped beneath the copse of trees that hid her canvas. Without asking, he pulled out the neatly folded material and spread it on the sand. Without speaking, they sat down side by side.

The tide was out. The waves whispered softly as they rode gently up the beach a ways and then retreated. Here and there, a gull called, but the night was otherwise quiet.

Justin looked at her. Moonlight bathed her features in a soft glow, accenting the gold in her hair, making it rich and lustrous. She'd worn it in curls tonight, and its sheen was lovely. Justin captured a curl between his fingers. Its springy texture coiled around his fingers, and he pulled slowly, stretching it until it reached nearly to her bottom.

Justin had never felt this way about Alicia. His bond to her had been superficial, except for the debt he had owed her father. Peter Kimball, Sr., had saved Hannah Lee, Justin's mother, from drowning when her carriage had slid off into the river. That was something Justin could never repay. Mr. Kimball, Sr., was alone now, because his son and daughter were dead. And Justin, who should have been the one to console him, hadn't even been able to offer his condolences when Peter had died.

Close now to reaching his goal, Justin had to bide his time. He also had to steel his heart against invasion by the beautiful sister of his nemesis. Life for the next few weeks would be difficult for Justin. The prospect of spending Christmas with Thalia suddenly became almost unbearable.

Thalia glanced up at him. His profile was strong, but there was a sadness sometimes in his eyes that she couldn't really define. Maybe his life was as miserable as hers. No, that couldn't be. Men didn't have to face the same problems as women. Men were automatically accepted, and their opinions heard with real interest. Men could walk away from an unpleasant situation more easily than a woman. Men, who were the real culprits, often got a woman or girl in trouble and didn't suffer any censure, while the woman was ostracized forever, along with her child.

And then there was marriage. Men did the choosing, and women had to make it work.

She looked at Justin with new regard. Marriage? Donald desperately wanted her to marry. Of course, he wanted her to marry Randolph. Thalia decided that if there were any way for a woman to trap a man into marriage, she was going to find out what it was and exploit it. She was going to marry Justin Lion-heart, if it was the last thing she ever did.

Justin knew that Thalia needed comforting now. No matter how angry he was at Donald, he couldn't just let Thalia suffer. The predator would have to wait. Justin hugged her closer, beneath the live oak, and kissed her forehead. ''Don't worry, Thalia. Everything is going to work out.''

Thalia looked up at him, relishing the tenderness of his touch. *Everything is going to work out, all right,* she decided. *But it's going to be because I'm the one doing the maneuvering. Fate can stand aside. I'm at the helm of this ship, now.*

She melted into his arms, deliberately pressing her breasts against him. Hearing his sharp intake of breath, she raised her mouth to meet his. When his lips touched hers, she opened her mouth wide, darting her tongue into his mouth and then probing, meeting his tongue and sparring.

Thalia's heart flew with the sureness of an eagle. She'd caught Justin off guard, and he'd responded passionately to her kisses. With a lilting laugh, she broke free of his embrace and ran breathlessly back to the house. Nothing made a man want a woman more than knowing he couldn't have her. She'd left him wanting more, the more that he wouldn't get. She'd left him wanting, and the only way for him to get her would be to marry her.

Justin didn't know what to think. He'd followed her to the beach, intent on comforting her, but his little wounded kitten had turned into a tigress in his arms.

Chapter Sixteen

Early the next morning, the Misty Glade slaves brought out long tables and placed them down near the beach. The guests who'd stayed overnight, as well as those who lived on the island, strolled down to the beach at dinnertime.

The young black boys who were the sons of Misty Glade slaves, had spent the day gathering the whitefoot oysters that were so abundant on the beaches of Edisto Island. Great fires had been set on the beach, and hundreds of the oysters were dumped on the coals to cook. The oysters, tender and succulent, were served on platters to all the guests.

"These are delicious," Randolph said, wiping away a juicy trail that led from his mouth to his chin. "I've never tasted better."

"Thank you. We pride ourselves on our seafood, particularly the oysters," Donald said, sliding a knife into an oyster shell.

Thalia glared at her brother. He'd done nothing to plan the ball, and even less for the oyster roast, yet he was accepting all the accolades as if he'd prepared the oysters himself. She turned the other way, no longer able to listen to his bragging.

After the grand feast of roasted oysters, a fine dinner was served beneath the trees. The guests ate fresh roasted flounder, a tasty chowder, greens from Sea Mist's gardens, and a delicious flummery. Many were heard to say that they couldn't even rise from their seats.

The younger people played several games of quoits. Thalia proved to have a good eye, and several of her tosses ringed the pegs in the ground and stayed. Justin and Donald wagered about who would come the closer, and Justin won almost every time.

But Donald didn't seem to be worrying very much. Justin never asked for money to back up the bets. Randolph hung around, vowing that he was no good at the game. When he was finally persuaded to play, Thalia had to agree with him. He simply had no prowess when it came to tossing the rings.

As evening approached, everyone sauntered back to the house. Though nobody seemed hungry, Princess produced a supper of roast pork and sweet potatoes. At the end of the meal, there was nothing left on the platters.

Thalia finally climbed the stairs and headed for bed. As she approached her room, she hesitated. Agatha, Margaret, Lenore and Pansy were there, and Thalia could hear them laughing. They were still in a jovial mood, while Thalia's was pensive. She could stand it for one more night.

Dawn found her standing on the piazza, already fully clothed. In just a few short hours, she could return to Sea Mist. Most of the guests were leaving this morning, though a few of Donald's friends would remain until after the New Year. Horse races, boat races, and other amusements were planned, but Thalia didn't have to participate.

She was going home. She had hardly seen Lenore. Edward Nelson had arrived with the Calhouns, and had taken almost all of her time. But that was all right with Thalia, because she had discovered that she had little in common with her best friend. Thalia found that thought disturbing. When they had been little girls, she and Lenore had vowed to remain best friends forever.

Lenore, along with her mother, had helped Thalia to survive some difficult days. Immediately after the deaths of her aunt and uncle, Lenore had come and stayed to comfort Thalia. When Thalia's father had died, Lenore had been there, quietly helping Thalia to see that none of the agony she'd suffered through the years because of her father's rejection had been her fault. Lenore, in her own silly way, had pointed out that there was no need for Thalia, a mere child, to feel guilty about something her father, a grown man, had done.

Before Lenore left Misty Glade, Thalia drew her aside. She hugged her friend gratefully, having accepted the fact that Lenore would always be a lovable twit. As Uncle Martin had always said about Lenore, "When the Lord was handin' out common sense, somebody jiggled his hand."

No matter what happened, the two women would be friends for life. Thalia, however, said a prayer of thanks that they didn't live closer together. Now her thoughts turned to Randolph and Pansy. How could she bring them closer together?

Thalia decided that there was little she could do for the present. She'd have to wait until February, until Race Week, to do anything at all.

Home again. Thalia ran up the front steps. Justin, Pansy and the others trailed after her. She went to her room, changed into her work clothes and rode out to look for Adam. She found him in the vegetable gardens, overseeing the harvest of onions, potatoes, greens and cabbages.

"Hello." She dismounted and hugged him impulsively. "How is it going?"

"We'll have a feast this Christmas," Adam declared, rubbing his chin thoughtfully. "I've already sent a roast of beef to the kitchen, along with a turkey and some hams. We're going to roast a hog down in the slave quarters."

"Mmm, sounds good." Thalia surveyed her fields. Almost anything would grow in this rich black soil. The climate was so moderate that they could cultivate two crops a year of many varieties. "Make sure that there's plenty for everybody. I've ordered extra fruit, too. Our people will have the best Christmas ever. Make sure they know that they're supposed to come to the big house in the morning."

Christmas Eve, she thought as she rode back to the stable. As a child, she'd always loved Christmas here at Sea Mist Plantation. Aunt Molly had made sure that there were gifts for everyone, especially Thalia. Uncle Martin had brought in vast quantities of meats and vegetables, and the feasting had gone on all day. Christmas had been a magical time. A time of giving and loving and forgiving. A time when the animals in the barns talked, or so the story went. A time to celebrate the birth of Christ.

This year, Thalia had ordered that no work was to be done for two days, except what was necessary to feed everyone. Those who had jobs to do would have extra time off later. This celebration would be the most special ever.

And Justin would be here.

Christmas Eve was a quiet time at Sea Mist. Supper was delicious, but everyone was too excited to really notice. Curiosity was running high among the house servants and the slaves, but Thalia said nothing. Their special day would begin early in the morning.

But this evening belonged to her and her friends. Thalia had asked the Woodsleys to join her at supper, along with Justin and Pansy. After the meal, the small group retired to the parlor to celebrate their Christmas Eve together.

Thalia handed out the presents. She'd found a pretty shawl for Irene, who was always cold. For Adam, Thalia had bought a new hat. With childish delight, she watched as Pansy opened her gift, the beautiful ivory-and-lace fan and the matching shawl.

Then she handed Justin his gift. He took it and peered at the thin package for a moment as if he were afraid to open it. He smiled at her and removed the paper and lace bow wrapping the gift. When he lifted the painting and gazed at it for a long time, she didn't know what to do. She couldn't tell if he liked it or hated it.

Finally, he turned to look at her. With a slight catch in his voice, he said, "Thank you, Thalia. I shall treasure this always. Regardless of where I am, I'll always have the *Spirit of Justice* with me.

Thalia received a little dish of scented soap flakes from Pansy. "Where did you get this?" Thalia asked, knowing Pansy hadn't been off the island.

"I asked Lenore to get it for me." Pansy hugged herself nervously. "Do you like it? It's rose-scented, like you always wear."

"I adore it. Thank you, so much." Thalia took her package from Irene and opened it. "Oh, what a pretty mirror." Thalia lifted it and looked at herself. It was a hand mirror, silver, with a curved handle that fitted right in her hand.

Irene blushed and smiled happily. "I bought it with some of my money. I . . . I never had any money of my own before."

"Well, you shouldn't have spent it on me," Thalia scolded. She realized what a prize she had in Irene. She hadn't expected a gift at all. "Thank you both."

Justin watched all the others exchanging gifts. He had something for Thalia, but he wanted to wait until they were alone to give it to her. He caught her gaze and hoped that his expression conveyed that he'd give her a present later.

"Thalia, don't you play the piano?" Pansy asked. "Play for us. We'll sing."

Thalia moved to the piano stool and sat down. She played a few light pieces, and then began to play Christmas carols. They sang and danced and played for a long time, until they were all exhausted. Around midnight, Thalia stood and said, "I think it's time for bed. We have a busy day tomorrow—starting very early."

At that, Adam and Irene left. Pansy soon excused herself and went upstairs, leaving Thalia alone with Justin. They settled on the sofa near the fire, and for a long time they watched the flames leaping and playing along the logs. The smell and feel of Christmas was everywhere, and Thalia felt happy and content that her first Christmas at home was going to be wonderful.

And then Justin kissed her. She melted into his arms, savoring the passion that seemed to dwell just beneath the surface to be rekindled at a single touch. When he drew away, she looked at him, puzzled.

"This is for you." He took a small box from his waistcoat and handed it to her.

Thalia felt the weight of the small box and knew that it must be jewelry. With shaking fingers, she opened it. Inside, nestled in a bed of cotton, she found a silver necklace with a large square sapphire in the center and several smaller ones clustered around it. Beneath the necklace were earrings that matched.

"Oh, Justin, I never had anything this lovely." She felt tears mist her eyes, knowing that he was kind and honest, and that she was using every womanly trick to trap him into marrying her. Her guilt was almost overwhelming. "I . . . I can't accept anything so expensive. Oh, but it's lovely . . . truly lovely."

"Take it, Thalia," he urged. The sapphires meant little enough to him, except for the way they'd look on Thalia. He hoped that one day when he had to leave her, she'd think of him every time she wore them. The expensive jewelry was his way of saying how sorry he was—before he had to abandon her. "They were made especially for you."

"Made for me?" she asked as she slipped the necklace around her neck and tried to fasten it. Her fingers were shaking too badly.

Justin moved her hands gently and did the job for her. "They're the exact color of your eyes when I kiss you."

She looked up into his eyes, eyes that were warm and wonderful now, with the beautiful blue-gray color she loved so much. She smiled a little and pursed her lips. "Prove it," she said, holding up her mirror.

He didn't need to be asked twice. He kissed her, deeply, plunging his tongue into her mouth and pressing her back on the brocade sofa. She went limp in his arms, and the mirror dropped from her hand, thudding softly on the plush Aubusson carpet beneath the sofa.

The house all around them was silent, with everyone sleeping in anticipation of the coming festivities. Thalia and Justin slid from the sofa to the floor, still locked in an embrace. She caught her breath when he moved from her lips to her cheek and trailed kisses down her neck to the soft mounds of her breasts.

Justin wanted to rip Thalia's gown off, but he took his time, unbuttoning each pearl button and finally slipping the softly rustling dress and crinolines over her head. He lifted her hips and pulled off her pantalets, then concentrated on his own clothing. Within a span of seconds, they both lay naked, except for the sapphires Thalia wore, in front of the Christmas tree.

The fragrance of cedar mingled with that of roses, the crackle of a dying fire and the soft glow of candlelight combined to furnish the two lovers with a romantic ambience that neither could have consciously planned. Thalia's hair, now coming loose from its braids, lay in a soft circle around her head, and

Justin wrapped his hands in it, luxuriating in the silken texture.

For what seemed a long time, they lay there, gently exploring each other's bodies. Thalia shyly traced the dark curly hair of his chest down his stomach to that mysterious place, and touched him there for the first time. The throbbing length felt firm in her hand, and yet the skin was soft.

Justin groaned and turned her onto her back. His fingers dancing over her skin, he kissed her long and hard, imprisoning her with one hand and teasing her with the other. And then he slid over her silky legs and entered her.

Thalia didn't feel a sharp pain this time, though the discomfort returned for a few moments. His slow motion gradually obliterated any uneasiness she might have had, and she joined joyfully in the steadily increasing rhythm.

This time, Justin waited until he knew she was near to gaining satisfaction, and then slowed his pace. Again and again, he brought her to the brink of rapture and drew her back, insisting on prolonging the pleasure.

When she thought she could stand no more, she met his thrusts vigorously, clinging to him and demanding, "Now, Justin, love me now."

Her words were like liquid passion pouring over him. Justin could no longer control his movements. Their hips met in wild abandon until both were satisfied and spent. He remained inside her, kissing her, cuddling her, murmuring sweet words to her, until he made love to her again. This time, their lovemaking was sweet and gentle at first, slow and deliberate. As the pace increased, the candles on the Christmas tree began to wink out, leisurely concealing their satiated bodies in the dying light.

The scent of their joyous union mingled with the Christmas fragrances, and for a few moments they lay there, gazing at each other in the very last vestiges of light. Thalia fell asleep with her head on Justin's shoulder.

Justin held her as if she were the most fragile piece of fine crystal he'd ever possessed. Her sweet, trusting face was a form of accusation that he couldn't deny. He knew that his coming victory over Donald would hurt her terribly, maybe irreparably. He pushed that thought aside. He kept trying to concentrate on the fact that she was a planter's daughter and, as such, would eventually display the self-centeredness he loathed. If—and when—she did, he would feel much better about what he had to do. He hoped he would. He prayed he would.

Somewhere deep in the house, a clock struck three o'clock. Justin knew that he couldn't expose Thalia in her current naked state to the inquisitive eyes of servants and friends. He kissed her gently, teasing her awake with his caresses. "Come, Thalia, my darling, let me take you to your room."

Thalia awoke sluggishly. She'd been dreaming of Justin, of his kind face, a face that was somehow shrouded with mystery. She wanted desperately to know what he was hiding, and how it would affect her. She slipped silently into her room, where a lamp burned low.

Justin tossed her clothes onto the rocking chair and helped her into bed. He wanted to linger there, but knew that Clover would be in early to awaken Thalia. He kissed her gently and then whispered, "Good night, love."

Thalia's eyes sprang open. He'd called her *love*. Her plan was working. She wondered if she could live with herself after using every womanly wile she could discover. She'd never been a deceitful woman, and she hated herself for becoming one, but she knew no other way.

She had to keep Sea Mist and she feared that if she didn't marry soon Donald would somehow cheat her out of it. Thalia decided that she must remain committed to her present path. She'd have the rest of their lives to make it up to Justin.

Morning came too soon at Sea Mist on Christmas Day. Thalia dragged herself out of bed and splashed water on her face. She wore nothing except the sapphires Justin had given her. The necklace lay accusingly about her neck. What she was doing was wrong, and she knew it. But she was desperate to maintain her hold on Sea Mist.

She dressed quickly and went downstairs. At seven o'clock she went out back and rang the plantation bell. Its first peal jarred her nerves, but as she rang it she found that the bell's deep musical tones, echoing across the plantation, pleased her.

Soon, black people were coming from everywhere. There were more than a hundred of them, counting the children. Everyone, including Justin and Pansy, gathered in the nearly empty ballroom, because they couldn't all get into the parlor. Thalia sat by the huge pile of gifts and handed them out as the slaves came by. Several of them had made presents for her—a cake, a little wooden bird carved from cypress, a tiny arrangement of dried flowers in a small basket. She was touched by their thoughtfulness. Many whispered that they were happy to have her back home.

She gave all the children extra portions of fruit. Thalia had bought a small wooden toy for each of the children, as well as some warm clothing. For each of the adults, she had a new outfit that included a warm cloak. When all the slaves who worked outside had been given their gifts, Thalia stood and surveyed the room. Everyone looked happy. She asked Princess to bring in the feast.

Because there were no tables, everybody, including Thalia, sat on the floor and ate heartily. After dinner, the slaves sang some of their haunting spirituals, leaving tears in Thalia's eyes. Thalia asked several to remain after the others left. Gradually mothers took small dark hands and returned to the cabins for nap time. All the rest of the slaves soon followed, leaving only the house servants and those Thalia had selected to remain.

About twelve or fifteen expectant gazes followed her as she paced for a moment. She turned and smiled at them. "I want to... Each of you has been chosen for a reason. I've worked with you, talked with you, and listened to you. And I have another gift for you."

A whisper crossed the room and gradually died down. She continued, "I want to teach you all to read. I've heard some of you lament that you can't read the Bible, and I'm going to make sure that there are enough of you who can read so that everyone on this plantation can hear the word of God. Maybe later you can teach others to read." Thalia paused and looked at her chosen students. "But you must keep this a secret. You all know that teaching slaves to read is a crime."

One woman jumped up and embraced Thalia. "Praise the Lord! Hallelujah! Praise be to the name of Jesus!"

Several amens were heard around the room, and Thalia smiled. "We'll begin very soon after the New Year's celebration." She handed each of them a little Bible that would be their first reading text. "Go back to your families now."

So far, Thalia had withheld the house servants' gifts. When they were finally alone, Thalia handed each one of them the gift she had chosen. The shawls, aprons and new shoes for the women, the new shoes, the cloak and the new shirts for Ebenezer. As they finished opening their presents, Thalia gave each of them the envelope that Mr. Stevens had sent her.

None of them could read. They simply stared at the official documents enclosed. Thalia dabbed at the corners of her eyes. The time had come for her to reveal that each of the three slaves sitting before her was no longer a slave. Thalia sat back down. They looked at her expectantly, and she said, "When I teach you to read, this will be the document—after the Bible, I hope—that you will treasure most. Those are your official release papers. You are no longer slaves."

She'd expected a lot of things, but not the silence that resulted. After a moment, they turned to each other and then back to her. Clover finally said, "Miss Thalia, does that mean we has to leave?"

Thalia breathed a sigh of relief. "No, Clover, it means that you'll be getting wages for what you now do. But you may leave if you wish."

"But we don't have to go, do we?" Ebenezer asked, fingering his new clothes as if they'd be taken back.

"No, Ebenezer." Thalia hugged him. "You're always welcome here. You and I—all of us, I guess—belong together. But now we'll be together because we want to be, not because one of us owns the others."

"Then I'm still gonna be your cook? And I can still take the leavin's home to my cabin?" Princess asked, staring at the important paper. "I like to cook, Miss Thalia. I like to cook for you. I was born here, and I been cooking here since before Mistah Martin and Miz Molly was married."

"You'll always cook here at Sea Mist Plantation, Princess." Thalia hugged each of her friends. They'd been part of her life since she'd first come to Sea Mist. Now they could stay or go. She believed they'd all stay. "I've arranged a wage for you. Mr. Stevens will be out one day to talk to you about it. He'll set it aside for you, and you can do whatever you want with it. Now, go on and enjoy your holiday. Don't worry about us. We'll have leftovers.''

The three servants left. They had all carefully tucked their envelopes into the Bibles they'd received. Thalia, Pansy and Justin were finally alone to spend a quiet day together.

Justin left soon after Christmas. He couldn't stand being with Thalia, knowing what he had to do. The longer he stayed with her, the more difficult his task would be, because he was becoming dangerously involved with her. When he reached Charleston, he took the first cargo he could find and sailed for the Bahama Islands. He planned to stay gone for at least a month while he plotted his revenge.

Thalia spent the next few weeks cleaning the house, putting everything in order again and getting ready for the spring planting. Pansy helped with the house, but she seemed a little distant. After a long silence one day, Thalia placed her hands on Pansy's shoulders and pressed her into a chair. ''All right, tell me what's troubling you.''

''Me? Why, nothing,'' Pansy said, fingering the fabric of her skirt.

''Pansy, I know when something is wrong.'' Thalia sat down and sighed. She missed Justin, and hadn't heard from him in several weeks. ''Please trust me enough to confide in me.''

Pansy fidgeted for a few seconds longer. ''Thalia, I really like Randolph Taylor, and I know he's mad for you. I'm trying not to . . . to like him so much, but—''

Thalia whooped with laughter. It felt so good to laugh again as she had as a child. ''Oh, Pansy.'' Thalia tried to compose herself. ''Don't you worry about hurting my feelings. I've been attempting to find a way to bring you and Randolph together, but I didn't know exactly how to go about it.''

''You're not angry?'' Pansy asked, blushing under Thalia's gaze.

''No, I'm not. I'm delighted.'' Thalia studied her friend for a moment. ''I think we both need a trip to Charleston to get us out of the winter doldrums. Why not go to town for Race Week?''

"Both of us?" Pansy shifted uncomfortably. "I don't know if I'm ready to go to an event like that."

"Of course, you are," Thalia replied. She decided that Pansy could spend a little more time with Randolph, perhaps draw his interest. "We'll have a splendid time."

"Where would we stay...if we went?" Pansy wasn't sure she wanted to go, no matter what Thalia said. She hadn't been back to Charleston since she'd left with Walter Rice. "I'm afraid of what people might say, Thalia. What if Walter went back to Charleston and said something?"

"Nonsense. When I was there, I made sure that Mrs. Kirkley understood that you were here as my guest and that you had money of your own." Thalia was growing angry, not because of Pansy's shyness about returning to the city, but because of the nature of people. They always seemed to look for a weakness and pick at it until the poor victim either slunk ignominiously away or died. "I'll be damned if I'll let that happen to you."

"Thalia!" Pansy exclaimed, gaping at her friend. "I've never heard such talk from you."

Thalia leapt to her feet and began to pace. There were many examples of injustice in the world that she could cite to her friend, but none would really convince Pansy of the need to fight back. She knew that Pansy would rise to the occasion and do whatever was necessary when the time came. "Pansy, we're not going to let those...those gossiping old snipes keep you from enjoying your stay in Charleston. We'll find an ally. I think Randolph will do nicely. We'll stop in to see him first thing."

"I'm not sure..." Pansy saw the determination in Thalia's face and sighed. It was no use to argue with Thalia when she set her mouth that way. She was going back to Charleston.

Thalia smiled. She hadn't heard from Justin, except for a note thanking her for her hospitality during Christmas. His words had been kind, thoughtful, but somehow sterile, and yet, Thalia thought, the touch of him could be felt through the ink and paper. She missed the touch of him, but his scent lingered on the note, and she put it in her little casket of treasures.

She would go to Charleston to see Justin. By the end of Race Week, she expected to be engaged to him.

Chapter Seventeen

Race Week in Charleston began the first Wednesday in February. People came from all over the state, from all over the country—even from other countries—for the festivities. Visitors to the state during Race Week were given ribbons that admitted them to all events without charge.

Thalia and Pansy descended from their carriage and walked beneath the covered archway into the ladies' stand. They went upstairs to the viewing room, one wall of which was all windows, and sat down to await the beginning of the first heat.

"I didn't come last year," Thalia said, peering right and left to see who had arrived. "Everyone will be here."

Pansy sat quite still. "I hope not."

"Silly, Mr. Rice can't get in here. Even if he came to the race, he'd have to sit in the citizens' stand." Thalia slipped her arm around Pansy's shoulders. "Don't worry. Let's go out onto the balcony where we can see better."

"If you insist," Pansy replied, rising to follow her.

They arrived on the balcony in time for the first heat of the day. The race was an exciting one. Pansy seemed to forget her problems for a little while, and Thalia was glad. During the time between races, she spotted Donald, Randolph and Justin.

Now she faced a dilemma. She could try to let Justin notice her and take the chance that Donald and Randolph would see her, as well, or she could simply forget about seeing Justin. No matter how much she wanted to see Justin, she didn't want to face her brother right now.

Thalia returned her attention to the races. There were several heats for each event. Many of Charleston's best-known citizens had horses entered, and there were horses from all over the country, as well. Maybe Sea Mist would have an entry one day.

Justin glanced at the ladies' stand. His eye was immediately drawn to the golden chignon and blue hat that Thalia was wearing. He'd felt someone staring at him; now he knew who it was. If he hadn't been with Donald and Randolph, he felt sure, Thalia would have joined him.

He wondered where she was staying. Since Donald was in town, Justin felt sure she had taken a room at the Charleston Hotel. He would see her there later. No matter how hard Justin tried, he couldn't keep his eyes off her. He hadn't seen her in about six weeks, and the time had been agonizing.

Thalia knew she had caught Justin's eye. She felt warm inside, as if he were sending her waves of heat, even across the distance. With a smile that spoke volumes, she finally averted her eyes. She knew where he was staying, and she would see him later.

The South Carolina Jockey Club Ball was to be held on Friday night. Thalia had been busy with Mr. Stevens at the bank and with Mr. Saunders, the cotton buyer, before the races began, but there was little she could do now, because all the most important businesses in Charleston closed for Race Week. Fortunately, planning for the new crop of cotton took little time, since this year she had only Sea Mist Plantation with which to concern herself.

Thalia was walking up the street one afternoon when she spotted Donald and Randolph. She glanced around, trying to find someplace to hide until they passed, but all she saw was the tavern. Inhaling deeply, she hurried up the steps and opened the door. Without wasting a single moment, she ducked inside and closed the door behind her. If she could stand there for about one minute, they would pass and she could return to the street.

"Hello, Thalia. How nice to see you again." Justin stood there, smiling, hoping she was still speaking to him, even though he hadn't been to see her recently. He had expected to meet with her at the hotel or someplace else; he'd never thought to see her again in the tavern.

"Oh . . . hello, Justin," Thalia replied, trying to smile.

"Am I foolish to hope you were looking for me?" he asked, walking over to her side.

"Uh, no. Well, not precisely." She leaned forward enough to peer out the window. Donald and Randolph had passed by, apparently without seeing her. It was unfortunate that she'd run into Justin in the tavern, but lucky that she'd evaded Donald. She wouldn't even have minded seeing Randolph, because she wanted to direct his attention to Pansy once again. "I was . . ."

Justin looked past her and out the window. He, too, saw Donald and Randolph walking down the street. "You were avoiding your brother? That's why you came in here?"

"If you must know, yes." Thalia wished Justin would suggest that they leave the tavern. Even though she hadn't been accosted by a drunk yet, the possibility existed.

Justin shook his head sadly and opened the door. "You might have saved yourself the effort. He already knows you're in town. Shall we go?"

Thalia stepped back into the sunlight and waited for Justin. "How does he know? Did you tell him after seeing me at Washington Race Course?"

"Afraid not." Justin took her arm. "He already knew. Mrs. Kirkley, I believe, told Lenore, and she went directly to Donald's town house to see you. Unfortunately, Donald was at home at the time."

"I suppose he knows where I'm staying, then." Thalia didn't want to see Donald, but she did want to stay in town long enough for the ball.

Justin shook his head. "No. He asked me if I knew, and I just asked why he thought I should know."

"You answered his question with a question and avoided answering it at all." Thalia laughed. "That's good enough for Donald."

"I'll see you back to the hotel, if that's where you're going." Justin took her arm and looked down into her eyes. He'd forgotten just how blue Thalia's eyes could be at times. *No, I haven't forgotten,* he told himself, *I just chose not to remember.*

But he had remembered. Every night away from her had been filled with dreams of her—when he could sleep. He'd thought of almost nothing else. His crew found him grouchy and avoided him. Edward, when he was around, complained about Justin's ill temper and persistent bad mood. Even though he'd tried to concentrate on achieving his goal of revenge, Justin had hardly been able to concentrate. No, he hadn't forgotten.

Thalia felt the power of his touch, something she'd dreamed of ever since Christmas. A surge of heat seemed to ride along every bone in her body and then radiate out until her body fairly tingled with excitement. Oh, how she'd missed him. She set her mind to capture him for sure during this visit.

Justin glanced down at Thalia as they walked. "Are you attending the ball on Friday evening?"

"I... Pansy and I haven't decided." Thalia looked back over her shoulder to make sure Donald wasn't following her. She didn't want him to see where she went. Nor did she want Donald to suspect that she had plans for Justin, big plans. By the end of this week, she and Justin Lionheart would be engaged to be married.

They reached the hotel, and Thalia smiled prettily when they stopped outside her room. "Thank you for walking with me, Justin. I seem to run into you every time I go into that tavern. I can't imagine why."

Justin laughed and propped his hand on the wall behind her. His face was hardly more than an inch from hers, and he was becoming quickly intoxicated by her fragrance and her magnetism. "Could it be that you've been in that tavern only twice?"

Thalia felt that if she moved, even to answer his question, her lips would touch his. She wanted him to kiss her; she craved the intimacy that they'd shared. But she wanted to leave him unsatisfied. "Could be," she answered, ducked beneath his arm and went inside, closing the door behind her.

Thalia leaned against the door, breathing heavily, for a few seconds. She'd almost given in. If she'd stood there another second, she would have kissed him.

Pansy walked into the room and stared at Thalia for a minute. "What happened? You look as if you've seen a ghost."

"Almost, Pansy, almost." Thalia took her cloak off and laid it on a chair. "I nearly missed running into Donald. Fortunately, I stepped inside a tavern door, and—"

"Thalia Payton Freemont, you know you didn't!" Pansy exclaimed, her eyes wide with shock.

"Oh, gracious, Pansy, it's just a restaurant where men go. It's not a—a bordello, or anything like that."

"Thalia! You know a lady doesn't go into either place," Pansy scolded, dropping into a chair near the fire. "And she never, but never, mentions a bordello. You shouldn't even know what that is."

"Pansy, don't get so worked up over nothing. I merely stepped inside the door," Thalia said, defending her actions. "I'd rather have gone into a bordello than to have talked with Donald."

"Lord, save us," Pansy prayed aloud. "You're certainly turning into a hoyden. I declare, you're getting as bad as Lenore."

"Now, Pansy, be serious. You know I didn't want to see Donald." Thalia walked over to the fireplace and held out her hands. "It's chilly outside. Besides, I didn't even want him to know I was in town."

"Well, did he see you?"

"No, he didn't, thank God." Thalia sat down on the sofa and tucked her feet beneath her. She smiled at Pansy. "But I did see Justin Lionheart."

Pansy sat a little straighter and raised her eyebrows thoughtfully. "Where did you see him?"

"In the tavern," Thalia replied thoughtfully. "Pansy, I'm going to somehow get that man to ask me to marry him. And he'll do it this week."

Thalia could hardly contain her excitement about the ball. In reality, she cared little about the ball itself, but the prospect of seeing Justin again—and working her wiles on him—thrilled her. She dressed carefully, making sure that her hair was styled perfectly.

Her gown, the blue taffeta that she'd ordered last fall from Mrs. Kirkley, looked beautiful with the lace shawl. Clover wound sapphire-colored ribbon through Thalia's hair and tucked in a few blue flowers as an accent.

"That's a beautiful gown, Thalia," Pansy said, appraising her friend's appearance.

"You look wonderful, Pansy." Thalia looked in the mirror one last time, fastened Justin's necklace about her neck and smiled at herself. The necklace would bring her good luck tonight. She gazed back at Pansy. "I'll bet Randolph Taylor will fall in love with you this very night."

Pansy stared vacantly at Thalia for a moment and then said, "I don't know. He's so smitten with you...."

"When he knows I'm not going to marry him," Thalia reminded Pansy, "he'll discover you. I'm sure of it. Let's go."

By the time they arrived at the ball, many people were already there. Thalia and Pansy walked into the ballroom and glanced around. Justin hadn't arrived yet. Donald and Randolph had. They spotted her immediately and came over.

"Hello, Thalia," Donald said, kissing her on the cheek. "How have you been?"

"I'm fine, Donald." Thalia glanced toward the door, hoping Justin would come in. "Good evening, Randolph."

Thalia stood there for a few minutes while Donald, Randolph and Pansy talked. She didn't even listen to the conversation. When Lenore walked in with Edward, Thalia's heart fluttered because she'd thought that Justin might come with Edward. He hadn't.

The orchestra began to play, and couples drifted toward the dance floor. Randolph smiled at Thalia. "Would you dance with me, Thalia?"

"Well, Randolph, I don't want to leave Pansy—"

"Pansy will dance with me, won't you, Pansy?" Donald asked, cutting off Thalia's rejection of Randolph's request.

"There seems to be no reason, Thalia." Randolph took her hand and led her to the dance floor.

The music droned on interminably. When the first dance was over, Randolph held her hand and kept her from leaving the floor. "We'll just dance again."

Thalia tried to smile, but failed miserably. "Wouldn't you like to dance with Pansy?"

"No. Why should I?" Randolph asked, pulling Thalia much closer, as the next set started. "I'm with *my* girl."

Thalia's eyes bulged in disbelief. What had Donald told Randolph? Dread washed over her, but she could do nothing other than allow Randolph to drag her all over the dance floor. When the dance was over, she smiled sweetly and said, "I'm sorry, Randolph, but I have to... to go to the powder room. You'll excuse me, I'm sure."

Without waiting for his answer, she strode quickly off the dance floor and disappeared into the crowd. Thalia didn't know what she was going to do, but she had to find a way to convince Donald that she was never going to marry Randolph.

Thalia made sure she danced with every man she knew. Avoiding Randolph was her primary objective. Occasionally she caught the look of disapproval in Donald's eyes, but she didn't care. She would have to deal with him later.

Donald finally caught up to her and led her onto the dance floor. "Why are you avoiding Randolph?"

"I've already danced twice with him." Thalia peered over Donald's shoulder. She was still looking for Justin.

"Thalia, I insist that you be kinder to Randolph," Donald said, squeezing her hand. "I insist. You're going to marry him. Nobody else will have you."

"Nobody?" she asked, wondering what he could mean. "Donald, what are you up to?"

"Nothing, Thalia, dear," Donald answered with a vague smile. He whirled her around the floor and stopped beside Randolph. "Here, Randolph, I believe my sister wants to dance with you."

Randolph's eyes brightened, and he grinned foolishly. "You don't know how happy that makes me."

Thalia danced once again with Randolph. She was so angry with Donald that she couldn't even think of a way to escape from Randolph. At least he was harmless. He was clearly smitten with her, and would do nothing to upset her.

Looking over Randolph's shoulder, she grimaced when he stepped on her toes. She tried to smile, knowing that he couldn't help being clumsy.

Thalia longed for Justin. He was an excellent dancer, one who tested her own skills with his intricate steps. She'd always managed to keep up. But Justin hadn't appeared, and she began to wonder if he was coming at all. Maybe he'd been trying to tell her that when they'd met at the tavern.

When the music stopped, Thalia hurried off the dance floor. She found Pansy and began to chat. "Why, Randolph, I haven't seen you dance with Pansy tonight."

Randolph blushed. "Miss Monroe, could I have this dance?"

Pansy smiled. It was a beautiful smile that reached her warm brown eyes. "Why, yes, Mr. Taylor. I'd love to dance with you."

No matter what she had to do, Thalia didn't intend to dance with Randolph again. She watched her friend smile shyly at Randolph as he stepped on her feet. *Better Pansy than I,* Thalia thought. Pansy's in love with him. Let her have the aching toes in the morning.

The evening was nearly over. Thalia could hardly dance another step, and she could see Randolph coming toward her. Her feet rebelled, and she sneaked out of the ballroom, hoping he hadn't seen which way she'd gone.

Randolph watched Thalia leave the ballroom. He hurried over to Donald. "What should I do?"

Donald thought a moment. "Go after her. If we can get her into a compromising situation, she'll have to marry you."

"Donald, I don't know. If she dislikes me, why should—"

"She adores you. I'm positive she's just acting coy to... to make you chase her even harder. You know how women are." Donald pushed Randolph toward the door. "Go on. Catch up to her. I'll be along in a moment. She won't want me to raise a ruckus when I catch the two of you together. She'll do anything for you then."

Thalia hurried along the pathway into the garden and settled into a little nook in the rosebushes. They didn't provide much cover themselves, but the little nook was surrounded by tall boxwoods. Disappointment enveloped her. All her carefully laid plans for entrapping Justin had come to nothing. He hadn't even come to the ball.

She heard a noise. Her heart began to pitter-patter. Could Justin have arrived late and seen her leave the ballroom? Or could it be Randolph? She prayed it was Justin.

Thalia couldn't have been more wrong. Randolph stepped into the little garden and sat down.

"Oh, Thalia, my dearest," he began, and grabbed her. He pulled her close, pressing wet kisses on her cheeks and then her mouth.

"Stop it, Randolph," she demanded, trying to wrest free of him. "Whatever has come over you?"

"You, darling. You are irresistible." Randolph slipped his hand around far enough to capture one of her breasts. "Ah, Thalia, I know making love to you would be wonderful."

"I don't know what's happened to you, but—"

Randolph cut off her words with a deep kiss. His tongue groped in her mouth, pillaging like a victorious warrior, as he slipped his hand inside her gown, tearing the bodice.

Rage swept through Thalia like fire through dry kindling. She bit his tongue as hard as she could and then pushed with all her might. Randolph caught at her, but got only her necklace, and he fell back off the bench, howling in pain.

A second man entered the nook, and Randolph looked up with pleading in his eyes. "Tell her, Donald, tell her it was your plan for me to—"

Hatred raced through Justin. Before he knew what was happening, he drew back his fist and smashed Randolph squarely in the face. "You're a low, cowardly bastard, and I'll—"

As he was getting ready to hit him again, Thalia recovered sufficiently to stop him. "No, Justin," Thalia cried, catching his hand before it crunched into Randolph's face again. "It's not his fault. Donald put him up to it, I'm sure. Help me find my necklace."

Justin searched the brick walkway and found her broken necklace. "Is this the necklace I gave you?"

"Yes," she cried, taking it in her hand. She treasured that necklace, valued it above all her other possessions—except Sea Mist.

Justin took it back and stuck it in his pocket. "I'll have it fixed, love. Don't worry."

Justin enfolded Thalia in his arms. The top of her dress lay open, tattered by Randolph's outrageous molestation. "Are you ... Did he ... Are you all right?"

"I'm all right." Thalia looked down at her gown. The bodice was in shreds. "I can't go back into the ballroom like this."

"Come, I'll take you back to the hotel." Justin held her close for a moment. "Did you wear a cloak?"

"Yes, I have a blue velvet pelisse." Thalia held her breath for a moment as she stepped over Randolph. "Forget it. Maybe Pansy will bring it when she comes."

Justin removed his cloak and wrapped it around her shoulders. He took her around the outside of the building and hailed a carriage. Making sure she was tucked in and warm, he said, "I'll be right back. I want to tell Pansy where you went."

"All right." Thalia lay back against the soft leather seat. Her anger at Randolph had lessened, but her rage at Donald was undiminished. She'd find a way to get even, if it killed her.

Justin looked over the dancers. He didn't see Pansy right away, but soon found her talking to Mrs. Calhoun. He walked over and greeted both ladies. "Miss Monroe, I'm afraid that Miss Freemont has become ill. She wants you to remain and have a good time." Justin glanced at Mrs. Calhoun. "Mrs. Calhoun, I hate to ask this of you, but would you be sure that Miss Monroe gets safely back to the Charleston Hotel?"

Wilhemina smiled. She liked Justin, and, more than that, she knew he loved Thalia. The two of them were right for each other. She knew that Thalia wasn't ill. She had seen Thalia leave, and then she'd seen Randolph go after her. She suspected foul play and was delighted to see that Captain Lionheart had stepped in, possibly to prevent some mishap. "Captain, you're so kind. I appreciate your taking Thalia back to the hotel. Please don't worry about Pansy. I'll take care of her."

Justin thanked Mrs. Calhoun and then turned to Pansy. "Miss Monroe, if you'll bring Thalia's...Miss Freemont's pelisse, I'd appreciate it. I've given her my own cloak to keep her warm during the carriage ride back to the hotel."

Nodding at the two ladies, he left quickly. He spotted Donald and started to speak to him, but decided against it. He had heard what Randolph had said about Donald's having planned the whole sordid affair, and he might lose his temper. He couldn't risk that, not when he was so close to reaching his goal.

Justin stepped into the carriage and sat down beside Thalia. She was huddled in the corner, as if she were afraid someone would see her. He wrapped his arms around her and drew her close. She must be bewildered about what had happened. First, she had nearly been raped. Then, even worse, she had found out that her brother had arranged it all. Her emotions must be pretty fragile right now.

They arrived at the hotel, and Justin lifted her out of the carriage. He handed the driver a few coins and then took Thalia into the hotel. He whispered, "I doubt anyone is around right now. Everybody's probably still at the dance."

Thalia didn't care. She just wanted to get back to her room and take off her dress. The idea of Randolph's having touched her was repulsive, and she was going to wash before collapsing into bed.

"Thalia," Justin said when they reached her door, "we're leaving first thing in the morning. I'm taking you back to Sea Mist."

More than ready to go herself, Thalia merely nodded. She couldn't really talk right now, because she was still so furious with Donald.

They went into the parlor of her rooms. Clover came out and looked from one of them to the other. Then she saw Thalia's torn dress. Without speaking, she grabbed a flatiron from the hearth and ran towards Justin.

"No, no, Clover!" Thalia shouted, trying to grab the woman's hands. Thalia missed, and Clover got to Justin.

Fortunately, Thalia had delayed her long enough for Justin to prepare himself. When she reached him, he snatched the iron from her hands.

"Clover, please," Thalia pleaded, holding on to her friend with every ounce of strength she could muster. "He didn't do it."

Clover hesitated a few seconds, but continued to glare at Justin. "If he didn't do it, who did?"

Thalia continued to hold Clover. "Randolph."

"That Mistah Taylor that's Mistah Donald's friend?" she asked, peering at Thalia suspiciously. "I never did like that fool."

Releasing Clover, Thalia sighed. She dropped onto a chair and bowed her head. "It wasn't Randolph's fault."

"Then jus' whose fault was it?" Clover eyed Thalia through narrow slits that indicated the depth of her anger. "Don't you be tellin' me you the cause of this."

"No, Clover. I was trying to get away from him." Thalia tucked her feet beneath her until she noticed Clover's glare and sat up properly. "This is all Donald's fault."

Clover stared at Thalia as if she couldn't believe what she was hearing. Then she nodded and looked back at Justin. "How come you let this happen?"

"I'm sorry I allowed this to happen, truly I am." Justin shook his head sadly. "If I could have gotten there any sooner, I would have. If Thalia hadn't stopped me, I'd probably have beaten the man to death."

Clover nodded. She would have done the same. "How come you the one bringing her home?"

"I promise, Clover, I had nothing to do with it. I..." Justin thought that being interrogated by Clover was worse than when Mrs. Calhoun had questioned him. "When I arrived, I looked for Thalia and couldn't find her. I saw Randolph leave the ballroom and followed him. I knew he was up to no good."

"Miss Thalia," Clover said, crossing her arms and sighing heavily, "that brother o' yours ain't no better than a snake in the grass. If he come to Sea Mist while I'm alive, he'll be mighty sorry!"

"Now, Clover," Thalia said soothingly. "He had an unhappy childhood. Remember that his mother—"

"That ain't got nothing to do with what he does. That man's just evil." Clover scowled, looking from Thalia to Justin. "Ain't no two ways about it. Evil. The devil done took that man's mind."

Chapter Eighteen

Thalia listened to the slapping of waves on the side of the boat. Justin had insisted on taking her back to Sea Mist without her seeing Donald. As soon as the sun had risen this morning, he'd come to collect their trunks.

Pansy, already homesick for the plantation, had agreed with Justin, and Thalia had gladly acquiesced.

True to his prediction, the trip from Charleston to Edisto Island was much smoother with Justin at the helm. The cornflower-blue sky, punctuated by a bright February sun, warmed them as they sailed the forty miles home.

For now, Thalia could think of little but getting home to Sea Mist, where she always felt safe and protected. Justin's presence was wonderful, calming. It was as if things were settled between them, even though no words had been spoken. Randolph, in his bumbling attempt to molest her, had probably succeeded in doing what she might never have done. The protective man in Justin had suddenly resurfaced. It was that man, the protector of innocents, that Thalia meant to reach.

When they arrived at the docks on Edisto Island, Justin sent a boy ahead to Sea Mist to get a wagon. They waited for a short period of time before Thalia spotted Adam driving the wagon. Guinevere and another horse, a black, were tied to the back.

"Oh, thank God," Thalia exclaimed when she saw her horse. "I won't have to ride in the wagon."

Justin and Adam loaded the trunks onto the wagon bed. Pansy and Clover found places to sit comfortably. Thalia looked at Pansy. She felt bad about leaving her to ride in the wagon, but she couldn't do anything about it. "I'm sorry, Pansy."

"Go ahead. I know you'll want to get home in a hurry." Pansy settled herself more comfortably and leaned against a trunk. "Besides, the sun's nice and warm. Clover and I will be fine."

Thalia and Justin rode away from the dock at a gallop. Sea Mist wasn't very far away and she wanted to get home as quickly as possible. After a short distance, Justin waved to her to stop.

"What is it?" she asked, looking at him with a puzzled expression on her face.

"Let's take the beach route," Justin suggested.

Thalia nodded, and they cut through to the beach. It was a little farther this way, but much nicer. They rode for a while, enjoying the scenery and the warm breeze from the ocean.

Before long, they had reached Sea Mist. Thalia urged Guinevere into a gallop, and they were at the barn quickly.

Justin finally caught up and dismounted. He took her hand as they walked toward the house. "One of these days, we'll have to race."

She gazed at him with steady eyes, though her heart was pounding. "I'm not a gambler."

"Oh?" Justin said, a hint of surprise in his voice. "I think you are."

Thalia didn't answer. She hurried into the house. "Princess!" she called. "We're home."

Irene came in, wiped her hands on her apron and greeted them. "Princess is out back. She'll be in after a while, unless you need her now."

"No," Thalia admitted. "I just wanted to tell her that we're home."

"I'll tell her, then." Irene looked past Thalia at Justin. "Shall I have Princess prepare supper for company?"

"Yes," Thalia said, and turned to go up to her room. "Oh, Irene, tell her to make something special. Maybe chicken and dumplings. Nobody makes dumplings like Princess." She smiled at Justin. "I'll see you at supper."

Thalia went up to her room. She left Justin and Irene in the downstairs hallway. She removed her boots and lay across her bed, thinking of what had happened and what was going to happen. She knew that Justin wanted to be alone with her, but she'd avoided that as much as possible until they'd ridden from the dock. And then she'd stayed far enough ahead of him to keep conversation to a minimum. Tonight, she knew, would be the night he asked her. Butterflies filled her stomach, flitting and flying and sending shivers of anticipation throughout her body. Could she wait until tonight?

Supper was over. Justin had been gazing at Thalia all through the meal. She had hardly eaten, even though she loved chicken and dumplings.

After everyone rose and went to the parlor, Justin said, "Thalia, would you like to take a walk?"

Her heart pounding, she smiled. "Why, yes, I believe I would."

They walked around the piazza and down the steps. From there, they crossed the lawn, ducked under some low-hanging live-oak limbs, and started walking along the beach. Frogs, crickets and night birds all sang as Thalia and Justin strolled. The waves rushed up near their feet, whispering across the hard-packed sand and then falling back toward the sea.

"Let's sit over there by those trees for a few minutes," Justin suggested, taking her arm.

Where he touched her, waves of sensation began, waves that rippled through her. Thalia followed along, heady with anticipation and hardly able to breathe for the tension that seemed to sizzle in the air between the two of them.

Removing his coat, Justin said, "Sit on my coat. I don't want to get your dress dirty." He grinned mischievously. "And I certainly don't want to make Clover angry with me."

Thalia laughed uncertainly; it was a nervous little laugh that seemed to startle the wildlife, for all the sounds stopped, except for the pounding of the surf and the pounding of her blood rushing through her veins.

When she was seated comfortably, Justin dropped down beside her. For a long time, they sat there watching the waves. The moon kissed the waves with a silvery glow that seemed to dance along the tide. Thalia wondered what Justin was thinking, what was taking him so long.

Justin gazed at Thalia. She was incredibly beautiful in the silvery moonbeams, and she seemed to have some inner beauty, some glow, that defied explanation. "Thalia, dearest..." he began, trying to think of a way of asking what he must ask, but afraid of taking this step.

She turned slightly to look up at him. "Yes, Justin?"

Her voice was low and throaty, as if she'd been making love. Justin loved that sound, and longed to hear it more. Thalia was everything he could want in a wife—if he wanted a wife, that is—but the words seemed to become garbled in his throat. Once more he tried. "Thalia, love...my sweet, this is not an easy thing to say." Gaining courage, he continued. "I have never wanted a wife, but now I find my thoughts on you constantly. You must know how much I care for you, how deeply my feelings run."

Thalia's breath was all but swept away. She could hardly utter a sound. "Yes, Justin, I think...I believe I know how you feel."

"Tell me that you feel the same as I." He slid his arms around her and kissed her lightly. "Is this love? Do we share the same tender feelings? Or have I imagined all this?"

"I...I don't think it's your imagination," Thalia whispered against his lips.

Justin kissed her. He needed the time to think. All day he'd tried to think of words that would ensure a positive response from her, but he'd failed. There seemed to be no way to be sure of a woman's feelings. He realized right away that kissing Thalia was a mistake, and he drew away. He decided to blurt out the words and see what happened. "Thalia, I love you, I adore you. I want to spend my life with you." He inhaled deeply and went on, "Please marry me and make me the happiest of men."

"Yes, yes, yes, Justin, yes, I'll marry you," she murmured, her emotions clouding her eyes with tears of joy.

Justin closed his eyes for a moment, reveling in the happiness those words brought to him. He removed a ring from his pocket and slipped it on her finger. "For you, a sapphire to match your necklace." His kisses were gentler now, loving, as they embraced and sealed their agreement with passion. He slowly pushed Thalia back on his cloak and kissed her again and again. Thalia answered his kisses with as much fervor as she knew how and slid her fingers inside his shirt.

"No, my love," Justin whispered, kissing the tip of her turned-up nose. "We must go back to the house. Our passion can wait for our wedding night." He stood and pulled her to her feet.

Embracing her one last time before they returned to the house, Justin tried to memorize the curves of her body as she pressed herself against him. "Darling," he murmured against her hair. "Set our wedding date soon. I'm not a patient man."

Thalia didn't sleep that night. Early the next morning, she was out of bed and dancing around the room, holding her hand out so that she could admire her new ring.

Clover came in and stared at Thalia for a few seconds. "Is you gone mad?"

"No, no, no, I'm happy. I'm in love." She whirled over to Clover and hugged her. "Look, Clover, Justin and I are going to get married."

"Lawsy mercy! I ain't never seen a rock that big on a lady's finger." Clover twisted Thalia's finger to get a better view. "I'm a striped hound if that ain't the purtiest ring I ever seen."

"Help me dress. I can't wait to show Pansy," Thalia said, drawing her nightgown over her head. She flung it back at the bed. "Oh, Clover, I've never been this happy in my life."

"You ain't never been that naked when your brother come in either, and he's downstairs, madder'n a wildcat in quicksand." As Thalia put on her crinolines, Clover selected a prim-looking light wool dress and then pulled it over Thalia's head.

Clover started to braid Thalia's hair, but she waved her away. "I want to get rid of Donald. Never mind my hair. I'll just brush it."

Thalia brushed her hair until it shone. The cream-colored dress was sedate, but pretty enough for company. "Don't worry. I'll handle Donald."

With a swish of her skirts, Thalia left the room. She walked slowly down the stairs, thinking that it wouldn't hurt Donald to wait for once in his life. She hesitated at the parlor door for an instant, then opened it and walked in. "Hello, Donald."

Donald, who was staring out the window, whirled and glared at Thalia. "How dare you scorn Randolph after I told you to accept his proposal?"

"Lower your voice, Donald, or you'll awaken everyone." Thalia walked across the room and sat down. "How dare you suggest to Randolph that I'd welcome his—his mauling?"

"Do you think I give a damn about that?" Donald screamed, placing his hands on the chair in which she was sitting and glaring down into her face. "You'll marry him, and that's final!"

Thalia stared back at him until he averted his eyes, lifted his hands and stepped back. "Donald, I am going to say this to you only once more." She stood and walked toward him as steadily as she could. "I am never, ever marrying Randolph. As of last night, I am engaged to—"

"To me, Donald." Wearing nothing but his trousers, Justin burst into the room, anger etching across his face. "If you could have seen what that imbecile did to Thalia . . . He actually ripped her gown and . . . God only knows what else. He *says* that you encouraged him to do so. That it was your idea." Justin put himself between Donald and Thalia. "If I discover that is the truth—"

"Preposterous!" Donald shouted, falling back onto the sofa. He'd never seen a man as furious as Justin. Trying desperately to find a way to calm him, he shook his head furiously. "The nerve of the man to lie like that." Donald looked over Justin's shoulder at Thalia, who was standing slightly behind him. "I had no idea . . . Thalia, dear sister, I apologize most humbly."

Justin stepped back and wrapped his arms around Thalia. He knew Donald was lying, but he didn't know exactly how Thalia felt. For a few seconds, he'd come close to losing whatever advantage he had over Donald. "Donald, forgive me. When I heard that you'd— I mean, he said you were responsible."

Thalia looked up at Justin with questioning eyes. "You believe him?"

Justin looked back at Donald and said, "I don't know." Justin stared at Donald for a long moment. "If I ever find out that you did what Randolph said, I'll tie you up and drag you behind my ship all the way to Charleston."

Donald knew that Justin meant every word of his threat. Standing, he walked over to Thalia and took her hand. "Thalia, I promise you, I never said anything remotely like that to Randolph. He must... He was drinking heavily. You know that punch he loves so much. That must have been what caused the horrible incident."

Justin felt sick; he'd never known a more despicable man. "Donald, Thalia and I are to be married as soon as we can arrange the wedding. We hope you'll give us your blessing."

"Well, of course, I— I mean—" Donald stuttered, wondering what he could say.

"Not that it matters. We're getting married whether you like it or not." Thalia slid her arm around Justin's waist and studied Donald carefully. He was in turmoil, but she smiled. "So there's nothing left to discuss. Thank you for stopping in to see us."

Donald smiled and shook Justin's hand. "Of course, you have my blessing." He kissed Thalia on the forehead. "All I ever wanted was for you to be happy."

When Donald had gone, Justin looked down, wriggled his bare toes and said, "Maybe I'd better go—"

"What's all the shouting about?" Pansy asked, stepping into the room and rubbing her eyes. "Justin!"

"Just leaving. Sorry if I've embarrassed you." Justin started out of the room and then backed slowly in again. "Hold on, Clover, I'm not the culprit this time, either."

"That snake left yet?" Clover was once again brandishing a flatiron. "I'll straighten him out."

Thalia's life was a whirlwind for the next few weeks. She made several trips to Charleston to purchase clothes, order an orchestra, food, all the things she'd need for a wedding. She and Justin were going to be married in March at Sea Mist. She'd sent invitations to everyone she knew, both in Charleston and on Edisto Island.

"Justin," she said one afternoon as she was going over her list again, "isn't there someone I need to invite for you? I mean, you haven't given me a single name to add to the list."

Justin shifted uncomfortably. Yes, there were people he wanted to invite, but he couldn't. He didn't think he'd ever see his parents again, nor his younger brother, Samuel. Justin wondered what Samuel was doing, whether he'd ever gotten over killing a man. Justin smiled at Thalia. "No, love. We know all the same people."

Thalia studied him for a moment. "I mean out-of-town people. Aren't there any…Lionhearts in Virginia you'd like to invite?"

For a long time, he'd planned to simply disappear on the day of the wedding. Donald would be humiliated. Justin would call in all his markers, and Donald's property would belong to Justin. Then he would reveal his identity.

His plans had changed somewhat. He'd decided to go through with the wedding. No matter how angry he was with Donald, Justin simply couldn't embarrass Thalia, as he knew he would if he didn't marry her. Now she was asking a question he didn't want to answer.

No, there were no Lionhearts in Virginia. Justin had wrestled with the name problem, too. He'd never taken the name Lionheart legally. Though many people changed names and never did so with the courts' blessing, Justin would have felt better giving Thalia his real name. But the chance of someone discovering who he really was was too great.

Finally, he shrugged and said, "Nobody, Thalia. There's nobody to invite."

Thalia had to be content with that. Wedding presents were coming in from all around Charleston, and her days were filled with cataloging the gifts and writing the necessary thank-you notes. She'd never been happier.

Justin spent as much time as possible at Sea Mist, but he still had his ship to maintain. He took as few trips as possible, trips already contracted for, no others for now. His revenge was nearing completion.

Donald paced back and forth. Thalia's wedding was but days away. He could see everything he owned slipping through his fingers. What had happened to Pansy Monroe and her family was going to happen to Donald. Of course, his debts to Justin would have to be forgiven, if they were to be family, but Donald's other creditors were becoming more intimidating. He just owed too much to too many people. There was no way out, unless...

Sea Mist Plantation was decorated with thousands of flowers and beautiful white bows. All along the road from the dock and the village, white streamers were strung from posts to mark the way. Sea Mist itself was filled with flowers and white bows. The spicy smells of a wedding feast were spread all over the island with every breeze that blew.

Thalia was about to have a fit. She'd paced the floor all night long, wondering how she could go through with this ceremony. She'd tricked Justin into marrying her.

"Miss Thalia, you gonna ruin that gown, you keep pacin' the floor like a first-time daddy," Clover admonished her, straightening her veil. "All brides scared on they wedding day, but they ain't nothin' to worry about."

Thalia gazed at Clover. Obviously Clover thought that she was concerned about her wedding night. That was the least of her problems. She smiled. "I'll be fine, Clover."

From downstairs, the sound of music reached Thalia. "I—I guess it's time to go."

Clover's eyes misted over, and she hugged Thalia. "My baby gittin' married."

"Don't worry, Clover, everything will be all right. I'll make it all right." Thalia opened the door and went downstairs to join Justin. She paused at the entrance to the ballroom. Everybody was there, staring at her, as she took her first step toward the little altar Adam and some of the other men had made.

Justin looked resplendent in his new clothes. His waistcoat and trousers were of black satin and hugged his every muscle. Thalia thought she'd never seen him look better. When she reached him, he smiled down at her, and she suddenly thought everything *would* be all right, despite the fact that both Donald and Randolph were attending the festivities.

For Thalia, the rest of the day was a blur. She mumbled the correct responses, smiled at all their guests, tried to be a perfect hostess. But her senses were simply overloaded with the weight of the day's proceedings and from having attended more than a dozen parties given in her honor during the past few weeks.

Around midnight, Justin took Thalia's hand, and the two of them walked up the stairs, amid the calls of all the young men and the giggles of the maidens. When they reached the top of the stairs, Justin lifted Thalia and carried her into her room, which had been prepared for both of them.

The sounds of merrymaking wafted up to the two of them from downstairs. Thalia undressed nervously, while Justin went to his room on some pretext or other. By the time he returned, she'd slipped into bed.

Justin entered the room quietly. The lamp was turned so low that he could hardly see the bed, but his eyes adjusted quickly. He slid into bed and drew Thalia into his arms. Justin had never considered that marrying Thalia would make him this happy. She felt so right in his arms, so full of love and life. "Why, my love, you're naked."

Thalia laughed and kissed him. "So I am, Captain Lionheart."

Her laughter was like food to a starving man. Justin caressed her silken body, playing his fingers along the sensitive flesh of her breasts and stomach and legs. His mouth covered hers, hungry for the sustenance only she could provide. He knew that he'd been right to wait until this night after he'd asked for her hand. Their passions were explosive after the long days of being together without making love.

"Thalia, my darling, I love you more than life itself." Justin held her face between his hands and kissed her and then drew his hands down to her passion-swollen breasts. Already the nipples were hard and erect, tight little buds that he caressed, first with his fingers and then with his tongue.

"Justin, love, you've kept me waiting all these weeks. Do not linger any longer than is necessary," Thalia chided gently, nuzzling him with her kisses. "I'm not a patient woman."

With her body pressed so close to his that he could feel the steady rhythm of her heart, Justin had to agree. "I fear I've married a wild woman."

"Wild for you, my love." Thalia pushed him back and slid her body over him.

She was untutored in many ways, but she wanted to give Justin a night he'd never forget. Thalia slowly eased herself down onto him. It seemed he exploded into her, suddenly filling her more completely than ever before. She rocked back and forth, gradually letting all of him penetrate her, until she thought she would burst from the exquisite pain.

For a moment, Thalia didn't know what was happening, but gradually she felt a tingle begin low in her stomach. The tingling grew into a wave of sensation, and she felt ripples of heat scorch every part of her. She arched her neck and groaned with a pleasure that surpassed anything she'd ever known.

After a moment she rolled over, and Justin came with her, still inside her, filling her. He started a steady motion that brought her back to him. Within a few minutes, she knew, she would reach that peak of pleasure again. Astonished that he had such an effect on her, she relaxed and allowed him to love her completely. Her body no longer belonged to her; it was his to do with as he chose.

Justin knew Thalia had reached her gratification soon after she'd straddled him, but he wanted this night of all nights to be special to them both. He slowed his pace and made sure that she was ready for him to begin again. When her body seemed to match his rhythm, he moved a little faster, until something deep within him took over. Something primal, something animal, exploded within him, and a blinding light filled him as he felt his seed spill into Thalia.

After a few more kisses, Thalia fell asleep in his arms. Several times during the night, she awoke to find him kissing her or caressing her. After three times, she stopped counting. To Thalia, it seemed that her entire wedding night was spent making love.

When morning came, she awoke, and Justin was gone. Had she dreamed it all? No, her wedding dress lay across the chair by the fireplace. Where could he be?

Then she heard him. That loud, joyful, off-key singing was coming from downstairs. She stumbled from the bed and washed as quickly as possible. By the time Clover came in, Thalia had on her pantalets and crinolines.

"Lord, that man sing like a scalded hound." Clover scowled at the crumpled wedding gown and shook her head. After a moment she smiled. "But he sho' sound happy."

After a series of visits from neighbors and friends, life at Sea Mist settled down into a routine. Pansy went back to Charleston with Mrs. Calhoun for a few weeks to give the newlyweds a chance to adjust, but Thalia made her promise to return soon.

Justin knew a little about planting, but not much about cotton. He spent hours listening to Thalia and Adam discuss certain qualities, certain seed.

"You know, Justin," Thalia said, with eyes that glittered like the waters of the Caribbean, "it's said that Edisto Island cotton isn't sold. It's contracted for before it's ever planted."

Justin was proud of his wife, and of her energetic interest in everything around her. He'd forced her to slow down a little, but he couldn't stop her completely. Irene was a help. She ran the household as if it were her own, with little interference from "the missus," as she now called Thalia.

Thalia suspected that she was with child. She fought the sickness, but it came each morning, just when she needed to be in the fields, directing the workers. Thalia knew she'd better get as much done as possible, because after she began to swell she couldn't very well ride into the fields.

Clover came in one morning while Thalia was naked and slammed the door behind her. "You just take that ridin' outfit off, 'cause you ain't going out to that cotton field today."

"What are you talking about?" Thalia asked, staring at Clover in shock. "Of course, I'm going to the fields. Why wouldn't I?"

"'Cause you is standin' behind a baby, that's why." Clover crossed her arms and propped against the door. "It ain't right for you to go traipsin' across them fields. What would happen if you was to lose that baby?"

Thalia stood stock-still. She knew Clover was right. Thalia simply hadn't considered that she might be endangering her baby's life. She'd been so concerned with the planting and weeding that she'd put her own safety, and that of her baby, second. But she wasn't sure that she was pregnant. "What makes you think I'm going to have a baby?"

"Anybody with eyes that can see knows you is." Clover flew away from the door as it opened from the outside.

Justin peered around the door. "Sorry, Clover, didn't know you were—"

He gazed at Thalia with an apologetic smile. He thought he'd heard Clover talking about a baby. He stared at Thalia in disbelief. For the first time, he noticed that her stomach was slightly rounded and her breasts were even fuller. He walked in and closed the door behind him. "Thalia, why didn't you tell me?"

Thalia glowered at Clover and then looked at Justin. "I—I don't think I really knew until this moment. I mean, I suspected, but I didn't know. Are you angry?"

Justin bolted across the room and lifted Thalia in his arms. "Angry? I'm ecstatic!" He whirled around and placed Thalia on the bed. "Rest today. You've been working too hard." He turned to Clover and danced around her. "We're going to have a baby. I'll just bet she's the prettiest baby ever born in South Carolina—except her mother, of course."

Clover chuckled. "I always knowed you was a fool, Mistah Justin." She shook her head and walked to the door. "Miss Thalia, if you even act like you goin' to git on a horse, I'll tie you up and put you in that bed till our baby comes."

When she was gone, Justin lay down beside his naked wife. He ran his hands over her stomach and then placed his ear there. "I can't hear her."

"Oh, silly, what makes you think you could hear her, and what makes you think it's a 'her'?" Thalia giggled. She'd never given much thought to becoming a mother. A mother. Her own mother had died giving birth. She was suddenly frightened.

Justin saw the changes in her face, and knew immediately what she was thinking. He moved up and cuddled her in his arms. "Thalia, everything will be all right. I promise you."

Thalia held on to Justin for a moment, thinking of all the possibilities. "Justin," she said finally, "promise me one thing."

"Anything, love," he promised, resting his hands on the place where his child slept inside Thalia's body.

"Promise me that if something happens to...to me." She gulped, and felt tears sting her eyes. "Please promise to love our baby. Don't blame her—or him—if . . . if something bad happens."

Justin felt his heart breaking. He'd never hurt this bad in his life. Nothing, not Alicia's death, not Peter's, not even having to leave his home forever, had ever hurt Justin as much as those words. "Thalia, my love, my life," Justin whispered, holding her as tight as he could. "Nothing bad will happen."

"Promise, please promise, Justin," she pleaded, the tears now rimming her eyelids.

"I promise, my darling, I promise." Justin kissed her hair and her forehead and her lips. "But I'll make one more promise. Nothing will ever happen to you. I won't let it."

He looked down at her. If he could have cried, he would have. Now was the time to tell her all about himself. "Thalia, you've questioned me about my family, about my past. . . ."

Thalia gazed up at him. Through her unshed tears, he was a little blurry, but she tried to smile. "Yes, Justin?"

His gaze swept down her body and came to rest on her rounded belly. "I . . . We'll talk about all this after the baby comes. I promise."

"What, Justin?" she asked as he rose from the bed. "What are you talking about?"

"Nothing, love. Don't you worry about a thing." Justin smiled, as brightly as he could. "I've got to go out and learn how to manage a cotton plantation. I'm going to be a father."

Life was about as good as it could ever get—under the circumstances. He had Donald exactly where he wanted him. There was little the man could do. Donald had thought, had even suggested, that since Justin was now his brother-in-law all the markers he held should be torn up. Justin had surprised him by refusing to do so.

Donald had threatened to tell Thalia, but Justin had just laughed. "Thalia cares little what goes on between us. She certainly won't mind if I foreclose on Misty Glade. But if you dare upset her, I'll make sure that you're the laughingstock of Charleston."

In a fit of fury, Donald had sworn to get even. He'd left Sea Mist in a rage. When he'd gotten back to Misty Glade, he'd decided that he'd better urge fate along, or he'd be terribly embarrassed.

From his desk drawer, he'd pulled the papers the investigator had provided. He didn't want to use them, but Justin had made it necessary. First, he would show them to Thalia. That should spoil her little love nest. Then he would kill both Thalia and Justin. When the sheriff arrived, he would produce the papers and swear that Justin had killed Thalia and then himself.

Donald chuckled. At last. He'd be rid of Thalia, and have all her lovely money and that damnable Sea Mist that had nearly destroyed him. He'd sell it to the highest bidder without a thought.

Samuel hadn't seen his brother in several years, but he knew that Justin was in trouble. Ever since that misty morning in the glade, Samuel had been unable to assuage the guilt he felt for shooting Peter Kimball and thereby sealing Justin's fate. Justin had been unwilling to let Samuel take the blame, and had left Virginia forever.

The time had come for Samuel to confess. But before he did, he wanted to make sure Justin knew that someone was investigating him—and that he was free to return to Virginia. Samuel had left a note for his father, explaining the entire situation. He hoped his parents would understand that he was doing what he had to do. Samuel Lee, like his older brother, was an honorable man.

Chapter Nineteen

Samuel Lee arrived in Charleston. He'd discovered that a man from Charleston, a private investigator, had come to Virginia looking for information about a Justin Lionheart. The investigator had connected Justin Lionheart with Justin Lee.

The younger Lee brother sat in a tavern and watched the men around him drinking. He'd heard that Justin frequented this particular tavern, but he didn't understand why. None of the patrons here looked like men Justin would associate with.

Then a well-dressed man entered and sat down. Nobody joined him, and he said nothing. Samuel decided that this man might know Justin personally.

He rose and went over. "Hello, sir, I'm looking for Justin Lee—Lionheart. Do you know of him?"

Edward Nelson looked at the young man. He was almost Justin's double. Edward smiled and indicated that the young man should join him. "You must be his brother."

"You know him? You know he has a brother?" Samuel asked, thrilled to finally meet someone who could help.

"Well, I certainly know the lucky devil, but I didn't know about you until you showed your face here. He doesn't say much about his past." Edward signaled to the barkeep. "Ale, here." He returned his attention to the young man. "I'm Edward Nelson, best friend of Captain Justin Lionheart."

"Captain? What do you mean, lucky?" Samuel asked, sitting down. "Oh, I'm Samuel Lee . . . Lionheart."

"Well, Samuel. What are you doing in Charleston?" Edward asked, lighting a cigar.

"I'm looking for Justin. I need to see him at once." Samuel didn't know how much he could trust this man, though he seemed like a friend. "This is an urgent matter, Mr. Nelson."

Edward studied Samuel over the tankard of ale the tavernkeeper had brought him. Cigar smoke curled over the table and gradually wafted away. "Well, if you're here on urgent business, I'd suggest you hop the next ferry for Edisto Island."

"Edisto Island?" Samuel asked, rising from his chair. "Where can I get a ferry?"

"Hold on, boy," Edward said, and caught Samuel's arm. "I'll show you."

Edward took Samuel down to the wharves and showed him which boat to board. "And, when you get to Edisto, here's how to get to Sea Mist Plantation."

After a moment, Samuel nodded happily. "I'm real good with directions, sir. Thank you."

The ferry seemed to take forever, though in truth it took no more than three hours and a half. When the ship docked, Samuel was the first off. He borrowed a horse and rode as quickly as he could for Sea Mist.

When he arrived, he rode straight up to the front door. He tethered his horse and ran up the steps, three at a time. Excitement pounded in his chest. He was going to see his brother for the first time in years. He wondered if Justin would recognize him.

He rapped on the door, and a black woman answered almost immediately. She took one look at him and stepped back. "Lawsy mercy! You must be Mistah Justin's brother or something!"

"I am. My name is Samuel Lee, and I'm here to see Justin." Samuel stepped inside when the woman indicated.

"Come on in here. Mistah Justin ain't here right now, but his wife is." Clover pointed to the parlor, turned and ran up the stairs.

When she reached Thalia's morning room, she knocked and then burst through the door. "Miss Thalia! Guess who come!"

"Who, Clover? And why are you in such a dither?" Thalia looked up from her sewing. She was making a little nightshirt for her baby.

"Mistah Justin's brother." Clover beamed with pleasure. "He down in the parlor right now."

Thalia dropped her sewing and hurried down the stairs. She went into the parlor without hesitating. The young man was unmistakably related to her husband. "Hello. Welcome to Sea Mist. I'm Thalia—"

"You're Justin's wife?" Samuel looked at her appreciatively. Justin had good taste in women. "Mrs. Lee, I'm Samuel Lee, Justin's younger brother."

"Lee?" Thalia repeated and sat down. So Justin *had* used a false name, as she'd suspected. Her first thought was for her child, their child. What name would the child bear? She looked at Samuel. He was young, and probably impulsive. He'd be the talkative sort. "Samuel, please be seated. You must call me Thalia."

"Thalia." Samuel sat down by her. "I never thought about Justin being married, after what Alicia did, and all."

Thalia swallowed hard, nearly choking. "Alicia?"

"Yes, ma'am. She and Justin were engaged, but she, well, I guess Justin's told you all this." Samuel smiled at her, wondering when Justin would return. "Will Justin be back soon?"

"Oh, yes, he'll be here in time for dinner." Thalia tried to smile. She patted Samuel on the hand. "Now, tell me all about Justin when he was in Virginia."

"Well, I guess he told you that he had to leave on account of me." Samuel hung his head in his hands. Then he glanced at Thalia. "But I guess he didn't do too bad. I reckon he found that guy that got Alicia pregnant." Samuel tried to see if Thalia was following the conversation. She nodded. "There just wasn't no stopping her brother, though. And Justin wouldn't tell him that she was carrying another man's baby. No, he wouldn't. Justin's too honorable. He just vowed to get revenge on that guy. Did I tell you Justin was older than me?"

"Yes, I believe you did." Thalia could feel her world shattering under her. Everything she and Justin had built together was crumbling like the sand castles she had built on the beach as a child. "I'll bet you wanted to be just like him, didn't you?"

"Sure did." Samuel shook his head sadly. "I messed up everything. Peter shot him, all right. Guess he has a scar. Justin wouldn't even shoot back. So I hid in the trees and shot Peter. But it didn't do Justin any good." Samuel tried to smile. "Justin tried to protect me. But this fellow Henry who was Peter's second, started thinking about the shooting one day. Now he's started a rumor that I was really the one who shot Peter."

"Thalia!" Justin's voice boomed out from the back of the house. He hurried down the hallway and started up the stairs.

Thalia could hardly speak. She didn't have to. Samuel jumped up and ran into the parlor.

"Justin!" he exclaimed, throwing himself into his brother's arms.

At first, Justin was so happy to see Samuel that he didn't think of the implications. When Justin saw the look on Thalia's face, he knew what had happened. She rose slowly, looked at him as if she could see clear through him, and walked up the stairs.

"Wait here, Samuel. Go on into the dining room and get something to eat." Justin raced up the stairs. He had to talk to Thalia, to make her understand. Justin swung open the door to their room. Thalia was just standing there, looking at the bed. "Thalia, love, let me explain."

She turned around slowly and stared at him. "Explain? Why? Samuel just told me everything. Even my name."

"Thalia, listen to me. All this is unimportant." He tried to convince himself that it *was* unimportant, but one look at her face and he knew he was wrong.

"Get out, Justin. Leave me alone." Thalia sank into her rocking chair, hugging herself as if to protect their child. "Please, go. I don't ever want to see you again."

Justin walked slowly down the stairs. He knew that after Thalia thought this over he could reason with her. Hell, he'd even forgive Donald if it would make her happy. After all the years of searching, Justin would simply give up seeking his revenge to keep her. Justin sat down on the bottom step. He had the terrible feeling that his life was truly ending.

"Justin?" Samuel asked. "What's wrong?"

"Wrong? Nothing, Samuel...and everything." Justin stood up. "Did you bring your trunks?"

"No, I left them at the hotel in Charleston," Samuel said, removing the napkin from his shirt. "I guess we aren't going to eat now."

"No, we're going to Charleston for a day or two." Justin took Samuel by the arm and led him out the front door. If he gave Thalia some time, everything would work out. It had to.

Thalia stood at her window and watched Justin leave. She should have given him time to explain. There had to be a reasonable explanation. He was wanted for murder. She remembered having wondered about that at one time. But Samuel had committed the murder, not Justin. Justin Lee. Thalia Lee. It didn't have the same romantic ring as Justin and Thalia Lionheart. She wished fervently that she'd listened to him.

Justin had never been so drunk in his entire life. He wobbled back and forth as Samuel tried to help him from the tavern. As they stumbled down the street, a carriage stopped, and a woman poked her head out.

"Justin? Is that you?" She opened the door and climbed down. "Gracious, I never saw you this—" She looked at Samuel. "Here, boy, put him in my carriage."

"Yes, ma'am." Samuel helped Justin into the carriage, where he immediately passed out. Samuel looked at the woman. She was pretty in a way, but not nearly as beautiful as Thalia. "Do you know my brother very well?"

"Oh, yes. We're the closest of friends," the woman said with a smile. "So Justin's your brother, is he? I'm Eugenia Prentiss, and I can't say how delighted I am to meet Captain Lionheart's brother."

Donald walked slowly down the street. He'd had to give fifty of his slaves to Randolph to discharge his debt to him. Donald wasn't happy. Even though he'd promised Randolph that he'd be paid within a few days, Randolph had refused to listen. Everything was falling down around Donald's shoulders. He had to speed up his plan.

As he walked along near Eugenia's house, he spotted Justin and a young man he didn't know coming out of the house. *So, here's a little fuel for the fire I'm about to start.*

Donald ducked into the gate next to Eugenia's and waited until Justin had passed. *Ah, victory is mine,* he thought.

He headed straight back to Edisto Island. Without stopping by Misty Glade, he rode directly to Sea Mist. He hurried up the steps, humming a jaunty tune.

Thalia paced back and forth in her morning room. Where was Justin? He'd been gone overnight, and she was worried about him. She had treated him badly. He didn't deserve such ill treatment from her. After all, she'd tricked him into marrying her.

She heard a lilting tune through the open window and looked out, thinking that Justin had returned. But it was Donald.

She knew that she'd have to see him, no matter what. She might as well get it over with. Thalia walked down the stairs and met him at the front door. "Donald, to what do I owe this pleasure?"

Donald caught the sarcasm in her voice. "I've come with grave news, dear sister."

Her eyes widened. "Donald, you're not telling me that Justin's...that he's... Oh, God forbid, he's not dead, is he?"

Thalia felt dizzy. She swayed and could hardly stand.

Donald reached out and caught her. "Clover," he shouted. "Clover, where the hell are you, woman?" Donald carried Thalia into the parlor and laid her on the sofa.

Clover ran into the room. "Lawsy, my baby dead!"

"No, she's just fainted." Donald glared at the black woman. "Go and get her smelling salts."

"Lord, don't let that baby die." Clover hurried from the room, praying as she ran. "Please, Lord, don't let Miss Thalia's baby die."

Donald gaped at Thalia. *She was pregnant!*

Thalia opened her eyes. "Donald, please tell me he isn't..."

"No, Thalia, my dear, he isn't dead." Donald moved from the sofa to the nearest chair. "I sent that crazy woman of yours after your smelling salts."

Thalia tried to sit up. "Clover isn't crazy."

"No, she ain't," Clover said as she entered the room again. "And she ain't forgot what you done in Charleston, either,

Mistah Donald. I promised the Lord that if you ever come here I'd kill you."

"Clover, please," Thalia pleaded.

Clover left the room, mumbling as she went.

Donald looked at Thalia and smiled. "I'm afraid I have bad news, dear sister," Donald repeated. How he relished telling his sister this little tidbit. "I saw Justin coming out of Eugenia's very early this morning. Apparently he spent the night there."

Thalia waved her hand. "That doesn't matter to me, Donald. As long as he's safe."

Donald felt deflated. He had been sure the news would cause Thalia to become upset. "There's more."

"More?" she asked, closing her eyes. Why didn't he just leave her alone?

"Yes. I've discovered that Justin Lionheart is none other than Justin Lee, a wanted murderer from Virginia." Donald smiled brightly. This information ought to shatter her trust in the man. "I've already notified the sheriff that I believe Justin's a criminal."

"Donald, how could you?" Thalia jumped up, wavered for a moment, but regained her composure. "Get out. Leave now."

"Don't you care?" Donald asked incredulously. "Your husband—if he is your husband—is a murderer."

"I won't bandy words with you, Donald, but if you've done anything that will harm Justin or his reputation, I'll personally tie you up and drag you to Charleston behind his sailboat." Thalia glared at him and pointed to the door. "Leave immediately before I go and get one of Uncle Martin's prized pistols and shoot your worthless hide."

Donald left. A pregnant woman simply didn't think rationally. Maybe he could use that to his advantage, too. After all, Alicia had been pregnant. Maybe he could make the sheriff believe that Justin actually killed Alicia because she was pregnant. Donald would make sure the sheriff knew that Thalia was pregnant, as well. Ought to make a tidy little case against Justin. Nobody would ever think to look suspiciously at Donald.

Justin held his aching head as he looked at the tankard of ale in front of him. God, but his head hurt this morning.

He had to go back to Sea Mist. He had to talk to Thalia. Somehow they would work this out. There had to be a way.

"Look, Samuel." Justin swilled down the last of his ale. "I'm going out to talk to Thalia. You stay here. Send a telegram to Father and tell him where you are. Wait for an answer. Then get all your things together and come over to Edisto Island on the morning ferry. I'll have Ebenezer at the dock to pick you up."

Samuel didn't like the idea of Justin going back to Sea Mist alone, especially in his condition, but Justin refused to listen to his arguments.

Justin left. He sailed his schooner back to Edisto Island, thinking that at that particular moment he wasn't much of a sailor. When he arrived at the dock, he hired a carriage to take him out to Sea Mist. He slept all the way.

Donald was heading for Charleston. Today he wanted to make sure the sheriff sent a telegram to the sheriff in Richmond to inquire about Justin. He made it a quick trip. The sheriff didn't really want to do anything of the sort, but Donald finally convinced him that it was urgent, that his sister's life might be in danger.

Without waiting for a reply from Virginia, Donald hurried back to Edisto Island. When the sheriff arrived, it would be too late.

"Justin," she purred, holding as tightly as she could. "Why didn't you trust me enough to tell me?"

"Thalia, how could I? He's your brother." Justin lifted her and carried her to the nearest chair. He sat down, with Thalia on his lap. "I was foolish, but it's all in the past. I've forgiven Donald for everything."

"Did you . . . did you really love her?" Thalia asked, thinking of the poor girl who'd committed suicide because of Donald.

"No," Justin answered honestly. "Her father saved my mother's life. Ever since I was a child, he kept saying that Alicia and I were perfect for each other. I wanted to believe it, because of the debt I owed him."

"What of Peter? Why didn't you tell him the truth?" Thalia asked, feeling a great pity for the two families that Donald had destroyed—nearly three, the last being her own.

"I couldn't. Peter worshiped his sister," Justin explained. "From the moment she was born, he adored her. I couldn't break his heart by telling him that she'd been unfaithful to me. He was almost dead inside already."

"Oh, what a terrible story." Thalia laid her head on Justin's shoulder and let the tears flow. She was crying for the poor girl, Alicia, for Justin, for dear Samuel, who had loved Justin enough to kill for him. "It's all over, Justin. Nothing bad can happen to us now."

Justin hugged her and prayed that it could be so. He still had to go back to Virginia to help defend Samuel. No matter how hard Justin had talked, Samuel refused to continue with the deception. "The time has come to tell the truth," he'd said.

"Justin," Thalia said, a quiet hesitation in her voice. "I have something to tell you, too."

Justin kissed her and snuggled closer. "What is it, love?"

"I...I conspired to trick you into marrying me." Thalia breathed a sigh of relief. Now the truth was out between them. All the lies and deception had passed.

"Conspired? Trick?" Justin asked, drawing back to stare at her. "What do you mean?"

"Donald wanted me to marry that imbecile Randolph so badly because Randolph had promised Sea Mist to Donald. I overheard them talking," Thalia confessed, hoping that Justin wouldn't hate her. "So I decided right then that I'd marry you. I'd do anything within my power to trap you into marrying me."

"Oh, so you tricked me, did you?" Justin laughed and hugged her. "Sounds like we're a bunch of liars and deceivers. Better beware."

"You're not angry?" Thalia asked. At that moment she felt the baby kick for the first time. "Oh, he kicked me!"

"He? I thought we'd agreed to have a she." Justin winked at her and placed his hand on her stomach. "Make her kick again."

Thalia laughed. "I can't 'make' her or him. Babies do whatever they—oh, he did it again!"

"I think we may just have a boy and a girl. Each of them has kicked you." Justin kissed Thalia. He could hardly wait to see their child.

"Twins? Oh, gracious, I don't know what I'd do with two babies." Thalia considered the idea for the first time.

"Have twice the fun," Justin suggested. "One for you and one for me."

Chapter Twenty

Donald went into his mother's rose garden. The early roses were starting to bloom. He'd tended this garden for almost twenty years. His mother had loved these roses. He took an ax and began to whack at the roses. As the bushes fell, the thorns caught at his hands, tearing into his flesh. He didn't care. Tears rolled down his cheeks. He hated Thalia for killing his mother. He hated his mother for dying. Nobody had ever loved him. Even Thalia, who'd killed their mother and father, had been loved. Everybody loved her.

He'd fix her. He hated her. He hated her. He hated her. The chant matched the blows of the ax as rosebush after rosebush fell dying at his feet. He didn't stop until every single one was level with the ground.

As he walked back over the broken bushes, he stopped to pick up a rosebud. It was as red as blood. He liked that. He'd take it to Thalia.

Donald rode up to Sea Mist again, for the last time of his life, he hoped. His Uncle Martin had a well-stocked gun room; Donald wondered if Thalia had changed anything. He decided that she hadn't. She liked everything to stay the same. She'd like this rose.

Now was the time he would get even with her. She'd killed his mother. She'd made his father hate him. Thalia had made his life miserable from the moment she was born. He relished the idea of getting even.

He hated her. The hatred had festered for years. What fun he'd have killing her. He'd put this rose in her hands. He'd even stick the thorns into her flesh and make her bleed. He liked that

dea. All these years she'd painted these roses. She liked them.
He could tell. He'd just see how she liked them when they made
er bleed.

Sea Mist was in sight. Revenge for all his years of pain was
within his grasp. Donald dismounted and walked calmly up the
teps. He knocked like a gentleman.

Clover came to the door. "What you doin' here again?"

"I've come to see my sister. I have to talk to her." Donald
wanted to throw Clover out. He might even shoot her after he
hot Justin and Thalia. He'd never liked her.

Clover stepped to one side and motioned to Donald to come
n. "They's in the parlor."

Donald didn't wait to be announced. He barged right in.
Thalia was sitting on Justin's lap, and they were giggling like
children. They wouldn't for long.

Thalia noticed him first. "Donald? What are you doing
here?"

"I've— Thalia, I'm sorry. I've been a fool." He held out the
rose to her and smiled. "I cut this from one of Mother's roses.
She said she wants you to have it."

Thalia gaped at him in stunned disbelief. "Donald, what are
you talking about? What happened to your hands?"

Donald looked at his hands for the first time. They were
bleeding where the thorns had torn his flesh. "I was, well . . . I
was tending the roses, and the thorns got me. When they were
falling down."

Justin looked from Thalia to Donald. He didn't understand
what was happening between them, but Donald had a wild-eyed
appearance that he didn't like at all. "Donald," he said, sliding out from under Thalia. "Let's go have a talk."

Donald stared at Justin and then smiled. "All right." He
handed the rose to Thalia. "Put this in your hair. It'll look
pretty." He walked out of the room. "Let's go see Uncle Martin's guns. Do you know where they are? He has a great collection."

"Stay here, Thalia. Donald and I are going to have a talk,"
Justin said.

"No, Justin, there's something wrong. Donald is . . . I think
he's ill. Please, let me send for someone," Thalia begged,
hanging on to Justin's hand. She tucked the rose in her chignon and tried to decide what to do.

"Don't worry, love. We'll be all right." Justin followe
Donald along the hallway and into the gun room.

Thalia paced back and forth. Something was wrong wit
Donald. She looked at the rose. She recognized it. Donald ha
said it had been one of their mother's favorites, because it ha
always bloomed first. What had he meant about all the bushe
falling down? How had he hurt his hands?

Samuel walked out of the hotel and right into his fathe
"Father! What are you doing here?"

"I've come for you. Have you found your brother?" Au
gustus Lee asked, turning around.

"Yes, he's on Edisto Island. We can just catch the ferry if w
hurry."

Justin went into the gun room and looked around. "Look
like your uncle had a fine collection."

Donald walked very slowly by all the guns. He reached ou
and touched some of them. They felt good to him, cool an
smooth. He took one down and rubbed his fingers across th
cold barrel. It was loaded. So much like rose petals. Excep
cold. Cold like death.

Justin walked toward Donald. "Say, Donald, it's about tim
for dinner. I think Princess is making chicken and dumpling
today."

Donald whirled around, the gun in his hand. "Your fun i
over, Justin Lionheart. Justin Lee. I know all about you, an
I've told the sheriff. He's probably on his way out here righ
now."

Justin stopped moving. He didn't want to scare Donald. I
his state, anything could make him fire. "That's good. Com
on, Donald. Let's go eat. Did I tell you that Thalia's going t
have a baby?" Justin chuckled, trying to get Donald to com
back to reality. "Boy, I know things are going to change aroun
here."

Donald glowered at Justin. "My baby killed somebody. Jus
like Thalia killed my mother."

"No, Donald, you've got it all wrong." Justin felt the ten
sion in Donald. He was really worried now. "Your mother die
because of some complications of childbirth, not because o
Thalia. Your baby... It didn't kill Alicia."

"You know her? You know about Alicia?" Donald laughed. "I remember. You were the man who was going to marry her. I got her with child. That's why you're going to die. You made Thalia pregnant."

"Come, Donald, let's talk about this." Justin glanced around quickly. He couldn't reach a gun fast enough to defend himself. He didn't even know which ones were loaded. He spotted a half-full brandy decanter. "Let's have a drink and talk about this."

"I don't want to talk." Donald stared at Justin. "I'm going to kill you, and then Thalia."

Thalia went to the doorway. She listened. She could hear Justin and Donald talking, but couldn't understand what they were saying. Suddenly she knew what Donald was going to do.

She ran down the hallway. "Clover," she called when she reached the back of the house. "Go find Adam right away. It's an emergency. Run!"

Thalia hurried back to the hallway and stopped outside the gun room. She heard Donald talking. He said he was going to kill Justin and then her.

Thalia peered into the room. Donald was standing with his side to her, but he wasn't paying any attention to the door. Wondering what she should do, she decided that her only alternative was to jump Donald and somehow wrest the gun from his hand. While she was struggling with Donald, Justin could escape.

Slipping back a little, she kept listening as she slid her crinolines off and left them where they lay. Her skirt was full, but it wouldn't be nearly as noticeable as it was with the hoops beneath it. Thalia edged closer.

Donald still hadn't noticed her. He was smirking at Justin.

Justin saw Thalia at the door. He wanted to cry out, to warn her to run, but he was afraid that if he did, Donald would shoot. Justin was helpless.

Then he realized what Thalia was doing. She was sneaking into the room, hoping to attack Donald from the rear. Justin would do his part. He smiled at Donald. "Look, Donald, you don't want to do this. You have your whole life ahead of you. We'll give you whatever you want."

"You don't have to give me anything." Donald sneered, leveling the gun at Justin without wavering. "It's all mine. It always was. Thalia just got in the way. The money should have been mine from the beginning. Father just... She bewitched him or tricked him. That's it. He probably liked me a lot, but she tricked him."

"Donald," Justin began, using a calm, soothing tone. Thalia was inside the room now, moving stealthily behind Donald. Somehow, Justin had to keep Donald occupied long enough for Thalia to reach him. "I'm sure your father loved you very much. You're a bright boy. He left you a beautiful plantation. Of course, he loved you."

"Yes, but he gave lots of money to Thalia." Donald grimaced. "I know my father wouldn't do that. He loved me."

"But, Donald, don't you remember?" Justin asked quietly. Thalia was less than two yards from Donald. Justin prayed silently that she wouldn't make a noise and give herself away. "He gave you money, too. Much more than he gave Thalia. I'd say that he loved you a lot more than he loved her."

"He hated her. She killed my mother. Thalia doesn't need any money. She doesn't deserve anything." Donald's eyes opened wider. They had a wild, glazed look about them. "I hate her. I always hated her. She's nothing but a greedy bitch."

"Now, Donald," Justin said softly, trying to look directly at Donald, but keeping Thalia within his line of vision. "That's not fair. Thalia's helped you. She paid for the overseer at Misty Glade. She sent money to you just recently."

Thalia prayed that she'd have enough time to reach Donald before reason abandoned him completely. He sounded mad, insane, and full of hatred for the whole world. Fear held her back. What would happen if he heard her before she made her final move? He'd shoot her without even thinking about it. He didn't care. Paralyzed for a few seconds, she forced herself to breathe deeply. She had to find the courage to attack soon.

"It's *my* money!" Donald screamed, tears beginning to shine in his eyes. "I'm going to kill you. Then she'll come in here and see you. She'll cry and beg for mercy, but I won't listen. She's a bitch. I'm going to kill her—and that bastard baby of hers."

Donald's last words jarred Thalia into action. She leapt at him from behind with her full body weight, making sure she hit the hand holding the pistol. Donald fell forward, but he still managed to grip the gun, albeit unsteadily. Thalia shouted, "Run, Justin, please run!"

Thalia wrestled with Donald. He pummeled her with his fist, but she held on tenaciously. Justin searched the gun racks and finally found another loaded pistol. Following the pair rolling on the floor with the barrel of the gun, Justin knew complete frustration and anguish. His wife, his beloved Thalia, was being beaten, and he couldn't kill the bastard who was beating her.

The rose fell out of Thalia's hair and landed on the carpet along with several hairpins. When Donald rolled over, the thorns tore into his back. "Aagh!" he screamed, and hit her even harder as she tried to wrest the gun from his other hand.

Justin could wait no longer. He shouted, "Stop! I've got a gun, Donald."

Donald hesitated, but his hand snaked out, and he aimed his pistol at Justin. He got to his feet, dragging Thalia with him as a barrier. Then he rested the barrel of the gun against her temple. "Drop your gun, Justin. I swear I'll shoot her and never lose a moment's sleep."

"No, Justin," Thalia warned. "Don't do it. He's...he's bluffing."

"You know I mean what I say." Donald smiled wickedly, wrenching Thalia closer.

Justin saw the situation becoming utterly hopeless. Donald had the upper hand. He wouldn't hesitate to kill Thalia. The only option Justin had was to drop the gun and try to talk Donald out of this madness. "All right." The gun fell from Justin's hand.

Then Justin saw Samuel at the door. If he made any sign, Donald would turn and shoot him. The situation was becoming more and more complicated. But, if things worked out, maybe the three of them could overpower Donald. Justin would have to watch every movement very carefully.

"Now, who's first?" Donald asked, noticing that Justin was looking at the door. "Oh, no. You don't have a chance of sneaking out." Donald dragged Thalia with him and moved between Justin and the door.

Now was Samuel's chance. "Stop!" He launched himself at Donald.

Donald whirled around to face the door. Thalia, seeing an opportunity, pretended to faint. As she fell out of Donald's arms, she struck him as Samuel hit Donald in the face and the gun dropped to the carpeted floor. The two men tumbled to the ground, scrambling for the gun.

For an eternity, Samuel and Donald fought for control of the gun. It fired. Thalia stood stock-still. Justin was rooted to the floor. The bullet struck Samuel, and he fell backwards. Thalia screamed and threw herself at Donald. Justin rushed over and pulled her off, taking the opportunity to strike a few blows to Donald's face and stomach. Donald's hand closed over the butt of the gun.

Augustus Lee and the sheriff ran through the door. The sheriff, seeing what was happening, leveled his gun at Donald. "All right, Mr. Freemont, ease the gun onto the floor. You're under arrest."

Augustus Lee rushed over to Samuel, who looked up at his father and smiled. "I'm just as brave as Justin, right, Father?" He glanced at Justin and Thalia. "I know you're going to be real happy. She's a real nice girl, Justin...."

Samuel's eyes closed, and his head rolled to one side. He was dead.

Donald looked about frantically. He was under arrest. Thalia was fine, and he was under arrest. Once again, she'd found a way to beat him. Not anymore. Donald lifted the gun shakily. Without making another sound, he pulled the trigger.

The sound of the shot echoed through the house. Thalia screamed. Donald's head sagged against his chest. He, too, was dead.

There were questions to be answered, but Justin insisted that Thalia go to bed. He sent for the doctor to make sure that Donald hadn't injured her when he'd beaten her.

Later, Justin went back downstairs to speak with his father for the first time in years. "Father, I...I'm sorry for all this. It's my fault that Samuel is dead."

"No, son." Augustus Lee embraced his eldest—and now his only—son. "Samuel left me a letter telling me everything. I've arranged with the sheriff here to convey a letter of confession from Samuel that will clear your name. You're free to return to Virginia."

"That's right, son," the sheriff said. "There's been a lot of bloodshed here today, but there's not a mark against you. You're free."

Justin shook his head sadly. "Perhaps free from legal charges, but I'll never be free of the scars that mark my soul."

"Maybe not for a long time," Thalia said from the stairs. She walked over to Justin and put her arms around him. "But when our baby comes—our little Samuel, if it's a boy—everything will be all right again. Time, and the joy of a new life, will heal many things."

Augustus Lee smiled at his new daughter-in-law. "That's the most sensible thing I've heard in a long time."

"Thalia, I'd like you to meet my father, Augustus Lee." Justin smiled down at her and kissed her forehead. "Father, this is my wife, Thalia Lionheart."

"Lionheart?" Augustus asked, rubbing his chin. "What's wrong with Lee?"

"Nothing at all, but we're Lionhearts. Both of us." Justin laughed and patted Thalia's stomach. "Our baby, too. We'll make it right with the courts as soon as we can arrange it. Mr. and Mrs. Justin Caswell Lee Lionheart."

Thalia nodded vigorously and touched her father-in-law's cheek. "We've learned a great deal about each other in the past few days. We've learned that we're like newborn kittens, just exploring a new world. But," she continued, "when threatened, our lionhearts become predominant."

"The Lionhearts of Sea Mist Plantation." Justin tried the sound. "I think I like that. Our future is together, here at Sea Mist. We've got a lot of living to make up for. We've both had some sad times, but now we're going to live and love for the future. Together in everything we do."

"Everything?" Thalia asked, patting her stomach.

"Well, almost." Justin laughed and hugged her close. "Some plant the seeds, some harvest the crop, but whatever happens, we'll be together to the end."

* * * * *

Harlequin®

JANELLE TAYLOR

Valley of Fire

HARLEQUIN IS PROUD TO PRESENT *VALLEY OF FIRE* **BY JANELLE TAYLOR—AUTHOR OF TWENTY-TWO BOOKS, INCLUDING SIX** *NEW YORK TIMES* **BESTSELLERS**

VALLEY OF FIRE—the warm and passionate story of Kathy Alexander, a famous romance author, and Steven Winngate, entrepreneur and owner of the magazine that intended to expose the real Kathy "Brandy" Alexander to her fans.

Don't miss VALLEY OF FIRE, available in May.

Following the success of WITH THIS RING,
Harlequin cordially invites you to enjoy the
romance of the wedding season with

BARBARA BRETTON
RITA CLAY ESTRADA
SANDRA JAMES
DEBBIE MACOMBER

A collection of romantic stories that celebrate the joy,
excitement, and mishaps of planning that special day
by these four award-winning Harlequin authors.

Available in April at your favorite Harlequin
retail outlets.